Collected Short Stories of Aldous Huxley

COLLECTED
SHORT STORIES

ALDOUS HUXLEY

Elephant Paperbacks
IVAN R. DEE, PUBLISHER, CHICAGO

First ELEPHANT PAPERBACK edition published 1992 by
Ivan R. Dee, Inc., 1332 North Halsted Street, Chicago 60622.
Manufactured in the United States of America and printed
on acid-free paper.

Library of Congress Cataloging-in-Publication Data:
Huxley, Aldous, 1894–1963.
[Short stories. Selections. 1992]
Collected short stories / Aldous Huxley. — 1st Elephant
paperback ed.
p.   cm.
"Elephant paperbacks"
ISBN 0-929587-81-2
I. Title.
PR6015.U9A6   1992
823'.912—dc20   91-35171

CONTENTS

Collected Short Stories of
Aldous Huxley

Happily Ever After

I

AT the best of times it is a long way from Chicago to Blaybury in Wiltshire, but war has fixed between them a great gulf. In the circumstances, therefore, it seemed an act of singular devotion on the part of Peter Jacobsen to have come all the way from the Middle West, in the fourth year of war, on a visit to his old friend Petherton, when the project entailed a single-handed struggle with two Great Powers over the question of passports and the risk, when they had been obtained, of perishing miserably by the way, a victim of frightfulness.

At the expense of much time and more trouble Jacobsen had at last arrived; the gulf between Chicago and Blaybury was spanned. In the hall of Petherton's house a scene of welcome was being enacted under the dim gaze of six or seven brown family portraits by unknown masters of the eighteenth and nineteenth centuries.

Old Alfred Petherton, a grey shawl over his shoulders—for he had to be careful, even in June, of draughts and colds—was shakin his guest's hand with interminable cordiality.

"My dear boy," he kept repeating, "it *is* a pleasure to see you. My dear boy . . ."

Jacobsen limply abandoned his forearm and waited in patience.

"I can never be grateful enough," Mr Petherton went on—"never grateful enough to you for having taken all this endless trouble to come and see an old decrepit man—for that's what I am now, that's what I am, believe me."

"Oh, I assure you . . ." said Jacobsen, with vague deprecation. "Le vieux crétin qui pleurniche," he said to himself. French was a wonderfully expressive language, to be sure.

"My digestion and my heart have got much worse since I saw you last. But I think I must have told you about that in my letters."

"You did indeed, and I was most grieved to hear it."

"Grieved"—what a curious flavour that word had! Like somebody's tea which used to recall the most delicious blends of forty years ago. But it was decidedly the *mot juste*. It had the right obituary note about it.

"Yes," Mr Petherton continued, "my palpitations are very bad now. Aren't they, Marjorie?" He appealed to his daughter who was standing beside him.

"Father's palpitations are very bad," she replied dutifully.

It was as though they were talking about some precious heirloom long and lovingly cherished.

"And my digestion. . . . This physical infirmity makes all mental activity so difficult. All the same, I manage to do a little useful work. We'll discuss that later, though. You must be feeling tired and dusty after your journey down. I'll guide you to your room. Marjorie, will you get someone to take up his luggage?"

"I can take it myself," said Jacobsen, and he picked up a small Gladstone-bag that had been deposited by the door.

"Is that all?" Mr Petherton asked.

"Yes, that's all."

As one living the life of reason, Jacobsen objected to owning things. One so easily became the slave of things and not their master. He liked to be free; he checked his possessive instincts and limited his possessions to the strictly essential. He was as much or as little at home at Blaybury or Pekin. He could have explained all this if he liked. But in the present case it wasn't worth taking the trouble.

"This is your humble chamber," said Mr Petherton, throwing open the door of what was, indeed, a very handsome spare-room, bright with chintzes and cut flowers and silver candlesticks. "A poor thing, but your own."

Courtly grace! Dear old man! Apt quotation! Jacobsen unpacked his bag and arranged its contents neatly and methodically in the various drawers and shelves of the wardrobe.

It was a good many years now since Jacobsen had come in the course of his grand educational tour to Oxford. He spent a couple of years there, for he liked the place, and its inhabitants were a source of unfailing amusement to him.

A Norwegian, born in the Argentine, educated in the United States, in France, and in Germany; a man with no nationality and no prejudices, enormously old in experience, he found something very new and fresh and entertaining about his fellow-students with their comic public-school traditions and fabulous ignorance of the world. He had quietly watched them doing their little antics, feeling all the time that a row of bars separated them from himself, and that he ought, after each particularly amusing trick, to offer them a bun or a handful of pea-nuts. In the intervals of sightseeing in this strange and delightful Jardin des Plantes he read Greats, and it was through Aristotle that he had come into contact with Alfred Petherton, fellow and tutor of his college.

The name of Petherton is a respectable one in the academic world. You will find it on the title-page of such meritorious, if not exactly brilliant, books as *Plato's Predecessors*, *Three Scottish Meta-physicians*, *Introduction to the Study of Ethics*, *Essays in Neo-Idealism*. Some of his works are published in cheap editions as text-books.

One of those curious inexplicable friendships that often link the most unlikely people had sprung up between tutor and pupil, and had lasted unbroken for upwards of twenty years. Petherton felt a fatherly affection for the younger man, together with a father's pride, now that Jacobsen was a man of world-wide reputation, in having, as he supposed, spiritually begotten him. And now Jacobsen had travelled three or four thousand miles across a world at war just to see the old man. Petherton was profoundly touched.

"Did you see any submarines on the way over?" Marjorie asked, as she and Jacobsen were strolling together in the garden after breakfast the next day.

"I didn't notice any; but then I am very unobservant about these things."

There was a pause. At last, "I suppose there is a great deal of war-work being done in America now?" said Marjorie.

Jacobsen supposed so; and there floated across his mind a vision of massed bands, of orators with megaphones, of patriotic sky-signs, of streets made perilous by the organized highway robbery of Red Cross collectors. He was too lazy to describe it all; besides, she wouldn't see the point of it.

"I should like to be able to do some war-work," Marjorie explained apologetically. "But I have to look after father, and there's the housekeeping, so I really haven't the time."

Jacobsen thought he detected a formula for the benefit of

strangers. She evidently wanted to make things right about herself in people's minds. Her remark about the housekeeping made Jacobsen think of the late Mrs Petherton, her mother; she had been a good-looking, painfully sprightly woman with a hankering to shine in University society at Oxford. One quickly learned that she was related to bishops and country families; a hunter of ecclesiastical lions and a snob. He felt glad she was dead.

"Won't it be awful when there's no war-work," he said. "People will have nothing to do or think about when peace comes."

"I shall be glad. Housekeeping will be so much easier."

"True. There are consolations."

Marjorie looked at him suspiciously; she didn't like being laughed at. What an undistinguished-looking little man he was! Short, stoutish, with waxed brown moustaches and a forehead that incipient baldness had made interminably high. He looked like the sort of man to whom one says: "Thank you, I'll take it in notes with a pound's worth of silver." There were pouches under his eyes and pouches under his chin, and you could never guess from his expression what he was thinking about. She was glad that she was taller than he and could look down on him.

Mr Petherton appeared from the house, his grey shawl over his shoulders and the crackling expanse of *The Times* between his hands.

"Good morrow," he cried.

To the Shakespearean heartiness of this greeting Marjorie returned her most icily modern "Morning." Her father always said "Good morrow" instead of "Good morning," and the fact irritated her with unfailing regularity every day of her life.

"There's a most interesting account," said Mr Petherton, "by a young pilot of an air fight in to-day's paper," and as they walked up and down the gravel path he read the article, which was a column and a half in length.

Marjorie made no attempt to disguise her boredom, and occupied herself by reading something on the other side of the page, craning her neck round to see.

"Very interesting," said Jacobsen when it was finished.

Mr Petherton had turned over and was now looking at the Court Circular page.

"I see," he said, "there's someone called Beryl Camberley-

Belcher going to be married. Do you know if that's any relation of the Howard Camberley-Belchers, Majorie?"

"I've no idea who the Howard Camberley-Belchers are," Marjorie answered rather sharply.

"Oh, I thought you did. Let me see. Howard Camberley-Belcher was at college with me. And he had a brother called James—or was it William?—and a sister who married one of the Riders, or at any rate some relation of the Riders; for I know the Camberley-Belchers and the Riders used to fit in somewhere. Dear me, I'm afraid my memory for names is going."

Marjorie went indoors to prepare the day's domestic campaign with the cook. When that was over she retired to her sitting-room and unlocked her very private desk. She must write to Guy this morning. Marjorie had known Guy Lambourne for years and years, almost as long as she could remember. The Lambournes were old family friends of the Pethertons: indeed they were, distantly, connections; they "fitted in somewhere," as Mr Petherton would say—somewhere, about a couple of generations back. Marjorie was two years younger than Guy; they were both only children; circumstances had naturally thrown them a great deal together. Then Guy's father had died, and not long afterwards his mother, and at the age of seventeen Guy had actually come to live with the Pethertons, for the old man was his guardian. And now they were engaged; had been, more or less, from the first year of the war.

Marjorie took pen, ink, and paper. "DEAR GUY," she began— ("*We* aren't sentimental," she had once remarked, with a mixture of contempt and secret envy, to a friend who had confided that she and her fiancé never began with anything less than Darling.) —"I am longing for another of your letters...." She went through the usual litany of longing. "It was father's birthday yesterday; he is sixty-five. I cannot bear to think that some day you and I will be as old as that. Aunt Ellen sent him a Stilton cheese—a useful war-time present. How boring housekeeping is. By dint of thinking about cheeses my mind is rapidly turning into one—a Gruyère; where there isn't cheese there are just holes, full of vacuum . . ."

She didn't really mind housekeeping so much. She took it for granted, and did it just because it was there to be done. Guy, on the contrary, never took anything for granted; she made these demonstrations for his benefit.

"I read Keats's letters, as you suggested, and thought them *too* beautiful . . ."

At the end of a page of rapture she paused and bit her pen. What was there to say next? It seemed absurd one should have to write letters about the books one had been reading. But there was nothing else to write about; nothing ever happened. After all, what had happened in her life? Her mother dying when she was sixteen; then the excitement of Guy coming to live with them; then the war, but that hadn't meant much to her; then Guy falling in love, and their getting engaged. That was really all. She wished she could write about her feelings in an accurate, complicated way, like people in novels; but when she came to think about it, she didn't seem to have any feelings to describe.

She looked at Guy's last letter from France. "Sometimes," he had written, "I am tortured by an intense physical desire for you. I can think of nothing but your beauty, your young, strong body. I hate that; I have to struggle to repress it. Do you forgive me?" It rather thrilled her that he should feel like that about her: he had always been so cold, so reserved, so much opposed to sentimentality—to the kisses and endearments she would, perhaps, secretly have liked. But he had seemed so right when he said, "We must love like rational beings, with our minds, not with our hands and lips." All the same . . .

She dipped her pen in the ink and began to write again. "I know the feelings you spoke of in your letter. Sometimes I long for you in the same way. I dreamt the other night I was holding you in my arms, and woke up hugging the pillow." She looked at what she had written. It was too awful, too vulgar! She would have to scratch it out. But no, she would leave it in spite of everything, just to see what he would think about it. She finished the letter quickly, sealed and stamped it, and rang for the maid to take it to the post. When the servant had gone, she shut up her desk with a bank. Bang—the letter had gone, irrevocably.

She picked up a large book lying on the table and began to read. It was the first volume of the *Decline and Fall*. Guy had said she must read Gibbon; she wouldn't be educated till she had read Gibbon. And so yesterday she had gone to her father in his library to get the book.

"Gibbon," Mr Petherton had said, "certainly, my dear. How

delightful it is to look at these grand old books again. One always finds something new every time."

Marjorie gave him to understand that she had never read it. she felt rather proud of her ignorance.

Mr Petherton handed the first of eleven volumes to her. "A great book," he murmured—"an essential book. It fills the gap between your classical history and your mediaeval stuff."

"Your" classical history, Marjorie repeated to herself, "your" classical history indeed! Her father had an irritating way of taking it for granted that she knew everything, that classical history was as much hers as his. Only a day or two before he had turned to her at luncheon with, "Do you remember, dear child, whether it was Pomponazzi who denied the personal immortality of the soul, or else that queer fellow, Laurentius Valla? It's gone out of my head for the moment." Marjorie had quite lost her temper at the question—much to the innocent bewilderment of her poor father.

She had set to work with energy on the Gibbon; her bookmarker registered the fact that she had got through one hundred and twenty-three pages yesterday. Marjorie started reading. After two pages she stopped. She looked at the number of pages still remaining to be read—and this was only the first volume. She felt like a wasp sitting down to eat a vegetable marrow. Gibbon's bulk was not perceptibly diminished by her first bite. It was too long. She shut the book and went out for a walk. Passing the Whites' house, she saw her friend, Beatrice White that was, sitting on the lawn with her two babies. Beatrice hailed her, and she turned in.

"Pat a cake, pat a cake," she said. At the age of ten months, baby John had already learnt the art of patting cakes. He slapped the outstretched hand offered him, and his face, round and smooth and pink like an enormous peach, beamed with pleasure.

"Isn't he a darling!" Marjorie exclaimed. "You know, I'm sure he's grown since I last saw him, which was on Tuesday."

"He put on eleven ounces last week," Beatrice affirmed.

"How wonderful! His hair's coming on splendidly . . ."

It was Sunday the next day. Jacobsen appeared at breakfast in the neatest of black suits. He looked, Marjorie thought, more than ever like a cashier. She longed to tell him to hurry up or he'd miss the 8.53 for the second time this week and the manager would be annoyed. Marjorie herself was, rather consciously, not in Sunday best.

"What is the name of the Vicar?" Jacobsen inquired, as he helped himself to bacon.

"Trubshaw. Luke Trubshaw, I believe."

"Does he preach well?"

"He didn't when I used to hear him. But I don't often go to church now, so I don't know what he's like these days."

"Why don't you go to church?" Jacobsen inquired, with a silkiness of tone which veiled the crude outlines of his leading question.

Marjorie was painfully conscious of blushing. She was filled with rage against Jacobsen. "Because," she said firmly, "I don't think it necessary to give expression to my religious feelings by making a lot of"—she hesitated a moment—"a lot of meaningless gestures with a crowd of other people."

"You used to go," said Jacobsen.

"When I was a child and hadn't thought about these things."

Jacobsen was silent, and concealed a smile in his coffee-cup. Really, he said to himself, there ought to be religious conscription for women—and for most men, too. It was grotesque the way these people thought they could stand by themselves—the fools, when there was the infinite authority of organized religion to support their ridiculous feebleness.

"Does Lambourne go to church?" he asked maliciously, and with an air of perfect naïveté and good faith.

Marjorie coloured again, and a fresh wave of hatred surged up within her. Even as she had said the words she had wondered whether Jacobsen would notice that the phrase "meaningless gestures" didn't ring very much like one of her own coinages. "Gesture"—that was one of Guy's words, like "incredible", "exacerbate", "impinge", "sinister". Of course all her present views about religion had come from Guy. She looked Jacobsen straight in the face and replied:

"Yes, I think he goes to church pretty regularly. But I really don't know: his religion has nothing to do with me."

Jacobsen was lost in delight and admiration.

Punctually at twenty minutes to eleven he set out for church. From where she was sitting in the summer-house Marjorie watched him as he crossed the garden, incredibly absurd and incongruous in his black clothes among the blazing flowers and the young emerald of the trees. Now he was hidden behind the sweet-briar hedge, all except the hard black melon of his bowler hat, which she could see bobbing along between the topmost sprays.

She went on with her letter to Guy. ". . . What a strange man Mr Jacobsen is. I suppose he is very clever, but I can't get very much out of him. We had an argument about religion at breakfast this morning; I rather scored off him. He has now gone off to church all by himself;—I really couldn't face the prospect of going with him—I hope he'll enjoy old Mr Trubshaw's preaching!"

Jacobsen did enjoy Mr Trubshaw's preaching enormously. He always made a point, in whatever part of Christendom he happened to be, of attending divine service. He had the greatest admiration of churches as institutions. In their solidity and unchangeableness he saw one of the few hopes for humanity. Further, he derived great pleasure from comparing the Church as an institution—splendid, powerful, eternal—with the childish imbecility of its representatives. How delightful it was to sit in the herded congregation and listen to the sincere outpourings of an intellect only a little less limited than that of an Australian aboriginal! How restful to feel oneself a member of a flock, guided by a good shepherd—himself a sheep! Then there was the scientific interest (he went to church as student of anthropology, as a Freudian psychologist) and the philosophic amusement of counting the undistributed middles and tabulating historically the exploded fallacies in the parson's discourse.

To-day Mr Trubshaw preached a topical sermon about the Irish situation. His was the gospel of the *Morning Post*, slightly tempered by Christianity. It was our duty, he said, to pray for the Irish first of all, and if that had no effect upon recruiting, why, then, we must conscribe them as zealously as we had prayed before.

Jacobsen leaned back in his pew with a sigh of contentment. A connoisseur, he recognized that this was the right stuff.

"Well," said Mr Petherton over the Sunday beef at lunch, "how did you like our dear Vicar?"

"He was splendid," said Jacobsen, with grave enthusiasm. "One of the best sermons I've ever heard."

"Indeed? I shall really have to go and hear him again. It must be nearly ten years since I listened to him."

"He's inimitable."

Marjorie looked at Jacobsen carefully. He seemed to be perfectly serious. She was more than ever puzzled by the man.

The days went slipping by, hot blue days that passed like a flash almost without one's noticing them, cold grey days, seeming interminable and without number, and about which one spoke with a sense of justified grievance, for the season was supposed to be summer. There was fighting going on in France—terrific battles, to judge from the headlines in *The Times*; but, after all, one day's paper was very much like another's. Marjorie read them dutifully, but didn't honestly take in very much; at least she forgot about things very soon. She couldn't keep count with the battles of Ypres, and when somebody told her that she ought to go and see the photographs of the *Vindictive*, she smiled vaguely and said Yes, without remembering precisely what the *Vindictive* was —a ship, she supposed.

Guy was in France, to be sure, but he was an Intelligence Officer now, so that she was hardly anxious about him at all. Clergymen used to say that the war was bringing us all back to a sense of the fundamental realities of life. She supposed it was true: Guy's enforced absences were a pain to her, and the difficulties of housekeeping continually increased and multiplied.

Mr Petherton took a more intelligent interest in the war than did his daughter. He prided himself on being able to see the thing as a whole, on taking an historical God's-eye view of it all. He talked about it at meal-times, insisting that the world must be made safe for democracy. Between meals he sat in the library working at his monumental *History of Morals*. To his dinner-table disquisitions Marjorie would listen more or less attentively, Jacobsen with an unfailing, bright, intelligent politeness. Jacobsen himself rarely volunteered a remark about the war; it was taken for granted that he thought about it in the same way as all other right-thinking folk. Between meals he worked in his room or discussed the morals of the Italian Renaissance with his host. Marjorie could write to Guy that nothing was happening, and that but for his absence and the weather interfering so much with tennis, she would be perfectly happy.

Into the midst of this placidity there fell, delightful bolt from

the blue, the announcement that Guy was getting leave at the
end of July. "DARLING," Marjorie wrote, "I am so excited to
think that you will be with me in such a little—such a long, long
time." Indeed, she was so excited and delighted that she realized
with a touch of remorse how comparatively little she had thought
of him when there seemed no chance of seeing him, how dim a
figure in absence he was. A week later she heard that George
White had arranged to get leave at the same time so as to see
Guy. She was glad; George was a charming boy, and Guy was so
fond of him. The Whites were their nearest neighbours, and ever
since Guy had come to live at Blaybury he had seen a great deal
of young George.

"We shall be a most festive party," said Mr Petherton. "Roger
will be coming to us just at the same time as Guy."

"I'd quite forgotten Uncle Roger," said Marjorie. "Of course,
his holidays begin then, don't they?"

The Reverend Roger was Alfred Petherton's brother and a
master at one of our most glorious public schools. Marjorie hardly
agreed with her father in thinking that his presence would add
anything to the "festiveness" of the party. It was a pity he should
be coming at this particular moment. However, we all have our
little cross to bear.

Mr Petherton was feeling playful. "We must bring down," he
said, "the choicest Falernian, bottled when Gladstone was consul,
for the occasion. We must prepare wreaths and unguents and hire
a flute player and a couple of dancing girls . . ."

He spent the rest of the meal in quoting Horace, Catullus,
the Greek Anthology, Petronius, and Sidonius Apollinaris.
Marjorie's knowledge of the dead languages was decidedly
limited. Her thoughts were elsewhere, and it was only dimly and
as it were through a mist that she heard her father murmuring—
whether merely to himself or with the hope of eliciting an answer
from somebody, she hardly knew—"Let me see: how does that
epigram go?—that one about the different kinds of fish and the
garlands of roses, by Meleager, or is it Poseidippus? . . ."

II

Guy and Jacobsen were walking in the Dutch garden, an incongruous couple. On Guy military servitude had left no out-

wardly visible mark; out of uniform, he still looked like a tall, untidy undergraduate; he stooped and drooped as much as ever; his hair was still bushy and, to judge by the dim expression of his face, he had not yet learnt to think imperially. His khaki always looked like a disguise, like the most absurd fancy dress. Jacobsen trotted beside him, short, fattish, very sleek, and correct. They talked in a desultory way about things indifferent. Guy, anxious for a little intellectual exercise after so many months of discipline, had been trying to inveigle his companion into a philosophical discussion. Jacobsen consistently eluded his efforts; he was too lazy to talk seriously; there was no profit that he could see to be got out of this young man's opinions, and he had not the faintest desire to make a disciple. He preferred, therefore, to discuss the war and the weather. It irritated him that people should want to trespass on the domain of thought—people who had no right to live anywhere but on the vegetative plane of mere existence. He wished they would simply be content to *be* or *do*, not try, so hopelessly, to think, when only one in a million can think with the least profit to himself or anyone else.

Out of the corner of his eye he looked at the dark, sensitive face of his companion; he ought to have gone into business at eighteen, was Jacobsen's verdict. It was bad for him to think; he wasn't strong enough.

A great sound of barking broke upon the calm of the garden. Looking up, the two strollers saw George White running across the green turf of the croquet lawn with a huge fawn-coloured dog bounding along at his side.

"Morning," he shouted. He was hatless and out of breath. "I was taking Bella for a run, and thought I'd look in and see how you all were."

"What a lovely dog!" Jacobsen exclaimed.

"An old English mastiff—our one aboriginal dog. She has a pedigree going straight back to Edward the Confessor."

Jacobsen began a lively conversation with George on the virtues and short-comings of dogs. Bella smelt his calves and then lifted up her gentle black eyes to look at him. She seemed satisfied.

He looked at them for a little; they were too much absorbed in their doggy conversation to pay attention to him. He made a gesture as though he had suddenly remembered something, gave a little grunt, and with a very preoccupied expression on his face turned to go towards the house. His elaborate piece of by-play escaped the notice of the intended spectators; Guy saw that it had, and felt more miserable and angry and jealous than ever. They would think he had slunk off because he wasn't wanted—which was quite true—instead of believing that he had something very important to do, which was what he had intended they should believe.

A cloud of self-doubt settled upon him. Was his mind, after all, worthless, and the little things he had written—rubbish, not potential genius as he had hoped? Jacobsen was right in preferring George's company. George was perfect, physically, a splendid creature; what could he himself claim?

"I'm second-rate," he thought—"second-rate, physically, morally, mentally. Jacobsen is quite right."

The best he could hope to be was a pedestrian literary man with quiet tastes.

NO, no, no! He clenched his hands and, as though to register his resolve before the universe, he said, aloud:

"I will do it; I will be first-rate, I will."

He was covered with confusion on seeing a gardener pop up, surprised from behind a bank of rose-bushes. Talking to himself— the man must have thought him mad!

He hurried on across the lawn, entered the house, and ran upstairs to his room. There was not a second to lose; he must begin at once. He would write something—something that would last, solid, hard, shining. . . .

"Damn them all! I will do it, I can . . ."

There were writing materials and a table in his room. He selected a pen—with a Relief nib he would be able to go on for hours without getting tired—and a large square sheet of writing-paper.

> "HATCH HOUSE,
> BLAYBURY,
> WILTS.
>
> Station: Cogham, 3 miles; Nobes
> Monacorum, 4½ miles"

Stupid of people to have their stationery printed in red, when black or blue is so much nicer! He inked over the letters.

He held up the paper to the light; there was a watermark, "Pimlico Bond". What an admirable name for the hero of a novel! Pimlico Bond. . . .

> "*There's be-eef in the la-arder*
> *And du-ucks in the pond;*
> *Crying dilly dilly, dilly dilly* . . ."

He bit the end of his pen. "What I want to get," he said to himself, "is something very hard, very external. Intense emotion, but one will somehow have got outside it." He made a movement of hands, arms, and shoulders, tightening his muscles in an effort to express to himself physically that hardness and tightness and firmness of style after which he was struggling.

He began to draw on his virgin paper. A woman, naked, one arm lifted over her head, so that it pulled up her breast by that wonderful curving muscle that comes down from the shoulder. The inner surface of the thighs, remember, is slightly concave. The feet, seen from the front, are always a difficulty.

It would never do to leave that about. What would the servants think? He turned the nipples into eyes, drew heavy lines for nose, mouth, and chin, slopped on the ink thick; it made a passable face now—though an acute observer might have detected the original nudity. He tore it up into very small pieces.

A crescendo booming filled the house. It was the gong. He looked at his watch. Lunch-time, and he had done nothing. O God! . . .

III

It was dinner-time on the last evening of Guy's leave. The uncovered mahogany table was like a pool of brown unruffled water within whose depths flowers and the glinting shapes of glass and silver hung dimly reflected. Mr Petherton sat at the head of the board, flanked by his brother Roger and Jacobsen. Youth, in the persons of Marjorie, Guy, and George White, had collected at the other end. They had reached the stage of dessert.

"This is excellent port," said Roger, sleek and glossy like a well-fed black cob under his silken clerical waistcoat. He was a strong, thick-set man of about fifty, with a red neck as thick as his head. His hair was cropped with military closeness; he liked to set a good example to the boys, some of whom showed distressing "aesthetic" tendencies and wore their hair long.

"I'm glad you like it. I mayn't touch it myself, of course. Have another glass." Alfred Petherton's face wore an expression of dyspeptic melancholy. He was wishing he hadn't taken quite so much of that duck.

"Thank you, I will." Roger took the decanter with a smile of satisfaction. "The tired schoolmaster is worthy of his second glass. White, you look rather pale; I think you must have another." Roger had a hearty, jocular manner, calculated to prove to his pupils that he was not one of the slimy sort of parsons, not a Creeping Jesus.

There was an absorbing conversation going on at the youthful end of the table. Secretly irritated at having been thus interrupted in the middle of it, White turned round and smiled vaguely at Roger.

"Oh, thank you, sir," he said, and pushed his glass forward to be filled. The "sir" slipped out unawares; it was, after all, such a little while since he had been a schoolboy under Roger's dominion.

"One is lucky," Roger went on seriously, "to get any port wine at all now. I'm thankful to say I bought ten dozen from my old college some years ago to lay down; otherwise I don't know what I should do. My wine merchant tells me he couldn't let me have a single bottle. Indeed, he offered to buy some off me, if I'd sell. But I wasn't having any. A bottle in the cellar is worth ten shillings in the pocket these days. I always say that port has become a necessity now one gets so little meat. Lambourne! you are another of our brave defenders; you deserve a second glass."

"No, thanks," said Guy, hardly looking up. "I've had enough." He went on talking to Marjorie—about the different views of life held by the French and the Russians.

Roger helped himself to cherries. "One has to select them carefully," he remarked for the benefit of the unwillingly listening George. "There is nothing that gives you such stomachaches as unripe cherries."

"I expect you're glad, Mr Petherton, that holidays have begun at last?" said Jacobsen.

"Glad? I should think so. One is utterly dead beat at the end of the summer term. Isn't one, White?"

White had taken the opportunity to turn back again and listen to Guy's conversation; recalled, like a dog who has started off on a forbidden scent, he obediently assented that one did get tired at the end of the summer term.

"I suppose," said Jacobsen, "you still teach the same old things —Cæsar, Latin verses, Greek grammar, and the rest? We Americans can hardly believe that all that still goes on."

"Thank goodness," said Roger, "we still hammer a little solid stuff into them. But there's been a great deal of fuss lately about new curriculums and so forth. They do a lot of science now and things of that kind, but I don't believe the children learn anything at all. It's pure waste of time."

"So is all education, I dare say," said Jacobsen lightly.

"Not if you teach them discipline. That's what's wanted—discipline. Most of these little boys need plenty of beating, and they don't get enough now. Besides, if you can't hammer knowledge in at their heads, you can at least beat a little in at their tails."

"You're very ferocious, Roger," said Mr Petherton, smiling. He was feeling better; the duck was settling down.

"No, it's the vital thing. The best thing the war has brought us is discipline. The country had got slack and wanted tightening up." Roger's face glowed with zeal.

From the other end of the table Guy's voice could be heard saying, "Do you know César Franck's 'Dieu s'avance à travers la lande'? It's one of the finest bits of religious music I know."

Mr Petherton's face lighted up; he leaned forward. "No," he said, throwing his answer unexpectedly into the midst of the young people's conversation. "I don't know it; but do you know this? Wait a minute." He knitted his brows, and his lips moved as though he were trying to recapture a formula. "Ah, I've got it. Now, can you tell me this? The name of what famous piece of religious music do I utter when I order an old carpenter, once a Liberal but now a renegade to Conservatism, to make a hive for bees?"

Guy gave it up; his guardian beamed delightedly.

"Hoary Tory, oh, Judas! Make a bee-house," he said. "Do you see? Oratorio *Judas Maccabeus*."

Guy could have wished that this bit of flotsam from Mr Petherton's sportive youth had not been thus washed up at his feet. He felt that he had been peeping indecently close into "the dark backward and abysm of time".

"That was a good one," Mr Petherton chuckled. "I must see if I can think of some more."

Roger, who was not easily to be turned away from his favourite topic, waited till this irrelevant spark of levity had quite expired, and continued: "It's a remarkable and noticeable fact that you never seem to get discipline combined with the teaching of science or modern languages. Who ever heard of a science master having a good house at a school? Scientists' houses are always bad."

"How very strange!" said Jacobsen.

"Strange, but a fact. It seems to me a great mistake to give them houses at all if they can't keep discipline. And then there's the question of religion. Some of these men never come to chapel except when they're on duty. And then, I ask you, what happens when they prepare their boys for Confirmation? Why, I've known boys come to me who were supposed to have been prepared by one or other of these men, and, on asking them, I've found that they know nothing whatever about the most solemn facts of the Eucharist.—May I have some more of those excellent cherries please, White?—Of course, I do my best in such cases to tell the boys what I feel personally about these solemn things. But there generally isn't the time; one's life is so crowded; and so they go into Confirmation with only the very haziest knowledge of what it's all about. You see how absurd it is to let anyone but the classical men have anything to do with the boys' lives."

"Shake it well, dear," Mr Petherton was saying to his daughter, who had come with his medicine.

"What is that stuff?" asked Roger.

"Oh, it's merely my peptones. I can hardly digest at all without it, you know."

"You have all my sympathies. My poor colleague, Flexner, suffers from chronic colitis. I can't imagine how he goes on with his work."

"No, indeed. I find I can do nothing strenuous."

Roger turned and seized once more on the unhappy George. "White," he said, "let this be a lesson to you. Take care of your inside; it's the secret of a happy old age."

Guy looked up quickly. "Don't worry about his old age," he said in a strange harsh voice, very different from the gentle, elaborately modulated tone in which he generally spoke. "He won't have an old age. His chances against surviving are about fourteen to three if the war goes on another year."

"Come," said Roger, "don't let's be pessimistic."

"But I'm not. I assure you, I'm giving you a most rosy view of George's chance of reaching old age."

It was felt that Guy's remarks had been in poor taste. There was a silence; eyes floated vaguely and uneasily, trying not to encounter one another. Roger cracked a nut loudly. When he had sufficiently relished the situation, Jacobsen changed the subject by remarking:

"That was a fine bit of work by our destroyers this morning, wasn't it?"

"It did one good to read about it," said Mr Petherton. "Quite the Nelson touch."

Roger raised his glass. "Nelson!" he said, and emptied it at a gulp. "What a man! I am trying to persuade the Headmaster to make Trafalgar Day a holiday. It is the best way of reminding boys of things of that sort."

"A curiously untypical Englishman to be a national hero, isn't he?" said Jacobsen. "So emotional and lacking in Britannic phlegm."

The Reverend Roger looked grave. "There's one thing I've never been able to understand about Nelson, and that is, how a man who was so much the soul of honour and of patriotism could have been—er—immoral with Lady Hamilton. I know people say that it was the custom of the age, that these things meant nothing then, and so forth; but all the same, I repeat, I cannot understand how a man who was so intensely a patriotic Englishman could have done such a thing."

"I fail to see what patriotism has got to do with it," said Guy.

Roger fixed him with his most pedagogic look and said slowly and gravely. "Then I am sorry for you. I shouldn't have thought it was necessary to tell an Englishman that purity of morals is a national tradition: you especially, a public-school man."

"Let us go and have a hundred up at billiards," said Mr Petherton. "Roger, will you come? And you, George, and Guy?"

"I'm so incredibly bad," Guy insisted, "I'd really rather not."

"So am I," said Jacobsen.

"Then, Marjorie, you must make the fourth."

The billiard players trooped out; Guy and Jacobsen were left alone, brooding over the wreckage of dinner. There was a long silence. The two men sat smoking, Guy sitting in a sagging, crumpled attitude, like a half-empty sack abandoned on a chair, Jacobsen very upright and serene.

"Do you find you can suffer fools gladly?" asked Guy abruptly.

"Perfectly gladly."

"I wish I could. The Reverend Roger has a tendency to make my blood boil."

"But such a good soul," Jacobsen insisted.

"I dare say, but a monster all the same."

"You should take him more calmly. I make a point of never letting myself be moved by external things. I stick to my writing and thinking. Truth is beauty, beauty is truth, and so forth: after all, they're the only things of solid value." Jacobsen looked at the young man with a smile as he said these words. There is no doubt, he said to himself, that that boy ought to have gone into business; what a mistake this higher education is, to be sure.

"Of course, they're the only things," Guy burst out passionately. "You can afford to say so because you had the luck to be born twenty years before I was, and with five thousand miles of good deep water between you and Europe. Here am I, called upon to devote my life, in a very different way from which you devote yours to truth and beauty—to devote my life to—well, what? I'm not quite sure, but I pseserve a touching faith that it is good. And you tell me to ignore external circumstances. Come and live in Flanders a little and try..." He launched forth into a tirade about agony and death and blood and putrefaction.

"What is one to do?" he concluded despairingly. "What the devil is right? I had meant to spend my life writing and thinking, trying to create something beautiful or discover something true. But oughtn't one, after all, if one survives, to give up everything else and try to make this hideous den of a world a little more habitable."

"I think you can take it that a world which has let itself be dragooned into this criminal folly is pretty hopeless. Follow your inclinations; or, better, go into a bank and make a lot of money."

Guy burst out laughing, rather too loudly. "Admirable, admirable!" he said. "To return to our old topic of fools: frankly, Jacobsen, I cannot imagine why you should elect to pass your time with my dear old guardian. He's a charming old man, but one must admit——" He waved his hand.

"One must live somewhere," said Jacobsen. "I find your guardian a most interesting man to be with.—Oh, do look at that dog!" On the hearth-rug Marjorie's little Pekingese, Confucius, was preparing to lie down and go to sleep. He went assiduously through the solemn farce of scratching the floor, under the impression, no doubt, that he was making a comfortable nest to lie in. He turned round and round, scratching earnestly and methodically. Then he lay down, curled himself up in a ball, and was asleep in the twinkling of an eye.

"Isn't that too wonderfully human!" exclaimed Jacobsen delightedly. Guy thought he could see now why Jacobsen enjoyed living with Mr Petherton. The old man was so wonderfully human.

Later in the evening, when the billiards was over and Mr Petherton had duly commented on the anachronism of introducing the game into Antony and Cleopatra, Guy and Marjorie went for·a stroll in the garden. The moon had risen above the trees and lit up the front of the house with its bright pale light that could not wake the sleeping colours of the world.

"Moonlight is the proper architectural light," said Guy, as they stood looking at the house. The white light and the hard black shadows brought out all the elegance of its Georgian symmetry.

"Look, here's the ghost of a rose." Marjorie touched a big cool flower, which one guessed rather than saw to be red, a faint equivocal lunar crimson. "And, oh, smell the tobacco-plant flowers. Aren't they delicious!"

"I always think there's something very mysterious about perfume drifting through the dark like this. It seems to come from some perfectly different immaterial world, peopled by unembodied sensations, phantom passions. Think of the spiritual effect of incense in a dark church. One isn't surprised that people have believed in the existence of the soul."

They walked on in silence. Sometime, accidentally, his hand would brush against hers in the movement of their march. Guy felt an intolerable emotion of expectancy, akin to fear. It made him feel almost physically sick.

"Do you remember," he said abruptly, "that summer holiday our families spent together in Wales? It must have been nineteen four or five. I was ten and you were eight or thereabouts."

"Of course I remember," cried Marjorie. "Everything. There was that funny little toy railway from the slate quarries."

"And do you remember our gold-mine? All those tons of yellow ironstone we collected and hoarded in a cave, fully believing they were nuggets. How incredibly remote it seems!"

"And you had a wonderful process by which you tested whether the stuff was real gold or not. It all passed triumphantly as genuine, I remember!"

"Having that secret together first made us friends, I believe."

"I dare say," said Marjorie. "Fourteen years ago—what a time! And you began educating me even then: all that stuff you told me about gold-mining, for instance."

"Fourteen years," Guy repeated reflectively, "and I shall be going out again to-morrow . . ."

"Don't speak about it. I am so miserable when you're away." She genuinely forgot what a delightful summer she had had, except for the shortage of tennis.

"We must make this the happiest hour of our lives. Perhaps it may be the last we shall be together." Guy looked up at the moon, and he perceived, with a sudden start, that it was a sphere islanded in an endless night, not a flat disk stuck on a wall not so very far away. It filled him with an infinite dreariness; he felt too insignificant to live at all.

"Guy, you mustn't talk like that," said Marjorie appealingly.

"We've got twelve hours," said Guy in a meditative voice, "but that's only clock-work time. You can give an hour the quality of everlastingness, and spend years which are as though they had never been. We get our immortality here and now; it's a question of quality, not of quantity. I don't look forward to golden harps or anything of that sort. I know that when I am dead, I shall be dead; there isn't any afterwards. If I'm killed, my immortality will be in your memory. Perhaps, too, somebody will read the things I've written, and in his mind I shall survive, feebly and partially. But in your mind I shall survive intact and whole."

"But I'm sure we shall go on living after death. It can't be the end." Marjorie was conscious that she had heard those words before. Where? Oh yes, it was earnest Evangeline who had spoken them at the school debating society.

"I wouldn't count on it," Guy replied, with a little laugh.

"You may get such a disappointment when you die." Then in an altered voice, "I don't want to die. I hate and fear death. But probably I shan't be killed after all. All the same . . ." His voice faded out. They stepped into a tunnel of impenetrable darkness between two tall hornbeam hedges. He had become nothing but a voice, and now that had ceased; he had disappeared. The voice began again, low, quick, monotonous, a little breathless. "I remember once reading a poem by one of the old Provençal troubadours, telling how God had once granted him supreme happiness; for the night before he was to set out for the Crusade, it had been granted him to hold his lady in his arms—all the short eternal night through. Ains que j'aille oltre mer: when I was going beyond sea." The voice stopped again. They were standing at the very mouth of the hornbeam alley, looking out from that close-pent river of shadow upon an ocean of pale moonlight.

"How still it is." They did not speak; they hardly breathed. They became saturated with the quiet.

Marjorie broke the silence. "Do you want me as much as all that, Guy?" All through that long, speechless minute she had been trying to say the words, repeating them over to herself, longing to say them aloud, but paralysed, unable to. And at last she had spoken them, impersonally, as though through the mouth of someone else. She heard them very distinctly, and was amazed at the matter-of-factness of the tone.

Guy's answer took the form of a question. "Well, suppose I were killed now," he said, "should I ever have really lived?"

They had stepped out of the cavernous alley into the moonlight. She could see him clearly now, and there was something so drooping and dejected and pathetic about him, he seemed so much of a great, overgrown child that a wave of passionate pitifulness rushed through her, reinforcing other emotions less maternal. She longed to take him in her arms, stroke his hair, lullaby him, baby-fashion, to sleep under her breast. And Guy, on his side, desired nothing better than to give his fatigues and sensibilities to her maternal care, to have his eyes kissed fast, and sleep to her soothing. In his relations with women—but his experience in this direction was deplorably small—he had, unconsciously at first but afterwards with a realization of what he was doing, played this child part. In moments of self-analysis he laughed at himself for acting the "child stunt", as he called it. Here he was—he hadn't noticed it yet—doing it again, drooping, dejected, wholly pathetic, feeble . . .

Marjorie was carried away by her emotion. She would give herself to her lover, would take possession of her helpless, pitiable child. She put her arms round his neck, lifted her face to his kisses, whispered something tender and inaudible.

Guy drew her towards him and began kissing the soft, warm mouth. He touched the bare arm that encircled his neck; the flesh was resilient under his fingers; he felt a desire to pinch it and tear it. It had been just like this with that little slut Minnie. Just the same—all horrible lust. He remembered a curious physiological fact out of Havelock Ellis. He shuddered as though he had touched something disgusting, and pushed her away.

"No, no, no. It's horrible; it's odious. Drunk with moonlight and sentimentalizing about death. . . . Why not just say with Biblical frankness, Lie with me—Lie with me?"

That this love, which was to have been so marvellous and new and beautiful, should end libidinously and bestially like the affair, never remembered without a shiver of shame, with Minnie (the vulgarity of her!)—filled him with horror.

Marjorie burst into tears and ran away, wounded and trembling. into the solitude of the hornbeam shadow. "Go away, go away," she sobbed, with such intensity of command that Guy, moved by an immediate remorse and the sight of tears to stop her and ask forgiveness, was constrained to let her go her ways.

A cool, impersonal calm had succeeded almost immediately to his outburst. Critically, he examined what he had done, and judged it, not without a certain feeling of satisfaction, to be the greatest "floater" of his life. But at least the thing was done and couldn't be undone. He took the weak-willed man's delight in the irrevocability of action. He walked up and down the lawns smoking a cigarette and thinking, clearly and quietly—remembering the past, questioning the future. When the cigarette was finished he went into the house.

He entered the smoking-room to hear Roger saying, ". . . It's the poor who are having the good time now. Plenty to eat, plenty of money, and no taxes to pay. No taxes—that's the sickening thing. Look at Alfred's gardener, for instance. He gets twenty-five or thirty bob a week and an uncommon good house. He's married, but only has one child. A man like that is uncommonly well off.

He ought to be paying income-tax; he can perfectly well afford it."

Mr Petherton was listening somnolently, Jacobsen with his usual keen, intelligent politeness; George was playing with the blue Persian kitten.

It had been arranged that George should stay the night, because it was such a bore having to walk that mile and a bit home again in the dark. Guy took him up to his room and sat down on the bed for a final cigarette, while George was undressing. It was the hour of confidence—that rather perilous moment when fatigue has relaxed the fibres of the mind, making it ready and ripe for sentiment.

"It depresses me so much," said Guy, "to think that you're only twenty and that I'm just on twenty-four. You will be young and sprightly when the war ends; I shall be an old antique man."

"Not so old as all that," George answered, pulling off his shirt. His skin was very white, face, neck, and hands seeming dark brown by comparison; there was a sharply demarcated high-water mark of sunburn at throat and wrist.

"It horrifies me to think of the time one is wasting in this bloody war, growing stupider and grosser every day, achieving nothing at all. It will be five, six—God knows how many—years cut clean out of one's life. You'll have the world before you when it's all over, but I shall have spent my best time."

"Of course, it doesn't make so much difference to me," said George through a foam of tooth-brushing; "I'm not capable of doing anything of any particular value. It's really all the same whether I lead a blameless life broking stocks or spend my time getting killed. But for you, I agree, it's too bloody. . . ."

Guy smoked on in silence, his mind filled with a languid resentment against circumstance. George put on his pyjamas and crept under the sheet; he had to curl himself up into a ball, because Guy was lying across the end of the bed, and he couldn't put his feet down.

"I suppose," said Guy at last, meditatively—"I suppose the only consolations are, after all, women and wine. I shall really have to resort to them. Only women are mostly so fearfully boring and wine is so expensive now."

"But not all women!" George, it was evident, was waiting to get a confidence off his chest.

"I gather you've found the exceptions."

George poured forth. He had just spent six months at Chelsea—six dreary months on the barrack square; but there had been lucid intervals between the drills and the special courses, which he had filled with many notable voyages of discovery among unknown worlds. And chiefly, Columbus to his own soul, he had discovered all those psychological intricacies and potentialities, which only the passions bring to light. *Nosce teipsum*, it has been commanded; and a judicious cultivation of the passions is one of the surest roads to self-knowledge. To George, at barely twenty, it was all so amazingly new and exciting, and Guy listened to the story of his adventures with admiration and a touch of envy. He regretted the dismal and cloistered chastity—broken only once, and how sordidly! Wouldn't he have learnt much more, he wondered—have been a more real and better human being if he had had George's experiences? He would have profited by them more than George could ever hope to do. There was the risk of George's getting involved in a mere foolish expense of spirit in a waste of shame. He might not be sufficiently an individual to remain himself in spite of his surroundings; his hand would be coloured by the dye he worked in. Guy felt sure that he himself would have run no risk; he would have come, seen, conquered, and returned intact and still himself, but enriched by the spoils of a new knowledge. Had he been wrong after all? Had life in the cloister of his own philosophy been wholly unprofitable?

He looked at George. It was not surprising that the ladies favoured him, glorious ephebus that he was.

"With a face and figure like mine," he reflected, "I shouldn't have been able to lead his life, even if I'd wanted to." He laughed inwardly.

"You really must meet her," George was saying enthusiastically.

Guy smiled. "No, I really mustn't. Let me give you a bit of perfectly good advice. Never attempt to share your joys with anyone else. People will sympathize with pain, but not with pleasure. Good night, George."

He bent over the pillow and kissed the smiling face that was as smooth as a child's to his lips.

Guy lay awake for a long time, and his eyes were dry and aching before sleep finally came upon him. He spent those dark interminable hours thinking—thinking hard, intensely, painfully.

No sooner had he left George's room than a feeling of intense unhappiness took hold of him. "Distorted with misery," that was how he described himself; he loved to coin such phrases, for he felt the artist's need to express as well as to feel and think. Distorted with misery, he went to bed; distorted with misery, he lay and thought and thought. He had, positively, a sense of physical distortion: his guts were twisted, he had a hunched back, his legs were withered. . . .

He had the right to be miserable. He was going back to France to-morrow, he had trampled on his mistress's love, and he was beginning to doubt himself, to wonder whether his whole life hadn't been one ludicrous folly.

He reviewed his life, like a man about to die. Born in another age, he would, he supposed, have been religious. He had got over religion early, like the measles—at nine a Low Churchman, at twelve a Broad Churchman, and at fourteen an Agnostic—but he still retained the temperament of a religious man. Intellectually he was a Voltairian, emotionally a Bunyanite. To have arrived at this formula was, he felt, a distinct advance in self-knowledge. And what a fool he had been with Marjorie! The priggishness of his attitude—making her read Wordsworth when she didn't want to. Intellectual love—his phrases weren't always a blessing; how hopelessly he had deceived himself with words! And now this evening the crowning outrage, when he had behaved to her like a hysterical anchorite dealing with a temptation. His body tingled, at the recollection, with shame.

An idea occurred to him; he would go and see her, tiptoe downstairs to her room, kneel by her bed, ask for her forgiveness. He lay quite still imagining the whole scene. He even went so far as to get out of bed, open the door, which made a noise in the process like a peacock's scream, quite unnerving him, and creep to the head of the stairs. He stood there a long time, his feet growing colder and colder, and then decided that the adventure was really too sordidly like the episode at the beginning of Tolstoy's *Resurrection*. The door screamed again as he returned; he lay in bed, trying to persuade himself that his self-control had been admirable and at the same time cursing his absence of courage in not carrying out what he had intended.

He remembered a lecture he had given Marjorie once on the subject of Sacred and Profane Love. Poor girl, how she had listened in patience? He could see her attending with such a serious expression on her face that she looked quite ugly. She looked so beautiful when she was laughing or happy; at the Whites, for instance, three nights ago, when George and she had danced after dinner and he had sat, secretly envious, reading a book in the corner of the room and looking superior. He wouldn't learn to dance, but always wished he could. It was a barbarous, aphrodisiacal occupation, he said, and he preferred to spend his time and energies in reading. Salvationist again! What a much wiser person George had proved himself than he. He had no prejudices, no theoretical views about the conduct of life; he just lived, admirably, naturally, as the spirit or the flesh moved him. If only he could live his life again, if only he could abolish this evening's monstrous stupidity. . . .

Marjorie also lay awake. She too felt herself distorted with misery. How odiously cruel he had been, and how much she longed to forgive him! Perhaps he would come in the dark, when all the house was asleep, tiptoeing into the room very quietly to kneel by her bed and ask to be forgiven. Would he come, she wondered? She stared into the blackness above her and about her, willing him to come, commanding him—angry and wretched because he was so slow in coming, because he didn't come at all. They were both of them asleep before two.

Seven hours of sleep make a surprising difference to the state of mind. Guy, who thought he was distorted for life, woke to find himself healthily normal. Marjorie's angers and despairs had subsided. The hour they had together between breakfast and Guy's departure was filled with almost trivial conversation. Guy was determined to say something about last night's incident. But it was only at the very last moment, when the dog-cart was actually at the door, that he managed to bring out some stammered repentance for what had happened last night.

"Don't think about it," Marjorie had told him. So they had kissed and parted, and their relations were precisely the same as they had been before Guy came on leave.

George was sent out a week or two later, and a month after that they heard at Blaybury that he had lost a leg—fortunately below the knee.

"Poor boy!" said Mr Petherton. "I must really write a line to his mother at once."

Jacobsen made no comment, but it was a surprise to him to find how much he had been moved by the news. George White had lost a leg; he couldn't get the thought out of his head. But only below the knee; he might be called lucky. Lucky—things are deplorably relative, he reflected. One thanks God because He has thought fit to deprive one of His creatures of a limb.

"Neither delighteth He in any man's legs," eh? Nous avons changé tout cela.

George had lost a leg. There would be no more of that Olympian speed and strength and beauty. Jacobsen conjured up before his memory a vision of the boy running with his great fawn-coloured dog across green expanses of grass. How glorious he had looked, his fine brown hair blowing like fire in the wind of his own speed, his cheeks flushed, his eyes very bright. And how easily he ran, with long, bounding strides, looking down at the dog that jumped and barked at his side!

He had had a perfection, and now it was spoilt. Instead of a leg he had a stump. *Moignon*, the French called it; there was the right repulsive sound about *moignon* which was lacking in "stump". Soignons le moignon en l'oignant d'oignons.

Often, at night before he went to sleep, he couldn't help thinking of George and the war and all the millions of *moignons* there must be in the world. He had a dream one night of slimy red knobbles, large polyp-like things, growing as he looked at them, swelling between his hands—*moignons*, in fact.

George was well enough in the late autumn to come home. He had learnt to hop along on his crutches very skilfully, and his preposterous donkey-drawn bath-chair soon became a familiar object in the lanes of the neighbourhood. It was a grand sight to behold when George rattled past at the trot, leaning forward like a young Phœbus in his chariot and urging his unwilling beast with voice and crutch. He drove over to Blaybury almost every day; Marjorie and he had endless talks about life and love and Guy and other absorbing topics. With Jacobsen he played piquet and discussed a thousand subjects. He was always gay and happy—that was what especially lacerated Jacobsen's heart with pity.

IV

The Christmas holidays had begun, and the Reverend Roger was back again at Blaybury. He was sitting at the writing-table in the drawing-room, engaged, at the moment, in biting the end of his pen and scratching his head. His face wore an expression of perplexity; one would have said that he was in the throes of literary composition. Which indeed he was: "Beloved ward of Alfred Petherton . . ." he said aloud. "Beloved ward . . ." He shook his head doubtfully.

The door opened and Jacobsen came into the room. Roger turned round at once.

"Have you heard the grievous news?" he said.

"No. What?"

"Poor Guy is dead. We got the telegram half an hour ago."

"Good God!" said Jacobsen in an agonized voice which seemed to show that he had been startled out of the calm belonging to one who leads the life of reason. He had been conscious ever since George's mutilation that his defences were growing weaker; external circumstance was steadily encroaching upon him. Now it had broken in and, for the moment, he was at its mercy. Guy dead. . . . He pulled himself together sufficiently to say, after a pause, "Well, I suppose it was only to be expected sooner or later. Poor boy."

"Yes, it's terrible, isn't it?" said Roger, shaking his head. "I am just writing out an announcement to send to *The Times*. One can hardly say 'the beloved ward of Alfred Petherton,' can one? It doesn't sound quite right; and yet one would like somehow to give public expression to the deep affection Alfred felt for him. 'Beloved ward'—no, decidedly it won't do."

"You'll have to get round it somehow," said Jacobsen. Roger's presence somehow made a return to the life of reason easier.

"Poor Alfred," the other went on. "You've no idea how hardly he takes it. He feels as though he had given a son."

"What a waste it is!" Jacobsen exclaimed. He was altogether too deeply moved.

"I have done my best to console Alfred. One must always bear in mind for what Cause he died."

"All those potentialities destroyed. He was an able fellow, was

Guy." Jacobsen was speaking more to himself than to his companion, but Roger took up the suggestion.

"Yes, he certainly was that. Alfred thought he was very promising. It is for his sake I am particularly sorry. I never got on very well with the boy myself. He was too eccentric for my taste. There's such a thing as being too clever, isn't there? It's rather inhuman. He used to do most remarkable Greek iambics for me when he was a boy. I dare say he was a very good fellow under all that cleverness and queerness. It's all very distressing, very grievous."

"How was he killed?"

"Died of wounds yesterday morning. Do you think it would be a good thing to put in some quotation at the end of the announcement in the paper? Something like, 'Dulce et Decorum', or 'Sed Miles, sed Pro Patria', or 'Per Ardua ad Astra'?"

"It hardly seems essential," said Jacobsen.

"Perhaps not." Roger's lips moved silently; he was counting. "Forty-two words. I suppose that counts as eight lines. Poor Marjorie! I hope she won't feel it too bitterly. Alfred told me they were unofficially engaged. "

"So I gathered."

"I am afraid I shall have to break the news to her. Alfred is too much upset to be able to do anything himself. It will be a most painful task. Poor girl! I suppose as a matter of fact they would not have been able to marry for some time, as Guy had next to no money. These early marriages are very rash. Let me see: eight times three shillings is one pound four, isn't it? I suppose they take cheques all right?"

"How old was he?" asked Jacobsen.

"Twenty-four and a few months."

Jacobsen was walking restlessly up and down the room. "Just reaching maturity! One is thankful these days to have one's own work and thoughts to take the mind off these horrors."

"It's terrible, isn't it?—terrible. So many of my pupils have been killed now that I can hardly keep count of the number."

There was a tapping at the French window; it was Marjorie asking to be let in. She had been cutting holly and ivy for the Christmas decorations, and carried a basket full of dark, shining leaves.

Jacobsen unbolted the big window and Marjorie came in, flushed with the cold and smiling. Jacobsen had never seen her looking so handsome: she was superb, radiant, like Iphigenia coming in her wedding garments to the sacrifice.

"The holly is very poor this year," she remarked. "I am afraid we shan't make much of a show with our Christmas decorations."

Jacobsen took the opportunity of slipping out through the French window. Although it was unpleasantly cold, he walked up and down the flagged paths of the Dutch garden, hatless and overcoatless, for quite a long time.

Marjorie moved about the drawing-room fixing sprigs of holly round the picture frames. Her uncle watched her, hesitating to speak; he was feeling enormously uncomfortable.

"I am afraid," he said at last, "that your father's very upset this morning." His voice was husky; he made an explosive noise to clear his throat.

"Is it his palpitations?" Marjorie asked coolly; her father's infirmities did not cause her much anxiety.

"No, no." Roger realized that his opening gambit had been a mistake. "No. It is—er—a more mental affliction, and one which, I fear, will touch you closely too. Marjorie, you must be strong and courageous; we have just heard that Guy is dead."

"Guy dead?" She couldn't believe it; she had hardly envisaged the possibility; besides, he was on the Staff. "Oh, Uncle Roger, it isn't true."

"I am afraid there is no doubt. The War Office telegram came just after you had gone out for the holly."

Marjorie sat down on the sofa and hid her face in her hands. Guy dead; she would never see him again, never see him again, never; she began to cry.

Roger approached and stood, with his hand on her shoulder, in the attitude of a thought-reader. To those overwhelmed by sorrow the touch of a friendly hand is often comforting. They have fallen into an abyss, and the touching hand serves to remind them that life and God and human sympathy still exist, however bottomless the gulf of grief may seem. On Marjorie's shoulder her uncle's hand rested with a damp, heavy warmth that was peculiarly unpleasant.

"Dear child, it is very grievous, I know; but you must try and be strong and bear it bravely. We all have our cross to bear. We shall be celebrating the Birth of Christ in two days' time; remember with what patience He received the cup of agony. And then remember for what Cause Guy has given his life. He has died a hero's death, a martyr's death, witnessing to Heaven against the powers of evil." Roger was unconsciously slipping into the words of his last sermon in the school chapel. "You should feel pride in his death as well as sorrow. There, there, poor child." He patted her shoulder two or three times. "Perhaps it would be kinder to leave you now."

For some time after her uncle's departure Marjorie sat motionless in the same position, her body bent forward, her face in her hands. She kept on repeating the words, "Never again," and the sound of them filled her with despair and made her cry. They seemed to open up such a dreary grey infinite vista—"never again". They were as a spell evoking tears.

She got up at last and began walking aimlessly about the room. She paused in front of a little old black-framed mirror that hung near the window and looked at her reflection in the glass. She had expected somehow to look different, to have changed. She was surprised to find her face entirely unaltered: grave, melancholy perhaps, but still the same face she had looked at when she was doing her hair this morning. A curious idea entered her head; she wondered whether she would be able to smile now, at this dreadful moment. She moved the muscles of her face and was overwhelmed with shame at the sight of the mirthless grin that mocked her from the glass. What a beast she was! She burst into tears and threw herself again on the sofa, burying her face in a cushion. The door opened, and by the noise of shuffling and tapping Marjorie recognized the approach of George White on his crutches. She did not look up. At the sight of the abject figure on the sofa, George halted, uncertain what he should do. Should he quietly go away again, or should he stay and try to say something comforting? The sight of her lying there gave him almost physical pain. He decided to stay.

He approached the sofa and stood over her, suspended on his crutches. Still she did not lift her head, but pressed her face deeper into the smothering blindness of the cushion, as though to shut out from her consciousness all the external world. George looked down at her in silence. The little delicate tendrils of hair on the nape of her neck were exquisitely beautiful.

"I was told about it," he said at last, "just now, as I came in. It's too awful. I think I cared for Guy more than for almost anyone in the world. We both did, didn't we?"

She began sobbing again. George was overcome with remorse, feeling that he had somehow hurt her, somehow added to her pain by what he had said. "Poor child, poor child," he said, almost aloud. She was a year older than he, but she seemed so helplessly and pathetically young now that she was crying.

Standing up for long tired him, and he lowered himself, slowly and painfully, into the sofa beside her. She looked up at last and began drying her eyes.

"I'm so wretched, George, so specially wretched because I feel I didn't act rightly towards darling Guy. There were times, you know, when I wondered whether it wasn't all a great mistake, our being engaged. Sometimes I felt I almost hated him. I'd been feeling so odious about him these last weeks. And now comes this, and it makes me realize how awful I've been towards him." She found it a relief to confide and confess; George was so sympathetic, he would understand. "I've been a beast."

Her voice broke, and it was as though something had broken in George's head. He was overwhelmed with pity; he couldn't bear it that she should suffer.

"You mustn't distress yourself unnecessarily, Marjorie dear," he begged her, stroking the back of her hand with his large hard palm. "Don't."

Marjorie went on remorselessly. "When Uncle Roger told me just now, do you known what I did? I said to myself, Do I really care? I couldn't make out. I looked in the glass to see if I could tell from my face. Then I suddenly thought I'd see whether I could laugh, and I did. And that made me feel how detestable I was, and I started crying again. Oh, I have been a beast, George, haven't I?"

She burst into a passion of tears and hid her face once more in the friendly cushion. George couldn't bear it at all. He laid his hand on her shoulder and bent forward, close to her, till his face almost touched her hair. "Don't," he cried. "Don't, Marjorie. You mustn't torment yourself like this. I know you loved Guy; we both loved him. He would have wanted us to be happy and brave and to go on with life—not make his death a source of hopeless despair." There was a silence, broken only by the agonizing sound of sobbing. "Marjorie, darling, you mustn't cry."

"There, I'm not," said Marjorie through her tears. "I'll try to stop. Guy wouldn't have wanted us to cry for him. You're right;

he would have wanted us to live for him—worthily, in his splendid way."

"We who knew him and loved him must make our lives a memorial of him." In ordinary circumstances George would have died rather than make a remark like that. But in speaking of the dead, people forget themselves and conform to the peculiar obituary convention of thought and language. Spontaneously, unconsciously, George had conformed.

Marjorie wiped her eyes. "Thank you, George. You know so well what darling Guy would have liked. You've made me feel stronger to bear it. But, all the same, I do feel odious for what I thought about him sometimes. I didn't love him enough. And now it's too late. I shall never see him again." The spell of that "never" worked again: Marjorie sobbed despairingly.

George's distress knew no bounds. He put his arm round Marjorie's shoulders and kissed her hair. "Don't cry, Marjorie. Everybody feels like that sometimes, even towards the people they love most. You really mustn't make yourself miserable."

Once more she lifted her face and looked at him with a heart-breaking, tearful smile. "You have been too sweet to me, George. I don't know what I should have done without you."

"Poor darling!" said George. "I can't bear to see you unhappy." Their faces were close to one another, and it seemed natural that at this point their lips should meet in a long kiss. "We'll remember only the splendid, glorious things about Guy," he went on—"what a wonderful person he was, and how much we loved him." He kissed her again.

"Perhaps our darling Guy is with us here even now," said Marjorie, with a look of ecstasy on her face.

"Perhaps he is," George echoed.

It was at this point that a heavy footstep was heard and a hand rattled at the door. Marjorie and George moved a little farther apart. The intruder was Roger, who bustled in, rubbing his hands with an air of conscious heartiness, studiously pretending that nothing untoward had occurred. It is our English tradition that we should conceal our emotions. "Well, well," he said, "I think we had better be going in to luncheon. The bell has gone."

Eupompus Gave Splendour to Art by Numbers

"**I** HAVE made a discovery," said Emberlin as I entered his room. "What about?" I asked.

"A discovery," he replied, "about *Discoveries*." He radiated an unconcealed satisfaction; the conversation had evidently gone exactly as he had intended it to go. He had made his phrase, and, repeating it lovingly—"A discovery about *Discoveries*"—he smiled benignly at me, enjoying my look of mystification—an expression which, I confess, I had purposely exaggerated in order to give him pleasure. For Emberlin, in many ways so childish, took an especial delight in puzzling and nonplussing his acquaintances; and these small triumphs, these little " scores" off people afforded him some of his keenest pleasures. I always indulged his weakness when I could, for it was worth while being in Emberlin's good books. To be allowed to listen to his post-prandial conversation was a privilege indeed. Not only was he himself a consummately good talker, but he had also the power of stimulating others to talk well. He was like some subtle wine, intoxicating just to the Meredithian level of tipsiness. In his company you would find yourself lifted to the sphere of nimble and mercurial conceptions; you would suddenly realize that some miracle had occurred, that you were living no longer in a dull world of jumbled things but somewhere above the hotch-potch in a glassily perfect universe of ideas, where all was informed, consistent, symmetrical. And it was Emberlin who, godlike, had the power of creating this new and real world. He built it out of words, this crystal Eden, where no belly-going snake, devourer of quotidian dirt, might ever enter and disturb its harmonies. Since I first knew Emberlin I have come to have a greatly enhanced respect for magic and all the formulas of its liturgy. If by words Emberlin can create a new world for me, can make my spirit slough off completely the domination of the old, why should not he or I or anyone, having found the suitable phrases, exert by means of them an influence more vulgarly miraculous upon the world of mere things? Indeed when I compare Emberlin and the common or garden black magician of commerce, it seems to me that Emberlin is the greater thaumaturge. But let that pass; I am straying from my purpose, which was to give some description of the man who so confidently whispered to me that he had made a discovery about *Discoveries*.

In the best sense of the word, then, Emberlin was academic. For us who knew him his rooms were an oasis of aloofness planted secretly in the heart of the desert of London. He exhaled an atmosphere that combined the fantastic speculativeness of the undergraduate with the more mellowed oddity of incredibly wise and antique dons. He was immensely erudite, but in a wholly unencyclopædic way—a mine of irrelevant information, as his enemies said of him. He wrote a certain amount, but, like Mallarmé, avoided publication, deeming it akin to "the offence of exhibitionism." Once, however, in the folly of youth, some dozen years ago, he had published a volume of verses. He spent a good deal of time now in assiduously collecting copies of his book and burning them. There can be but very few left in the world now. My friend Cope had the fortune to pick one up the other day —a little blue book, which he showed me very secretly. I am at a loss to understand why Emberlin wishes to stamp out all trace of it. There is nothing to be ashamed of in the book; some of the verses, indeed, are, in their young ecstatic fashion, good. But they are certainly conceived in a style that is unlike that of his present poems. Perhaps it is that which makes him so implacable against them. What he writes now for very private manuscript circulation is curious stuff. I confess I prefer the earlier work; I do not like the stony, hard-edged quality of this sort of thing—the only one I can remember of his later productions. It is a sonnet on a porcelain figure of a woman, dug up at Cnossus:

> *"Her eyes of bright unwinking glaze*
> *All imperturbable do not*
> *Even make pretences to regard*
> *The jutting absence of her stays*
> *Where many a Syrian gallipot*
> *Excites desire with spilth of nard.*
> *The bistred rims above the fard*
> *Of cheeks as red as bergamot*
> *Attest that no shamefaced delays*
> *Will clog fulfilment nor retard*

> Full payment of the Cyprian's praise
> Down to the last remorseful jot.
> Hail priestess of we know not what
> Strange cult of Mycenean days!"

Regrettably, I cannot remember any of Emberlin's French poems. His peculiar muse expresses herself better, I think, in that language than in her native tongue.

Such is Emberlin; such, I should rather say, *was* he, for, as I propose to show, he is not now the man that he was when he whispered so confidentially to me, as I entered the room, that he had made a discovery about *Discoveries*.

I waited patiently till he had finished his little game of mystification and, when the moment seemed ripe, I asked him to explain himself. Emberlin was ready to open out.

"Well," he began, "these are the facts—a tedious introduction, I fear, but necessary. Years ago, when I was first reading Ben Jonson's *Discoveries*, that queer jotting of his, 'Eupompus gave splendour to Art by Numbers', tickled my curiosity. You yourself must have been struck by the phrase, everybody must have noticed it; and everybody must have noticed too that no commentator has a word to say on the subject. That is the way of commentators—the obvious points fulsomely explained and discussed, the hard passages, about which one might want to know something passed over in the silence of sheer ignorance. 'Eupompus gave splendour to Art by Numbers'—the absurd phrase stuck in my head. At one time it positively haunted me. I used to chant it in my bath, set to music as an anthem. It went like this, so far as I remember"—and he burst into song: "'Eupompus, Eu-u-pompus gave sple-e-e-endour . . .'" and so on, through all the repetitions, the dragged-out rises and falls of a parodied anthem.

"I sing you this," he said when he had finished, "just to show you what a hold that dreadful sentence took upon my mind. For eight years, off and on, its senselessness has besieged me. I have looked up Eupompus in all the obvious books of reference, of course. He is there all right—Alexandrian artist, eternized by some wretched little author in some even wretcheder little anecdote, which at the moment I entirely forget; it had nothing, at any rate, to do with the embellishment of art by numbers.

Long ago I gave up the search as hopeless; Eupompus remained for me a shadowy figure of mystery, author of some nameless outrage, bestower of some forgotten benefit upon the art that he practised. His history seemed wrapt in an impenetrable darkness. And then yesterday I discovered all about him and his art and his numbers. A chance discovery, than which few things have given me a greater pleasure.

"I happened upon it, as a I say, yesterday when I was glancing through a volume of Zuylerius. Not, of course, the Zuylerius one knows," he added quickly, "otherwise one would have had the heart out of Eupompus' secret years ago."

"Of course," I repeated, "not the familiar Zuylerius."

"Exactly," said Emberlin, taking seriously my flippancy, "not the familiar John Zuylerius, Junior, but the elder Henricus Zuylerius, a much less—though perhaps undeservedly so—renowned figure than his son. But this is not the time to discuss their respective merits. At any rate, I discovered in a volume of critical dialogues by the elder Zuylerius, the reference, to which, without doubt, Jonson was referring in his note. (It was of course a mere jotting, never meant to be printed, but which Jonson's literary executors pitched into the book with all the rest of the available posthumous materials.) 'Eupompus gave splendour to Art by Numbers'—Zuylerius gives a very circumstantial account of the process. He must, I suppose, have found the sources for it in some writer now lost to us."

Emberlin paused a moment to muse. The loss of the work of any ancient writer gave him the keenest sorrow. I rather believe he had written a version of the unrecovered books of Petronius. Some day I hope I shall be permitted to see what conception Emberlin has of the *Satyricon* as a whole. He would, I am sure, do Petronius justice—almost too much, perhaps.

"What was the story of Eupompus?" I asked. "I am all curiosity to know."

Emberlin heaved a sigh and went on.

"Zuylerius' narrative," he said, "is very bald, but on the whole lucid; and I think it gives one the main points of the story. I will give it you in my own words; that is preferable to reading his Dutch Latin. Eupompus, then, was one of the most fashionable portrait-painters of Alexandria. His clientele was large, his business immensely profitable. For a half-length in oils the great courtesans would pay him a month's earnings. He would paint likenesses of the merchant princes in exchange for the costliest of their outlandish treasures. Coal-black potentates would come a thousand miles out of Ethiopia to have a miniature limned on some specially choice panel of ivory; and for payment there would be camel-loads of gold and spices. Fame, riches, and honour came to him while he was yet young; an unparalleled career seemed to lie before him. And then, quite suddenly, he gave it all up—refused to paint another portrait. The doors of his studio were closed. It was in vain that clients, however rich, however distinguished, demanded admission; the slaves had their order; Eupompus would see no one but his own intimates."

Emberlin made a pause in his narrative.

"What was Eupompus doing?" I asked.

"He was, of course," said Emberlin, "occupied in giving splendour to Art by Numbers. And this, as far as I can gather from Zuylerius, is how it all happened. He just suddenly fell in love with numbers—head over ears, amorous of pure counting. Number seemed to him to be the sole reality, the only thing about which the mind of man could be certain. To count was the one thing worth doing, because it was the one thing you could be sure of doing right. Thus, art, that it may have any value at all, must ally itself with reality—must, that is, possess a numerical foundation. He carried the idea into practice by painting the first picture in his new style. It was a gigantic canvas, covering several hundred square feet—I have no doubt that Eupompus could have told you the exact area to an inch—and upon it was represented an illimitable ocean covered, as far as the eye could reach in every direction, with a multitude of black swans. There were thirty-three thousand of these black swans, each, even though it might be but a speck on the horizon, distinctly limned. In the middle of the ocean was an island, upon which stood a more or less human figure having three eyes, three arms and legs, three breasts and three navels. In the leaden sky three suns were dimly expiring. There was nothing more in the picture; Zuylerius describes it exactly. Eupompus spent nine months of hard work in painting it. The privileged few who were allowed to see it pronounced it, finished, a masterpiece. They gathered round Eupompus in a little school, calling themselves the Philarithmics. They would sit for hours in front of his great work, contemplating the swans and counting them; according to the Philarithmics, to count and to contemplate were the same thing.

Eupompus' next picture, representing an orchard of identical trees set in quincunxes, was regarded with less favour by the connoisseurs. His studies of crowds were, however, more highly esteemed; in these were portrayed masses of people arranged in groups that exactly imitated the number and position of the stars making up various of the more famous constellations. And then there was his famous picture of the amphitheatre, which created a furore among the Philarithmics. Zuylerius again gives us a detailed description. Tier upon tier of seats are seen, all occupied by strange Cyclopean figures. Each tier accommodates more people than the tier below, and the number rises in a complicated but regular progression. All the figures seated in the amphitheatre possess but a single eye, enormous and luminous, planted in the middle of the forehead: and all these thousands of single eyes are fixed, in a terrible and menacing scrutiny, upon a dwarf-like creature cowering pitiably in the arena. . . . He alone of the multitude possesses two eyes.

"I would give anything to see that picture," Emberlin added, after a pause. "The colouring, you know; Zuylerius gives no hint, but I feel somehow certain that the dominant tone must have been a fierce brick-red—a red granite amphitheatre filled with a red-robed assembly, sharply defined against an implacable blue sky."

"Their eyes would be green," I suggested.

Emberlin closed his eyes to visualize the scene and then nodded a slow and rather dubious assent.

"Up to this point," Emberlin resumed at length, "Zuylerius' account is very clear. But his descriptions of the later philarithmic art become extremely obscure; I doubt whether he understood in the least what it was all about. I will give you such meaning as I manage to extract from his chaos. Eupompus seems to have grown tired of painting merely numbers of objects. He wanted now to represent Number itself. And then he conceived the plan of rendering visible the fundamental ideas of life through the medium of those purely numerical terms into which, according to him, they must ultimately resolve themselves. Zuylerius speaks vaguely of a picture of Eros, which seems to have consisted of a series of interlacing planes. Eupompus' fancy seems next to have been taken by various of the Socratic dialogues upon the nature of general ideas, and he made a series of illustrations for them in the same arithmogeometric style. Finally there is Zuylerius' wild description of the last picture that Eupompus ever painted. I can make very little of it. The subject of the work, at least, is clearly stated; it was a representation of Pure Number, or God and the Universe, or whatever you like to call that pleasingly inane conception of totality. It was a picture of the cosmos seen, I take it, through a rather Neoplatonic *camera obscura*—very clear and in small. Zuylerius suggests a design of planes radiating out from a single point of light. I dare say something of the kind came in. Actually, I have no doubt, the work was a very adequate rendering in visible form of the conception of the one and the many, with all the intermediate stages of enlightenment between matter and the *Fons Deitatis*. However, it's no use speculating what the picture may have been going to look like. Poor old Eupompus went mad before he had completely finished it and, after he had dispatched two of the admiring Philarithmics with a hammer, he flung himself out of the window and broke his neck. That was the end of him, and that was how he gave splendour, regrettably transient, to Art by Numbers."

Emberlin stopped. We brooded over our pipes in silence; poor old Eupompus!

That was four months ago, and to-day Emberlin is a confirmed and apparently irreclaimable Philarithmic, a quite wholehearted Eupompian.

It was always Emberlin's way to take up the ideas that he finds in books and to put them into practice. He was once, for example, a working alchemist, and attained to considerable proficiency in the Great Art. He studied mnemonics under Bruno and Raymond Lully, and constructed for himself a model of the latter's syllogizing machine, in hopes of gaining that universal knowledge which the Enlightened Doctor guaranteed to its user. This time it is Eupompianism, and the thing has taken hold of him. I have held up to him all the hideous warnings that I can find in history. But it is no use.

There is the pitiable spectacle of Dr Johnson under the tyranny of an Eupompian ritual, counting the posts and the paving-stones of Fleet Street. He himself knew best how nearly a madman he was.

And then I count as Eupompians all gamblers, all calculating boys, all interpreters of the prophecies of Daniel and the Apocalypse; then too the Elberfeld horses, most complete of all Eupompians.

And here was Emberlin joining himself to this sect, degrading himself to the level of counting beasts and irrational children and men, more or less insane. Dr Johnson was at least born with a strain of the Eupompian aberration in him; Emberlin is busily and consciously acquiring it. My expostulations, the expostulations of all his friends, are as yet unavailing. It is in vain that I tell Emberlin that counting is the easiest thing in the world to do, that when I am utterly exhausted, my brain, for lack of ability to perform any other work, just counts and reckons, like a machine, like an Elberfeld horse. It all falls on deaf ears; Emberlain merely smiles and shows me some new numerical joke that he has discovered. Emberlin can never enter a tiled bathroom now without counting how many courses of tiles there are from floor to ceiling. He regards it as an interesting fact that there are twenty-six rows of tiles in his bathroom and thirty-two in mine, while all the public lavatories in Holborn have the same number. He knows now how many paces it is from any one point in London to any other. I have given up going for walks with him. I am always made so distressingly conscious by his preoccupied look, that he is counting his steps.

His evenings, too, have become profoundly melancholy; the conversation, however well it may begin, always comes round to the same nauseating subject. We can never escape numbers; Eupompus haunts us. It is not as if we were mathematicians and could discuss problems of any interest or value. No, none of us are mathematicians, least of all Emberlin. Emberlin likes talking about such points as the numerical significance of the Trinity, the immense importance of its being three in one, not forgetting the even greater importance of its being one in three. He likes giving us statistics about the speed of light or the rate of growth in fingernails. He loves to speculate on the nature of odd and even numbers. And he seems to be unconscious how much he has changed for the worse. He is happy in an exclusively absorbing interest. It is as though some mental leprosy had fallen upon his intelligence.

In another year or so, I tell Emberlin, he may almost be able to compete with the calculating horses on their own ground. He will have lost all traces of his reason, but he will be able to extract cube roots in his head. It occurs to me that the reason why Eupompus killed himself was not that he was mad; on the contrary, it was because he was, temporarily, sane. He had been mad for years, and then suddenly the idiot's self-complacency was lit up by a flash of sanity. By its momentary light he saw into what gulfs of imbecility he had plunged. He saw and understood, and the full horror, the lamentable absurdity of the situation made him desperate. He vindicated Eupompus against Eupompianism, humanity against the Philarithmics. It gives me the greatest pleasure to think that he disposed of two of that hideous crew before he died himself.

Cynthia

WHEN, some fifty years hence, my grandchildren ask me what I did when I was at Oxford in the remote days towards the beginning of our monstrous century, I shall look back across the widening gulf of time and tell them with perfect good faith that I never worked less than eight hours a day, that I took a keen interest in Social Service, and that coffee was the strongest stimulant in which I indulged. And they will very justly say—but I hope I shall be out of hearing. That is why I propose to write my memoirs as soon as possible, before I have had time to forget, so that having the truth before me I shall never in time to come be able, consciously or unconsciously, to tell lies about myself.

At present I have no time to write a complete account of that decisive period in my history. I must content myself therefore with describing a single incident of my undergraduate days. I have selected this one because it is curious and at the same time wholly characteristic of Oxford life before the war.

My friend Lykeham was an Exhibitioner at Swellfoot College. He combined blood (he was immensely proud of his Anglo-Saxon descent and the derivation of his name from Old English *lycam*, a corpse) with brains. His tastes were eccentric, his habits deplorable, the range of his information immense. As he is now dead, I will say no more about his character.

To proceed with my anecdote: I had gone one evening, as was my custom, to visit him in his rooms at Swellfoot. It was just after nine when I mounted the stairs, and great Tom was still tolling.

> "*In Thomae laude*
> *Resono bim bam sine fraude,*"

as the charmingly imbecile motto used to run, and to-night he was living up to it by bim-bamming away in a persistent *basso profondo* that made an astonishing background of discord to the sound of frantic guitar playing which emanated from Lykeham's room. From the fury of his twanging I could tell that something more than usually cataclysmic had happened, for mercifully it was only in moments of the greatest stress that Lykeham touched his guitar.

I entered the room with my hands over my ears. "For God's sake——" I implored. Through the open window Tom was shouting a deep E flat, with a spread chord of under- and over-tones, while the guitar gibbered shrilly and hysterically in D natural. Lykeham laughed, banged down his guitar on to the sofa with such violence that it gave forth a trembling groan from all its strings, and ran forward to meet me. He slapped me on the shoulder with painful heartiness; his whole face radiated joy and excitement.

I can sympathize with people's pains, but not with their pleasures. There is something curiously boring about somebody else's happiness.

"You are perspiring," I said coldly.

Lykeham mopped himself, but went on grinning.

"Well, what is it this time?" I asked. "Are you engaged to be married again?"

Lykeham burst forth with the triumphant pleasure of one who has at last found an opportunity of disburdening himself of an oppressive secret. "Far better than that," he cried.

I groaned. "Some more than usually unpleasant amour, I suppose." I knew that he had been in London the day before, a pressing engagement with the dentist having furnished an excuse to stay the night.

"Don't be gross," said Lykeham, with a nervous laugh which showed that my suspicions had been only too well founded.

"Well, let's hear about the delectable Flossie or Effie or whatever her name was," I said, with resignation.

"I tell you she was a goddess."

"The goddess of reason, I suppose."

"A goddess," Lykeham continued; "the most wonderful creature I've ever seen. And the extraordinary thing is," he added confidentially, and with ill-supposed pride, "that it seems I myself am a god of sorts."

"Of gardens; but do come down to facts."

"I'll tell you the whole story. It was like this: Last night I was in town, you know, and went to see that capital play that's running at the Prince Consort's. It's one of those ingenious combinations of melodrama and problem play, which thrill you to the marrow and at the same time give you a virtuous feeling that you've been to see something serious. Well, I rolled in rather late, having secured an admirable place in the front row of the dress circle. I trampled in over the populace, and casually observed that there was a girl sitting next me, whom I apologized to for treading on her toes. I thought no more about her during the first act. In the interval, when the lights were on again, I turned round to look at things in general and discovered that there was a goddess sitting next me. One only had to look at her to see she was a goddess. She was quite incredibly beautiful—rather pale and virginal and slim, and at the same time very stately. I can't describe her; she was simply perfect—there's nothing more to be said."

"Perfect," I repeated, "but so were all the rest."

"Fool!" Lykeham answered impatiently. "All the rest were just damned women. This was a goddess, I tell you. Don't interrupt me any more. As I was looking with astonishment at her profile, she turned her head and looked squarely at me. I've never seen anything so lovely; I almost swooned away. Our eyes met——"

"What an awful novelist's expression!" I expostulated.

"I can't help it; there's no other word. Our eyes did meet, and we both fell simultaneously in love."

"Speak for yourself."

"I could see it in her eyes. Well, to go on. We looked at one another several times during that first interval, and then the second act began. In the course of the act, entirely accidentally, I knocked my programme on to the floor, and reaching down to get it I touched her hand. Well, there was obviously nothing else to do but to take hold of it."

"And what did she do?"

"Nothing. We sat like that the whole of the rest of the act, rapturously happy and—"

"And quietly perspiring palm to palm. I know exactly, so we can pass that over. Proceed."

"Of course you don't know in the least; you've never held a goddess's hand. When the lights went up again I reluctantly dropped her hand, not liking the thought of the profane crowd seeing us, and for want of anything better to say, I asked her if she actually was a goddess. She said it was a curious question, as she'd been wondering what god I was. So we said, how incredible: and I said I was sure she was a goddess, and she said she was certain I was a god, and I bought some chocolates, and the third act began. Now, it being a melodrama, there was of course in the third act a murder and burglary scene, in which all the lights were turned out. In this thrilling moment of total blackness I suddenly felt her kiss me on the cheek."

"I thought you said she was virginal."

"So she was—absolutely, frozenly virginal; but she was made of a sort of burning ice, if you understand me. She was virginally passionate—just the combination you'd expect to find in a goddess. I admit I was startled when she kissed me, but with infinite presence of mind I kissed her back, on the mouth. Then the murder was finished and the lights went on again. Nothing much more happened till the end of the show, when I helped her on with her coat and we went out together, as if it were the most obvious thing in the world, and got into a taxi. I told the man to drive somewhere where we could get supper, and he drove there."

"Not without embracements by the way?"

"No, not without certain embracements."

"Always passionately virginal?"

"Always virginally passionate."

"Proceed."

"Well, we had supper—a positively Olympian affair, nectar and ambrosia and stolen hand-pressures. She became more and more wonderful every moment. My God, you should have seen her eyes! The whole soul seemed to burn in their depths, like fire under the sea——"

"For narrative," I interrupted him, "the epic or heroic style is altogether more suitable than the lyrical."

"Well, as I say, we had supper, and after that my memory becomes a sort of burning mist."

"Let us make haste to draw the inevitable veil. What was her name?"

Lykeham confessed that he didn't know; as she was a goddess, it didn't really seem to matter what her earthly name was. How did he expect to find her again? He hadn't thought of that, but knew she'd turn up somehow. I told him he was a fool, and asked which particular goddess he thought she was and which particular god he himself.

"We discussed that," he said. "We first thought Ares and Aphrodite; but she wasn't my idea of Aphrodite, and I don't know that I'm very much like Ares."

He looked pensively in the old Venetian mirror which hung over the fireplace. It was a complacent look, for Lykeham was rather vain about his personal appearance, which was, indeed, repulsive at first sight, but had, when you looked again, a certain strange and fascinating ugly beauty. Bearded, he would have made a passable Socrates. But Ares—no, certainly he wasn't Ares.

"Perhaps you're Hephæstus," I suggested; but the idea was received coldly.

Was he sure that she was a goddess? Mightn't she just have been a nymph of sorts? Europa, for instance. Lykeham repudiated the implied suggestion that he was a bull, nor would he hear of himself as a swan or a shower of gold. It was possible, however, he thought, that he was Apollo and she Daphne, reincarnated from her vegetable state. And though I laughed heartily at the idea of his being Phœbus Apollo, Lykeham stuck to the theory with increasing obstinacy. The more he thought of it the more it seemed to him probable that his nymph, with her burning cold virginal passion was Daphne, while to doubt that he himself was Apollo seemed hardly to occur to him.

It was about a fortnight later, in June, towards the end of term, that we discovered Lykeham's Olympian identity. We had gone, Lykeham and I, for an after-dinner walk. We set out through the pale tranquillity of twilight, and following the towpath up the river as far as Godstow, halted at the inn for a glass of port and a talk with the glorious old female Falstaff in black silk who kept it. We were royally entertained with gossip and old wine, and after Lykeham had sung a comic song which had reduced the old lady to a quivering jelly of hysterical laughter, we set out once more, intending to go yet a little farther up the river before we turned back. Darkness had fallen by this time; the stars were lighted in the sky; it was the sort of summer night to which Marlowe compared Helen of Troy. Over the meadows invisible peewits wheeled and uttered their melancholy cry; the far-off thunder of the weir bore a continuous, even burden to all the other small noises of the night. Lykeham and I walked on in silence. We had covered perhaps a quarter of a mile when all at once my companion stopped and began looking fixedly westward towards Witham Hill. I paused too, and saw that he was staring at the thin crescent of the moon, which was preparing to set in the dark woods that crowned the eminence.

"What are you looking at?" I asked.

But Lykeham paid no attention, only muttered something to himself. Then suddenly he cried out, "It's she!" and started off at full gallop across the fields in the direction of the hill. Conceiving that he had gone suddenly mad, I followed. We crashed through the first hedge twenty yards apart. Then came the backwater; Lykeham leapt, flopped in three-quarters of the way across, and scrambled oozily ashore. I made a better jump and landed among the mud and rushes of the farther bank. Two more hedges and a ploughed field, a hedge, a road, a gate, another field, and then we were in Witham Wood itself. It was pitch black under the trees, and Lykeham had perforce to slacken his pace a little. I followed him by the noise he made crashing through the undergrowth and cursing when he hurt himself. That wood was a nightmare, but we got through it somehow and into the open glade at the top of the hill. Through the trees on the farther side of the clearing shone the moon, seeming incredibly close at hand. Then, suddenly, along the very path of the moonlight, the figure of a woman came walking through the trees into the open. Lykeham rushed towards her and flung himself at her feet and embraced her knees; she stooped down and smoothed his ruffled hair. I turned and walked away; it is not for a mere mortal to look on at the embracements of the gods.

As I walked back, I wondered who on earth—or rather who in heaven—Lykeham could be. For here was chaste Cynthia giving herself to him in the most unequivocal fashion. Could he be Endymion? No, the idea was too preposterous to be entertained for a moment. But I could think of no other loved by the virgin moon. Yet surely I seemed dimly to recollect that there had been some favoured god; for the life of me I could not remember who. All the way back along the river path I searched my mind for his name, and always it eluded me.

But on my return I looked up the matter in Lemprière, and almost died of laughing when I discovered the truth. I thought of

Lykeham's Venetian mirror and his complacent side glances at his own image, and his belief that he was Apollo, and I laughed and laughed. And when, considerably after midnight, Lykeham got back to college, I met him in the porch and took him quietly by the sleeve, and in his ear I whispered, "GOAT-FOOT," and then I roared with laughter once again.

The Bookshop

IT seemed indeed an unlikely place to find a bookshop. All the other commercial enterprises of the street aimed at purveying the barest necessities to the busy squalor of the quarter. In this, the main arterial street, there was a specious glitter and life produced by the swift passage of the traffic. It was almost airy, almost gay. But all around great tracts of slum pullulated dankly. The inhabitants did their shopping in the grand street; they passed, holding gobbets of meat that showed glutinous even through the wrappings of paper; they cheapened linoleum at upholstery doors; women, black-bonneted and black-shawled, went shuffling to their marketing with dilapidated bags of straw plait. How should these, I wondered, buy books? And yet there it was, a tiny shop; and the windows were fitted with shelves, and there were the brown backs of books. To the right a large emporium over-flowed into the street with its fabulously cheap furniture; to the left the curtained, discreet windows of an eating-house announced in chipped white letters the merits of sixpenny dinners. Between, so narrow as scarcely to prevent the junction of food and furniture, was the little shop. A door and four feet of dark window, that was the full extent of frontage. One saw here that literature was a luxury; it took its proportionable room here in this place of necessity. Still, the comfort was that it survived, definitely survived.

The owner of the shop was standing in the doorway, a little man, grizzle-bearded and with eyes very active round the corners of the spectacles that bridged his long, sharp nose.

"Trade is good?" I inquired.

"Better in my grandfather's day," he told me, shaking his head sadly.

"We grow progressively more Philistine," I suggested.

"It is our cheap press. The ephemeral overwhelms the permanent, the classical."

"This journalism," I agreed, "or call it rather this piddling quotidianism, is the curse of our age."

"Fit only for——" He gesticulated clutchingly with his hands as though seeking the word.

"For the fire."

The old man was triumphantly emphatic with his, "No: for the sewer."

I laughed sympathetically at his passion. "We are delightfully at one in our views," I told him. "May I look about me a little among your treasures?"

Within the shop was a brown twilight, redolent with old leather and the smell of that fine subtle dust that clings to the pages of forgotten books, as though preservative of their secrets—like the dry sand of Asian deserts beneath which, still incredibly intact, lie the treasures and the rubbish of a thousand years ago. I opened the first volume that came to my hand. It was a book of fashion-plates, tinted elaborately by hand in magenta and purple, maroon and solferino and puce and those melting shades of green that a yet earlier generation had called "The Sorrows of Werther." Beauties in crinolines swam with the amplitude of pavilioned ships across the pages. Their feet were represented as thin and flat and black, like tea-leaves shyly protruding from under their petticoats. Their faces were egg-shaped, sleeked round with hair of glossy black, and expressive of an immaculate purity. I thought of our modern fashion figures, with their heels and their arch of instep, their flattened faces and smile of pouting invitation. It was difficult not to be a deteriorationist. I am easily moved by symbols; there is something of a Quarles in my nature. Lacking the philosophic mind, I prefer to see my abstractions concretely imaged. And it occurred to me then that if I wanted an emblem to picture the sacredness of marriage and the influence of the home I could not do better than choose two little black feet like tea-leaves peeping out decorously from under the hem of wide, disguising petticoats. While heels and thoroughbred insteps should figure—oh well, the reverse.

The current of my thoughts was turned aside by the old man's voice. "I expect you are musical," he said.

Oh yes, I was a little; and he held out to me a bulky folio.

"Did you ever hear this?" he asked.

Robert the Devil: no, I never had. I did not doubt that it was a gap in my musical education.

The old man took the book and drew up a chair from the dim

penetralia of the shop. It was then that I noticed a surprising fact: what I had, at a careless glance, taken to be a common counter I perceived now to be a piano of a square, unfamiliar shape. The old man sat down before it. "You must forgive any defects in its tone," he said, turning to me. "An early Broadwood, Georgian, you know, and has seen a deal of service in a hundred years."

He opened the lid, and the yellow keys grinned at me in the darkness like the teeth of an ancient horse.

The old man rustled pages till he found a desired place. "The ballet music," he said: "it's fine. Listen to this."

His bony, rather tremulous hands began suddenly to move with an astonishing nimbleness, and there rose up, faint and tinkling against the roar of the traffic, a gay pirouetting music. The instrument rattled considerably and the volume of sound was thin as the trickle of a drought-shrunken stream: but, still it kept tune and the melody was there, filmy, aerial.

"And now for the drinking-song," cried the old man, warming excitedly to his work. He played a series of chords that mounted modulating upwards towards a breaking-point; so supremely operatic as positively to be a parody of that moment of tautening suspense, when the singers are bracing themselves for a burst of passion. And then it came, the drinking chorus. One pictured to oneself cloaked men, wildly jovial over the emptiness of cardboard flagons.

> "*Versiam' a tazza piena*
> *Il generoso umor . . .*"

The old man's voice was cracked and shrill, but his enthusiasm made up for any defects in execution. I had never seen anyone so wholeheartedly a reveller.

He turned over a few more pages. "Ah, the 'Valse Infernale,'" he said. "That's good." There was a little melancholy prelude and then the tune, not so infernal perhaps as one might have been led to expect, but still pleasant enough. I looked over his shoulder at the words and sang to his accompaniment.

> "*Demoni fatali*
> *Fantasmi d'orror,*
> *Dei regni infernali*
> *Plaudite al signor.*"

A great steam-driven brewer's lorry roared past with its annihilating thunder and utterly blotted out the last line. The old man's hands still moved over the yellow keys, my mouth opened and shut; but there was no sound of words or music. It was as though the fatal demons, the phantasms of horror, had made a sudden irruption into this peaceful, abstracted place.

I looked out through the narrow door. The traffic ceaselessly passed; men and women hurried along with set faces. Phantasms of horror, all of them: infernal realms wherein they dwelt. Outside, men lived under the tyranny of things. Their every action was determined by the orders of mere matter, by money, and the tools of their trade and the unthinking laws of habit and convention. But here I seemed to be safe from things, living at a remove from actuality; here where a bearded old man, improbable survival from some other time, indomitably played the music of romance, despite the fact that the phantasms of horror might occasionally drown the sound of it with their clamour.

"So: will you take it?" The voice of the old man broke across my thoughts. "I will let you have it for five shillings." He was holding out the thick, dilapidated volume towards me. His face wore a look of strained anxiety. I could see how eager he was to get my five shillings, how necessary, poor man! for him. He has been, I thought with an unreasonable bitterness—he has been simply performing for my benefit, like a trained dog. His aloofness, his culture—all a business trick. I felt aggrieved. He was just one of the common phantasms of horror masquerading as the angel of this somewhat comic paradise of contemplation. I gave him a couple of half-crowns and he began wrapping the book in paper.

"I tell you," he said, "I'm sorry to part with it. I get attached to my books, you know; but they always have to go."

He sighed with such an obvious genuineness of feeling that I repented of the judgment I had passed upon him. He was a reluctant inhabitant of the infernal realms, even as was I myself.

Outside they were beginning to cry the evening papers: a ship sunk, trenches captured, somebody's new stirring speech. We looked at one another—the old bookseller and I—in silence. We understood one another without speech. Here were we in particular, and here was the whole of humanity in general, all faced by the hideous triumphs of things. In this continued massacre of men, in this old man's enforced sacrifice, matter equally triumphed.

And walking homeward through Regent's Park, I too found matter triumphing over me. My book was unconscionably heavy, and I wondered what in the world I should do with a piano score of *Robert the Devil* when I had got it home. It would only be another thing to weigh me down and hinder me; and at the moment it was very, oh, abominably, heavy. I leaned over the railings that ring round the ornamental water, and as unostentatiously as I could, I let the book fall into the bushes.

I often think it would be best not to attempt the solution of the problem of life. Living is hard enough without complicating the process by thinking about it. The wisest thing, perhaps, is to take for granted the "wearisome condition of humanity, born under one law, to another bound," and to leave the matter at that, without an attempt to reconcile the incompatibles. Oh, the absurd difficulty of it all! And I have, moreover, wasted five shillings, which is serious, you know, in these thin times.

The Death of Lully

THE sea lay in a breathing calm, and the galley, bosomed in its transparent water, stirred rhythmically to the slow pulse of its sleeping life. Down below there, fathoms away through the crystal-clear Mediterranean, the shadow of the ship lazily swung, moving, a long dark patch, very slowly back and forth across the white sand of the sea-bottom—very slowly, a scarcely perceptible advance and recession of the green darkness. Fishes sometimes passed, now hanging poised with idly tremulous fins, now darting onwards, effortless and incredibly swift; and always, as it seemed, utterly aimless, whether they rested or whether they moved; as the life of angels their life seemed mysterious and unknowable.

All was silence on board the ship. In their fetid cage below decks the rowers slept where they sat, chained, on their narrow benches. On deck the sailors lay sleeping or sat in little groups playing at dice. The fore-part of the deck was reserved, it seemed, for passengers of distinction. Two figures, a man and a woman, were reclining there on couches, their faces and half-bared limbs flushed in the coloured shadow that was thrown by the great red awning stretched above them.

It was a nobleman, the sailors had heard, and his mistress that they had on board. They had taken their passage at Scanderoon, and were homeward bound for Spain. Proud as sin these Spaniards were; the man treated them like slaves or dogs. As for the woman, she was well enough, but they could find as good a face and pair of breasts in their native Genoa. If anyone so much as looked at her from half the ship's length away it sent her possessor into a rage. He had struck one man for smiling at her. Damned Catalonian, as jealous as a stag; they wished him the stag's horns as well as its temper.

It was intensely hot even under the awning. The man woke from his uneasy sleep and reached out to where on a little table beside him stood a deep silver cup of mixed wine and water. He drank a gulp of it; it was as warm as blood and hardly cooled his throat. He turned over and, leaning on his elbow, looked at his companion. She on her back, quietly breathing through parted lips, still asleep. He leaned across and pinched her on the breast, so that she woke up with a sudden start and cry of pain.

"Why did you wake me?" she asked.

He laughed and shrugged his shoulders. He had, indeed, had no reason for doing so, except that he did not like it that she should be comfortably asleep, while he was awake and unpleasantly conscious of the heat.

"It is hotter than ever," he said, with a kind of gloomy satisfaction at the thought that she would now have to suffer the same discomforts as himself. "The wine scorches instead of cooling; the sun seems no lower down the sky."

The woman pouted. "You pinched me cruelly," she said. "And I still do not know why you wanted to wake me."

He smiled again, this time with a good-humoured lasciviousness. "I wanted to kiss you," he said. He passed his hand over her body possessively, as a man might caress a dog.

Suddenly the quiet of the afternoon was shattered. A great clamour rose up, ragged and uneven, on the air. Shrill yells pierced the dull rumbling growl of bass voices, pierced the sound of beaten drums and hammered metal.

"What are they doing in the town?" asked the woman anxiously of her lover.

"God knows," he answered. "Perhaps the heathen hounds are making some trouble with our men."

He got up and walked to the rail of the ship. A quarter of a mile away, across the smooth water of the bay, stood the little African town at which they had stopped to call. The sunlight showed everything with a hard and merciless definition. Sky, palms, white houses, domes, and towers seemed as though made from some hard enamelled metal. A ridge of low red hills rolled away to right and left. The sunshine gave to everything in the scene the same clarity of detail, so that to the eye of the onlooker there was no impression of distance. The whole thing seemed to be painted in flat upon a single plane.

The young man returned to his couch under the awning and lay down. It was hotter than ever, or seemed so, at least, since he had made the exertion of getting up. He thought of high cool pastures in the hills, with the pleasant sound of streams, far down and out of sight in their deep channels. He thought of winds that were fresh and scented—winds that were not mere breaths of dust and fire. He thought of the shade of cypresses, a narrow opaque strip of darkness; and he thought too of the green coolness, more diffused and fluid and transparent, of chestnut groves. And he thought of the people he remembered sitting under the trees—young people, gay and brightly dressed, whose life was all gaiety and deliciousness. There were the songs that they sang—he recalled the voices and the dancing of the strings. And there were perfumes and, when one drew closer, the faint intoxicating fragrance of a woman's body. He thought of the stories they told; one in particular came to his mind, a capital tale of a sorcerer who offered to change a peasant's wife into a mare, and how he gulled the husband and enjoyed the woman before his eyes, and the delightful excuses he made when she failed to change her shape. He smiled to himself at the thought of it, and stretching out a hand touched his mistress. Her bosom was soft to his fingers and damp with sweat; he had an unpleasant notion that she was melting in the heat.

"Why do you touch me?" she asked.

He made no reply, but turned away from her. He wondered how it would come to pass that people would rise again in the body. It seemed curious, considering the manifest activities of worms. And suppose one rose in the body that one possessed in age. He shuddered, picturing to himself what this woman would be like when she was sixty, seventy. She would be beyond words repulsive. Old men too were horrible. They stank, and their eyes were rheumy and rosiny, like the eyes of deer. He decided that he would kill himself before he grew old. He was eight-and-twenty now. He would give himself twelve years more. Then he would end it. His thoughts dimmed and faded away into sleep.

The woman looked at him as he slept. He was a good man, she thought, though sometimes cruel. He was different from all the other men she had known. Once, when she was sixteen and a beginner in the business of love, she had thought that all men were always drunk when they made love. They were all dirty and like beasts; she had felt herself superior to them. But this man was a nobleman. She could not understand him; his thoughts were always obscure. She felt herself infinitely inferior to him. She was afraid of him and his occasional cruelty; but still he was a good man, and he might do what he liked with her.

From far off came the sound of oars, a rhythmical splash and creak. Somebody shouted, and from startlingly close at hand one of the sailors hallooed back.

The young man woke up with a start.

"What is it?" he asked, turning with an angry look to the girl, as though he held her to be responsible for this breaking in upon his slumbers.

"The boat, I think," she said, "It must be coming back from the shore."

The boat's crew came up over the side, and all the stagnant life of the ship flowed excitedly round them. They were the centre of a vortex towards which all were drawn. Even the young Catalonian, for all his hatred of these stinking Genoese shipmen, was sucked into the eddy. Everybody was talking at once, and in the general hubbub of question and answer there was nothing coherent to be made out. Piercingly distinct above all the noise came the voice of the little cabin-boy, who had been to shore with the boat's crew. He was running round to everyone in turn repeating: "I hit one of them. You know. I hit one. With a stone on the forehead. Didn't he bleed, ooh! didn't he just!" And he would dance with uncontrollable excitement.

The captain held up his hand and shouted for silence. "One at a time, there," he ordered, and when order had a little been restored, added grumblingly, "Like a pack of dogs on a bone. You talk, boatswain."

"I hit one of them," said the boy. Somebody cuffed him over the head, and he relapsed into silence.

When the boatswain's story had rambled through labyrinths of digression, over countless obstacles of interruptions and emendations, to its conclusion, the Spaniard went back to join his companion under the awning. He had assumed again his habitual indifference.

"Nearly butchered," he said languidly, in response to her eager questions. "They"—he jerked a hand in the direction of the town —"they were pelting an old fellow who had come there preaching the Faith. Left him dead on the beach. Our men had to run for it."

She could get no more out of him; he turned over and pretended to go to sleep.

Towards evening they received a visit from the captain. He was a large, handsome man, with gold ear-rings glinting from among a bush of black hair.

"Divine Providence," he remarked sententiously, after the usual courtesies had passed, "has called upon us to perform a very notable work."

"Indeed?" said the young man.

"No less a work," continued the captain, "than to save from the clutches of the infidels and heathen the precious remains of a holy martyr."

The captain let fall his pompous manner. It was evident that he had carefully prepared these pious sentences, they rolled so roundly off his tongue. But he was eager now to get on with his story, and it was in a homelier style that he went on: "If you knew these seas as well as I—and it's near twenty years now that I've been sailing them—you'd have some knowledge of this same holy man that—God rot their souls for it!—these cursed Arabs have done to death here. I've heard of him more than once in my time, and not always well spoken of; for, to tell the honest truth, he does more harm with his preachments to good Christian traders than ever he did good to black-hearted heathen dogs. Leave the bees alone, I say, and if you can get a little honey out of them quietly, so much the better; but he goes about among the beehives with a pole, stirring up trouble for himself and others too. Leave them alone to their damnation, is what I say, and get what you can from them this side of hell. But, still, he has died a holy martyr's death. God rest his soul! A martyr is a wonderful thing, you know, and it's not for the likes of us to understand what they mean by it all.

"They do say, too, that he could make gold. And, to my mind, it would have been a thing more pleasing to God and man if he had stopped at home minting money for poor folks and dealing it round, so that there'd be no need to work any more and break oneself for a morsel of bread. Yes, he was great at gold-making and at the books too. They tell me he was called the Illuminated Doctor. But I know him still as plain Lully. I used to hear of him from my father, plain Lully, and no better once than he should have been.

"My father was a shipwright in Minorca in those days—how long since? Fifty, sixty years perhaps. He knew him then; he has often told me the tale. And a raffish young dog he was. Drinking, drabbing, and dicing, he outdid them all, and between the bouts wrote poems, they say, which was more than the rest could do. But he gave it all up on the sudden. Gave away his lands, quitted his former companions, and turned hermit up in the hills, living alone like a fox in his burrow, high up above the vines. And all because of a woman and his own qualmish stomach."

The shipmaster paused and helped himself to a little wine. "And what did this woman do?" the girl asked curiously.

"Ah, it's not what she did but what she didn't do," the captain answered, with a leer and wink. "She kept him at his distance—all but once, all but once; and that was what put him on the road to being a martyr. But there, I'm outrunning myself. I must go more soberly.

"There was a lady of some consequence in the island—one of the Castellos, I think she was; her first name has quite slipped my memory—Anastasia, or something of the kind. Lully conceives a passion for her, and sighs and importunes her through I know not how many months and years. But her virtue stands steady as the judgment seat. Well, in the end, what happens was this. The story leaked out after it was all over, and he was turned hermit in the mountains. What happened, I say, was this. She tells him at last that he may come and see her, fixing some solitary twilight place and time, her own room at nightfall. You can guess how he washes and curls and scents himself, shaves his chin, chews anises, musks over whatever of the goat may cling about the body. Off he goes, dreaming swoons and ecstasies, foretasting inconceivable sweets. Arrived, he finds the lady a little melancholy—her settled humour, but a man might expect a smile at such a time. Still, nothing abashed, he falls at her feet and pours out his piteous case, telling her he has sighed through seven years, not closed an eye for above a hundred nights, is forepined to a shadow, and, in a word, will perish unless she show some mercy. She, still melancholy—her settled humour, mark you—makes answer that she is ready to yield, and that her body is entirely his. With that, she lets herself be done with as he pleases, but always sorrowfully. 'You are all mine,' says he—'all mine'—and unlaces her gorgeret to prove the same. But he was wrong. Another lover was already in her bosom, and his kisses had been passionate—oh, burning passionate, for he had kissed away half her left breast. From the nipple down it had all been gnawed away by a cancer.

"Bah, a man may see as bad as that any day in the street or at church-doors where beggars most congregate. I grant you that it is a nasty sight, worm-eaten flesh, but still—not enough, you will agree, to make yourself a hermit over. But there, I told you he had a queasiness of the stomach. But doubtless it was all in God's plan to make a holy martyr of him. But for that same queasiness of his, he would still be living there, a superannuated rake; or else have died in very foul odour, instead of passing, all embalmed with sanctity, to Paradise Gate.

"I know not what happened to him between his hermit-hood and his quest for martyrdom. I saw him first a dozen years ago, down Tunis way. They were always clapping him into prison or pulling out his beard for preaching. This time, it seems, they have made a holy martyr of him, done the business thoroughly with no bungling. Well, may he pray for our souls at the throne of God. I go in secretly to-night to steal his body. It lies on the shore there beyond the jetty. It will be a notable work, I tell you, to bring back so precious a corpse to Christendom. A most notable work. . . ."

The captain rubbed his hands.

It was after midnight, but there was still a bustle of activity on board the galley. At any moment they were expecting the arrival of the boat with the corpse of the martyr. A couch, neatly draped in black, with at its head and foot candles burning two by two, had been set out on the poop for the reception of the body. The captain called the young Spaniard and his mistress to come and see the bier.

"That's a good bit of work for you," he said, with justifiable pride. "I defy anyone to make a more decent resting-place for a martyr than that is. It could hardly have been done better on shore, with every appliance at hand. But we sailors, you know, can make anything out of nothing. A truckle-bed, a strip of tarred canvas, and four tallow dips from the cabin lanterns—there you are, a bier for a king."

He hurried away, and a little later the young man and the girl could hear him giving orders and cursing somewhere down below.

The candles burned almost without a tremor in the windless air, and the reflections of the stars were long, thin tracks of fire along the utterly calm water.

"Were there but perfumed flowers and the sound of a lute," said the young Spaniard, "the night would tremble into passion of its own accord. Love should come unsought on such a night as this, among these black waters and the stars that sleep so peacefully on their bosom."

He put his arm round the girl and bent his head to kiss her. But she averted her face. He could feel a shudder run her through the body.

"Not to-night," she whispered. "I think of the poor dead man. I would rather pray."

"No, no," he cried. "Forget him. Remember only that we are alive, and that we have but little time and none to waste."

He drew her into the shadow under the bulwark, and, sitting down on a coil of rope, crushed her body to his own and began kissing her with fury. She lay, at first, limp in his arms, but gradually she kindled to his passion.

A plash of oars announced the approach of the boat. The captain hallooed into the darkness: "Did you find him?"

"Yes, we have him here," came back the answer.

"Good. Bring him alongside and we'll hoist him up. We have the bier in readiness. He shall lie in state to-night."

"But he's not dead," shouted back the voice from the night.

"Not dead?" repeated the captain, thunderstruck. "But what about the bier, then?"

A thin, feeble voice came back. "Your work will not be wasted, my friend. It will be but a short time before I need your bier."

The captain, a little abashed, answered in a gentler tone, "We thought, holy father, that the heathens had done their worst and that Almighty God had already given you the martyr's crown."

By this time the boat had emerged from the darkness. In the stern sheets an old man was lying, his white hair and beard stained with blood, his Dominican's robe torn and fouled with dust. At the sight of him, the captain pulled off his cap and dropped upon his knees.

"Give us your blessing, holy father," he begged.

The old man raised his hand and wished him peace.

They lifted him on board and, at his own desire, laid him upon the bier which had been prepared for his dead body. "It would be a waste of trouble," he said, "to put me anywhere else, seeing I shall in any case be lying there so soon."

So there he lay, very still under the four candles. One might have taken him for dead already, but that his eyes, when he opened them, shone so brightly.

He dismissed from the poop everyone except the young Spaniard. "We are countrymen," he said, "and of noble blood, both of us. I would rather have you near me than anyone else."

The sailors knelt for a blessing and disappeared; soon they could be heard weighing the anchor; it was safest to be off before day. Like mourners at either side of the lighted bier crouched the Spaniard and his mistress. The body of the old man, who was not yet dead, lay quiet under the candles. The martyr was silent for some time, but at last he opened his eyes and looked at the young man and the woman.

"I too," he said, "was in love, once. In this year falls the jubilee of my last earthly passion; fifty years have run since last I longed after the flesh—fifty years since God opened my eyes to the hideousness of the corruption that man has brought upon himself.

"You are young, and your bodies are clean and straight, with no blotch or ulcer or leprous taint to mar their much-desired beauty; but because of your outward pride, your souls, it may be, fester inwardly the more.

"And yet God made all perfect; it is but accident and the evil of will that causes defaults. All metals should be gold, were it not that their elements willed evilly in their desire to combine. And so with men: the burning sulphur of passion, the salt of wisdom, the nimble mercurial soul should come together to make a golden being, incorruptible and rustless. But the elements mingle jarringly, not in a pure harmony of love, and gold is rare, while lead and iron and poisonous brass that leaves a taste as of remorse behind it are everywhere common.

"God opened my eyes to it before my youth had too utterly wasted itself to rottenness. It was half a hundred years ago, but I see her still, my Ambrosia, with her white, sad face and her naked body and that monstrous ill eating away at her breast.

"I have lived since then trying to amend the evil, trying to restore, as far as my poor powers would go, some measure of original perfection to the corrupted world. I have striven to give to all metals their true nature, to make true gold from the false, the unreal, the accidental metals, lead and copper and tin and iron. And I have essayed that more difficult alchemy, the transformation of men. I die now in my effort to purge away that most foul dross of misbelief from the souls of these heathen men. Have I achieved anything? I know not."

The galley was moving now, its head turned seaward. The candles shivered in the wind of its speed, casting uncertain, changing shadows upon his face. There was a long silence on the poop. The oars creaked and splashed. Sometimes a shout would come up from below, orders given by the overseer of the slaves, a curse, the sound of a blow. The old man spoke again, more weakly now, as though to himself.

"I have had eighty years of it," he said—"eighty years in the midst of this corroding sea of hatred and strife. A man has need to keep pure and unalloyed his core of gold, that little centre of perfection with which all, even in his declination of time, are born. All other metal, though it be as tough as steel, as shining-hard as brass, will melt before the devouring bitterness of life. Hatred, lust, anger—the vile passions will corrode your will of iron, the warlike pomp of your front of brass. It needs the golden perfection of pure love and pure knowledge to withstand them.

"God has willed that I should be the stone—weak, indeed, in virtue—that has touched and transformed at least a little of baser metal into the gold that is above corruption. But it is hard work—thankless work. Man has made a hell of his world, and has set up gods of pain to rule it. Goatish gods, that revel and feast on the agony of it all, poring over the tortured world, like those hateful lovers, whose lust burns darkly into cruelty.

"Fever goads us through life in a delirium of madness. Thirsting for the swamps of evil whence the fever came, thirsting for the mirages of his own delirium, man rushes headlong he knows not whither. And all the time a devouring cancer gnaws at his entrails. It will kill him in the end, when even the ghastly inspiration of fever will not be enough to whip him on. He will lie there, cumbering the earth, a heap of rottenness and pain, until at last the cleansing fire comes to sweep the horror away.

"Fever and cancer; acids that burn and corrode. . . . I have had eighty years of it. Thank God, it is the end."

It was already dawn; the candles were hardly visible now in the light, fading to nothing, like souls in prosperity. In a little while the old man was asleep.

The captain tiptoed up on to the poop and drew the young Spaniard aside for a confidential talk.

"Do you think he will die to-day?" he asked.

The young man nodded.

"God rest his soul," said the captain piously. "But do you think it would be best to take his body to Minorca or to Genoa? At Minorca they would give much to have their own patron martyr. At the same time it would add to the glory of Genoa to possess so holy a relic, though he is in no way connected with the place. It's there is my difficulty. Suppose, you see, that my people of Genoa did not want the body, he being from Minorca and not one of them. I should look a fool then, bringing it in in state. Oh, it's hard, it's hard. There's so much to think about. I am not sure but what I hadn't better put in at Minorca first. What do you think?"

The Spaniard shrugged his shoulders. "I have no advice to offer."

"Lord," said the captain as he bustled away, "life is a tangled knot to unravel."

Sir Hercules

THE infant who was destined to become the fourth baronet
of the name of Lapith was born in the year 1740. He was a
very small baby, weighing not more than three pounds at birth,
but from the first he was sturdy and healthy. In honour of his
maternal grandfather, Sir Hercules Occam of Bishop's Occam,
he was christened Hercules. His mother, like many other mothers,
kept a notebook, in which his progress from month to month was
recorded. He walked at ten months, and before his second year
was out he had learnt to speak a number of words. At three years
he weighed but twenty-four pounds, and at six, though he could
read and write perfectly and showed a remarkable aptitude for
music, he was no larger and heavier than a well-grown child of
two. Meanwhile, his mother had borne two other children, a boy
and a girl, one of whom died of croup during infancy, while the
other was carried off by smallpox before it reached the age of five.
Hercules remained the only surviving child.

On his twelfth birthday Hercules was still only three feet and
two inches in height. His head, which was very handsome and
nobly shaped, was too big for his body, but otherwise he was
exquisitely proportioned and, for his size, of great strength and
agility. His parents, in the hope of making him grow, consulted all
the most eminent physicians of the time. Their various prescrip-
tions were followed to the letter, but in vain. One ordered a very
plentiful meat diet; another exercise; a third constructed a little
rack, modelled on those employed by the Holy Inquisition, on
which young Hercules was stretched, with excruciating torments,
for half an hour every morning and evening. In the course of the
next three years Hercules gained perhaps two inches. After that
his growth stopped completely, and he remained for the rest of his
life a pigmy of three feet and four inches. His father, who had
built the most extravagant hopes upon his son, planning for him
in his imagination a military career equal to that of Marlborough,
found himself a disappointed man. "I have brought an abortion
into the world," he would say, and he took so violent a dislike to
his son that the boy dared scarcely come into his presence. His

temper, which had been serene, was turned by disappointment to moroseness and savagery. He avoided all company (being, as he said, ashamed to show himself, the father of a *lusus naturæ*, among normal, healthy human beings), and took to solitary drinking, which carried him very rapidly to his grave; for the year before Hercules came of age his father was taken off by an apoplexy. His mother, whose love for him had increased with the growth of his father's unkindness, did not long survive, but little more than a year after her husband's death succumbed, after eating two dozen of oysters, to an attack of typhoid fever.

Hercules thus found himself at the age of twenty-one alone in the world, and master of a considerable fortune, including the estate and mansion of Crome. The beauty and intelligence of his childhood had survived into his manly age, and, but for his dwarfish stature, he would have taken his place among the handsomest and most accomplished young men of his time. He was well read in Greek and Latin authors, as well as in all the moderns of any merit who had written in English, French, or Italian. He had a good ear for music, and was no indifferent performer on the violin, which he used to play like a bass viol, seated on a chair with the instrument between his legs. To the music of the harpsichord and clavichord he was extremely partial, but the smallness of his hands made it impossible for him ever to perform upon these instruments. He had a small ivory flute made for him, on which, whenever he was melancholy, he used to play a simple country air or jig, affirming that this rustic music had more power to clear and raise the spirits than the most artificial productions of the masters. From an early age he practised the composition of poetry, but, though conscious of his great powers in this art, he would never publish any specimen of his writing. "My stature," he would say, "is reflected in my verses; if the public were to read them it would not be because I am a poet, but because I am a dwarf." Several MS. books of Sir Hercules's poems survive. A single specimen will suffice to illustrate his qualities as a poet.

> *In ancient days, while yet the world was young,*
> *Ere Abram fed his flocks or Homer sung;*
> *When blacksmith Tubal tamed creative fire,*
> *And Jabal dwelt in tents and Jubal struck the lyre;*
> *Flesh grown corrupt brought forth a monstrous birth*

And obscene giants trod the shrinking earth,
Till God, impatient of their sinful brood,
Gave rein to wrath and drown'd them in the Flood.
Teeming again, repeopled Tellus bore
The lubber Hero and the Man of War;
Huge towers of Brawn, topp'd with an empty Skull,
Witlessly bold, heroically dull.
Long ages pass'd and Man grown more refin'd,
Slighter in music but of vaster Mind,
Smiled at his grandsire's broadsword, bow and bill,
And learn'd to wield the Pencil and the Quill.
The glowing canvas and the written page
Immortaliz'd his name from age to age,
His name emblazon'd on Fame's temple wall;
For Art grew great as Humankind grew small.
Thus man's long progress step by step we trace;
The Giant dies, the hero takes his place;
The Giant vile, the dull heroic Block:
At one we shudder and at one we mock.
Man last appears. In him the Soul's pure flame
Burns brightlier in a not inord'nate frame.
Of old when Heroes fought and Giants swarmed,
Men were huge mounds of matter scarce inform'd;
Wearied by leavening so vast a mass,
The spirit slept and all the mind was crass.
The smaller carcase of these later days
Is soon inform'd; the Soul unwearied plays
And like a Pharos darts abroad her mental rays.
But can we think that Providence will stay
Man's footsteps here upon the upward way?
Mankind in understanding and in grace
Advanc'd so far beyond the Giants' race?
Hence impious thought! Still led by GOD'S own **Hand,**
Mankind proceeds towards the Promised Land.
A time will come (prophetic, I descry
Remoter dawns along the gloomy sky),
When happy mortals of a Golden Age
Will backward turn the dark historic page,
And in our vaunted race of Men behold
A form as gross, a Mind as dead and cold,

As we in Giants see, in warriors of old.
A time will come, wherein the soul shall be
From all superfluous matter wholly free:
When the light body, agile as a fawn's,
Shall sport with grace along the velvet lawns.
Nature's most delicate and final birth,
Mankind perfected shall possess the earth.
But ah, not yet! For still the Giants' race,
Huge, though diminish'd, tramps the Earth's fair face;
Gross and repulsive, yet perversely proud,
Men of their imperfections boast aloud.
Vain of their bulk, of all they still retain
Of giant ugliness absurdly vain;
At all that's small they point their stupid scorn
And, monsters, think themselves divinely born.
Sad is the Fate of those, ah, sad indeed,
The rare precursors of the nobler breed!
Who come man's golden glory to foretell,
But pointing Heav'nwards live themselves in Hell.

As soon as he came into the estate, Sir Hercules set about re-modelling his household. For though by no means ashamed of his deformity—indeed, if we may judge from the poem quoted above, he regarded himself as being in many ways superior to the ordinary race of man—he found the presence of full-grown men and women embarrassing. Realizing, too, that he must abandon all ambitions in the great world, he determined to retire absolutely from it and to create, as it were, at Crome a private world of his own, in which all should be proportionable to himself. Accordingly, he discharged all the old servants of the house and replaced them gradually, as he was able to find suitable successors, by others of dwarfish stature. In the course of a few years he had assembled about himself a numerous household, no member of which was above four feet high and the smallest among them scarcely two feet and six inches. His father's dogs, such as setters, mastiffs, greyhounds, and a pack of beagles, he sold or gave away as too large and too boisterous for his house, replacing them by pugs and King Charles spaniels and whatever other breeds of dog were the smallest. His father's stable was also sold. For his own use, whether riding or driving, he had six black Shetland ponies, with four very choice piebald animals of New Forest breed.

Having thus settled his household entirely to his own satisfaction, it only remained for him to find some suitable companion with whom to share this paradise. Sir Hercules had a susceptible heart, and had more than once, between the ages of sixteen and twenty, felt what it was to love. But here his deformity had been a source of the most bitter humiliation, for, having once dared to declare himself to a young lady of his choice, he had been received with laughter. On his persisting, she had picked him up and shaken him like an importunate child, telling him to run away and plague her no more. The story soon got about—indeed, the young lady herself used to tell it as a particularly pleasant anecdote—and the taunts and mockery it occasioned were a source of the most acute distress to Hercules. From the poems written at this period we gather that he meditated taking his own life. In course of time, however, he lived down this humiliation; but never again, though he often fell in love, and that very passionately, did he dare to make any advances to those in whom he was interested. After coming to the estate and finding that he was in a position to create his own world as he desired it, he saw that, if he was to have a wife—which he very much desired, being of an affectionate and, indeed, amorous temper—he must choose her as he had chosen his servants—from among the race of dwarfs. But to find a suitable wife was, he found, a matter of some difficulty; for he would marry none who was not distinguished by beauty and gentle birth. The dwarfish daughter of Lord Bemboro he refused on the ground that besides being a pigmy she was hunchbacked; while another young lady, an orphan belonging to a very good family in Hampshire, was rejected by him because her face, like that of so many dwarfs, was wizened and repulsive. Finally, when he was almost despairing of success, he heard from a reliable source that Count Titimalo, a Venetian nobleman, possessed a daughter of exquisite beauty and great accomplishments, who was but three feet in height. Setting out at once for Venice, he went immediately on his arrival to pay his respects to the count, whom he found living with his wife and five children in a very mean apartment in one of the poorer quarters of the town. Indeed, the count was so far reduced in his circumstances that he was even then negotiating (so it was rumoured) with a travelling

company of clowns and acrobats, who had had the misfortune
to lose their performing dwarf, for the sale of his diminutive
daughter Filomena. Sir Hercules arrived in time to save her from
this untoward fate, for he was so much charmed by Filomena's
grace and beauty, that at the end of three days' courtship he made
her a formal offer of marriage, which was accepted by her no
less joyfully than by her father, who perceived in an English
son-in-law a rich and unfailing source of revenue. After an
unostentatious marriage, at which the English ambassador acted
as one of the witnesses, Sir Hercules and his bride returned
by sea to England, where they settled down, as it proved, to a life
of uneventful happiness.

Crome and its household of dwarfs delighted Filomena, who
felt herself now for the first time to be a free woman living among
her equals in a friendly world. She had many tastes in common
with her husband, especially that of music. She had a beautiful
voice, of a power surprising in one so small, and could touch A in
alt without effort. Accompanied by her husband on his fine
Cremona fiddle, which he played, as we have noted before, as
one plays a bass viol, she would sing all the liveliest and tenderest
airs from the operas and cantatas of her native country. Seated
together at the harpsichord, they found that they could with their
four hands play all the music written for two hands of ordinary
size, a circumstance which gave Sir Hercules unfailing pleasure.

When they were not making music or reading together, which
they often did, both in English and Italian, they spent their time
in healthful outdoor exercises, sometimes rowing in a little boat on
the lake, but more often riding or driving, occupations in which,
because they were entirely new to her, Filomena especially delighted. When she had become a perfectly proficient rider,
Filomena and her husband used often to go hunting in the park,
at that time very much more extensive than it is now. They
hunted not foxes nor hares, but rabbits, using a pack of about
thirty black and fawn-coloured pugs, a kind of dog which, when
not overfed, can course a rabbit as well as any of the smaller
breeds. Four dwarf grooms, dressed in scarlet liveries and mounted
on white Exmoor ponies, hunted the pack, while their master and
mistress, in green habits, followed either on the black Shetlands or
on the piebald New Forest ponies. A picture of the whole hunt—
dogs, horses, grooms, and masters—was painted by William

Stubbs, whose work Sir Hercules admired so much that he invited him, though a man of ordinary stature, to come and stay at the mansion for the purpose of executing this picture. Stubbs likewise painted a portrait of Sir Hercules and his lady driving in their green enamelled calash drawn by four black Shetlands. Sir Hercules wears a plum-coloured velvet coat and white breeches; Filomena is dressed in flowered muslin and a very large hat with pink feathers. The two figures in their gay carriage stand out sharply against a dark background of trees; but to the left of the picture the trees fall away and disappear, so that the four black ponies are seen against a pale and strangely lurid sky that has the golden-brown colour of thunder-clouds lighted up by the sun.

In this way four years passed happily by. At the end of that time Filomena found herself great with child. Sir Hercules was overjoyed. "If God is good," he wrote in his day-book, "the name of Lapith will be preserved and our rarer and more delicate race transmitted through the generations until in the fullness of time the world shall recognize the superiority of those beings whom now it uses to make mock of." On his wife's being brought to bed of a son he wrote a poem to the same effect. The child was christened Ferdinando in memory of the builder of the house.

With the passage of the months a certain sense of disquiet began to invade the minds of Sir Hercules and his lady. For the child was growing with an extraordinary rapidity. At a year he weighed as much as Hercules had weighed when he was three. "Ferdinando goes *crescendo*," wrote Filomena in her diary. "It seems not natural." At eighteen months the baby was almost as tall as their smallest jockey, who was a man of thirty-six. Could it be that Ferdinando was destined to become a man of the normal, gigantic dimensions? It was a thought to which neither of his parents dared yet give open utterance, but in the secrecy of their respective diaries they brooded over it in terror and dismay.

On his third birthday Ferdinando was taller than his mother and not more than a couple of inches short of his father's height. "To-day for the first time," wrote Sir Hercules, "we discussed the situation. The hideous truth can be concealed no longer: Ferdinando is not one of us. On this, his third birthday, a day when we should have been rejoicing at the health, the strength, and beauty of our child, we wept together over the ruin of our happiness. God give us strength to bear this cross."

At the age of eight Ferdinando was so large and so exuberantly healthy that his parents decided, though reluctantly, to send him to school. He was packed off to Eton at the beginning of the next half. A profound peace settled upon the house. Ferdinando returned for the summer holidays larger and stronger than ever. One day he knocked down the butler and broke his arm. "He is rough, inconsiderate, unamenable to persuasion," wrote his father. "The only thing that will teach him manners is corporal chastisement." Ferdinando, who at this age was already seventeen inches taller than his father, received no corporal chastisement.

One summer holidays about three years later Ferdinando returned to Crome accompanied by a very large mastiff dog. He had bought it from an old man at Windsor who found the beast too expensive to feed. It was a savage, unreliable animal; hardly had it entered the house when it attacked one of Sir Hercules's favourite pugs, seizing the creature in its jaws and shaking it till it was nearly dead. Extremely put out by this occurrence, Sir Hercules ordered that the beast should be chained up in the stable-yard. Ferdinando sullenly answered that the dog was his, and he would keep it where he pleased. His father, growing angry, bade him take the animal out of the house at once, on pain of his utmost displeasure. Ferdinando refused to move. His mother at this moment coming into the room, the dog flew at her, knocked her down, and in a twinkling had very severely mauled her arm and shoulder; in another instant it must infallibly have had her by the throat, had not Sir Hercules drawn his sword and stabbed the animal to the heart. Turning on his son, he ordered him to leave the room immediately, as being unfit to remain in the same place with the mother whom he had nearly murdered. So awe-inspiring was the spectacle of Sir Hercules standing with one foot on the carcase of the gigantic dog, his sword drawn and still bloody, so commanding were his voice, his gestures, and the expression of his face, that Ferdinando slunk out of the room in terror and behaved himself for all the rest of the vacation in an entirely exemplary fashion. His mother soon recovered from the bites of the mastiff, but the effect on her mind of this adventure was ineradicable; from that time forth she lived always among imaginary terrors.

The two years which Ferdinando spent on the Continent, making the Grand Tour, were a period of happy repose for his parents. But even now the thought of the future haunted them; nor were they able to solace themselves with all the diversions of their younger days. The Lady Filomena had lost her voice and Sir Hercules was grown too rheumatical to play the violin. He, it is true, still rode after his pugs, but his wife felt herself too old and, since the episode of the mastiff, too nervous for such sports. At most, to please her husband, she would follow the hunt at a distance in a little gig drawn by the safest and oldest of the Shetlands.

The day fixed for Ferdinando's return came round. Filomena, sick with vague dreads and presentiments, retired to her chamber and her bed. Sir Hercules received his son alone. A giant in a brown travelling-suit entered the room. "Welcome home, my son," said Sir Hercules in a voice that trembled a little.

"I hope I see you well, sir." Ferdinando bent down to shake hands, then straightened himself up again. The top of his father's head reached to the level of his hip.

Ferdinando had not come alone. Two friends of his own age accompanied him, and each of the young men had brought a servant. Not for thirty years had Crome been desecrated by the presence of so many members of the common race of men. Sir Hercules was appalled and indignant, but the laws of hospitality had to be obeyed. He received the young gentlemen with grave politeness and sent the servants to the kitchen, with orders that they should be well cared for.

The old family dining-table was dragged out into the light and dusted (Sir Hercules and his lady were accustomed to dine at a small table twenty inches high). Simon, the aged butler, who could only just look over the edge of the big table, was helped at supper by the three servants brought by Ferdinando and his guests.

Sir Hercules presided, and with his usual grace supported a conversation on the pleasures of foreign travel, the beauties of art and nature to be met with abroad, the opera at Venice, the singing of the orphans in the churches of the same city, and on other topics of a similar nature. The young men were not particularly attentive to his discourses; they were occupied in watching the efforts of the butler to change the plates and replenish the glasses. They covered their laughter by violent and repeated fits of coughing or choking. Sir Hercules affected not to notice, but changed the subject of the conversation to sport. Upon this one of the young men asked whether it was true, as he had heard, that he used to hunt the rabbit with a pack of pug dogs. Sir Hercules replied that it was, and proceeded to describe the chase in some detail. The young men roared with laughter.

When supper was over, Sir Hercules climbed down from his chair and, giving as his excuse that he must see how his lady did, bade them good-night. The sound of laughter followed him up the stairs. Filomena was not asleep; she had been lying on her bed listening to the sound of enormous laughter and the tread of strangely heavy feet on the stairs and along the corridors. Sir Hercules drew a chair to her bedside and sat there for a long time in silence, holding his wife's hand and sometimes gently squeezing it. At about ten o'clock they were startled by a violent noise. There was a breaking of glass, a stamping of feet, with an outburst of shouts and laughter. The uproar continuing for several minutes, Sir Hercules rose to his feet and, in spite of his wife's entreaties, prepared to go and see what was happening. There was no light on the staircase, and Sir Hercules groped his way down cautiously, lowering himself from stair to stair and standing for a moment on each tread before adventuring on a new step. The noise was louder here; the shouting articulated itself into recognizable words and phrases. A line of light was visible under the dining-room door. Sir Hercules tiptoed across the hall towards it. Just as he approached the door there was another terrific crash of breaking glass and jangled metal. What could they be doing? Standing on tiptoe he managed to look through the keyhole. In the middle of the ravaged table old Simon, the butler, so primed with drink that he could scarcely keep his balance, was dancing a jig. His feet crunched and tinkled among the broken glass, and his shoes were wet with spilt wine. The three young men sat round, thumping the table with their hands or with the empty wine bottles, shouting and laughing encouragement. The three servants leaning against the wall laughed too. Ferdinando suddenly threw a handful of walnuts at the dancer's head, which so dazed and surprised the little man that he staggered and fell down on his back, upsetting a decanter and several glasses. They raised him up, gave him some brandy to drink, thumped him on the back. The old man smiled and hiccoughed, "To-morrow," said Ferdinando, "we'll have a concerted ballet of the whole household." "With father Hercules wearing his club and lion-skin," added one of his companions, and all three roared with laughter.

Sir Hercules would look and listen no further. He crossed the hall once more and began to climb the stairs, lifting his knees painfully high at each degree. This was the end; there was no place for him now in the world, no place for him and Ferdinando together.

His wife was still awake; to her questioning glance he answered, "They are making mock of old Simon. To-morrow it will be our turn." They were silent for a time.

At last Filomena said, "I do not want to see to-morrow."

"It is better not," said Sir Hercules. Going into his closet he wrote in his day-book a full and particular account of all the events of the evening. While he was still engaged in this task he rang for a servant and ordered hot water and a bath to be made ready for him at eleven o'clock. When he had finished writing he went into his wife's room, and preparing a dose of opium twenty times as strong as that which she was accustomed to take when she could not sleep, he brought it to her, saying, "Here is your sleeping-draught."

Filomena took the glass and lay for a little time, but did not drink immediately. The tears came into her eyes. "Do you remember the songs we used to sing, sitting out there *sulla terrazza* in summer-time?" She began singing softly in her ghost of a cracked voice a few bars from Stradella's "*Amor, amor, non dormir più.*" "And you playing on the violin. It seems such a short time ago, and yet so long, long, long. *Addio, amore. A rivederti.*" She drank off the draught and, laying back on the pillow, closed her eyes. Sir Hercules kissed her hand and tiptoed away, as though he were afraid of waking her. He returned to his closet, and having recorded his wife's last words to him, he poured into his bath the water that had been brought up in accordance with his orders. The water being too hot for him to get into the bath at once, he took down from the shelf his copy of Suetonius. He wished to read how Seneca had died. He opened the book at random. "But dwarfs," he read, "he held in abhorrence as being *lusus naturæ* and of evil omen." He winced as though he had been struck. This same Augustus, he remembered, had exhibited in the amphitheatre a young man called Lucius, of good family, who was not quite two feet in height and weighed seventeen pounds, but had a stentorian voice. He turned over the pages. Tiberius, Caligula, Claudius, Nero: it was a tale of growing horror. "Seneca his preceptor, he forced to kill himself." And there was Petronius, who had called his friends about him at the last, bidding them talk to him, not of the consolations of philosophy, but of love and gallantry, while the life was ebbing away through his opened veins. Dipping his pen once more in the ink he wrote on the last page of his diary: "He died a Roman death." Then, putting the toes of one foot into the water and finding that it was not too hot, he threw off his dressing-gown and, taking a razor in his hand, sat down in the bath. With one deep cut he severed the artery in his left wrist, then lay back and composed his mind to meditation. The blood oozed out, floating through the water in dissolving wreaths and spirals. In a little while the whole bath was tinged with pink. The colour deepened; Sir Hercules felt himself mastered by an invincible drowsiness; he was sinking from vague dream to dream. Soon he was sound asleep. There was not much blood in his small body.

The Gioconda Smile

I

"MISS SPENCE will be down directly, sir."

"Thank you," said Mr Hutton, without turning round. Janet Spence's parlourmaid was so ugly—ugly on purpose, it always seemed to him, malignantly, criminally ugly—that he could not bear to look at her more than was necessary. The door closed. Left to himself, Mr Hutton got up and began to wander round the room, looking with meditative eyes at the familiar objects it contained.

Photographs of Greek statuary, photographs of the Roman Forum, coloured prints of Italian masterpieces, all very safe and well known. Poor, dear Janet, what a prig—what an intellectual snob! Her real taste was illustrated in that water-colour by the pavement artist, the one she had paid half a crown for (and thirty-five shillings for the frame). How often he had heard her tell the story, how often expatiate on the beauties of that skilful imitation of an oleograph! "A real Artist in the streets," and you could hear the capital A in Artist as she spoke the words. She made you feel that part of his glory had entered into Janet Spence when she tendered him that half-crown for the copy of the oleograph. She was implying a compliment to her own taste and penetration. A genuine Old Master for half a crown. Poor, dear Janet!

Mr Hutton came to a pause in front of a small oblong mirror. Stooping a little to get a full view of his face, he passed a white, well-manicured finger over his moustache. It was as curly, as freshly auburn as it had been twenty years ago. His hair still retained its colour, and there was no sign of baldness yet—only a certain elevation of the brow. "Shakespearean," thought Mr Hutton, with a smile, as he surveyed the smooth and polished expanse of his forehead.

Others abide our question, thou are free. . . . Footsteps in the sea . . . Majesty. . . . Shakespeare, thou shouldst be living at this hour. No, that was Milton, wasn't it? Milton, the Lady of Christ's. There was no lady about him. He was what the women would call a manly man. That was why they liked him—for the curly auburn moustache and the discreet redolence of tobacco. Mr Hutton smiled again; he enjoyed making fun of himself. Lady of Christ's? No, no. He was the Christ of Ladies. Very pretty, very pretty. The Christ of Ladies. Mr Hutton wished there were somebody he could tell the joke to. Poor, dear Janet wouldn't appreciate it, alas!

He straightened himself up, patted his hair, and resumed his peregrination. Damn the Roman Forum; he hated those dreary photographs.

Suddenly he became aware that Janet Spence was in the room, standing near the door. Mr Hutton started, as though he had been taken in some felonious act. To make these silent and spectral appearances was one of Janet Spence's peculiar talents. Perhaps she had been there all the time, had seen him looking at himself in the mirror. Impossible! But, still, it was disquieting.

"Oh, you gave me such a surprise," said Mr Hutton, recovering his smile and advancing with outstretched hand to meet her.

Miss Spence was smiling too: her Gioconda smile, he had once called it in a moment of half-ironical flattery. Miss Spence had taken the compliment seriously, and always tried to live up to the Leonardo standard. She smiled on in silence while Mr Hutton shook hands; that was part of the Gioconda business.

"I hope you're well," said Mr Hutton. "You look it."

What a queer face she had! That small mouth pursed forward by the Gioconda expression into a little snout with a round hole in the middle as though for whistling—it was like a penholder seen from the front. Above the mouth a well-shaped nose, finely aquiline. Eyes large, lustrous, and dark, with the largeness, lustre, and darkness that seems to invite sties and an occasional bloodshot suffusion. They were fine eyes, but unchangingly grave. The penholder might do its Gioconda trick, but the eyes never altered in their earnestness. Above them, a pair of boldly arched, heavily pencilled black eyebrows lent a surprising air of power, as of a Roman matron, to the upper portion of the face. Her hair was dark and equally Roman; Agrippina from the brows upward.

"I thought I'd just look in on my way home," Mr Hutton went on. "Ah, it's good to be back here"—he indicated with a wave of his hand the flowers in the vases, the sunshine and greenery beyond the windows—"it's good to be back in the country after a stuffy day of business in town."

Miss Spence, who had sat down, pointed to a chair at her side.

"No, really, I can't sit down," Mr Hutton protested. "I must get back to see how poor Emily is. She was rather seedy this morning." He sat down, nevertheless. "It's these wretched liver chills. She's always getting them. Women——" He broke off and coughed, so as to hide the fact that he had uttered. He was about to say that women with weak digestions ought not to marry; but the remark was too cruel, and he didn't really believe it. Janet Spence, moreover, was a believer in eternal flames and spiritual attachments. "She hopes to be well enough," he added, "to see you at luncheon to-morrow. Can you come? Do!" He smiled persuasively. "It's my invitation too, you know."

She dropped her eyes, and Mr Hutton almost thought that he detected a certain reddening of the cheek. It was a tribute; he stroked his moustache.

"I should like to come if you think Emily's really well enough to have a visitor."

"Of course. You'll do her good. You'll do us both good. In married life three is often better company than two."

"Oh, you're cynical."

Mr Hutton always had a desire to say "Bow-wow-wow" whenever that last word was spoken. It irritated him more than any other word in the language. But instead of barking he made haste to protest.

"No, no. I'm only speaking a melancholy truth. Reality doesn't always come up to the ideal, you know. But that doesn't make me believe any the less in the ideal. Indeed, I believe in it passionately—the ideal of a matrimony between two people in perfect accord. I think it's realisable. I'm sure it is."

He paused significantly and looked at her with an arch expression. A virgin of thirty-six, but still unwithered; she had her charms. And there was something really rather enigmatic about her. Miss Spence made no reply, but continued to smile. There were times when Mr Hutton got rather bored with the Gioconda. He stood up.

"I must really be going now. Farewell, mysterious Gioconda." The smile grew intenser, focused itself, as it were, in a narrower snout. Mr Hutton made a Cinquecento gesture, and kissed her extended hand. It was the first time he had done such a thing; the action seemed not to be resented. "I look forward to to-morrow."

"Do you?"

For answer Mr Hutton once more kissed her hand, then turned to go. Miss Spence accompanied him to the porch.

"Where's your car?" she asked.

"I left it at the gate of the drive."

"I'll come and see you off."

"No, no." Mr Hutton was playful, but determined. "You must do no such thing. I simply forbid you."

"But I should like to come," Miss Spence protested, throwing a rapid Gioconda at him.

Mr Hutton held up his hand. "No," he repeated, and then, with a gesture that was almost the blowing of a kiss, he started to run down the drive, lightly, on his toes, with long, bounding strides like a boy's. He was proud of that run; it was quite marvellously youthful. Still, he was glad the drive was no longer. At the last bend, before passing out of sight of the house, he halted and turned round. Miss Spence was still standing on the steps, smiling her smile. He waved his hand, and this time quite definitely and overtly wafted a kiss in her direction. Then, breaking once more into his magnificent canter, he rounded the last dark promontory of trees. Once out of sight of the house he let his high paces decline to a trot, and finally to a walk. He took out his handkerchief and began wiping his neck inside his collar. What fools, what fools! Had there ever been such an ass as poor, dear Janet Spence? Never, unless it was himself. Decidedly he was the more malignant fool, since he, at least, was aware of his folly and still persisted in it. Why did he persist? Ah, the problem that was himself, the problem that was other people . . .

He had reached the gate. A large prosperous-looking motor was standing at the side of the road.

"Home, M'Nab." The chauffeur touched his cap. "And stop at the cross-roads on the way, as usual," Mr Hutton added, as he opened the door of the car. "Well?" he said, speaking into the obscurity that lurked within.

"Oh, Teddy Bear, what an age you've been!" It was a fresh and childish voice that spoke the words. There was the faintest hint of Cockney impurity about the vowel sounds.

Mr Hutton bent his large form and darted into the car with the agility of an animal regaining its burrow.

"Have I?" he said, as he shut the door. The machine began to move. "You must have missed me a lot if you found the time so long." He sat back in the low seat; a cherishing warmth enveloped him.

"Teddy Bear . . ." and with a sigh of contentment a charming little head declined on to Mr Hutton's shoulder. Ravished, he looked down sideways at the round, babyish face.

"Do you know, Doris, you look like the pictures of Louise de Kéroual." He passed his fingers through a mass of curly hair.

"Who's Louise de Kera-whatever-it-is?" Doris spoke from remote distances.

"She was, alas! *Fuit*. We shall all be 'was' one of these days. Meanwhile . . ."

Mr Hutton covered the babyish face with kisses. The car rushed smoothly along. M'Nab's back, through the front window, was stonily impressive, the back of a statue.

"Your hands," Doris whispered. "Oh, you mustn't touch me. They give me electric shocks."

Mr Hutton adored her for the virgin imbecility of the words. How late in one's existence one makes the discovery of one's body!

"The electricity isn't in me, it's in you." He kissed her again, whispering her name several times: Doris, Doris, Doris. The scientific appellation of the sea-mouse, he was thinking as he kissed the throat she offered him, white and extended like the throat of a victim awaiting the sacrificial knife. The sea-mouse was a sausage with iridescent fur: very peculiar. Or was Doris the sea-cucumber, which turns itself inside out in moments of alarm? He would really have to go to Naples again, just to see the aquarium. These sea creatures were fabulous, unbelievably fantastic.

"Oh, Teddy Bear!" (More zoology; but he was only a land animal. His poor little jokes!) "Teddy Bear, I'm so happy."

"So am I," said Mr Hutton. Was it true?

"But I wish I knew if it were right. Tell me, Teddy Bear, is it right or wrong?"

"Ah, my dear, that's just what I've been wondering for the last thirty years."

"Be serious, Teddy Bear. I want to know if this is right; if it's right that I should be here with you and that we should love one another, and that it should give me electric shocks when you touch me."

"Right? Well, it's certainly good that you should have electric shocks rather than sexual repressions, Read Freud; repressions are the devil."

"Oh, you don't help me. Why aren't you ever serious? If only you knew how miserable I am sometimes, thinking it's not right. Perhaps, you know, there is a hell, and all that. I don't know what to do. Sometimes I think I ought to stop loving you."

"But could you?" asked Mr Hutton, confident in the powers of his seduction and his moustache.

"No. Teddy Bear, you know I couldn't. But I could run away, I could hide from you, I could lock myself up and force myself not to come to you."

"Silly little thing!" He tightened his embrace.

"Oh, dear, I hope it isn't wrong. And there are times when I don't care if it is."

Mr Hutton was touched. He had a certain protective affection for this little creature. He laid his cheek against her hair and so, interlaced, they sat in silence, while the car, swaying and pitching a little as it hastened along, seemed to draw in the white road and the dusty hedges towards it devouringly.

"Good-bye, good-bye."

The car moved on, gathered speed, vanished round a curve, and Doris was left standing by the sign-post at the cross-roads, still dizzy and weak with the languor born of those kisses and the electrical touch of those gentle hands. She had to take a deep breath, to draw herself up deliberately, before she was strong enough to start her homeward walk. She had half a mile in which to invent the necessary lies.

Alone, Mr Hutton suddenly found himself the prey of an appalling boredom.

II

Mrs Hutton was lying on the sofa in her boudoir, playing Patience. In spite of the warmth of the July evening a wood fire was burning on the hearth. A black Pomeranian, extenuated by the heat and the fatigues of digestion, slept before the blaze.

"Phew! Isn't it rather hot in here?" Mr Hutton asked as he entered the room.

"You know I have to keep warm, dear." The voice seemed breaking on the verge of tears. "I get so shivery."

"I hope you're better this evening."

"Not much, I'm afraid."

The conversation stagnated. Mr Hutton stood leaning his back against the mantelpiece. He looked down at the Pomeranian lying at his feet, and with the toe of his right boot he rolled the little dog over and rubbed its white-flecked chest and belly. The creature lay in an inert ecstasy. Mrs Hutton continued to play Patience. Arrived at an *impasse*, she altered the position of one card, took back another, and went on playing. Her Patiences always came out.

"Dr Libbard thinks I ought to go to Llandrindod Wells this summer."

"Well, go, my dear—go, most certainly."

Mr Hutton was thinking of the events of the afternoon: how they had driven, Doris and he, up to the hanging wood, had left the car to wait for them under the shade of the trees, and walked together out into the windless sunshine of the chalk down.

"I'm to drink the waters for my liver, and he thinks I ought to have massage and electric treatment, too."

Hat in hand, Doris had stalked four blue butterflies that were dancing together round a scabious flower with a motion that was like the flickering of blue fire. The blue fire burst and scattered into whirling sparks; she had given chase, laughing and shouting like a child.

"I'm sure it will do you good, my dear."

"I was wondering if you'd come with me, dear."

"But you know I'm going to Scotland at the end of the month."

Mrs Hutton looked up at him entreatingly. "It's the journey," she said. "The thought of it is such a nightmare. I don't know if I can manage it. And you know I can't sleep in hotels. And then there's the luggage and all the worries. I can't go alone."

"But you won't be alone. You'll have your maid with you." He spoke impatiently. The sick woman was usurping the place of the healthy one. He was being dragged back from the memory of the sunlit down and the quick, laughing girl, back to this unhealthy, overheated room and its complaining occupant.

"I don't think I shall be able to go."

"But you must, my dear, if the doctor tells you to. And, besides, a change will do you good."

"I don't think so."

"But Libbard thinks so, and he knows what he's talking about."

"No, I can't face it. I'm too weak. I can't go alone." Mrs Hutton pulled a handkerchief out of her black silk bag, and put it to her eyes.

"Nonsense, my dear, you must make the effort."

"I had rather be left in peace to die here." She was crying in earnest now.

"O Lord! Now do be reasonable. Listen now, please." Mrs Hutton only sobbed more violently. "Oh, what is one to do?" He shrugged his shoulders and walked out of the room.

Mr Hutton was aware that he had not behaved with proper patience; but he could not help it. Very early in his manhood he had discovered that not only did he not feel sympathy for the poor, the weak, the diseased, and deformed; he actually hated them. Once, as an undergraduate, he spent three days at a mission in the East End. He had returned, filled with a profound and ineradicable disgust. Instead of pitying, he loathed the unfortunate. It was not, he knew, a very comely emotion, and he had been ashamed of it at first. In the end he had decided that it was temperamental, inevitable, and had felt no further qualms. Emily had been healthy and beautiful when he married her. He had loved her then. But now—was it his fault that she was like this?

Mr Hutton dined alone. Food and drink left him more benevolent than he had been before dinner. To make amends for his show of exasperation he went up to his wife's room and offered to read to her. She was touched, gratefully accepted the offer, and Mr Hutton, who was particularly proud of his accent, suggested a little light reading in French.

"French? I am so fond of French." Mrs Hutton spoke of the language of Racine as though it were a dish of green peas.

Mr Hutton ran down to the library and returned with a yellow volume. He began reading. The effort of pronouncing perfectly absorbed his whole attention. But how good his accent was! The fact of its goodness seemed to improve the quality of the novel he was reading.

At the end of fifteen pages an unmistakable sound aroused him. He looked up; Mrs Hutton had gone to sleep. He sat still for a little while, looking with a dispassionate curiosity at the sleeping face. Once it had been beautiful; once, long ago, the sight of it, the recollection of it, had moved him with an emotion profounder, perhaps, than any he had felt before or since. Now it was lined and cadaverous. The skin was stretched tightly over the cheekbones, across the bridge of the sharp, bird-like nose. The closed eyes were set in profound bone-rimmed sockets. The lamplight striking on the face from the side emphasized with light and shade its cavities and projections. It was the face of a dead Christ by Morales.

Le squelette était invisible
Au temps heureux de l'art païen.

He shivered a little, and tiptoed out of the room.

On the following day Mrs Hutton came down to luncheon. She had had some unpleasant palpitations during the night, but she was feeling better now. Besides, she wanted to do honour to her guest. Miss Spence listened to her complaints about Llandrindod Wells, and was loud in sympathy, lavish with advice. Whatever she said was always said with intensity. She leaned forward, aimed, so to speak, like a gun, and fired her words. Bang! the charge in her soul was ignited, the words whizzed forth at the narrow barrel of her mouth. She was a machine-gun riddling her hostess with sympathy. Mr Hutton had undergone similar bombardments, mostly of a literary or philosophic character—bombardments of Maeterlinck, of Mrs Besant, of Bergson, of William James. To-day the missiles were medical. She talked about insomnia, she expatiated on the virtues of harmless drugs and beneficent specialists. Under the bombardment Mrs Hutton opened out, like a flower in the sun.

Mr Hutton looked on in silence. The spectacle of Janet Spence evoked in him an unfailing curiosity. He was not romantic enough to imagine that every face masked an interior physiognomy of beauty or strangeness, that every woman's small talk was like a vapour hanging over mysterious gulfs. His wife, for example, and Doris; they were nothing more than what they seemed to be. But with Janet Spence it was somehow different. Here one could be sure that there was some kind of a queer face behind the Gioconda smile and the Roman eyebrows. The only question was: What exactly was there? Mr Hutton could never quite make out.

"But perhaps you won't have to go to Llandrindod after all," Miss Spence was saying. "If you get well quickly Dr Libbard will let you off."

"I only hope so. Indeed, I do really feel rather better to-day."

Mr Hutton felt ashamed. How much was it his own lack of sympathy that prevented her from feeling well every day? But he comforted himself by reflecting that it was only a case of feeling, not of being better. Sympathy does not mend a diseased liver or a weak heart.

"My dear, I wouldn't eat those red currants if I were you," he said, suddenly solicitous. "You know that Libbard has banned everything with skins and pips."

"But I am so fond of them," Mrs Hutton protested, "and I feel so well to-day."

"Don't be a tyrant," said Miss Spence, looking first at him and then at his wife. "Let the poor invalid have what she fancies; it will do her good." She laid her hand on Mrs Hutton's arm and patted it affectionately two or three times.

"Thank you, my dear." Mrs Hutton helped herself to the stewed currants.

"Well, don't blame me if they make you ill again."

"Do I ever blame you, dear?"

"You have nothing to blame me for," Mr Hutton answered playfully. "I am the perfect husband."

They sat in the garden after luncheon. From the island of shade under the old cypress tree they looked out across a flat expanse of lawn, in which the parterres of flowers shone with a metallic brilliance.

Mr Hutton took a deep breath of the warm and fragrant air. "It's good to be alive," he said.

"Just to be alive," his wife echoed, stretching one pale, knot-jointed hand into the sunlight.

A maid brought the coffee; the silver pots and the little blue cups were set on a folding table near the group of chairs.

"Oh, my medicine!" exclaimed Mrs Hutton. "Run in and fetch it, Clara, will you? The white bottle on the sideboard."

"I'll go," said Mr Hutton. "I've got to go and fetch a cigar in any case."

He ran in towards the house. On the threshold he turned round for an instant. The maid was walking back across the lawn. His wife was sitting up in her deck-chair, engaged in opening her white parasol. Miss Spence was bending over the table, pouring out the coffee. He passed into the cool obscurity of the house.

"Do you like sugar in your coffee?" Miss Spence inquired.

"Yes, please. Give me rather a lot. I'll drink it after my medicine to take the taste away."

Mrs Hutton leaned back in her chair, lowering the sunshade over her eyes, so as to shut out from her vision the burning sky.

Behind her, Miss Spence was making a delicate clinking among the coffee-cups.

"I've given you three large spoonfuls. That ought to take the taste away. And here comes the medicine."

Mr Hutton had reappeared, carrying a wine-glass, half full of a pale liquid.

"It smells delicious," he said, as he handed it to his wife.

"That's only the flavouring." She drank it off at a gulp, shuddered, and made a grimace. "Ugh, it's so nasty. Give me my coffee."

Miss Spence gave her the cup; she sipped at it. "You've made it like syrup. But it's very nice, after that atrocious medicine."

At half-past three Mrs Hutton complained that she did not feel as well as she had done, and went indoors to lie down. Her husband would have said something about the red currants, but checked himself; the triumph of an "I told you so" was too cheaply won. Instead, he was sympathetic, and gave her his arm to the house.

"A rest will do you good," he said. "By the way, I shan't be back till after dinner."

"But why? Where are you going?"

"I promised to go to Johnson's this evening. We have to discuss the war memorial, you know."

"Oh, I wish you weren't going." Mrs Hutton was almost in tears. "Can't you stay? I don't like being alone in the house."

"But, my dear, I promised—weeks ago." It was a bother having to lie like this. "And now I must get back and look after Miss Spence."

He kissed her on the forehead and went out again into the garden. Miss Spence received him aimed and intense.

"Your wife is dreadfully ill," she fired off at him.

"I thought she cheered up so much when you came."

"That was purely nervous, purely nervous. I was watching her closely. With a heart in that condition and her digestion wrecked —yes, wrecked—anything might happen."

"Libbard doesn't take so gloomy a view of poor Emily's health."
Mr Hutton held open the gate that led from the garden into the
drive; Miss Spence's car was standing by the front door.

"Libbard is only a country doctor. You ought to see a
specialist."

He could not refrain from laughing. "You have a macabre
passion for specialists."

Miss Spence held up her hand in protest. "I am serious. I
think poor Emily is in a very bad state. Anything might happen
—at any moment."

He handed her into the car and shut the door. The chauffeur
started the engine and climbed into his place, ready to drive off.

"Shall I tell him to start?" He had no desire to continue the
conversation.

Miss Spence leaned forward and shot a Gioconda in his
direction. "Remember, I expect you to come and see me again
soon."

Mechanically he grinned, made a polite noise, and, as the car
moved forward, waved his hand. He was happy to be alone.

A few minutes afterwards Mr Hutton himself drove away.
Doris was waiting at the cross-roads. They dined together twenty
miles from home, at a roadside hotel. It was one of those bad, expensive meals which are only cooked in country hotels frequented
by motorists. It revolted Mr Hutton, but Doris enjoyed it. She
always enjoyed things. Mr Hutton ordered a not very good brand
of champagne. He was wishing he had spent the evening in his
library.

When they started homewards Doris was a little tipsy and extremely affectionate. It was very dark inside the car, but looking
forward, past the motionless form of M'Nab, they could see a
bright and narrow universe of forms and colours scooped out of
the night by the electric head-lamps.

It was after eleven when Mr Hutton reached home. Dr
Libbard met him in the hall. He was a small man with delicate
hands and well-formed features that were almost feminine. His
brown eyes were large and melancholy. He used to waste a great
deal of time sitting at the bedside of his patients, looking sadness
through those eyes and talking in a sad, low voice about nothing
in particular. His person exhaled a pleasing odour, decidedly anti-
septic but at the same time suave and discreetly delicious.

"Libbard?" said Mr Hutton in surprise. "You here? Is my wife ill?"

"We tried to fetch you earlier," the soft, melancholy voice replied. "It was thought you were at Mr Johnson's, but they had no news of you there."

"No, I was detained. I had a break-down," Mr Hutton answered irritably. It was tiresome to be caught out in a lie.

"Your wife wanted to see you urgently."

"Well, I can go now." Mr Hutton moved towards the stairs.

Dr Libbard laid a hand on his arm. "I am afraid it's too late."

"Too late?" He began fumbling with his watch; it wouldn't come out of the pocket.

"Mrs Hutton passed away half an hour ago."

The voice remained even in its softness, the melancholy of the eyes did not deepen. Dr Libbard spoke of death as he would speak of a local cricket match. All things were equally vain and equally deplorable.

Mr Hutton found himself thinking of Janet Spence's words. At any moment—at any moment. She had been extraordinarily right.

"What happened?" he asked. "What was the cause?"

Dr Libbard explained. It was heart failure brought on by a violent attack of nausea, caused in its turn by the eating of something of an irritant nature. Red currants? Mr Hutton suggested. Very likely. It had been too much for the heart. There was chronic valvular disease: something had collapsed under the strain. It was all over; she could not have suffered much.

III

"It's a pity they should have chosen the day of the Eton and Harrow match for the funeral," old General Grego was saying as he stood, his top hat in his hand, under the shadow of the lych gate, wiping his face with his handkerchief.

Mr Hutton overheard the remark and with difficulty restrained a desire to inflict grievous bodily pain on the General. He would have liked to hit the old brute in the middle of his big red face. Monstrous great mulberry, spotted with meal! Was there no respect for the dead? Did nobody care? In theory he didn't much care; let the dead bury their dead. But here, at the graveside, he had found himself actually sobbing. Poor Emily, they had been pretty happy once. Now she was lying at the bottom of a seven-foot hole. And here was Grego complaining that he couldn't go to the Eton and Harrow match.

Mr Hutton looked round at the groups of black figures that were drifting slowly out of the churchyard towards the fleet of cabs and motors assembled in the road outside. Against the brilliant background of the July grass and flowers and foliage, they had a horribly alien and unnatural appearance. It pleased him to think that all these people would soon be dead too.

That evening Mr Hutton sat up late in his library reading the life of Milton. There was no particular reason why he should have chosen Milton; it was the book that first came to hand, that was all. It was after midnight when he had finished. He got up from his armchair, unbolted the French windows, and stepped out on to the little paved terrace. The night was quiet and clear. Mr Hutton looked at the stars and at the holes between them, dropped his eyes to the dim lawns and hueless flowers of the garden, and let them wander over the farther landscape, black and grey under the moon.

He began to think with a kind of confused violence. There were the stars, there was Milton. A man can be somehow the peer of stars and night. Greatness, nobility. But is there seriously a difference between the noble and the ignoble? Milton, the stars, death, and himself—himself. The soul, the body; the higher and the lower nature. Perhaps there was something in it, after all. Milton had a god on his side and righteousness. What had he? Nothing, nothing whatever. There were only Doris's little breasts. What was the point of it all? Milton, the stars, death, and Emily in her grave, Doris and himself—always himself . . .

Oh, he was a futile and disgusting being. Everything convinced him of it. It was a solemn moment. He spoke aloud: "I will, I will." The sound of his own voice in the darkness was appalling; it seemed to him that he had sworn that infernal oath which binds even the gods: "I will, I will." There had been New Year's days and solemn anniversaries in the past, when he had felt the same contritions and recorded similar resolutions. They had all thinned away, these resolutions, like smoke, into nothingness. But this was a greater moment and he had pronounced a more fearful oath. In the future it was to be different. Yes, he would live by reason, he would be industrious, he would curb his appetites, he would devote his life to some good purpose. It was resolved and it would be so.

In practice he was himself spending his mornings in agricultural pursuits, riding round with the bailiff, seeing that his land was farmed in the best modern way—silos and artificial manures and continuous cropping, and all that. The remainder of the day should be devoted to serious study There was that book he had been intending to write for so long—*The Effect of Diseases on Civilization.*

Mr Hutton went to bed humble and contrite, but with a sense that grace had entered into him. He slept for seven and a half hours, and woke to find the sun brilliantly shining. The emotions of the evening before had been transformed by a good night's rest into his customary cheerfulness. It was not until a good many seconds after his return to conscious life that he remembered his resolution, his Stygian oath. Milton and death seemed somehow different in the sunlight. As for the stars, they were not there. But the resolutions were good; even in the daytime he could see that. He had his horse saddled after breakfast, and rode round the farm with the bailiff. After luncheon he read Thucydides on the plague at Athens. In the evening he made a few notes on malaria in Southern Italy. While he was undressing he remembered that there was a good anecdote in Skelton's jest-book about the Sweating Sickness. He would have made a note of it if only he could have found a pencil.

On the sixth morning of his new life Mr Hutton found among his correspondence an envelope addressed in that peculiarly vulgar handwriting which he knew to be Doris's. He opened it, and began to read. She didn't know what to say; words were so inadequate. His wife dying like that, and so suddenly—it was too terrible. Mr Hutton sighed, but his interest revived somewhat as he read on:

"Death is so frightening, I never think of it when I can help it. But when something like this happens, or when I am feeling ill or depressed, then I can't help remembering it is there so close, and I think about all the wicked things I have done and about you and me, and I wonder what will happen, and I am so frightened.

I am so lonely, Teddy Bear, and so unhappy, and I don't know what to do. I can't get rid of the idea of dying, I am so wretched and helpless without you. I didn't mean to write to you; I meant to wait till you were out of mourning and could come and see me again, but I was so lonely and miserable, Teddy Bear, I had to write. I couldn't help it. Forgive me, I want you so much; I have nobody in the world but you. You are so good and gentle and understanding; there is nobody like you. I shall never forget how good and kind you have been to me, and you are so clever and know so much, I can't understand how you ever came to pay any attention to me, I am so dull and stupid, much less like me and love me, because you do love me a little, don't you, Teddy Bear?"

Mr Hutton was touched with shame and remorse. To be thanked like this, worshipped for having seduced the girl—it was too much. It had just been a piece of imbecile wantonness. Imbecile, idiotic: there was no other way to describe it. For, when all was said, he had derived very little pleasure from it. Taking all things together, he had probably been more bored than amused. Once upon a time he had believed himself to be a hedonist. But to be a hedonist implies a certain process of reasoning, a deliberate choice of known pleasures, a rejection of known pains. This had been done without reason, against it. For he knew beforehand—so well, so well—that there was no interest or pleasure to be derived from these wretched affairs. And yet each time the vague itch came upon him he succumbed, involving himself once more in the old stupidity. There had been Maggie, his wife's maid, and Edith, the girl on the farm, and Mrs Pringle, and the waitress in London, and others—there seemed to be dozens of them. It had all been so stale and boring. He knew it would be; he always knew. And yet, and yet . . . Experience doesn't teach.

Poor little Doris! He would write to her kindly, comfortingly, but he wouldn't see her again. A servant came to tell him that his horse was saddled and waiting. He mounted and rode off. That morning the old bailiff was more irritating than usual.

Five days later Doris and Mr Hutton were sitting together on the pier at Southend; Doris, in white muslin with pink garnishings, radiated happiness; Mr Hutton, legs outstretched and chair tilted, had pushed the panama back from his forehead, and was trying to feel like a tripper. That night, when Doris was asleep, breathing and warm by his side, he recaptured, in this moment of darkness and physical fatigue, the rather cosmic emotion which had possessed him that evening, not a fortnight ago, when he had made his great resolution. And so his solemn oath had already gone the way of so many other resolutions. Unreason had triumphed; at the first itch of desire he had given way. He was hopeless, hopeless.

For a long time he lay with closed eyes, ruminating his humiliation. The girl stirred in her sleep. Mr Hutton turned over and looked in her direction. Enough faint light crept in between the half-drawn curtains to show her bare arm and shoulder, her neck, and the dark tangle of hair on the pillow. She was beautiful, desirable. Why did he lie there moaning over his sins? What did it matter? If he were hopeless, then so be it; he would make the best of his hopelessness. A glorious sense of irresponsibility suddenly filled him. He was free, magnificently free. In a kind of exaltation he drew the girl towards him. She woke, bewildered, almost frightened under his rough kisses.

The storm of his desire subsided into a kind of serene merriment. The whole atmosphere seemed to be quivering with enormous silent laughter.

"Could anyone love you as much as I do, Teddy Bear?" The question came faintly from distant worlds of love.

"I think I know somebody who does," Mr Hutton replied. The submarine laughter was swelling, rising, ready to break the surface of silence and resound.

"Who? Tell me. What do you mean?" The voice had come very close; charged with suspicion, anguish, indignation, it belonged to this immediate world.

"A—ah!"

"Who?"

"You'll never guess." Mr Hutton kept up the joke until it began to grow tedious, and then pronounced the name: "Janet Spence."

Doris was incredulous. "Miss Spence of the Manor? That old woman?" It was too ridiculous. Mr Hutton laughed too.

"But it's quite true," he said. "She adores me." Oh, the vast joke! He would go and see her as soon as he returned—see and conquer. "I believe she wants to marry me," he added. "But you wouldn't . . . you don't intend . . ."

The air was fairly crepitating with humour. Mr Hutton laughed aloud. "I intend to marry you," he said. It seemed to him the best joke he had ever made in his life.

When Mr Hutton left Southend he was once more a married man. It was agreed that, for the time being, the fact should be kept secret. In the autumn they would go abroad together, and the world should be informed. Meanwhile he was to go back to his own house and Doris to hers.

The day after his return he walked over in the afternoon to see Miss Spence. She received him with the old Gioconda.

"I was expecting you to come."

"I couldn't keep away," Mr Hutton gallantly replied.

They sat in the summer-house. It was a pleasant place—a little old stucco temple bowered among dense bushes of evergreen. Miss Spence had left her mark on it by hanging up over the seat a blue-and-white Della Robbia plaque.

"I am thinking of going to Italy this autumn," said Mr Hutton. He felt like a ginger-beer bottle, ready to pop with bubbling humorous excitement.

"Italy. . . ." Miss Spence closed her eyes ecstatically. "I feel drawn there too."

"Why not let yourself be drawn?"

"I don't know. One somehow hasn't the energy and initiative to set out alone."

"Alone. . . ." Ah, sound of guitars and throaty singing! "Yes, travelling alone isn't much fun."

Miss Spence lay back in her chair without speaking. Her eyes were still closed. Mr Hutton stroked his moustache. The silence prolonged itself for what seemed a very long time.

Pressed to stay to dinner, Mr Hutton did not refuse. The fun had hardly started. The table was laid in the loggia. Through its arches they looked out on to the sloping garden, to the valley below and the farther hills. Light ebbed away; the heat and silence were oppressive. A huge cloud was mounting up the sky, and there were distant breathings of thunder. The thunder drew nearer, a wind began to blow, and the first drops of rain fell. The table was cleared. Miss Spence and Mr Hutton sat on in the growing darkness.

Miss Spence broke a long silence by saying meditatively:

"I think everyone has a right to a certain amount of happiness, don't you?"

"Most certainly." But what was she leading up to? Nobody makes generalizations about life unless they mean to talk about themselves. Happiness: he looked back on his own life, and saw a cheerful, placid existence disturbed by no great griefs or discomforts or alarms. He had always had money and freedom; he had been able to do very much as he wanted. Yes, he supposed he had been happy—happier than most men. And now he was not merely happy; he had discovered in irresponsibility the secret of gaiety. He was about to say something about his happiness when Miss Spence went on speaking.

"People like you and me have a right to be happy some time in our lives."

"Me?" said Mr Hutton, surprised.

"Poor Henry! Fate hasn't treated either of us very well."

"Oh, well, it might have treated me worse."

"You're being cheerful. That's brave of you. But don't think I can't see behind the mask."

Miss Spence spoke louder and louder as the rain came down more and more heavily. Periodically the thunder cut across her utterances. She talked on, shouting against the noise.

"I have understood you so well and for so long."

A flash revealed her, aimed and intent, leaning towards him. Her eyes were two profound and menacing gun-barrels. The darkness re-engulfed her.

"You were a lonely soul seeking a companion soul. I could sympathize with you in your solitude. Your marriage . . ."

The thunder cut short the sentence. Miss Spence's voice became audible once more with the words:

". . . could offer no companionship to a man of your stamp. You needed a soul mate."

A soul mate—he! a soul mate. It was incredibly fantastic. "Georgette Leblanc, the ex-soul mate of Maurice Maeterlinck." He had seen that in the paper a few days ago. So it was thus that Janet Spence had painted him in her imagination—as a soulmater. And for Doris he was a picture of goodness and the cleverest man in the world. And actually, really, he was what?— Who knows?

"My heart went out to you. I could understand; I was lonely, too." Miss Spence laid her hand on his knee. "You were so patient." Another flash. She was still aimed, dangerously. "You never complained. But I could guess—I could guess."

"How wonderful of you!" So he was an *âme incomprise*. "Only a woman's intuition . . ."

The thunder crashed and rumbled, died away, and only the sound of the rain was left. The thunder was his laughter, magnified, externalized. Flash and crash, there it was again, right on top of them.

"Don't you feel that you have within you something that is akin to this storm?" He could imagine her leaning forward as she uttered the words. "Passion makes one the equal of the elements."

What was his gambit now? Why, obviously, he should have said "Yes," and ventured on some unequivocal gesture. But Mr Hutton suddenly took fright. The ginger beer in him had gone flat. The woman was serious—terribly serious. He was appalled.

Passion? "No," he desperately answered. "I am without passion."

But his remark was either unheard or unheeded, for Miss Spence went on with a growing exaltation, speaking so rapidly, however, and in such a burningly intimate whisper that Mr Hutton found it very difficult to distinguish what she was saying. She was telling him, as far as he could make out, the story of her life. The lightning was less frequent now, and there were long intervals of darkness. But at each flash he saw her still aiming towards him, still yearning forward with a terrifying intensity. Darkness, the rain, and then flash! her face was there, close at hand. A pale mask, greenish white; the large eyes, the narrow barrel of the mouth, the heavy eyebrows. Agrippina, or wasn't it rather—yes, wasn't it rather George Robey?"

He began devising absurd plans for escaping. He might suddenly jump up, pretending he had seen a burglar—Stop thief! stop thief!—and dash off into the night in pursuit. Or should he say that he felt faint, a heart attack? or that he had seen a ghost—Emily's ghost—in the garden? Absorbed in his childish plotting, he had ceased to pay any attention to Miss Spence's words. The spasmodic clutching of her hand recalled his thoughts.

"I honoured you for that, Henry," she was saying.

Honoured him for what?

"Marriage is a sacred tie, and your respect for it, even when the marriage was, as it was in your case, an unhappy one, made me respect you and admire you, and—shall I dare say the word?——"

Oh, the burglar, the ghost in the garden! But it was too late.

". . . yes, love you, Henry, all the more. But we're free now, Henry."

Free? There was a movement in the dark, and she was kneeling on the floor by his chair.

"Oh, Henry, Henry, I have been unhappy too."

Her arms embraced him, and by the shaking of her body he could feel that she was sobbing. She might have been a suppliant crying for mercy.

"You mustn't, Janet," he protested. Those tears were terrible, terrible. "Not now, not now! You must be calm; you must go to bed." He patted her shoulder, then got up, disengaging himself from her embrace. He left her still crouching on the floor beside the chair on which he had been sitting.

Groping his way into the hall, and without waiting to look for his hat, he went out of the house, taking infinite pains to close the front door noiselessly behind him. The clouds had blown over, and the moon was shining from a clear sky. There were puddles all along the road, and a noise of running water rose from the gutters and ditches. Mr Hutton splashed along, not caring if he got wet.

How heartrendingly she had sobbed! With the emotions of pity and remorse that the recollection evoked in him there was a certain resentment: why couldn't she have played the game that he was playing—the heartless, amusing game? Yes, but he had known all the time that she wouldn't, she couldn't, play that game; he had known and persisted.

What had she said about passion and the elements? Something absurdly stale, but true, true. There she was, a cloud black-bosomed and charged with thunder, and he, like some absurd little Benjamin Franklin, had sent up a kite into the heart of the menace. Now he was complaining that his toy had drawn the lightning.

She was probably still kneeling by that chair in the loggia, crying.

But why hadn't he been able to keep up the game? Why had

his irresponsibility deserted him, leaving him suddenly sober in a cold world? There were no answers to any of his questions. One idea burned steady and luminous in his mind—the idea of flight. He must get away at once.

IV

"What are you thinking about, Teddy Bear?"

"Nothing."

There was a silence. Mr Hutton remained motionless, his elbows on the parapet of the terrace, his chin in his hands, looking down over Florence. He had taken a villa on one of the hilltops to the south of the city. From a little raised terrace at the end of the garden one looked down a long fertile valley on to the town and beyond it to the bleak mass of Monte Morello and, eastward of it, to the peopled hill of Fiesole, dotted with white houses. Everything was clear and luminous in the September sunshine.

"Are you worried about anything?"

"No, thank you."

"Tell me, Teddy Bear."

"But, my dear, there's nothing to tell." Mr Hutton turned round, smiled, and patted the girl's hand. "I think you'd better go in and have your siesta. It's too hot for you here."

"Very well, Teddy Bear. Are you coming too?"

"When I've finished my cigar."

"All right. But do hurry up and finish it, Teddy Bear." Slowly, reluctantly, she descended the steps of the terrace and walked towards the house.

Mr Hutton continued his contemplation of Florence. He had need to be alone. It was good sometimes to escape from Doris and the restless solicitude of her passion. He had never known the pains of loving hopelessly, but he was experiencing now the pains of being loved. These last weeks had been a period of growing discomfort. Doris was always with him, like an obsession, like a guilty conscience. Yes, it was good to be alone.

He pulled an envelope out of his pocket and opened it, not without reluctance. He hated letters; they always contained something unpleasant—nowadays, since his second marriage. This was from his sister. He began skimming through the insulting home-truths of which it was composed. The words "indecent haste", "social suicide", "scarcely cold in her grave", "person of the lower classes", all occurred. They were inevitable now in any communication from a well-meaning and right-thinking relative. Impatient, he was about to tear the stupid letter to pieces when his eye fell on a sentence at the bottom of the third page. His heart beat with uncomfortable violence as he read it. It was too monstrous! Janet Spence was going about telling everyone that he had poisoned his wife in order to marry Doris. What damnable malice! Ordinarily a man of the suavest temper, Mr Hutton found himself trembling with rage. He took the childish satisfaction of calling names—he cursed the woman.

Then suddenly he saw the ridiculous side of the situation. The notion that he should have murdered anyone in order to marry Doris! If they only knew how miserably bored he was. Poor, dear Janet! She had tried to be malicious; she had only succeeded in being stupid.

A sound of footsteps aroused him; he looked round. In the garden below the little terrace the servant girl of the house was picking fruit. A Neapolitan, strayed somehow as far north as Florence, she was a specimen of the classical type—a little debased. Her profile might have been taken from a Sicilian coin of a bad period. Her features, carved floridly in the grand tradition, expressed an almost perfect stupidity. Her mouth was the most beautiful thing about her; the calligraphic hand of nature had richly curved it into an expression of mulish bad temper. . . . Under her hideous black clothes, Mr Hutton divined a powerful body, firm and massive. He had looked at her before with a vague interest and curiosity. To-day the curiosity defined and focused itself into a desire. An idyll of Theocritus. Here was the woman; he, alas, was not precisely like a goatherd on the volcanic hills. He called to her.

"Armida!"

The smile with which she answered him was so provocative, attested so easy a virtue, that Mr Hutton took fright. He was on the brink once more—on the brink. He must draw back, oh! quickly, quickly, before it was too late. The girl continued to look up at him.

"*Ha chiamato?*" she asked at last.

Stupidity or reason? Oh, there was no choice now. It was imbecility every time.

"*Scendo,*" he called back to her. Twelve steps led from the garden to the terrace. Mr Hutton counted them. Down, down, down, down. . . . He saw a vision of himself descending from one circle of the inferno to the next—from a darkness full of wind and hail to an abyss of sinking mud.

V

For a good many days the Hutton case had a place on the front page of every newspaper. There had been no more popular murder trial since George Smith had temporarily eclipsed the European War by drowning in a warm bath his seventh bride. The public imagination was stirred by this tale of a murder brought to light months after the date of the crime. Here, it was felt, was one of those incidents in human life, so notable because they are so rare, which do definitely justify the ways of God to man. A wicked man had been moved by an illicit passion to kill his wife. For months he had lived in sin and fancied security— only to be dashed at last more horribly into the pit he had prepared for himself. Murder will out, and here was a case of it. The readers of the newspapers were in a position to follow every movement of the hand of God. There had been vague, but persistent, rumours in the neighbourhood; the police had taken action at last. Then came the exhumation order, the post-mortem examination, the inquest, the evidence of the experts, the verdict of the coroner's jury, the trial, the condemnation. For once Providence had done its duty, obviously, grossly, didactically, as in a melodrama. The newspapers were right in making of the case the staple intellectual food of a whole season.

Mr Hutton's first emotion when he was summoned from Italy to give evidence at the inquest was one of indignation. It was a monstrous, a scandalous thing that the police should take such idle, malicious gossip seriously. When the inquest was over he would bring an action for malicious prosecution against the Chief Constable; he would sue the Spence woman for slander.

The inquest was opened; the astonishing evidence unrolled itself. The experts had examined the body, and had found traces of arsenic; they were of opinion that the late Mrs Hutton had died of arsenic poisoning.

Arsenic poisoning. . . . Emily had died of arsenic poisoning?

After that, Mr Hutton learned with surprise that there was enough arsenicated insecticide in his greenhouses to poison an army.

It was now, quite suddenly, that he saw it: there was a case against him. Fascinated, he watched it growing, growing, like some monstrous tropical plant. It was enveloping him, surrounding him; he was lost in a tangled forest.

When was the poison administered? The experts agreed that it must have been swallowed eight or nine hours before death. About lunch-time? Yes, about lunch-time. Clara, the parlourmaid, was called. Mrs Hutton, she remembered, had asked her to go and fetch her medicine. Mr Hutton had volunteered to go instead; he had gone alone. Miss Spence—ah, the memory of the storm, the white aimed face! the horror of it all!—Miss Spence confirmed Clara's statement, and added that Mr Hutton had come back with the medicine already poured out in a wine-glass, not in the bottle.

Mr Hutton's indignation evaporated. He was dismayed, frightened. It was all too fantastic to be taken seriously, and yet this nightmare was a fact—it was actually happening.

M'Nab had seen them kissing, often. He had taken them for a drive on the day of Mrs Hutton's death. He could see them reflected in the wind-screen, sometimes out of the tail of his eye.

The inquest was adjourned. That evening Doris went to bed with a headache. When he went to her room after dinner, Mr Hutton found her crying.

"What's the matter?" He sat down on the edge of her bed and began to stroke her hair. For a long time she did not answer, and he went on stroking her hair mechanically, almost unconsciously; sometimes, even, he bent down and kissed her bare shoulder. He had his own affairs, however, to think about. What had happened? How was it that the stupid gossip had actually come true? Emily had died of arsenic poisoning. It was absurd, impossible. The order of things had been broken, and he was at the mercy of an irresponsibility. What had happened, what was going to happen? He was interrupted in the midst of his thoughts.

"It's my fault—it's my fault!" Doris suddenly sobbed out. "I shouldn't have loved you; I oughtn't to have let you love me. Why was I ever born?"

Mr Hutton didn't say anything, but looked down in silence at the abject figure of misery lying on the bed.

"If they do anything to you I shall kill myself."

She sat up, held him for a moment at arm's length, and looked at him with a kind of violence, as though she were never to see him again.

"I love you, I love you, I love you." She drew him, inert and passive, towards her, clasped him, pressed herself against him. "I didn't know you loved me as much as that, Teddy Bear. But why did you do it—why did you do it?"

Mr Hutton undid her clasping arms and got up. His face became very red. "You seem to take it for granted that I murdered my wife," he said. "It's really too grotesque. What do you all take me for? A cinema hero?" He had begun to lose his temper. All the exasperation, all the fear and bewilderment of the day, was transformed into a violent anger against her. "It's all such damned stupidity. Haven't you any conception of a civilized man's mentality? Do I look the sort of man who'd go about slaughtering people? I suppose you imagined I was so insanely in love with you that I could commit any folly. When will you women understand that one isn't insanely in love? All one asks for is a quiet life, which you won't allow one to have. I don't know what the devil ever induced me to marry you. It was all a damned stupid, practical joke. And now you go about saying I'm a murderer. I won't stand it."

Mr Hutton stamped towards the door. He had said horrible things, he knew—odious things that he ought speedily to unsay. But he wouldn't. He closed the door behind him.

"Teddy Bear!" He turned the handle; the latch clicked into place. "Teddy Bear!" The voice that came to him through the closed door was agonized. Should he go back? He ought to go back. He touched the handle, then withdrew his fingers and quickly walked away. When he was half-way down the stairs he halted. She might try to do something silly—throw herself out of the window or God knows what! He listened attentively; there was no sound. But he pictured her very clearly, tiptoeing across the room, lifting the sash as high as it would go, leaning out into the cold night air. It was raining a little. Under the window lay the paved terrace. How far below? Twenty-five or thirty feet? Once, when he was walking along Piccadilly, a dog had jumped out of a third-storey window of the Ritz. He had seen it fall; he had heard it strike the pavement. Should he go back? He was damned if he would; he hated her.

He sat for a long time in the library. What had happened? What was happening? He turned the question over and over in his mind and could find no answer. Suppose the nightmare dreamed itself out to its horrible conclusion. Death was waiting for him. His eyes filled with tears; he wanted so passionately to live. "Just to be alive." Poor Emily had wished it too, he remembered: "Just to be alive." There were still so many places in this astonishing world unvisited, so many queer delightful people still unknown, so many lovely women never so much as seen. The huge white oxen would still be dragging their wains along the Tuscan roads, the cypresses would still go up, straight as pillars, to the blue heaven; but he would not be there to see them. And the sweet southern wines — Tear of Christ and Blood of Judas— others would drink them, not he. Others would walk down the obscure and narrow lanes between the bookshelves in the London Library, sniffing the dusty perfume of good literature, peering at strange titles, discovering unknown names, exploring the fringes of vast domains of knowledge. He would be lying in a hole in the ground. And why, why? Confusedly he felt that some extraordinary kind of justice was being done. In the past he had been wanton and imbecile and irresponsible. Now Fate was playing as wantonly, as irresponsibly, with him. It was tit for tat, and God existed after all.

He felt that he would like to pray. Forty years ago he used to kneel by his bed every evening. The nightly formula of his childhood came to him almost unsought from some long unopened chamber of the memory. "God bless Father and Mother, Tom and Cissie and the Baby, Mademoiselle and Nurse, and everyone that I love, and make me a good boy. Amen." They were all dead now—all except Cissie.

His mind seemed to soften and dissolve; a great calm descended upon his spirit. He went upstairs to ask Doris's forgiveness. He found her lying on the couch at the foot of the bed. On the floor beside her stood a blue bottle of liniment, marked "Not to be taken"; she seemed to have drunk about half of it.

"You didn't love me," was all she said when she opened her eyes to find him bending over her.

Dr Libbard arrived in time to prevent any very serious consequences. "You mustn't do this again," he said while Mr Hutton was out of the room.

"What's to prevent me?" she asked defiantly.

Dr Libbard looked at her with his large, sad eyes. "There's nothing to prevent you," he said. "Only yourself and your baby. Isn't it rather bad luck on your baby, not allowing it to come into the world because you want to go out of it?"

Doris was silent for a time. "All right," she whispered. "I won't."

Mr Hutton sat by her bedside for the rest of the night. He felt himself now to be indeed a murderer. For a time he persuaded himself that he loved this pitiable child. Dozing in his chair, he woke up, stiff and cold, to find himself drained dry, as it were, of every emotion. He had become nothing but a tired and suffering carcase. At six o'clock he undressed and went to bed for a couple of hours' sleep. In the course of the same afternoon the coroner's jury brought in a verdict of "Wilful Murder," and Mr Hutton was committed for trial.

VI

Miss Spence was not at all well. She had found her public appearances in the witness-box very trying, and when it was all over she had something that was very nearly a breakdown. She slept badly, and suffered from nervous indigestion. Dr Libbard used to call every other day. She talked to him a great deal—mostly about the Hutton case. . . . Her moral indignation was always on the boil? Wasn't it appalling to think that one had had a murderer in one's house? Wasn't it extraordinary that one could have been for so long mistaken about the man's character? (But she had had an inkling from the first.) And then the girl he had gone off with—so low class, so little better than a prostitute. The news that the second Mrs Hutton was expecting a baby—the posthumous child of a condemned and executed criminal—revolted her; the thing was shocking—an obscenity. Dr Libbard answered her gently and vaguely, and prescribed bromide.

One morning he interrupted her in the midst of her customary tirade. "By the way," he said in his soft, melancholy voice, "I suppose it was really you who poisoned Mrs Hutton."

Miss Spence stared at him for two or three seconds with enormous eyes, and then quietly said "Yes." After that she started to cry.

"In the coffee, I suppose."

She seemed to nod assent. Dr Libbard took out his fountain-pen, and in his neat, meticulous calligraphy wrote out a prescription for a sleeping-draught.

The Tillotson Banquet

I

YOUNG Spode was not a snob; he was too intelligent for that, too fundamentally decent. Not a snob; but all the same he could not help feeling very well pleased at the thought that he was dining, alone and intimately, with Lord Badgery. It was a definite event in his life, a step forward, he felt, towards that final success, social, material, and literary, which he had come to London with a fixed intention of making. The conquest and capture of Badgery was an almost essential strategical move in the campaign.

Edmund, forty-seventh Baron Badgery, was a lineal descendant of that Edmund, surnamed Le Blayreau, who landed on English soil in the train of William the Conqueror. Ennobled by William Rufus, the Badgerys had been one of the very few baronial families to survive the Wars of the Roses and all the other changes and chances of English history. They were a sensible and philoprogenitive race. No Badgery had ever fought in any war, no Badgery had ever engaged in any kind of politics. They had been content, to live and quietly to propagate their species in a huge machicolated Norman castle, surrounded by a triple moat, only sallying forth to cultivate their property and to collect their rents. In the eighteenth century, when life had become relatively secure, the Badgerys began to venture forth into civilized society. From boorish squires they blossomed into *grands seigneurs*, patrons of the arts, virtuosi. Their property was large, they were rich; and with the growth of industrialism their riches also grew. Villages on their estate turned into manufacturing towns, unsuspected coal was discovered beneath the surface of their barren moorlands. By the middle of the nineteenth century the Badgerys were among the richest of English noble families. The forty-seventh baron disposed of an income of at least two hundred thousand pounds a year. Following the great Badgery tradition, he had refused to have anything to do with politics or war. He occupied himself by collecting pictures; he took an interest in theatrical productions; he was the friend and patron of men of letters, of painters, and musicians. A personage, in a word, of considerable consequence

in that particular world in which young Spode had elected to
make his success.

Spode had only recently left the university. Simon Gollamy,
the editor of the *World's Review* (the "Best of all possible Worlds"),
had got to know him—he was always on the look out for youthful
talent—had seen possibilities in the young man, and appointed
him art critic of his paper. Gollamy liked to have young and
teachable people about him. The possession of disciples flattered
his vanity, and he found it easier, moreover, to run his paper with
docile collaborators than with men grown obstinate and case-
hardened with age. Spode had not done badly at his new job. At
any rate, his articles had been intelligent enough to arouse the
interest of Lord Badgery. It was, ultimately, to them that he owed
the honour of sitting to-night in the dining-room of Badgery House.

Fortified by several varieties of wine and a glass of aged brandy,
Spode felt more confident and at ease than he had done the whole
evening. Badgery was rather a disquieting host. He had an alarming habit of changing the subject of any conversation that had
lasted for more than two minutes. Spode had found it, for
example, horribly mortifying when his host, cutting across what
was, he prided himself, a particularly subtle and illuminating dis-
quisition on baroque art, had turned a wandering eye about the
room and asked him abruptly whether he liked parrots. He had
flushed and glanced suspiciously towards him, fancying that the
man was trying to be offensive. But no; Badgery's white, fleshy,
Hanoverian face wore an expression of perfect good faith. There
was no malice in his small greenish eyes. He evidently did genuinely want to know if Spode liked parrots. The young man
swallowed his irritation and replied that he did. Badgery then
told a good story about parrots. Spode was on the point of capping
it with a better story, when his host began to talk about Beethoven.
And so the game went on. Spode cut his conversation to suit his
host's requirements. In the course of ten minutes he had made a
more or less witty epigram on Benvenuto Cellini, Queen Victoria,
sport, God, Stephen Phillips, and Moorish architecture. Lord
Badgery thought him the most charming young man, and so
intelligent.

"If you've quite finished your coffee," he said, rising to his feet
as he spoke, "we'll go and look at the pictures."

Spode jumped up with alacrity, and only then realized that he had drunk just ever so little too much. He would have to be careful, talk deliberately, plant his feet consciously, one after the other.

"This house is quite cluttered up with pictures," Lord Badgery complained. "I had a whole wagon-load taken away to the country last week; but there are still far too many. My ancestors would have their portraits painted by Romney. Such a shocking artist, don't you think? Why couldn't they have chosen Gainsborough, or even Reynolds? I've had all the Romneys hung in the servants' hall now. It's such a comfort to know that one can never possibly see them again. I suppose you know all about the ancient Hittites?"

"Well . . ." the young man replied, with befitting modesty.

"Look at that, then." He indicated a large stone head which stood in a case near the dining-room door. "It's not Greek, or Egyptian, or Persian, or anything else; so if it isn't ancient Hittite, I don't know what it is. And that reminds me of that story about Lord George Sanger, the Circus King . . ." and, without giving Spode time to examine the Hittite relic, he led the way up the huge staircase, pausing every now and then in his anecdote to point out some new object of curiosity or beauty.

"I suppose you know Deburau's pantomimes?" Spode rapped out as soon as the story was over. He was in an itch to let out his information about Deburau. Badgery had given him a perfect opening with his ridiculous Sanger. "What a perfect man, isn't he? He used to . . ."

"This is my main gallery," said Lord Badgery, throwing open one leaf of a tall folding door. "I must apologize for it. It looks like a roller-skating rink." He fumbled with the electric switches and there was suddenly light—light that revealed an enormous gallery, duly receding into distance according to all the laws of perspective. "I dare say you've heard of my poor father," Lord Badgery continued. "A little insane, you know; sort of mechanical genius with a screw loose. He used to have a toy railway in this room. No end of fun he had, crawling about the floor after his trains. And all the pictures were stacked in the cellars. I can't tell you what they were like when I found them: mushrooms growing out of the Botticellis. Now I'm rather proud of this Poussin; he painted it for Scarron."

"Exquisite!" Spode exclaimed, making with his hand a gesture as though he were modelling a pure form in the air. "How splendid the onrush of those trees and leaning figures is! And the way they're caught up, as it were, and stemmed by that single godlike form opposing them with his contrary movement! And the draperies . . ."

But Lord Badgery had moved on, and was standing in front of a little fifteenth-century Virgin of carved wood.

"School of Rheims," he explained.

They "did" the gallery at high speed. Badgery never permitted his guest to halt for more than forty seconds before any work of art. Spode would have liked to spend a few moments of recollection and tranquillity in front of some of these lovely things. But it was not permitted.

The gallery done, they passed into a little room leading out of it. At the sight of what the lights revealed, Spode gasped.

"It's like something out of Balzac," he exclaimed. "Un de ces salons dorés où se déploie un luxe insolent. You know."

"My nineteenth-century chamber," Badgery explained. "The best thing of its kind, I flatter myself, outside the State Apartments at Windsor."

Spode tiptoed round the room, peering with astonishment at all the objects in glass, in gilded bronze, in china, in feathers, in embroidered and painted silk, in beads, in wax, objects of the most fantastic shapes and colours, all the queer products of a decadent tradition, with which the room was crowded. There were paintings on the walls—a Martin, a Wilkie, an early Landseer, several Ettys, a big Haydon, a slight pretty water-colour of a girl by Wainewright, the pupil of Blake and arsenic poisoner, and a score of others. But the picture which arrested Spode's attention was a medium-sized canvas representing Troilus riding into Troy among the flowers and plaudits of an admiring crowd, and oblivious (you could see from his expression) of everything but the eyes of Cressida, who looked down at him from a window, with Pandarus smiling over her shoulder.

"What an absurd and enchanting picture!" Spode exclaimed.

"Ah, you've spotted my Troilus." Lord Badgery was pleased.

"What bright harmonious colours! Like Etty's, only stronger, not so obviously pretty. And there's an energy about it that reminds one of Haydon. Only Haydon could never have done anything so impeccable in taste. Who is it by?" Spode turned to his host inquiringly.

"You were right in detecting Haydon," Lord Badgery answered. "It's by his pupil, Tillotson. I wish I could get hold of more of his work. But nobody seems to know anything about him. And he seems to have done so little."

This time it was the younger man who interrupted.

"Tillotson, Tillotson . . ." He put his hand to his forehead. A frown incongruously distorted his round, floridly curved face. "No . . . yes, I have it." He looked up triumphantly with serene and childish brows. "Tillotson, Walter Tillotson—the man's still alive."

Badgery smiled. "This picture was painted in 1846, you know."

"Well, that's all right. Say he was born in 1820, painted his masterpiece when he was twenty-six, and it's 1913 now; that's to say he's only ninety-three. Not as old as Titian yet."

"But he's not been heard of since 1860," Lord Badgery protested.

"Precisely. Your mention of his name reminded me of the discovery I made the other day when I was looking through the obituary notices in the archives of the *World's Review*. (One has to bring them up to date every year or so for fear of being caught napping if one of these old birds chooses to shuffle off suddenly.) Well there, among them—I remember my astonishment at the time—there I found Walter Tillotson's biography. Pretty full to 1860, and then a blank, except for a pencil note in the early nineteen hundreds to the effect that he had returned from the East. The obituary has never been used or added to. I draw the obvious conclusion: the old chap isn't dead yet. He's just been overlooked somehow."

"But this is extraordinary," Lord Badgery exclaimed. "You must find him, Spode—you must find him. I'll commission him to paint frescoes round this room. It's just what I've always vainly longed for—a real nineteenth-century artist to decorate this place for me. Oh, we must find him at once—at once."

Lord Badgery strode up and down in a state of great excitement.

"I can see how this room could be made quite perfect," he went on. "We'd clear away all these cases and have the whole of that wall filled by a heroic fresco of Hector and Andromache, or 'Distraining for Rent', or Fanny Kemble as Belvidera in 'Venice Preserved'—anything like that, provided it's in the grand manner of the 'thirties and 'forties. And here I'd have a landscape with lovely receding perspectives, or else something architectural and grand in the style of Belshazzar's feast. Then we'll have this Adam fireplace taken down and replaced by something Mauro-Gothic. And on these walls I'll have mirrors, or no! let me see . . ."

He sank into meditative silence, from which he finally roused himself to shout:

"The old man, the old man! Spode, we must find this astonishing old creature. And don't breathe a word to anybody. Tillotson shall be our secret. Oh, it's too perfect, it's incredible! Think of the frescoes."

Lord Badgery's face had become positively animated. He had talked of a single subject for nearly a quarter of an hour.

II

Three weeks later Lord Badgery was aroused from his usual after-luncheon somnolence by the arrival of a telegram. The message was a short one. "Found.—SPODE." A look of pleasure and intelligence made human Lord Badgery's clayey face of surfeit. "No answer," he said. The footman padded away on noiseless feet.

Lord Badgery closed his eyes and began to contemplate. Found! What a room he would have! There would be nothing like it in the world. The frescoes, the fireplace, the mirrors, the ceiling. . . . And a small, shrivelled old man clambering about the scaffolding, agile and quick like one of those whiskered little monkeys at the Zoo, painting away, painting away. . . . Fanny Kemble as Belvidera, Hector and Andromache, or why not the Duke of Clarence in the Butt, the Duke of Malmsey, the Butt of Clarence. . . . Lord Badgery was asleep.

Spode did not lag long behind his telegram. He was at Badgery House by six o'clock. His lordship was in the nineteenth-century chamber, engaged in clearing away with his own hands the bric-à-brac. Spode found him looking hot and out of breath.

"Ah, there you are," said Lord Badgery. "You see me already preparing for the great man's coming. Now you must tell me all about him."

"He's older even than I thought," said Spode. "He's ninety-seven this year. Born in 1816. Incredible, isn't it! There, I'm beginning at the wrong end."

"Begin where you like," said Badgery genially.

"I won't tell you all the incidents of the hunt. You've no idea what a job I had to run him to earth. It was like a Sherlock Holmes story, immensely elaborate, too elaborate. I shall write a book about it some day. At any rate, I found him at last."

"Where?"

"In a sort of respectable slum in Holloway, older and poorer and lonelier than you could have believed possible. I found out how it was he came to be forgotten, how he came to drop out of life in the way he did. He took it into his head, somewhere about the 'sixties, to go to Palestine to get local colour for his religious pictures—scapegoats and things, you know. Well, he went to Jerusalem and then on to Mount Lebanon and on and on, and then, somewhere in the middle of Asia Minor, he got stuck. He got stuck for about forty years."

"But what did he do all that time?"

"Oh, he painted, and started a mission, and converted three Turks, and taught the local Pashas the rudiments of English, Latin, and perspective, and God knows what else. Then, in about 1904, it seems to have occurred to him that he was getting rather old and had been away from home for rather a long time. So he made his way back to England, only to find that everyone he had known was dead, that the dealers had never heard of him and wouldn't buy his pictures, that he was simply a ridiculous old figure of fun. So he got a job as a drawing-master in a girls' school in Holloway, and there he's been ever since, growing older and older, and feebler and feebler, and blinder and deafer, and generally more gaga, until finally the school has given him the sack. He had about ten pounds in the world when I found him. He lives in a kind of black hole in a basement full of beetles. When his ten pounds are spent, I suppose he'll just quietly die there."

Badgery held up a white hand. "No more, no more. I find literature quite depressing enough. I insist that life at least shall be a little gayer. Did you tell him I wanted him to paint my room?"

"But he can't paint. He's too blind and palsied."

"Can't paint?" Badgery exclaimed in horror. "Then what's the good of the old creature?"

"Well, if you put it like that . . ." Spode began.

"I shall never have my frescoes. Ring the bell, will you?"

Spode rang.

"What right had Tillotson to go on existing if he can't paint?" went on Lord Badgery petulantly. "After all, that was his only justification for occupying a place in the sun."

"He doesn't have much sun in his basement."

The footman appeared at the door.

"Get someone to put all these things back in their places," Lord Badgery commanded, indicating with a wave of the hand the ravaged cases, the confusion of glass and china with which he had littered the floor, the pictures unhooked. "We'll go to the library, Spode; it's more comfortable there."

He led the way through the long gallery and down the stairs.

"I'm sorry old Tillotson has been such a disappointment," said Spode sympathetically.

"Let us talk about something else; he ceases to interest me."

"But don't you think we ought to do something about him? He's only got ten pounds between him and the workhouse. And if you'd seen the blackbeetles in his basement!"

"Enough—enough. I'll do everything you think fitting."

"I thought we might get up a subscription amongst lovers of the arts."

"There aren't any," said Badgery.

"No; but there are plenty of people who will subscribe out of snobbism."

"Not unless you give them something for their money."

"That's true. I hadn't thought of that." Spode was silent for a moment. "We might have a dinner in his honour. The Great Tillotson Banquet. Doyen of British Art. A Link with the Past. Can't you see it in the papers? I'd make a stunt of it in the *World's Review*. That ought to bring in the snobs."

"And we'll invite a lot of artists and critics—all the ones who can't stand one another. It will be fun to see them squabbling." Badgery laughed. Then his face darkened once again. "Still," he added, "it'll be a very poor second best to my frescoes. You'll stay to dinner, of course."

"Well, since you suggest it. Thanks very much."

III

The Tillotson Banquet was fixed to take place about three weeks later. Spode, who had charge of the arrangements, proved himself an excellent organizer. He secured the big banqueting-room at the Café Bomba, and was successful in bullying and cajoling the manager into giving fifty persons dinner at twelve shillings a head, including wine. He sent out invitations and collected subscriptions. He wrote an article on Tillotson in the *World's Review*—one of those charming, witty articles, couched in the tone of amused patronage and contempt with which one speaks of the great men of 1840. Nor did he neglect Tillotson himself. He used to go to Holloway almost every day to listen to the old man's endless stories about Asia Minor and the Great Exhibition of '51 and Benjamin Robert Haydon. He was sincerely sorry for this relic of another age.

Mr Tillotson's room was about ten feet below the level of the soil of South Holloway. A little grey light percolated through the area bars, forced a difficult passage through panes opaque with dirt, and spent itself, like a drop of milk that falls into an inkpot, among the inveterate shadows of the dungeon. The place was haunted by the sour smell of damp plaster and of woodwork that has begun to moulder secretly at the heart. A little miscellaneous furniture, including a bed, a washstand and chest of drawers, a table and one or two chairs, lurked in the obscure corners of the den or ventured furtively out into the open. Hither Spode now came almost every day, bringing the old man news of the progress of the banquet scheme. Every day he found Mr Tillotson sitting in the same place under the window, bathing, as it were, in his tiny puddle of light. "The oldest man that ever wore grey hairs," Spode reflected as he looked at him. Only there were very few hairs left on that bald, unpolished head. At the sound of the visitor's knock Mr Tillotson would turn in his chair, stare in the direction of the door with blinking, uncertain eyes. He was always full of apologies for being so slow in recognizing who was there.

"No discourtesy meant," he would say, after asking. "It's not as if I had forgotten who you were. Only it's so dark and my sight isn't what it was."

After that he never failed to give a little laugh, and, pointing out of the window at the area railings, would say:

"Ah, this is the place for somebody with good sight. It's the place for looking at ankles. It's the grand stand."

It was the day before the great event. Spode came as usual, and

Mr Tillotson punctually made his little joke about the ankles, and Spode as punctually laughed.

"Well, Mr Tillotson," he said, after the reverberation of the joke had died away, "to-morrow you make your re-entry into the world of art and fashion. You'll find some changes."

"I've always had such extraordinary luck," said Mr Tillotson, and Spode could see by his expression that he genuinely believed it, that he had forgotten the black hole and the blackbeetles and the almost exhausted ten pounds that stood between him and the workhouse. "What an amazing piece of good fortune, for instance, that you should have found me just when you did. Now, this dinner will bring me back to my place in the world. I shall have money, and in a little while—who knows?—I shall be able to see well enough to paint again. I believe my eyes are getting better, you know. Ah, the future is very rosy."

Mr Tillotson looked up, his face puckered into a smile, and nodded his head in affirmation of his words.

"You believe in the life to come?" said Spode, and immediately flushed for shame at the cruelty of the words.

But Mr Tillotson was in far too cheerful a mood to have caught their significance.

"Life to come," he repeated. "No, I don't believe in any of that stuff—not since 1859. The 'Origin of Species' changed my views, you know. No life to come for me, thank you! You don't remember the excitement, of course. You're very young, Mr Spode."

"Well, I'm not so old as I was," Spode replied. "You know how middle-aged one is as a schoolboy and undergraduate. Now I'm old enough to know I'm young."

Spode was about to develop this little paradox further, but he noticed that Mr Tillotson had not been listening. He made a note of the gambit for use in companies that were more appreciative of the subtleties.

"You were talking about the 'Origin of Species,'" he said.

"Was I?" said Mr Tillotson, waking from reverie.

"About its effect on your faith, Mr Tillotson."

"To be sure, yes. It shattered my faith. But I remember a fine thing by the Poet Laureate, something about there being more faith in honest doubt, believe me, than in all the . . . all the . . . I forget exactly what; but you see the train of thought. Oh, it was a bad time for religion. I am glad my master Haydon never lived to see it. He was a man of fervour. I remember him pacing up and down his studio in Lisson Grove, singing and shouting and praying all at once. It used almost to frighten me. Oh, but he was a wonderful man, a great man. Take him for all in all, we shall not look upon his like again. As usual, the Bard is right. But it was all very long ago, before your time, Mr Spode."

"Well, I'm not as old as I was," said Spode, in the hope of having his paradox appreciated this time. But Mr Tillotson went on without noticing the interruption.

"It's a very, very long time. And yet, when I look back on it, it all seems but a day or two ago. Strange that each day should seem so long and that many days added together should be less than an hour. How clearly I can see old Haydon pacing up and down! Much more clearly, indeed, than I see you, Mr Spode. The eyes of memory don't grow dim. But my sight is improving, I assure you; it's improving daily. I shall soon be able to see those ankles." He laughed, like a cracked bell—one of those little old bells, Spode fancied, that ring, with much rattling of wires, in the far-off servants' quarters of ancient houses. "And very soon," Mr Tillotson went on, "I shall be painting again. Ah, Mr Spode, my luck is extraordinary. I believe in it, I trust it. And after all, what is luck? Simply another name for Providence, in spite of the 'Origin of Species' and the rest of it. How right the Laureate was when he said that there was more faith in honest doubt, believe me, than in all the . . . er, the . . . er . . . well, you know. I regard you, Mr Spode, as the emissary of Providence. Your coming marked a turning-point in my life, and the beginning, for me, of happier days. Do you know, one of the first things I shall do when my fortunes are restored will be to buy a hedgehog."

"A hedgehog, Mr Tillotson?"

"For the blackbeetles. There's nothing like a hedgehog for beetles. It will eat blackbeetles till it's sick, till it dies of surfeit. That reminds me of the time when I told my poor great master Haydon—in joke, of course—that he ought to send in a cartoon of King John dying of a surfeit of lampreys for the frescoes in the new Houses of Parliament. As I told him, it's a most notable event in the annals of British liberty—the providential and exemplary removal of a tyrant."

Mr Tillotson laughed again—the little bell in the deserted

house; a ghostly hand pulling the cord in the drawing-room, and phantom footmen responding to the thin, flawed note.

"I remember he laughed, laughed like a bull in his old grand manner. But oh, it was a terrible blow when they rejected his designs, a terrible blow! It was the first and fundamental cause of his suicide."

Mr Tillotson paused. There was a long silence. Spode felt strangely moved, he hardly knew why, in the presence of this man, so frail, so ancient, in body three parts dead, in the spirit so full of life and hopeful patience, He felt ashamed. What was the use of his own youth and cleverness? He saw himself suddenly as a boy with a rattle scaring birds—rattling his noisy cleverness, waving his arms in ceaseless and futile activity, never resting in his efforts to scare away the birds that were always trying to settle in his mind. And what birds! wide-winged and beautiful, all those serene thoughts and faiths and emotions that only visit minds that have humbled themselves to quiet. Those gracious visitants he was for ever using all his energies to drive away. But this old man, with his hedgehogs and his honest doubts and all the rest of it—his mind was like a field made beautiful by the free coming and going, the unafraid alightings of a multitude of white, bright-winged creatures. He felt ashamed. But then, was it possible to alter one's life? Wasn't it a little absurd to risk a conversion? Spode shrugged his shoulders.

"I'll get you a hedgehog at once," he said. "They're sure to have some at Whiteley's."

Before he left that evening Spode made an alarming discovery. Mr Tillotson did not possess a dress-suit. It was hopeless to think of getting one made at this short notice, and, besides, what an unnecessay expense!

"We shall have to borrow a suit, Mr Tillotson. I ought to have thought of that before."

"Dear me, dear me." Mr Tillotson was a little chagrined by this unlucky discovery. "Borrow a suit?"

Spode hurried away for counsel to Badgery House. Lord Badgery surprisingly rose to the occasion. "Ask Boreham to come and see me," he told the footman who answered his ring.

Boreham was one of those immemorial butlers who linger on, generation after generation, in the houses of the great. He was over eighty now, bent, dried up, shrivelled with age.

"All old men are about the same size," said Lord Badgery. It was a comforting theory. "Ah, here he is. Have you got a spare suit of evening clothes, Boreham?"

"I have an old suit, my lord, that I stopped wearing in—let me see—was it nineteen seven or eight?"

"That's the very thing. I should be most grateful, Boreham, if you could lend it to me for Mr Spode here for a day."

The old man went out, and soon reappeared carrying over his arm a very old black suit. He held up the coat and trousers for inspection. In the light of day they were deplorable.

"You've no idea, sir," said Boreham deprecatingly to Spode— "you've no idea how easy things get stained with grease and gravy and what not. However careful you are, sir—however careful."

"I should imagine so." Spode was sympathetic.

"However careful, sir."

"But in artificial light they'll look all right."

"Perfectly all right," Lord Badgery repeated. "Thank you, Boreham; you shall have them back on Thursday."

"You're welcome, my lord, I'm sure." And the old man bowed and disappeared.

On the afternoon of the great day Spode carried up to Holloway a parcel containing Boreham's retired evening-suit and all the necessary appurtenances in the way of shirts and collars. Owing to the darkness and his own feeble sight Mr Tillotson was happily unaware of the defects in the suit. He was in a state of extreme nervous agitation. It was with some difficulty that Spode could prevent him, although it was only three o'clock, from starting his toilet on the spot.

"Take it easy, Mr Tillotson, take it easy. We needn't start till half-past seven, you know."

Spode left an hour later, and as soon as he was safely out of the room Mr Tillotson began to prepare himself for the banquet. He lighted the gas and a couple of candles, and, blinking myopically at the image that fronted him in the tiny looking-glass that stood on his chest of drawers, he set to work, with all the ardour of a young girl preparing for her first ball. At six o'clock, when the last touches had been given, he was not unsatisfied.

He marched up and down his cellar, humming to himself the gay song which had been so popular in his middle years:

*"Oh, oh, Anna Maria Jones!
Queen of the tambourine, the cymbals, and the bones!"*

Spode arrived an hour later in Lord Badgery's second Rolls-Royce. Opening the door of the old man's dungeon, he stood for a moment, wide-eyed with astonishment, on the threshold. Mr Tillotson was standing by the empty grate, one elbow resting on the mantelpiece, one leg crossed over the other in a jaunty and gentlemanly attitude. The effect of the candlelight shining on his face was to deepen every line and wrinkle with intense black shadow; he looked immeasurably old. It was a noble and pathetic head. On the other hand, Boreham's outworn evening-suit was simply buffoonish. The coat was too long in the sleeves and the tail; the trousers bagged in elephantine creases about his ankles. Some of the grease-spots were visible even in candlelight. The white tie, over which Mr Tillotson had taken infinite pains and which he believed in his purblindness to be perfect, was fantastically lop-sided. He had buttoned up his waistcoat in such a fashion that one button was widowed of its hole and one hole of its button. Across his shirt front lay the broad green ribbon of some unknown Order.

"Queen of the tambourine, the cymbals, and the bones," Mr Tillotson concluded in a gnat-like voice before welcoming his visitor.

"Well, Spode, here you are. I'm dressed already, you see. The suit, I flatter myself, fits very well, almost as though it had been made for me. I am all gratitude to the gentleman who was kind enough to lend it to me; I shall take the greatest care of it. It's a dangerous thing to lend clothes. For loan oft loseth both itself and friend. The Bard is always right."

"Just one thing," said Spode. "A touch to your waistcoat." He unbuttoned the dissipated garment and did it up again more symmetrically.

Mr Tillotson was a little piqued at being found so absurdly in the wrong. "Thanks, thanks," he said protestingly, trying to edge away from his valet. "It's all right, you know; I can do it myself. Foolish oversight. I flatter myself the suit fits very well."

"And perhaps the tie might . . ." Spode began tentatively. But the old man would not hear of it.

"No, no. The tie's all right. I can tie a tie, Mr Spode. The tie's all right. Leave it as it is, I beg."

"I like your Order."

Mr Tillotson looked down complacently at his shirt front. "Ah, you've noticed my Order. It's a long time since I wore that. It was given me by the Grand Porte, you know, for services rendered in the Russo-Turkish War. It's the Order of Chastity, the second class. They only give the first class to crowned heads, you know—crowned heads and ambassadors. And only Pashas of the highest rank get the second. Mine's the second. They only give the first class to crowned heads . . ."

"Of course, of course," said Spode.

"Do you think I look all right, Mr Spode?" Mr Tillotson asked, a little anxiously.

"Splendid, Mr Tillotson—splendid. The Order's magnificent."

The old man's face brightened once more. "I flatter myself," he said, "that this borrowed suit fits me very well. But I don't like borrowing clothes. For loan oft loseth both itself and friend, you know. And the Bard is always right."

"Ugh, there's one of those horrible beetles!" Spode exclaimed.

Mr Tillotson bent down and stared at the floor. "I see it," he said, and stamped on a small piece of coal, which crunched to powder under his foot. "I shall certainly buy a hedgehog."

It was time for them to start. A crowd of little boys and girls had collected round Lord Badgery's enormous car. The chauffeur, who felt that honour and dignity were at stake, pretended not to notice the children, but sat gazing, like a statue, into eternity. At the sight of Spode and Mr Tillotson emerging from the house a yell of mingled awe and derision went up. It subsided to an astonished silence as they climbed into the car. "Bomba's," Spode directed. The Rolls-Royce gave a faintly stertorous sigh and began to move. The children yelled again, and ran along beside the car, waving their arms in a frenzy of excitement. It was then that Mr Tillotson, with an incomparably noble gesture, leaned forward and tossed among the seething crowd of urchins his three last coppers.

IV

In Bomba's big room the company was assembling. The long gilt-edged mirrors reflected a singular collection of people. Middle-aged Academicians shot suspicious glances at youths whom they suspected, only too correctly, of being iconoclasts, organizers of Post-Impressionist Exhibitions. Rival art critics, brought suddenly face to face, quivered with restrained hatred. Mrs Nobes, Mrs Cayman, and Mrs Mandragore, those indefatigable hunters of artistic big game, came on one another all unawares in this well-stored menagerie, where each had expected to hunt alone, and were filled with rage. Through this crowd of mutually repellent vanities Lord Badgery moved with a suavity that seemed unconscious of all the feuds and hatreds. He was enjoying himself immensely. Behind the heavy waxen mask of his face, ambushed behind the Hanoverian nose, the little lustreless pig's eyes, the pale thick lips, there lurked a small devil of happy malice that rocked with laughter.

"So nice of you to have come, Mrs Mandragore, to do honour to England's artistic past. And I'm so glad to see you've brought dear Mrs Cayman. And is that Mrs Nobes, too? So it is! I hadn't noticed her before. How delightful! I knew we could depend on your love of art."

And he hurried away to seize the opportunity of introducing that eminent sculptor, Sir Herbert Herne, to the bright young critic who had called him, in the public prints, a monumental mason.

A moment later the Maître d'Hotel came to the door of the gilded saloon and announced, loudly and impressively, "Mr Walter Tillotson." Guided from behind by young Spode, Mr Tillotson came into the room slowly and hesitatingly. In the glare of the lights his eyelids beat heavily, painfully, like the wings of an imprisoned moth, over his filmy eyes. Once inside the door he halted and drew himself up with a conscious assumption of dignity. Lord Badgery hurried forward and seized his hand.

"Welcome, Mr Tillotson—welcome in the name of English art!"

Mr Tillotson inclined his head in silence. He was too full of emotion to be able to reply.

"I should like to introduce you to a few of your younger colleagues, who have assembled here to do you honour."

Lord Badgery presented everyone in the room to the old painter, who bowed, shook hands, made little noises in his throat, but still found himself unable to speak. Mrs Nobes, Mrs Cayman, and Mrs Mandragore all said charming things.

Dinner was served; the party took their places. Lord Badgery sat at the head of the table, with Mr Tillotson on his right hand and Sir Herbert Herne on his left. Confronted with Bomba's succulent cooking and Bomba's wines, Mr Tillotson ate and drank a good deal. He had the appetite of one who has lived on greens and potatoes for ten years among the blackbeetles. After the second glass of wine he began to talk, suddenly and in a flood, as though a sluice had been pulled up.

"In Asia Minor," he began, "it is the custom, when one goes to dinner, to hiccough as a sign of appreciative fullness. *Eructavit cor meum*, as the Psalmist has it; he was an Oriental himself."

Spode had arranged to sit next to Mrs Cayman; he had designs upon her. She was an impossible woman, of course, but rich and useful; he wanted to bamboozle her into buying some of his young friend's pictures.

"In a cellar?" Mrs Cayman was saying, "with blackbeetles? Oh, how dreadful! Poor old man! And he's ninety-seven, didn't you say? Isn't that shocking! I only hope the subscription will be a large one. Of course, one wishes one could have given more oneself. But then, you know, one has so many expenses, and things are so difficult now."

"I know, I know," said Spode, with feeling.

"It's all because of Labour," Mrs Cayman explained. "Of course, I should simply love to have him in to dinner sometimes. But, then, I feel he's really too old, too *farouche* and *gâteux*; it would not be doing a kindness to him, would it? And so you are working with Mr Gollamy now? What a charming man, so talented, such conversation . . ."

"*Eructavit cor meum*," said Mr Tillotson for the third time. Lord Badgery tried to head him off the subject of Turkish etiquette, but in vain.

By half-past nine a kinder vinolent atmosphere had put to sleep the hatreds and suspicions of before dinner. Sir Herbert Herne had discovered that the young Cubist sitting next him was not insane and actually knew a surprising amount about the Old Masters. For their part these young men had realized that their elders were not at all malignant; they were just very stupid and pathetic. It was only in the bosoms of Mrs Nobes, Mrs Cayman, and Mrs Mandragore that hatred still reigned undiminished. Being ladies and old-fashioned, they had drunk almost no wine.

The moment for speech-making arrived. Lord Badgery rose to

his feet, said what was expected of him, and called upon Sir Herbert to propose the toast of the evening. Sir Herbert coughed, smiled, and began. In the course of a speech that lasted twenty minutes he told anecdotes of Mr Gladstone, Lord Leighton, Sir Alma Tadema, and the late Bishop of Bombay; he made three puns, he quoted Shakespeare and Whittier, he was playful, he was eloquent, he was grave. . . At the end of his harangue Sir Herbert handed to Mr Tillotson a silk purse containing fifty-eight pounds ten shillings, the total amount of the subscription. The old man's health was drunk with acclamation.

Mr Tillotson rose with difficulty to his feet. The dry, snakelike skin of his face was flushed; his tie was more crooked than ever; the green ribbon of the Order of Chastity of the second class had somehow climbed up his crumpled and maculate shirt-front.

"My lord, ladies, and gentlemen," he began in a choking voice, and then broke down completely. It was a very painful and pathetic spectacle. A feeling of intense discomfort afflicted the minds of all who looked upon that trembling relic of a man, as he stood there weeping and stammering. It was as though a breath of the wind of death had blown suddenly through the room, lifting the vapours of wine and tobacco-smoke, quenching the laughter and the candle flames. Eyes floated uneasily, not knowing where to look. Lord Badgery, with great presence of mind, offered the old man a glass of wine. Mr Tillotson began to recover. The guests heard him murmur a few disconnected words.

"This great honour . . . overwhelmed with kindness . . . this magnificent banquet . . . not used to it . . . in Asia Minor . . . *eructavit cor meum.*"

At this point Lord Badgery plucked sharply at one of his long coat tails. Mr Tillotson paused, took another sip of wine, and then went on with a newly won coherence and energy.

"The life of the artist is a hard one. His work is unlike other men's work, which may be done mechanically, by rote and almost, as it were, in sleep. It demands from him a constant expense of spirit. He gives continually of his best life, and in return he receives much joy, it is true—much fame, it may be—but of material blessings, very few. It is eighty years since first I devoted my life to the service of art; eighty years, and almost every one of those years has brought me fresh and painful proof of what I have been saying: the artist's life is a hard one."

This unexpected deviation into sense increased the general feeling of discomfort. It became necessary to take the old man seriously, to regard him as a human being. Up till then he had been no more than an object of curiosity, a mummy in an absurd suit of evening-clothes with a green ribbon across the shirt front. People could not help wishing that they had subscribed a little more. Fifty-eight pounds ten—it wasn't enormous. But happily for the peace of mind of the company, Mr Tillotson paused to live up to his proper character by talking absurdly.

"When I consider the life of that great man, Benjamin Robert Haydon, one of the greatest men England has ever produced . . ." The audience heaved a sigh of relief; this was all as it should be. There was a burst of loud bravoing and clapping. Mr Tillotson turned his dim eyes round the room, and smiled gratefully at the misty figures he beheld. "That great man, Benjamin Robert Haydon," he continued, "whom I am proud to call my master and who, it rejoices my heart to see, still lives in your memory and esteem,—that great man, one of the greatest that England has ever produced, led a life so deplorable that I cannot think of it without a tear."

And with infinite repetitions and divagations, Mr Tillotson related the history of B. R. Haydon, his imprisonments for debt, his battle with the Academy, his triumphs, his failures, his despair, his suicide. Half-past ten struck. Mr Tillotson was declaiming against the stupid and prejudiced judges who had rejected Haydon's designs for the decoration of the new Houses of Parliament in favour of the paltriest German scribblings.

"That great man, one of the greatest England has ever produced, that great Benjamin Robert Haydon, whom I am proud to call my master and who, it rejoices me to see, still lives on in your memory and esteem—at that affront his great heart burst; it was the unkindest cut of all. He who had worked all his life for the recognition of the artist by the State, he who had petitioned every Prime Minister, including the Duke of Wellington, for thirty years, begging them to employ artists to decorate public buildings, he to whom the scheme for decorating the Houses of Parliament was undeniably due . . ." Mr Tillotson lost a grip on his syntax and began a new sentence. "It was the unkindest cut of all, it was the last straw. The artist's life is a hard one."

At eleven Mr Tillotson was talking about the pre-Raphaelites.

At a quarter-past he had begun to tell the story of B. R. Haydon all over again. At twenty-five minutes to twelve he collapsed quite speechless into his chair. Most of the guests had already gone away; the few who remained made haste to depart. Lord Badgery led the old man to the door and packed him into the second Rolls-Royce. The Tillotson Banquet was over; it had been a pleasant evening, but a little too long.

Spode walked back to his rooms in Bloomsbury, whistling as he went. The arc lamps of Oxford Street reflected in the polished surface of the road: canals of dark bronze. He would have to bring that into an article some time. The Cayman woman had been very successfully nobbled. "Voi che sapete," he whistled—somewhat out of tune, but he could not hear that.

When Mr Tillotson's landlady came in to call him on the following morning, she found the old man lying fully dressed on his bed. He looked very ill and very, very old; Boreham's dress-suit was in a terrible state, and the green ribbon of the Order of Chastity was ruined. Mr Tillotson lay very still, but he was not asleep. Hearing the sound of footsteps, he opened his eyes a little and faintly groaned. His landlady looked down at him menacingly.

"Disgusting!" she said; "disgusting, I call it. At your age."

Mr Tillotson groaned again. Making a great effort, he drew out of his trouser pocket a large silk purse, opened it, and extracted a sovereign.

"The artist's life is a hard one, Mrs Green," he said, handing her the coin. "Would you mind sending for the doctor? I don't feel very well. And oh, what shall I do about these clothes? What shall I say to the gentleman who was kind enough to lend them to me? Loan oft loseth both itself and friend. The Bard is always right."

Green Tunnels

"IN the Italian gardens of the thirteenth century . . ." Mr
Buzzacott interrupted himself to take another helping of the
risotto which was being offered him. "Excellent risotto this," he
observed. "Nobody who was not born in Milan can make it
properly. So they say."

"So they say," Mr Topes repeated in his sad, apologetic voice,
and helped himself in his turn.

"Personally," said Mrs Topes, with decision, "I find all Italian
cooking abominable. I don't like the oil—especially hot. No,
thank you." She recoiled from the proffered dish.

After the first mouthful Mr Buzzacott put down his fork. "In
the Italian gardens of the thirteenth century," he began again,
making with his long, pale hand a curved and flowery gesture
that ended with a clutch at his beard, "a frequent and most
felicitous use was made of green tunnels."

"Green tunnels?" Barbara woke up suddenly from her tranced
silence. "Green tunnels?"

"Yes, my dear," said her father. "Green tunnels. Arched alleys
covered with vines or other creeping plants. Their length was
very considerable."

But Barbara had once more ceased to pay attention to what he
was saying. Green tunnels—the words had floated down to her,
through profound depths of reverie, across great spaces of
abstraction, startling her like the sound of a strange-voiced bell.
Green tunnels—what a wonderful idea. She would not listen to
her father explaining the phrase into dullness. He made everything dull; an inverted alchemist, turning gold into lead. She
pictured caverns in a great aquarium, long vistas between rocks
and scarcely swaying weeds and pale, discoloured corals; endless
dim green corridors with huge lazy fishes loitering aimlessly along
them. Green-faced monsters with goggling eyes and mouths that
slowly opened and shut. Green tunnels . . .

"I have seen them illustrated in illuminated manuscripts of the
period," Mr Buzzacott went on; once more he clutched his pointed
brown beard—clutched and combed it with his long fingers.

Mr Topes looked up. The glasses of his round owlish spectacles flashed as he moved his head. "I know what you mean," he said.

"I have a very good mind to have one planted in my garden here."

"It will take a long time to grow," said Mr Topes. "In this sand, so close to the sea, you will only be able to plant vines. And they come up very slowly—very slowly indeed." He shook his head, and the points of light danced wildly in his spectacles. His voice drooped hopelessly, his grey moustache drooped, his whole person drooped. Then, suddenly, he pulled himself up. A shy, apologetic smile appeared on his face. He wriggled uncomfortably. Then, with a final rapid shake of the head, he gave vent to a quotation:

> *"But at my back I always hear*
> *Time's winged chariot hurrying near."*

He spoke deliberately, and his voice trembled a little. He always found it painfully difficult to say something choice and out of the ordinary; and yet what a wealth of remembered phrase, what apt new coinages were always surging through his mind!

"They don't grow so slowly as all that," said Mr Buzzacott confidently. He was only just over fifty, and looked a handsome thirty-five. He gave himself at least another forty years; indeed, he had not yet begun to contemplate the possibility of ever concluding.

"Miss Barbara will enjoy it, perhaps—your green tunnel." Mr Topes sighed and looked across the table at his host's daughter.

Barbara was sitting with her elbows on the table, her chin in her hands, staring in front of her. The sound of her own name reached her faintly. She turned her head in Mr Topes's direction and found herself confronted by the glitter of his round, convex spectacles. At the end of the green tunnel—she stared at the shining circles—hung the eyes of a goggling fish. They approached, floating, closer and closer, along the dim submarine corridor.

Confronted by this fixed regard, Mr Topes looked away. What thoughtful eyes! He couldn't remember ever to have seen eyes so full of thought. There were certain Madonnas of Montagna, he reflected, very like her: mild little blonde Madonnas with slightly snub noses and very, very young. But he was old; it would be many years, in spite of Buzzacott, before the vines grew up into a green tunnel. He took a sip of wine; then, mechanically, sucked his drooping grey moustache.

"Arthur!"

At the sound of his wife's voice Mr Topes started, raised his napkin to his mouth. Mrs Topes did not permit the sucking of moustaches. It was only in moments of absent-mindedness that he ever offended, now.

"The Marchese Prampolini is coming here to take coffee," said Mr Buzzacott suddenly. "I almost forgot to tell you."

"One of these Italian marquises, I suppose," said Mrs Topes, who was no snob, except in England. She raised her chin with a little jerk.

Mr Buzzacott executed an upward curve of the hand in her direction. "I assure you, Mrs Topes, he belongs to a very old and distinguished family. They are Genoese in origin. You remember their palace, Barbara? Built by Alessi."

Barbara looked up. "Oh yes," she said vaguely. "Alessi. I know." Alessi: Aleppo—where a malignant and a turbaned Turk. *And* a turbaned; that had always seemed to her very funny.

"Several of his ancestors," Mr Buzzacott went on, "distinguished themselves as viceroys of Corsica. They did good work in the suppression of rebellion. Strange, isn't it"—he turned parenthetically to Mr Topes—"the way in which sympathy is always on the side of rebels? What a fuss people made of Corsica! That ridiculous book by Gregorovius, for example. And the Irish, and the Poles, and all the rest of them. It always seems to me very superfluous and absurd."

"Isn't it, perhaps, a little natural?" Mr Topes began timorously and tentatively; but his host went on without listening.

"The present marquis," he said, "is the head of the local Fascisti. They have done no end of good work in this district in the way of preserving law and order and keeping the lower classes in their place."

"Ah, the Fascisti," Mrs Topes repeated approvingly. "One would like to see something of the kind in England. What with all these strikes . . ."

"He has asked me for a subscription to the funds of the organization. I shall give him one, of course."

"Of course," Mrs Topes nodded. "My nephew, the one who was a major during the war, volunteered in the last coal strike. He was sorry, I know, that it didn't come to a fight. 'Aunt Annie,' he said to me, when I saw him last, 'if there had been a fight we should have knocked them out completely—completely.'"

In Aleppo, the Fascisti, malignant *and* turbaned, were fighting, under the palm trees. Weren't they palm trees, those tufted green plumes?

"What, no ice to-day? *Niente gelato?*" inquired Mr Buzzacott as the maid put down the compote of peaches on the table.

Concetta apologized. The ice-making machine in the village had broken down. There would be no ice till to-morrow.

"Too bad," said Mr Buzzacott. "*Troppo male, Concetta.*"

Under the palm trees, Barbara saw them: they pranced about, fighting. They were mounted on big dogs, and in the trees were enormous many-coloured birds.

"Goodness me, the child's asleep." Mrs Topes was proffering the dish of peaches. "How much longer am I to hold this in front of your nose, Barbara?"

Barbara felt herself blushing. "I'm so sorry," she mumbled, and took the dish clumsily.

"Day-dreaming. It's a bad habit."

"It's one we all succumb to sometimes," put in Mr Topes deprecatingly, with a little nervous tremble of the head.

"You may, my dear," said his wife. "I do not."

Mr Topes lowered his eyes to his plate and went on eating.

"The *marchese* should be here at any moment now," said Mr Buzzacott, looking at his watch. "I hope he won't be late. I find I suffer so much from any postponement of my siesta. This Italian heat," he added, with growing plaintiveness, "one can't be too careful."

"Ah, but when I was with my father in India," began Mrs Topes in a tone of superiority: "he was an Indian civilian, you know . . ."

Aleppo, India—always the palm trees. Cavalcades of big dogs, and tigers too.

Concetta ushered in the marquis. Delighted. Pleased to meet. Speak English? Yés, yéss. *Pocchino.* Mrs Topes: and Mr Topes, the distinguished antiquarian. Ah, of course; know his name very well. My daughter. Charmed. Often seen the signorina bathing.

Admired the way she dives. Beautiful—the hand made a long, caressing gesture. These athletic English signorine. The teeth flashed astonishingly white in the brown face, the dark eyes glittered. She felt herself blushing again, looked away, smiled foolishly. The marquis had already turned back to Mr Buzzacott.

"So you have decided to settle in our Carrarese."

Well, not settled exactly; Mr Buzzacott wouldn't go so far as to say settled. A villino for the summer months. The winter in Rome. One was forced to live abroad. Taxation in England. . . . Soon they were all talking. Barbara looked at them. Beside the marquis they all seemed half dead. His face flashed as he talked; he seemed to be boiling with life. Her father was limp and pale, like something long buried from the light; and Mr Topes was all dry and shrivelled; and Mrs Topes looked more than ever like something worked by clockwork. They were talking about Socialism and Fascisti, and all that. Barbara did not listen to what they were saying; but she looked at them, absorbed.

Good-bye, good-bye. The animated face with its flash of a smile was turned like a lamp from one to another. Now it was turned on her. Perhaps one evening she would come, with her father, and the Signora Topes. He and his sister gave little dances sometimes. Only the gramophone, of course. But that was better than nothing, and the signorina must dance divinely—another flash—he could see that. He pressed her hand again. Good-bye.

It was time for the siesta.

"Don't forget to pull down the mosquito netting, my dear," Mr Buzzacott exhorted. "There is always a danger of ano-phylines."

"All right, father." She moved towards the door without turning round to answer him. He was always terribly tiresome about mosquito nets. Once they had driven through the Campagna in a hired cab, completely enclosed in an improvised tent of netting. The monuments along the Appian Way had loomed up mistily as through bridal veils. And how everyone had laughed. But her father, of course, hadn't so much as noticed it. He never noticed anything.

"Is it at Berlin, that charming little Madonna of Montagna's?" Mr Topes abruptly asked. "The one with the Donor kneeling in the left-hand corner as if about to kiss the foot of the Child." His spectacles flashed in Mr Buzzacott's direction.

"Why do you ask?"

"I don't know. I was just thinking of it."

"I think you must mean the one in the Mond Collection."

"Ah yes; very probably. In the Mond . . ."

Barbara opened the door and walked into the twilight of her shuttered room. It was hot even here; for another three hours it would hardly be possible to stir. And that old idiot, Mrs Topes, always made a fuss if one came in to lunch with bare legs and one's after-bathing tunic. "In India we always made a point of being properly and adequately dressed. An Englishwoman must keep up her position with natives, and to all intents and purposes Italians *are* natives." And so she always had to put on shoes and stockings and a regular frock just at the hottest hour of the day. What an old ass that woman was! She slipped off her clothes as fast as she could. That was a little better.

Standing in front of the long mirror in the wardrobe door she came to the humiliating conclusion that she looked like a piece of badly toasted bread. Brown face, brown neck and shoulders, brown arms, brown legs from the knee downwards; but all the rest of her was white, silly, effeminate, townish white. If only one could run about with no clothes on till one was like those little coppery children who rolled and tumbled in the burning sand! Now she was just underdone, half-baked, and wholly ridiculous. For a long time she looked at her pale image. She saw herself running bronzed all over, along the sand; or through a field of flowers, narcissus and wild tulips; or in soft grass under grey olive trees. She turned round with a sudden start. There, in the shadows behind her. . . . No, of course there was nothing. It was that awful picture in a magazine she had looked at, so many years ago, when she was a child. There was a lady sitting at her dressing-table, doing her hair in front of the glass; and a huge, hairy black monkey creeping up behind her. She always got the creeps when she looked at herself in a mirror. It was very silly. But still. She turned away from the mirror, crossed the room, and, without lowering the mosquito curtains, lay down on her bed. The flies buzzed about her, settled incessantly on her face. She shook her head, flapped at them angrily with her hands. There would be peace if she let down the netting. But she thought of the Appian Way seen mistily through the bridal veil and preferred to suffer the flies In the end she had to surrender; the brutes were too much for her. But, at any rate, it wasn't the fear of anophylines that made her lower the netting.

Undisturbed now and motionless, she lay stretched stiffly out under the transparent bell of gauze. A specimen under a glass case. The fancy possessed her mind. She saw a huge museum with thousands of glass cases, full of fossils and butterflies and stuffed birds and mediæval spoons and armour and Florentine jewellery and mummies and carved ivory and illuminated manuscripts. But in one of the cases was a human being, shut up there alive.

All of a sudden she became horribly miserable. "Boring, boring, boring," she whispered, formulating the words aloud. Would it never stop being boring? The tears came into her eyes. How awful everything was! And perhaps it would go on being as bad as this all her life. Seventeen from seventy was fifty-three. Fifty-three years of it. And if she lived to a hundred there would be more than eighty.

The thought depressed her all the evening. Even her bathe after tea did her no good. Swimming far out, far out, she lay there, floating on the warm water. Sometimes she looked at the sky, sometimes she turned her head towards the shore. Framed in their pinewood, the villas looked as small and smug as the advertisement of a seaside resort. But behind them, across the level plain, were the mountains. Sharp, bare peaks of limestone, green woodland slopes and grey-green expanses of terraced olive trees—they seemed marvellously close and clear in this evening light. And beautiful, beautiful beyond words. But that, somehow, only made things worse. And Shelley had lived a few miles farther up the coast, there, behind the headland guarding the Gulf of Spezia. Shelley had been drowned in this milk-warm sea. That made it worse too.

The sun was getting very low and red over the sea. She swam slowly in. On the beach Mrs Topes waited, disapprovingly. She had known somebody, a strong man, who had caught cramp from staying in too long. He sank like a stone. Like a stone. The queer people Mrs Topes had known! And the funny things they did, the odd things that happened to them!

Dinner that evening was duller than ever. Barbara went early to bed. All night long the same old irritating cicada scraped and scraped among the pine trees, monotonous and regular as clockwork. Zip, zip, zip, zip, zip. Boring, boring. Was the animal never bored by its own noise? It seemed odd that it shouldn't be. But, when she came to think of it, nobody ever did get bored with their own noise. Mrs Topes, for example; she never seemed to get bored. Zip zip, zip zip zip. The cicada went on without a pause.

Concetta knocked at the door at half-past seven. The morning was as bright and cloudless as all the mornings were. Barbara jumped up, looked from one window at the mountains, from the other at the sea; all seemed to be well with them. All was well with her too, this morning. Seated at the mirror, she did not so much as think of the big monkey in the far obscure corner of the room. A bathing dress and a bath-gown, sandals, a handkerchief round her head, and she was ready. Sleep had left no recollection of last night's mortal boredom. She ran downstairs.

"Good morning, Mr Topes."

Mr Topes was walking in the garden among the vines. He turned round, took off his hat, smiled a greeting.

"Good morning, Miss Barbara." He paused. Then, with an embarrassed wriggle of introduction he went on; a queer little falter came into his voice. "A real Chaucerian morning, Miss Barbara. A May-day morning—only it happens to be September. Nature is fresh and bright, and there is at least one specimen in this dream garden"—he wriggled more uncomfortably than ever, and there was a tremulous glitter in his round spectacle lenses— "of the poet's 'yonge fresshe folkes.'" He bowed in her direction, smiled deprecatingly, and was silent. The remark, it seemed to him, now that he had finished speaking, was somehow not as good as he had thought it would be.

Barbara laughed. "Chaucer! They used to make us read the *Canterbury Tales* at school. But they always bored me. Are you going to bathe?"

"Not before breakfast." Mr Topes shook his head. "One is getting a little too old for that."

"Is one?" Why did the silly old man always say 'one' when he meant 'I'? She couldn't help laughing at him. "Well, I must hurry, or else I shall be late for breakfast again, and you know how I catch it."

She ran out, through the gate in the garden wall, across the beach, to the striped red-and-white bathing cabin that stood before the house. Fifty yards away she saw the Marchese Prampolini, still dripping from the sea, running up towards his bathing hut. Catching sight of her, he flashed a smile in her direction, gave a military salute. Barbara waved her hand, then thought that the gesture had been a little too familiar—but at this hour of the morning it was difficult not to have bad jolly manners—and added the corrective of a stiff bow. After all, she had only met him yesterday. Soon she was swimming out to sea, and, ugh! what a lot of horrible huge jelly-fish there were.

Mr Topes had followed her slowly through the gate and across the sand. He watched her running down from the cabin, slender as a boy, with long, bounding strides. He watched her go jumping with great splashes through the deepening water, then throw herself forward and begin to swim. He watched her till she was more than a small dark dot far out.

Emerging from his cabin, the marquis met him walking slowly along the beach, his head bent down and his lips slightly moving as though he were repeating something, a prayer or a poem, to himself.

"Good morning, signore." The marquis shook him by the hand with a more than English cordiality.

"Good morning," replied Mr Topes, allowing his hand to be shaken. He resented this interruption of his thoughts.

"She swims very well, Miss Buzzacott."

"Very," assented Mr Topes, and smiled to himself to think what beautiful, poetical things he might have said, if he had chosen.

"Well, so, so," said the marquis, too colloquial by half. He shook hands again, and the two men went their respective ways.

Barbara was still a hundred yards from the shore when she heard the crescendo and dying boom of the gong floating out from the villa. Damn! she'd be late again. She quickened her stroke and came splashing out through the shallows, flushed and breathless. She'd be ten minutes late, she calculated; it would take her at least that to do her hair and dress. Mrs Topes would be on the warpath again; though what business that old woman had to lecture her as she did, goodness only knew. She always succeeded in making herself horribly offensive and unpleasant.

The beach was quite deserted as she trotted, panting, across it, empty to right and left as far as she could see. If only she had a horse to go galloping at the water's edge, miles and miles. Right

away down to Bocca d'Arno she'd go, swim the river—she saw
herself crouching on the horse's back, as he swam, with legs
tucked up on the saddle, trying not to get her feet wet—and gallop
on again, goodness only knew where.

In front of the cabin she suddenly halted. There in the ruffled
sand she had seen a writing. Big letters, faintly legible, sprawled
across her path.

O CLARA D'ELLÉBEUSE

She pieced the dim letters together. They hadn't been there when
she started out to bathe. Who? . . . She looked round. The beach
was quite empty. And what was the meaning? "O Clara
d'Ellébeuse." She took her bath-gown from the cabin, slipped on
her sandals, and ran back towards the house as fast as she could.
She felt most horribly frightened.

It was a sultry, headachey sort of morning, with a hot scirocco
that stirred the bunting on the flagstaffs. By midday the thunder-
clouds had covered half the sky. The sun still blazed on the sea,
but over the mountains all was black and indigo. The storm broke
noisily overhead just as they were drinking their after-luncheon
coffee.

"Arthur," said Mrs Topes, painfully calm, "shut the shutters,
please."

She was not frightened, no. But she preferred not to see the
lightning. When the room was darkened, she began to talk,
suavely and incessantly.

Lying back in her deep arm-chair, Barbara was thinking of
Clara d'Ellébeuse. What did it mean and who was Clara
d'Ellébeuse? And why had he written it there for her to see? He—
for there could be no doubt who had written it. The flash of teeth
and eyes, the military salute; she knew she oughtn't to have
waved to him. He had written it there while she was swimming
out. Written it and then run away. She rather liked that—just an
extraordinary word on the sand, like the footprint in *Robinson
Crusoe*.

"Personally," Mrs Topes was saying, "I prefer Harrod's."

The thunder crashed and rattled. It was rather exhilarating,
Barbara thought; one felt, at any rate, that something was
happening for a change. She remembered the little room half-
way up the stairs at Lady Thingumy's house, with the book-

shelves and the green curtains and the orange shade on the light; and that awful young man like a white slug who had tried to kiss her there, at the dance last year. But that was different—not at all serious; and the young man had been so horribly ugly. She saw the marquis running up the beach, quick and alert. Copper coloured all over, with black hair. He was certainly very handsome. But as for being in love, well . . . what did that exactly mean? Perhaps when she knew him better. Even now she fancied she detected something. O Clara d'Ellébeuse. What an extraordinary thing it was!

With his long fingers Mr Buzzacott combed his beard. This winter, he was thinking, he would put another thousand into Italian money when the exchange was favourable. In the spring it always seemed to drop back again. One could clear three hundred pounds on one's capital if the exchange went down to seventy. The income on three hundred was fifteen pounds a year, and fifteen pounds was now fifteen hundred lire. And fifteen hundred lire, when you came to think of it, was really sixty pounds. That was to say that one would make an addition of more than a pound a week to one's income by this simple little speculation. He became aware that Mrs Topes had asked him a question.

"Yes, yes, perfectly," he said.

Mrs Topes talked on; she was keeping up her morale. Was she right in believing that the thunder sounded a little less alarmingly loud and near?

Mr Topes sat, polishing his spectacles with a white silk handkerchief. Vague and myopic between their puckered lids, his eyes seemed lost, homeless, unhappy. He was thinking about beauty. There were certain relations between the eyelids and the temples, between the breast and the shoulder; there were certain successions of sounds. But what about them? Ah, that was the problem —that was the problem. And there was youth, there was innocence. But it was all very obscure, and there were so many phrases, so many remembered pictures and melodies; he seemed to get himself entangled among them. And he was so old and ineffective.

He put on his spectacles again, and definition came into the foggy world beyond his eyes. The shuttered room was very dark. He could distinguish the Renaissance profile of Mr Buzzacott, bearded and delicately featured. In her deep arm-chair Barbara appeared, faintly white, in an attitude relaxed and brooding. And Mrs Topes was nothing more than a voice in the darkness. She had got on to the marriage of the Prince of Wales. Who would they find for him?

Clara d'Ellébeuse, Clara d'Ellébeuse. She saw herself so clearly as the *marchesa*. They would have a house in Rome, a palace. She saw herself in the Palazzo Spada—it had such a lovely vaulted passage leading from the courtyard to the gardens at the back. "MARCHESA PRAMPOLINI, PALAZZO SPADA, ROMA"—a great big visiting-card beautifully engraved. And she would go riding every day in the Pincio. "*Mi porta il mio cavallo*," she would say to the footman, who answered the bell. *Porta?* Would that be quite correct? Hardly. She'd have to take some proper Italian lessons to talk to the servants. One must never be ridiculous before servants."*Voglio il mio cavallo*." Haughtily one would say it sitting at one's writing-table in a riding-habit, without turning round. It would be a green riding-habit, with a black tricorne hat, braided with silver.

"*Prendero la mia collazione al letto*." Was that right for breakfast in bed? Because she would have breakfast in bed, always. And when she got up there would be lovely looking-glasses with three panels where one could see oneself side-face. She saw herself leaning forward, powdering her nose, carefully, scientifically. With the monkey creeping up behind? Ooh! Horrible! *Ho paura di questa scimmia, questo scimmione.*

She would come back to lunch after her ride. Perhaps Prampolini would be there; she had rather left him out of the picture so far. "*Dov' è il Marchese?*" "*Nella sala di pranza, signora.*" I began without you, I was so hungry. *Pasta asciutta*. Where have you been, my love? Riding, my dove. She supposed they'd get into the habit of saying that sort of thing. Everyone seemed to. And you? I have been out with the Fascisti.

Oh, these Fascisti! Would life be worth living when he was always going out with pistols and bombs and things? They would bring him back one day on a stretcher. She saw it. Pale, pale, with blood on him. *Il signore è ferito. Nel petto. Gravamente. E morto.*

How could she bear it? It was too awful; too, too terrible. Her breath came in a kind of sob; she shuddered as though she had been hurt. *E morto. E morto.* The tears came into her eyes.

She was roused suddenly by a dazzling light. The storm had receded far enough into the distance to permit of Mrs Topes's opening the shutters.

"It's quite stopped raining."

To be disturbed in one's intimate sorrow and self-abandonment at a death-bed by a stranger's intrusion, an alien voice. . . . Barbara turned her face away from the light and surreptitiously wiped her eyes. They might see and ask her why she had been crying. She hated Mrs Topes for opening the shutters; at the inrush of the light something beautiful had flown, an emotion had vanished, irrecoverably. It was a sacrilege.

Mr Buzzacott looked at his watch. "Too late, I fear, for a siesta now," he said. "Suppose we ring for an early tea."

"An endless succession of meals," said Mr Topes, with a tremolo and a sigh. "That's what life seems to be—real life."

"I have been calculating"—Mr Buzzacott turned his pale green eyes towards his guest—"that I may be able to afford that pretty little *cinque cassone*, after all. It would be a bit of a squeeze." He played with his beard. "But still . . . "

After tea, Barbara and Mr Topes went for a walk along the beach. She didn't much want to go, but Mrs Topes thought it would be good for her; so she had to. The storm had passed and the sky over the sea was clear. But the waves were still breaking with an incessant clamour on the outer shallows, driving wide sheets of water high up the beach, twenty or thirty yards above the line where, on a day of calm, the ripples ordinarily expired. Smooth, shining expanses of water advanced and receded like steel surfaces moved out and back by a huge machine.Through the rain-washed air the mountains appeared with an incredible clarity. Above them hung huge masses of cloud.

"Clouds over Carrara," said Mr Topes, deprecating his remark with a little shake of the head and a movement of the shoulders. "I like to fancy sometimes that the spirits of the great sculptors lodge among these marble hills, and that it is their unseen hands that carve the clouds into these enormous splendid shapes. I imagine their ghosts"—his voice trembled—"feeling about among superhuman conceptions, planning huge groups and friezes and monumental figures with blowing draperies; planning, conceiving, but never quite achieving. Look, there's something of Michelangelo in that white cloud with the dark shadows underneath it." Mr Topes pointed, and Barbara nodded and said, "Yes, yes," though she wasn't quite sure which cloud he meant. "It's like Night on the Medici tomb; all the power and the passion are brooding inside it, pent up. And there, in that sweeping, gesticulating piece of vapour—you see the one I mean —there's a Bernini. All the passion's on the surface, expressed; the gesture's caught at its most violent. And that sleek, smug white fellow over there, that's a delicious absurd Canova." Mr Topes chuckled.

"Why do you always talk about art?" said Barbara. "You bring these dead people into everything. What do I know about Canova or whoever it is?" They were none of them alive. She thought of that dark face, bright as a lamp with life. He at least wasn't dead. She wondered whether the letters were still there in the sand before the cabin. No, of course not; the rain and the wind would have blotted them out.

Mr Topes was silent; he walked with slightly bent knees and his eyes were fixed on the ground; he wore a speckled black-and-white straw hat. He always thought of art; that was what was wrong with him. Like an old tree he was; built up of dead wood, with only a few fibres of life to keep him from rotting away. They walked on for a long time in silence.

"Here's the river," said Mr Topes at last.

A few steps more and they were on the bank of a wide stream that came down slowly through the plain to the sea. Just inland from the beach it was fringed with pine trees; beyond the trees one could see the plain, and beyond the plain were the mountains. In this calm light after the storm everything looked strange. The colours seemed deeper and more intense than at ordinary times. And though all was so clear, there was a mysterious air of remoteness about the whole scene. There was no sound, except the continuous breathing of the sea. They stood for a little while, looking; then turned back.

Far away along the beach two figures were slowly approaching. White flannel trousers, a pink skirt.

"Nature," Mr Topes enunciated, with a shake of the head. "One always comes back to nature. At a moment such as this, in surroundings like these, one realizes it. One lives now—more quietly, perhaps, but more profoundly. Deep waters. Deep waters. . . ."

The figures drew closer. Wasn't it the marquis? And who was with him? Barbara strained her eyes to see.

"Most of one's life," Mr Topes went on, "is one prolonged effort to prevent oneself thinking. Your father and I, we collect pictures and read about the dead. Other people achieve the same result by drinking, or breeding rabbits, or doing amateur carpentry. Anything rather than think calmly about the important things."

Mr Topes was silent. He looked about him, at the sea, at the mountains, at the great clouds, at his companion. A frail Montagna madonna, with the sea and the westering sun, the mountains and the storm, all eternity as a background. And he was sixty, with all a life, immensely long and yet timelessly short, behind him, an empty life. He thought of death and the miracles of beauty; behind his round, glittering spectacles he felt inclined to weep.

The approaching couple were quite near now.

"What a funny old walrus," said the lady.

"Walrus? Your natural history is quite wrong." The marquis laughed. "He's much too dry to be a walrus. I should suggest some sort of an old cat."

"Well, whatever he is, I'm sorry for that poor little girl. Think of having nobody better to go about with!"

"Pretty, isn't she?"

"Yes, but too young, of course."

"I like the innocence."

"Innocence? Cher ami! These English girls. Oh, la la! They may look innocent. But, believe me . . ."

"Sh, sh. They'll hear you."

"Pooh, they don't understand Italian."

The marquis raised his hand. "The old walrus . . ." he whispered; then addressed himself loudly and jovially to the newcomers.

"Good evening, signorina. Good evening, Mr Topes. After a storm the air is always the purest, don't you find, eh?"

Barbara nodded, leaving Mr Topes to answer. It wasn't his sister. It was the Russian woman, the one of whom Mrs Topes used to say that it was a disgrace she should be allowed to stay at the hotel. She had turned away, dissociating herself from the conversation; Barbara looked at the line of her averted face. Mr

Topes was saying something about the Pastoral Symphony. Purple face powder in the daylight; it looked hideous.

"Well, au revoir."

The flash of the marquis's smile was directed at them. The Russian woman turned back from the sea, slightly bowed, smiled languidly. Her heavy white eye-lids were almost closed; she seemed the prey of an enormous ennui.

"They jar a little," said Mr Topes when they were out of ear-shot—"they jar on the time, on the place, on the emotion. They haven't the innocence for this . . . this . . ."—he wriggled and tremoloed out the just, the all too precious word—"this pre-lapsarian landscape."

He looked sideways at Barbara and wondered what she was so thoughtfully frowning over. Oh, lovely and delicate young creature! What could he adequately say of death and beauty and tenderness? Tenderness . . .

"All this," he went on desperately, and waved his hand to indicate the sky, the sea, the mountains, "this scene is like something remembered, clear and utterly calm; remembered across great gulfs of intervening time."

But that was not really what he wanted to say.

"You see what I mean?" he asked dubiously. She made no reply. How could she see? "This scene is so clear and pure and remote; you need the corresponding emotion. Those people were out of harmony. They weren't clear and pure enough." He seemed to be getting more muddled than ever. "It's an emotion of the young and of the old. You could feel it, I could feel it. Those people couldn't." He was feeling his way through obscurities. Where would he finally arrive? "Certain poems express it. You know Francis Jammes? I have thought so much of his work lately. Art instead of life, as usual; but then I'm made that way. I can't help thinking of Jammes. Those delicate, exquisite things he wrote about Clara d'Ellébeuse."

"Clara d'Ellébeuse?" She stopped and stared at him.

"You know the lines?" Mr Topes smiled delightedly. "This place makes me think you make me think of them. '*J'aime dans les temps Clara d'Ellébeuse* . . .' But, my dear Barbara, what is the matter?"

She had started crying, for no reason whatever.

Nuns at Luncheon

"WHAT have I been doing since you saw me last?" Miss Penny repeated my question in her loud, emphatic voice. "Well, when did you see me last."

"It must have been June," I computed.

"Was that after I'd been proposed to by the Russian General?"

"Yes; I remember hearing about the Russian General."

Miss Penny threw back her head and laughed. Her long earrings swung and rattled—corpses hanging in chains: an agreeably literary simile. And her laughter was like brass, but that had been said before.

"That was an uproarious incident. It's sad you should have heard of it. I love my Russian General story. '*Vos yeux me rendent fou.*'" She laughed again.

Vos yeux—she had eyes like a hare's, flush with her head and very bright with a superficial and expressionless brightness.What a formidable woman. I felt sorry for the Russian General.

" '*Sans cœur et sans entrailles,*' " she went on, quoting the poor devil's words. "Such a delightful motto, don't you think? Like '*Sans peur et sans reproche.*' But let me think; what have I been doing since then?" Thoughtfully she bit into the crust of her bread with long, sharp, white teeth.

"Two mixed grills," I said parenthetically to the waiter.

"But of course," exclaimed Miss Penny suddenly. "I haven't seen you since my German trip. All sorts of adventures. My appendicitis; my nun."

"Your nun?"

"My marvellous nun. I must tell you all about her."

"Do." Miss Penny's anecdotes were always curious. I looked forward to an entertaining luncheon.

"You knew I'd been in Germany this autumn?"

"Well, I didn't, as a matter of fact. But still——"

"I was just wandering round." Miss Penny described a circle in the air with her gaudily jewelled hand. She always twinkled with massive and improbable jewellery. "Wandering round, living on three pounds a week, partly amusing myself, partly collecting materials for a few little articles. 'What it Feels Like to be a Conquered Nation'—sob-stuff for the Liberal press, you know—and 'How the Hun is Trying to Wriggle out of the Indemnity,' for the other fellows. One has to make the best of all possible worlds, don't you find? But we mustn't talk shop. Well, I was wandering round, and very pleasant I found it. Berlin, Dresden, Leipzig. Then down to Munich and all over the place. One fine day I got to Grauburg. You know Grauburg? It's one of those picture-book German towns with a castle on a hill, hanging beer-gardens, a Gothic church, an old university, a river, a pretty bridge, and forests all round. Charming. But I hadn't much opportunity to appreciate the beauties of the place. The day after I arrived there—bang!—I went down with appendicitis—screaming, I may add."

"But how appalling!"

"They whisked me off to hospital, and cut me open before you could say knife. Excellent surgeon, highly efficient Sisters of Charity to nurse me—I couldn't have been in better hands. But it was a bore being tied there by the leg for four weeks—a great bore. Still, the thing had its compensations. There was my nun, for example. Ah, here's the food, thank Heaven!"

The mixed grill proved to be excellent. Miss Penny's description of the nun came to me in scraps and snatches. A round, pink, pretty face in a winged coif; blue eyes and regular features; teeth altogether too perfect—false, in fact; but the general effect extremely pleasing. A youthful Teutonic twenty-eight.

"She wasn't my nurse," Miss Penny explained. "But I used to see her quite often when she came in to have a look at the *tolle Engländerin*. Her name was Sister Agatha. During the war, they told me, she had converted any number of wounded soldiers to the true faith—which wasn't surprising, considering how pretty she was."

"Did she try and convert you?" I asked.

"She wasn't such a fool." Miss Penny laughed, and rattled the miniature gallows of her ears.

I amused myself for a moment with the thought of Miss Penny's conversion—Miss Penny confronting a vast assembly of Fathers of the Church, rattling her ear-rings at their discourses on the Trinity, laughing her appalling laugh at the doctrine of the Immaculate Conception, meeting the stern look of the Grand

Inquisitor with a flash of her bright, emotionless hare's eyes. What was the secret of the woman's formidableness?

But I was missing the story. What had happened? Ah yes, the gist of it was that Sister Agatha had appeared one morning, after two or three days' absence, dressed, not as a nun, but in the overalls of a hospital charwoman, with a handkerchief instead of a winged coif on her shaven head.

"Dead," said Miss Penny; "she looked as though she were dead. A walking corpse, that's what she was. It was a shocking sight. I shouldn't have thought it possible for anyone to change so much in so short a time. She walked painfully, as though she had been ill for months, and she had great burnt rings round her eyes and deep lines in her face. And the general expression of unhappiness—that was something quite appalling."

She leaned out into the gangway between the two rows of tables, and caught the passing waiter by the end of one of his coat-tails. The little Italian looked round with an expression of surprise that deepened into terror on his face.

"Half a pint of Guinness," ordered Miss Penny. "And, after this, bring me some jam roll."

"No jam roll to-day, madam."

"Damn!" said Miss Penny. "Bring me what you like, then."

She let go of the waiter's tail, and resumed her narrative.

"Where was I? Yes, I remember. She came into my room, I was telling you, with a bucket of water and a brush, dressed like a charwoman. Naturally I was rather surprised. 'What on earth are you doing, Sister Agatha?' I asked. No answer. She just shook her head, and began to scrub the floor. When she'd finished, she left the room without so much as looking at me again. 'What's happened to Sister Agatha?' I asked my nurse when she next came in. 'Can't say.'—'Won't say,' I said. No answer. It took me nearly a week to find out what really had happened. Nobody dared tell me; it was *strengst verboten*, as they used to say in the good old days. But I wormed it out in the long run. My nurse, the doctor, the charwomen—I got something out of all of them. I always get what I want in the end." Miss Penny laughed like a horse.

"I'm sure you do," I said politely.

"Much obliged," acknowledged Miss Penny. "But to proceed. My information came to me in fragmentary whispers. 'Sister

Agatha ran away with a man.'—Dear me!—'One of the patients.'
—You don't say so.—'A criminal out of the jail.'—The plot
thickens.—'He ran away from her.'—It seems to grow thinner
again.—'They brought her back here; she's been disgraced.
There's been a funeral service for her in the chapel—coffin and
all. She had to be present at it—her own funeral. She isn't a nun
any more. She has to do charwoman's work now, the roughest in
the hospital. She's not allowed to speak to anybody, and nobody's
allowed to speak to her. She's regarded as dead.'" Miss Penny
paused to signal to the harassed little Italian. "My small
'Guinness,'" she called out.

"Coming, coming," and the foreign voice cried "Guinness"
down the lift, and from below another voice echoed, "Guinness."

"I filled in the details bit by bit. There was our hero, to begin
with; I had to bring him into the picture, which was rather
difficult, as I had never seen him. But I got a photograph of him.
The police circulated one when he got away; I don't suppose they
ever caught him." Miss Penny opened her bag. "Here it is," she
said. "I always carry it about with me; it's become a supersti-
tion. For years, I remember, I used to carry a little bit of heather
tied up with string. Beautiful, isn't it? There's a sort of Renaissance look about it, don't you think? He was half-Italian, you
know."

Italian. Ah, that explained it. I had been wondering how
Bavaria could have produced this thin-faced creature with the
big dark eyes, the finely modelled nose and chin, and the fleshy
lips so royally and sensually curved.

"He's certainly very superb," I said, handing back the picture.

Miss Penny put it carefully away in her bag. "Isn't he?" she
said. "Quite marvellous. But his character and his mind were even
better. I see him as one of those innocent, childlike monsters of
iniquity who are simply unaware of the existence of right and
wrong. And he had genius—the real Italian genius for engineering, for dominating and exploiting nature. A true son of the Roman
aqueduct builders he was, and a brother of the electrical engineers. Only Kuno—that was his name—didn't work in water;
he worked in women. He knew how to harness the natural energy
of passion; he made devotion drive his mills. The commercial
exploitation of love-power, that was his speciality. I sometimes
wonder," Miss Penny added in a different tone, "whether I shall

ever be exploited, when I get a little more middle-aged and celibate, by one of these young engineers of the passions. It would be humiliating, particularly as I've done so little exploiting from my side."

She frowned and was silent for a moment. No, decidedly, Miss Penny was not beautiful; you could not even honestly say that she had charm or was attractive. That high Scotch colouring, those hare's eyes, the voice, the terrifying laugh, and the size of her, the general formidableness of the woman. No, no, no.

"You said he had been in prison," I said. The silence, with all its implications, was becoming embarrassing.

Miss Penny sighed, looked up, and nodded. "He was fool enough," she said, "to leave the straight and certain road of female exploitation for the dangerous courses of burglary. We all have our occasional accesses of folly. They gave him a heavy sentence, but he succeeded in getting pneumonia, I think it was, a week after entering jail. He was transferred to the hospital. Sister Agatha, with her known talent for saving souls, was given him as his particular attendant. But it was he, I'm afraid, who did the converting."

Miss Penny finished off the last mouthful of the ginger pudding which the waiter had brought in lieu of jam roll.

"I suppose you don't smoke cheroots," I said, as I opened my cigar-case.

"Well, as a matter of fact, I do," Miss Penny replied. She looked sharply round the restaurant. "I must just see if there are any of those horrible little gossip paragraphers here to-day. One doesn't want to figure in the social and personal column to-morrow morning: 'A fact which is not so generally known as it ought to be, is that Miss Penny, the well-known woman journalist, always ends her luncheon with a six-inch Burma cheroot. I saw her yesterday in a restaurant—not a hundred miles from Carmelite Street—smoking like a house on fire.' You know the touch. But the coast seems to be clear, thank goodness."

She took a cheroot from the case, lit it at my proffered match, and went on talking.

"Yes, it was young Kuno who did the converting. Sister Agatha was converted back into the worldly Melpomene Fugger she had been before she became the bride of holiness."

"Melpomene Fugger?"

"That was her name. I had her history from my old doctor. He had seen all Grauburg, living and dying and propagating, for generations. Melpomene Fugger—why, he had brought little Melpel into the world, little Melpchen. Her father was Professor Fugger, the great Professor Fugger, the *berühmter Geolog*. Oh yes, of course, I know the name. So well . . . He was the man who wrote the standard work on Lemuria—you know, the hypothetical continent where the lemurs come from. I showed due respect. Liberal-minded he was, a disciple of Herder, a world-burgher, as they beautifully call it over there. Anglophile, too, and always ate porridge for breakfast—up till August 1914. Then, on the radiant morning of the fifth, he renounced it for ever, solemnly and with tears in his eyes. The national food of a people who had betrayed culture and civilization—how could he go on eating it? It would stick in his throat. In future he would have a lightly boiled egg. He sounded, I thought, altogether charming. And his daughter, Melpomene—she sounded charming, too; and such thick, yellow pigtails when she was young! Her mother was dead, and a sister of the great Professor's ruled the house with an iron rod. Aunt Bertha was her name. Well, Melpomene grew up, very plump and appetizing. When she was seventeen, something very odious and disagreeable happened to her. Even the doctor didn't know exactly what it was; but he wouldn't have been surprised if it had had something to do with the then Professor of Latin, an old friend of the family's, who combined, it seems, great erudition with a horrid fondness for very young ladies."

Miss Penny knocked half an inch of cigar ash into her empty glass.

"If I wrote short stories," she went on reflectively "(but it's too much bother), I should make this anecdote into a sort of potted life history, beginning with a scene immediately after this disagreeable event in Melpomene's life. I see the scene so clearly. Poor little Melpel is leaning over the bastions of Grauburg Castle, weeping into the June night and the mulberry trees in the gardens thirty feet below. She is besieged by the memory of what happened this dreadful afternoon. Professor Engelmann, her father's old friend, with the magnificent red Assyrian beard . . . Too awful—too awful! But then, as I was saying, short stories are really too much bother; or perhaps I'm too stupid to write them. I bequeath it to you. You know how to tick these things off."

"You're generous."

"Not at all," said Miss Penny. "My terms are a ten per cent commission on the American sale. Incidentally there won't be an American sale. Poor Melpchen's history is not for the chaste public of Those States. But let me hear what you propose to do with Melpomene now you've got her on the castle bastions."

"That's simple," I said. "I know all about German university towns and castles on hills. I shall make her look into the June night, as you suggest; into the violet night with its points of golden flame. There will be the black silhouette of the castle, with its sharp roofs and hooded turrets, behind her. From the hanging beer-gardens in the town below the voices of the students, singing in perfect four-part harmony, will float up through the dark-blue spaces. '*Röslein, Röslein, Röslein rot*' and '*Das Ringlein sprang in zwei*'—the heart-rendingly sweet old songs will make her cry all the more. Her tears will patter like rain among the leaves of the mulberry trees in the garden below. Does that seem to you adequate?"

"Very nice," said Miss Penny. "But how are you going to bring the sex problem and all its horrors into your landscape?"

"Well, let me think." I called to memory those distant foreign summers when I was completing my education. "I know. I shall suddenly bring a swarm of moving candles and Chinese lanterns under the mulberry trees. You imagine the rich lights and shadows, the jewel-bright leafage, the faces and moving limbs of men and women, seen for an instant and gone again. They are students and girls of the town come out to dance, this windless, blue June night, under the mulberry trees. And now they begin, thumping round and round in a ring, to the music of their own singing:

> '*Wir können spielen*
> *Vio-vio-vio-lin,*
> *Wir können spielen*
> *Vi-o-lin.*'

Now the rhythm changes, quickens:

> '*Und wir können tanzen Bumstarara,*
> *Bumstarara, Bumstarara,*
> *Und wir können tanzen Bumstarara,*
> *Bumstarara-rara.*'

The dance becomes a rush, an elephantine prancing on the dry lawn under the mulberry trees. And from the bastion Melpomene looks down and perceives, suddenly and apocalyptically, that everything in the world is sex, sex, sex. Men and women, male and female—always the same, and all, in the light of the horror of the afternoon, disgusting. That's how I should do it, Miss Penny."

"And very nice, too. But I wish you could find a place to bring in my conversation with the doctor. I shall never forget the way he cleared his throat and coughed before embarking on the delicate subject. 'You may know, ahem, gracious Miss,' he began —'you may know that religious phenomena are often, ahem, closely connected with sexual causes.' I replied that I had heard rumours which might justify me in believing this to be true among Roman Catholics, but that in the Church of England— and I for one was a practitioner of Anglicanismus—it was very different. That might be, said the doctor; he had had no opportunity in the course of his long medical career of personally studying Anglicanismus. But he could vouch for the fact that among his patients, here in Grauburg, mysticismus was very often mixed up with the *Geschlechtsleben*. Melpomene was a case in point. After that hateful afternoon she had become extremely religious; the Professor of Latin had diverted her emotions out of their normal channels. She rebelled against the placid Agnosticismus of her father, and at night, in secret, when Aunt Bertha's dragon eyes were closed, she would read such forbidden books as *The Life of St Theresa*, *The Little Flowers of St Francis*, *The Imitation of Christ*, and the horribly enthralling *Book of Martyrs*. Aunt Bertha confiscated these works whenever she came upon them; she considered them more pernicious than the novels of Marcel Prévost. The character of a good potential housewife might be completely undermined by reading of this kind. It was rather a relief for Melpomene when Aunt Bertha shuffled off, in the summer of 1911, this mortal coil. She was one of those indispensables of whom one makes the discovery, when they are gone, that one can get on quite as well without them. Poor Aunt Bertha!"

"One can imagine Melpomene trying to believe she was sorry, and horribly ashamed to find that she was really, in secret, almost glad." The suggestion seemed to me ingenious, but Miss Penny accepted it as obvious.

"Precisely," she said; " and the emotion would only further confirm and give new force to the tendencies which her aunt's death left her free to indulge as much as she liked. Remorse, contrition—they would lead to the idea of doing penance. And for one who was now wallowing in the martyrology, penance was the mortification of the flesh. She used to kneel for hours, at night, in the cold; she ate too little, and when her teeth ached, which they often did,—for she had a set, the doctor told me, which had given trouble from the very first,—she would not go and see the dentist, but lay awake at night, savouring to the full her excruciations, and feeling triumphantly that they must, in some strange way, be pleasing to the Mysterious Powers. She went on like that for two or three years, till she was poisoned through and through. In the end she went down with gastric ulcer. It was three months before she came out of hospital, well for the first time in a long space of years, and with a brand new set of imperishable teeth, all gold and ivory. And in mind, too, she was changed—for the better, I suppose. The nuns who nursed her had made her see that in mortifying herself she had acted supererogatively and through spiritual pride; instead of doing right, she had sinned. The only road to salvation, they told her, lay in discipline, in the orderliness of established religion, in obedience to authority. Secretly, so as not to distress her poor father, whose Agnosticism was extremely dogmatic, for all its unobtrusiveness, Melpomene became a Roman Catholic. She was twenty-two. Only a few months later came the war and Professor Fugger's eternal renunciation of porridge. He did not long survive the making of that patriotic gesture. In the autumn of 1914 he caught a fatal influenza. Melpomene was alone in the world. In the spring of 1915 there was a new and very conscientious Sister of Charity at work among the wounded in the hospital of Grauburg. Here," explained Miss Penny, jabbing the air with her forefinger, "you put a line of asterisks or dots to signify a six years' gulf in the narrative. And you begin again right in the middle of a dialogue between Sister Agatha and the newly convalescent Kuno."

"What's their dialogue to be about?" I asked.

"Oh, that's easy enough," said Miss Penny. "Almost anything would do. What about this, for example? You explain that the fever has just abated; for the first time for days the young man is fully conscious. He feels himself to be well, reborn, as it were, in

a new world—a world so bright and novel and jolly that he can't
help laughing at the sight of it. He looks about him; the flies on
the ceiling strike him as being extremely comic. How do they
manage to walk upside down? They have suckers on their feet,
says Sister Agatha, and wonders if her natural history is quite
sound. Suckers on their feet—ha, ha! What an uproarious notion!
Suckers on their feet—that's good that's damned good! You can
say charming, pathetic, positively tender things about the irrelevant mirth of convalescents—the more so in this particular case,
where the mirth is expressed by a young man who is to be taken
back to jail as soon as he can stand firmly on his legs. Ha, ha!
Laugh on, unhappy boy! It is the quacking of the Fates, the
Parcæ, the Norns!"

Miss Penny gave an exaggerated imitation of her own brassy
laughter. At the sound of it the few lunchers who still lingered at
the other tables looked up, startled.

"You can write pages about Destiny and its ironic quacking.
It's tremendously impressive, and there's money in every line."

"You may be sure I shall."

"Good! Then I can get on with my story. The days pass and
the first hilarity of convalescence fades away. The young man
remembers and grows sullen; his strength comes back to him, and
with it a sense of despair. His mind broods incessantly on the
hateful future. As for the consolations of religion, he won't listen
to them. Sister Agatha perseveres—oh, with what anxious
solicitude!—in the attempt to make him understand and believe
and be comforted. It is all so tremendously important, and in this
case, somehow, more important than in any other. And now you
see the *Geschlechtsleben* working yeastily and obscurely, and once
again the quacking of the Norns is audible. By the way," said
Miss Penny, changing her tone and leaning confidentially across
the table, "I wish you'd tell me something. Do you really—
honestly, I mean—do you seriously believe in literature?"

"Believe in literature?"

"I was thinking," Miss Penny explained, "of Ironic Fate and
the quacking of the Norns and all that."

" 'M yes."

"And then there's this psychology and introspection business;
and construction and good narrative and word pictures and *le
mot juste* and verbal magic and striking metaphors."

I remembered that I had compared Miss Penny's tinkling earrings to skeletons hanging in chains.

"And then, finally, and to begin with—Alpha and Omega—there's ourselves: two professionals gloating, with an absolute lack of sympathy, over a seduced nun, and speculating on the best method of turning her misfortunes into cash. It's all very curious, isn't it?—when one begins to think about it dispassionately."

"Very curious," I agreed. "But, then, so is everything else if you look at it like that."

"No, no," said Miss Penny. "Nothing's so curious as our business. But I shall never get to the end of my story if I get started on first principles."

Miss Penny continued her narrative. I was still thinking of literature. Do you believe in it? Seriously? Ah! Luckily the question was quite meaningless. The story came to me rather vaguely, but it seemed that the young man was getting better; in a few more days, the doctor had said, he would be well—well enough to go back to jail. No, no. The question was meaningless. I would think about it no more. I concentrated my attention again.

"Sister Agatha," I heard Miss Penny saying, "prayed, exhorted, indoctrinated. Whenever she had half a minute to spare from her other duties she would come running into the young man's room. 'I wonder if you fully realize the importance of prayer?' she would ask, and, before he had time to answer, she would give him a breathless account of the uses and virtues of regular and patient supplication. Or else it was: 'May I tell you about St Theresa?' or 'St Stephen, the first martyr—you know about him, don't you?' Kuno simply wouldn't listen at first. It seemed so fantastically irrelevant, such an absurd interruption to his thoughts, his serious, despairing thoughts about the future. Prison was real, imminent, and this woman buzzed about him with her ridiculous fairy-tales. Then, suddenly, one day he began to listen, he showed signs of contrition and conversion. Sister Agatha announced her triumph to the other nuns, and there was rejoicing over the one lost sheep. Melpomene had never felt so happy in her life, and Kuno, looking at her radiant face, must have wondered how he could have been such a fool as not to see from the first what was now so obvious. The woman had lost her head about him. And he had only four days now—four days in which to tap the tumultuous love power, to canalize it, to set it working for his escape. Why hadn't he started a week ago? He could have made certain of it then. But now? There was no knowing. Four days was a horribly short time."

"How did he do it?" I asked, for Miss Penny had paused.

"That's for you to say," she replied, and shook her ear-rings at me. "I don't know. Nobody knows, I imagine, except the two parties concerned and perhaps Sister Agatha's confessor. But one can reconstruct the crime, as they say. How would you have done it? You're a man, you ought to be familiar with the processes of amorous engineering."

"You flatter me," I answered. "Do you seriously suppose——" I extended my arms. Miss Penny laughed like a horse. "No. But, seriously, it's a problem. The case is a very special one. The person, a nun; the place, a hospital; the opportunities, few. There could be no favourable circumstances—no moonlight, no distant music; and any form of direct attack would be sure to fail. That audacious confidence which is your amorist's best weapon would be useless here."

"Obviously," said Miss Penny. "But there are surely other methods. There is the approach through pity and the maternal instincts. And there's the approach through Higher Things, through the soul. Kuno must have worked on those lines, don't you think? One can imagine him letting himself be converted, praying with her, and at the same time appealing for her sympathy and even threatening—with a great air of seriousness—to kill himself rather than go back to jail. You can write that up easily and convincingly enough. But it's the sort of thing that bores me so frightfully to do. That's why I can never bring myself to write fiction. What is the point of it all? And the way you literary men think yourselves so important—particularly if you write tragedies. It's all very queer, very queer indeed."

I made no comment. Miss Penny changed her tone and went on with the narrative.

"Well," she said, "whatever the means employed, the engineering process was perfectly successful. Love was made to find out a way. On the afternoon before Kuno was to go back to prison, two Sisters of Charity walked out of the hospital gates, crossed the square in front of it, glided down the narrow streets towards the river, boarded a tram at the bridge, and did not descend till the car had reached its terminus in the farther suburbs. They began to walk briskly along the high road out into the country. 'Look!' said one of them, when they were clear of the houses; and with the gesture of a conjurer produced from nowhere a red leather purse. 'Where did it come from?' asked the other, opening her eyes. Memories of Elisha and the ravens, of the widow's cruse, of the loaves and fishes, must have floated through the radiant fog in poor Melpomene's mind. 'The old lady I was sitting next to in the tram left her bag open. Nothing could have been simpler.' 'Kuno! You don't mean to say you stole it?' Kuno swore horribly. He had opened the purse. 'Only sixty marks. Who'd have thought that an old camel, all dressed up in silk and furs, would only have sixty marks in her purse. And I must have a thousand at least to get away.' It's easy to reconstruct the rest of the conversation down to the inevitable, 'For God's sake, shut up,' with which Kuno put an end to Melpomene's dismayed moralizing. They trudge on in silence. Kuno thinks desperately. Only sixty marks; he can do nothing with that. If only he had something to sell, a piece of jewellery, some gold or silver—anything, anything. He knows such a good place for selling things. Is he to be caught again for lack of a few marks? Melpomene is also thinking. Evil must often be done that good may follow. After all, had not she herself stolen Sister Mary of the Purification's clothes when she was asleep after night duty? Had not she run away from the convent, broken her vows? And yet how convinced she was that she was doing rightly! The mysterious Powers emphatically approved; she felt sure of it. And now there was the red purse. But what was a red purse in comparison with a saved soul—and, after all, what was she doing but saving Kuno's soul?" Miss Penny, who had adopted the voice and gestures of a debater asking rhetorical questions, brought her hand with a slap on to the table. "Lord, what a bore this sort of stuff is!" she exclaimed. "Let's get to the end of this dingy anecdote as quickly as possible. By this time, you must imagine, the shades of night were falling fast—the chill November twilight, and so on; but I leave the natural descriptions to you. Kuno gets into the ditch at the roadside and takes off his robes. One imagines that he would feel himself safer in trousers, more capable of acting with decision in a crisis. They tramp on for miles. Late in the evening they leave the high road and strike up through the fields towards the forest. At the fringe of the wood they find one of those wheeled huts where the shepherds sleep in the lambing season.

"The real 'Maison du Berger.' "

"Precisely," said Miss Penny, and she began to recite:

> *'Si ton cœur gémissant du poids de notre vie*
> *Se traine et se débat comme un aigle blessé. . . .'*

How does it go on? I used to adore it all so much when I was a girl:

> *'Le seuil est perfumé, l'alcôve est large et sombre,*
> *Et là parmi les fleurs, nous trouverons dans l'ombre,*
> *Pour nos cheveux unis un lit silencieux.'*

I could go on like this indefinitely."

"Do," I said.

"No, no. No, no. I'm determined to finish this wretched story. Kuno broke the padlock of the door. They entered. What happened in that little hut?" Miss Penny leaned forward at me. Her large hare's eyes glittered, the long ear-rings swung and faintly tinkled. "Imagine the emotions of a virgin of thirty, and a nun at that, in the terrifying presence of desire. Imagine the easy, familiar brutalities of the young man. Oh, there's pages to be made out of this—the absolutely impenetrable darkness, the smell of straw, the voices, the strangled crying, the movements! And one likes to fancy that the emotions pulsing about in that confined space made palpable vibrations like a deep sound that shakes the air. Why, it's ready-made literature, this scene. In the morning," Miss Penny went on, after a pause, "two woodcutters on their way to work noticed that the door of the hut was ajar. They approached the hut cautiously, their axes raised and ready for a blow if there should be need of it. Peeping in, they saw a woman in a black dress lying face downwards in the straw. Dead? No; she moved, she moaned. 'What's the matter?' A blubbered face, smeared with streaks of tear-clotted grey dust, is lifted towards them. 'What's the matter?'—'He's gone!' What a queer, indistinct utterance. The woodcutters regard one another. What does she say? She's a foreigner, perhaps. 'What's the matter?' they repeat once more. The woman bursts out violently crying. 'Gone, gone! He's gone,' she sobs out in her vague, in-

articulate way. 'Oh, gone. That's what she says. Who's gone?'—
'He's left me.'—'What?'—'Left me ...'—'What the devil ...?
Speak a little more distinctly.'—'I can't,' she wails; 'he's taken
my teeth.'—'Your what?'—'My teeth!'—and the shrill voice
breaks into a scream, and she falls back sobbing into the straw.
The woodcutters look significantly at one another. They nod.
One of them applies a thick yellow-nailed forefinger to his
forehead."

Miss Penny looked at her watch.

"Good heavens!" she said, "it's nearly half-past three. I must
fly. Don't forget about the funeral service," she added, as she put
on her coat. "The tapers, the black coffin in the middle of the
aisle, the nuns in their white-winged coifs, the gloomy chanting,
and the poor cowering creature without any teeth, her face all
caved in like an old woman's, wondering whether she wasn't
really and in fact dead—wondering whether she wasn't already
in hell. Good-bye."

Little Mexican

THE shopkeeper called it, affectionately, a little Mexican; and little, for a Mexican, it may have been. But in this Europe of ours, where space is limited and the scale smaller, the little Mexican was portentous, a giant among hats. It hung there, in the centre of the hatter's window, a huge black aureole, fit for a king among devils. But no devil walked that morning through the streets of Ravenna; only the mildest of literary tourists. Those were the days when very large hats seemed in my eyes very desirable, and it was on my head, all unworthy, that the aureole of darkness was destined to descend. On my head; for at the first sight of the hat, I had run into the shop, tried it on, found the size correct, and bought it, without bargaining, at a foreigner's price. I left the shop with the little Mexican on my head, and my shadow on the pavements of Ravenna was like the shadow of an umbrella pine.

The little Mexican is very old now, and moth-eaten and green. But I still preserve it. Occasionally, for old associations' sake, I even wear it. Dear Mexican! it represents for me a whole epoch of my life. It stands for emancipation and the first year at the university. It symbolizes the discovery of how many new things, new ideas, new sensations!—of French literature, of alcohol, of modern painting, of Nietzsche, of love, of metaphysics, of Mallarmé, of syndicalism, and of goodness knows what else. But, above all, I prize it because it reminds me of my first discovery of Italy. It re-evokes for me, my little Mexican, all the thrills and astonishments and virgin raptures of that first Italian tour in the early autumn of 1912. Urbino, Rimini, Ravenna, Ferrara, Modena, Mantua, Verona, Vicenza, Padua, Venice—my first impressions of all these fabulous names lie, like a hatful of jewels, in the crown of the little Mexican. Shall I ever have the heart to throw it away?

And then, of course, there is Tirabassi. Without the little Mexican I should never have made Tirabassi's acquaintance. He would never have taken me, in my small unemphatic English hat, for a painter. And I should never, in consequence, have seen the frescoes, never have talked with the old Count, never heard of the Colombella. Never. . . . When I think of that, the little Mexican seems to me more than ever precious.

It was, of course, very typical of Tirabassi to suppose, from the size of my hat, that I must be a painter. He had a neat military mind that refused to accept the vague disorder of the world. He was for ever labelling and pigeon-holing and limiting his universe; and when the classified objects broke out of their pigeon-holes and tore the labels from off their necks, Tirabassi was puzzled and annoyed. In any case, it was obvious to him from the first moment he saw me in the restaurant at Padua, that I must be a painter. All painters wear large black hats. I was wearing the little Mexican. Ergo, I was a painter. It was syllogistic, unescapable.

He sent the waiter to ask me whether I would do him the honour of taking coffee with him at his table. For the first moment, I must confess, I was a little alarmed. This dashing young lieutenant of cavalry—what on earth could he want with me? The most absurd fancies filled my mind: I had committed, all unconsciously, some frightful solecism; I had trodden on the toes of the lieutenant's honour, and he was about to challenge me to a duel. The choice of weapons, I rapidly reflected, would be mine. But what—oh, what on earth should I choose? Swords? I had never learnt to fence. Pistols? I had once fired six shots at a bottle, and missed it with every shot. Would there be time to write one or two letters, make some sort of a testament about my personal belongings? From this anguish of mind the waiter, returning a moment later with my fried octopus, delivered me. The Lieutenant Count, he explained in a whisper of confidence, had a villa on the Brenta, not far from Strà. A villa—he spread out his hands in a generous gesture—full of paintings. Full, full, full. And he was anxious that I should see them, because he felt sure that I was interested in paintings. Oh, of course—I smiled rather foolishly, for the waiter seemed to expect some sort of confirmatory interpolation from me—I *was* interested in paintings; very much. In that case, said the waiter, the Count would be delighted to take me to see them. He left me, still puzzled, but vastly relieved. At any rate, I was not being called upon to make the very embarrassing choice between swords and pistols.

Surreptitiously, whenever he was not looking in my direction,

I examined the Lieutenant Count. His appearance was not typically Italian (but then what is a typical Italian?). He was not, that is to say, blue-jowled, beady-eyed, swarthy, and aquiline. On the contrary, he had pale ginger hair, grey eyes, a snub nose, and a freckled complexion. I knew plenty of young Englishmen who might have been Count Tirabassi's less vivacious brothers.

He received me, when the time came, with the most exquisite courtesy, apologizing for the unceremonious way in which he had made my acquaintance. "But as I felt sure," he said, "that you were interested in art, I thought you would forgive me for the sake of what I have to show you." I couldn't help wondering why the Count felt so certain about my interest in art. It was only later, when we left the restaurant together, that I understood; for, as I put on my hat to go, he pointed with a smile at the little Mexican. "One can see," he said, "that you are a real artist." I was left at a loss, not knowing what to answer.

After we had exchanged the preliminary courtesies, the Lieutenant plunged at once, entirely for my benefit I could see, into a conversation about art. "Nowadays," he said, "we Italians don't take enough interest in art. In a modern country, you see . . ." He shrugged his shoulders, leaving the sentence unfinished. "But I don't think that's right. I adore art. Simply adore it. When I see foreigners going round with their guidebooks, standing for half an hour in front of one picture, looking first at the book, then at the picture"—and here he gave the most brilliantly finished imitation of an Anglican clergyman conscientiously "doing" the Mantegna chapel: first a glance at the imaginary guide-book held open in his two hands, then, with the movement of a chicken that drinks, a lifting of the face towards an imaginary fresco, a long stare between puckered eyelids, a falling open of the mouth, and finally a turning back of the eyes towards the inspired pages of Baedeker—"when I see them, I feel ashamed for us Italians." The Count spoke very earnestly, feeling, no doubt, that his talent for mimicry had carried him a little too far. "And if they stand for half an hour looking at the thing, I go and stand there for an hour. That's the way to understand great art. The only way." He leaned back in his chair and sipped his coffee. "Unfortunately," he added, after a moment, "one hasn't got much time."

I agreed with him. "When one can only get to Italy for a month at a stretch, like myself . . ."

"Ah, but if only I could travel about the world like you!" The Count sighed. "But here I am, cooped up in this wretched town. And when I think of the enormous capital that's hanging there on the walls of my house . . ." He checked himself, shaking his head. Then, changing his tone, he began to tell me about his house on the Brenta. It sounded altogether too good to be true. Carpioni, yes—I could believe in frescoes by Carpioni; almost any one might have those. But a hall by Veronese, but rooms by Tiepolo, all in the same house—that sounded incredible. I could not help believing that the Count's enthusiasm for art had carried him away. But, in any case, to-morrow I should be able to judge for myself; the Count had invited me to lunch with him.

We left the restaurant. Still embarrassed by the Count's references to my little Mexican, I walked by his side in silence up the arcaded street.

"I am going to introduce you to my father," said the Count. " He, too, adores the arts."

More than ever I felt myself a swindler. I had wriggled into the Count's confidence on false pretences; my hat was a lie. I felt that I ought to do something to clear up the misunderstanding. But the Count was so busy complaining to me about his father that I had no opportunity to put in my explanation. I didn't listen very attentively, I confess, to what he was saying. In the course of a year at Oxford, I had heard so many young men complain of their fathers. Not enough money, too much interference—the story was a stale one. And at that time, moreover, I was taking a very high philosophical line about this sort of thing. I was pretending that people didn't interest me—only books, only ideas. What a fool one can make of oneself at that age!

"*Eccoci*," said the Count. We halted in front of the Café Pedrochi. "He always comes here for his coffee."

And where else, indeed, should he come for his coffee? Who, in Padua, would go anywhere else?

We found him sitting out on the terrace at the farther end of the building. I had never, I thought, seen a jollier-looking old gentleman. The old Count had a red weather-beaten face, with white moustaches bristling gallantly upwards and a white imperial in the grand Risorgimento manner of Victor Emmanuel the

Second. Under the white tufty eyebrows, and set in the midst of a webwork of fine wrinkles, the eyes were brown and bright like a robin's. His long nose looked, somehow, more practically useful than the ordinary human nose, as though made for fine judicial sniffing, for delicate burrowing and probing. Thick set and strong, he sat there solidly in his chair, his knees apart, his hands clasped over the knob of his cane, carrying his paunch with dignity, nobly I had almost said, before him. He was dressed all in white linen—for the weather was still very hot—and his wide grey hat was tilted rakishly forward over his left eye. It gave one a real satisfaction to look at him; he was so complete, so perfect in his kind.

The young Count introduced me. "This is an English gentleman. Signor . . ." He turned to me for the name.

"Oosselay," I said, having learnt by experience that that was as near as any Italian could be expected to get to it.

"Signor Oosselay," the young Count continued, "is an artist."

"Well, not exactly an artist," I was beginning; but he would not let me make an end.

"He is also very much interested in ancient art," he continued. "To-morrow I am taking him to Dolo to see the frescoes. I know he will like them."

We sat down at the old Count's table; critically he looked at me and nodded. "*Benissimo*," he said, and then added, "Let's hope you'll be able to do something to help us sell the things."

This was startling. I looked in some perplexity towards the young Count. He was frowning angrily at his father. The old gentleman had evidently said the wrong thing; he had spoken, I guessed, too soon. At any rate, he took his son's hint and glided off serenely on another tack.

"The fervid phantasy of Tiepolo," he began rotundly, "the cool, unimpassioned splendour of Veronese—at Dolo you will see them contrasted." I listened attentively, while the old gentleman thundered on in what was evidently a set speech. When it was over, the young Count got up; he had to be back at the barracks by half-past two. I too made as though to go; but the old man laid his hand on my arm. "Stay with me," he said. "I enjoy your conversation infinitely." And as he himself had hardly ceased speaking for one moment since first I set eyes on him, I could well believe it. With the gesture of a lady lifting her skirts out of the mud (and those were the days when skirts still had to be lifted) the young Count picked up his trailing sabre and swaggered off, very military, very brilliant and glittering, like a soldier on the stage, into the sunlight, out of sight.

The old man's bird-bright eyes followed him as he went. "A good boy, Fabio," he said, turning back to me at last, "a good son." He spoke affectionately; but there was a hint, I thought, in his smile, in the tone of his voice, a hint of amusement, of irony. It was as though he were adding, by implication, "But good boys, after all, are fools to be so good." I found myself, in spite of my affectation of detachment, extremely curious about this old gentleman. And he, for his part, was not the man to allow any one in his company to remain for long in splendid isolation. He insisted on my taking an interest in his affairs. He told me all about them—or at any rate all about some of them—pouring out his confidences with an astonishing absence of reserve. Next to the intimate and trusted friend, the perfect stranger is the best of all possible confidants. There is no commercial traveller, of moderately sympathetic appearance, who has not, in the course of his days in the train, his evenings in the parlours of commercial hotels, been made the repository of a thousand intimate secrets—even in England. And in Italy—goodness knows what commercial travellers get told in Italy. Even I, a foreigner, speaking the language badly, and not very skilful anyhow in conducting a conversation with strangers, have heard queer things in the second-class carriages of Italian trains. . . . Here, too, on Pedrochi's terrace I was to hear queer things. A door was to be left ajar, and through the crack I was to have a peep at unfamiliar lives.

"What I should do without him," the old gentleman continued, "I really don't know. The way he manages the estate is simply wonderful." And he went rambling off into long digressions about the stupidity of peasants, the incompetence and dishonesty of bailiffs, the badness of the weather, the spread of phylloxera, the high price of manure. The upshot of it all was that, since Fabio had taken over the estate, everything had gone well; even the weather had improved. "It's such a relief," the Count concluded, "to feel that I have some one in charge on whom I can rely, some one I can trust, absolutely. It leaves me free to devote my mind to more important things."

I could not help wondering what the important things were; but it would have been impertinent, I felt, to ask. Instead, I put a more practical question. "But what will happen," I asked, "when your son's military duties take him away from Padua?"

The old Count gave me a wink and laid his forefinger, very deliberately, to the side of his long nose. The gesture was rich with significance. "They never will," he said. "It's all arranged. A little *combinazione*, you know. I have a friend in the Ministry. His military duties will always keep him in Padua." He winked again and smiled.

I could not help laughing, and the old Count joined in with a joyous ha-ha that was the expression of a profound satisfaction, that was, as it were, a burst of self-applause. He was evidently proud of his little *combinazione*. But he was prouder still of the other combination, about which he now confidentially leaned across the table to tell me. It was decidedly the subtler of the two.

"And it's not merely his military duties," he said, wagging at me the thick, yellow-nailed forefinger which he had laid against his nose, "it's not merely his military duties that'll keep the boy in Padua. It's his domestic duties. He's married. I married him." He leaned back in his chair, and surveyed me, smiling. The little wrinkles round his eyes seemed to be alive. "That boy, I said to myself, must settle down. He must have a nest, or else he'll fly away. He must have roots, or else he'll run. And his poor old father will be left in the lurch. He's young, I thought, but he must marry. He *must* marry. At once." And the old gentleman made great play with his forefinger. It was a long story. His old friend, the Avvocato Monaldeschi, had twelve children—three boys and nine girls. (And here there were digressions about the Avvocato and the size of good Catholic families.) The eldest girl was just the right age for Fabio. No money, of course; but a good girl and pretty, and very well brought up and religious. Religious —that was very important, for it was essential that Fabio should have a large family—to keep him more effectually rooted, the old Count explained—and with these modern young women brought up outside the Church one could never be certain of children. Yes, her religion was most important; he had looked into that very carefully before selecting her. Well, the next thing, of course, was that Fabio should be induced to select her. It had been a matter of bringing the horse to water *and* making him drink. Oh, a most difficult and delicate business! For Fabio prided himself on his independence; and he was obstinate, like a mule. Nobody should interfere with his affairs, nobody should make him do what he didn't want to. And he was so touchy, he was so pig-headed that often he wouldn't do what he really wanted, merely because somebody else had suggested that he ought to do it. So I could imagine—the old Count spread out his hands before me—just how difficult and delicate a business it had been. Only a consummate diplomat could have succeeded. He did it by throwing them together a great deal and talking, meanwhile, about the rashness of early marriages, the uselessness of poor wives, the undesirability of wives not of noble birth. It worked like a charm; within four months, Fabio was engaged; two months later he was married, and ten months after that he had a son and heir. And now he was fixed, rooted. The old gentleman chuckled, and I could fancy that I was listening to the chuckling of some old white-haired tyrant of the quattrocento, congratulating himself on the success of some peculiarly ingenious stroke of policy—a rich city induced to surrender itself by fraud, a dangerous rival lured by fair words into a cage and trapped. Poor Fabio, I thought; and also, what a waste of talent!

Yes, the old Count went on, now he would never go. He was not like his younger brother, Lucio. Lucio was a rogue, *furbo*, sly; he had no conscience. But Fabio had ideas about duty, and lived up to them. Once he had engaged himself, he would stick to his engagements, obstinately, with all the mulishness of his character. Well, now he lived on the estate, in the big painted house at Dolo. Three days a week he came into Padua for his military duties, and the rest of his time he devoted to the estate. It brought in, now, more than it had ever done before. But goodness knew, the old man complained, that was little enough. Bread and oil, and wine and milk, and chickens and beef—there was plenty of those and to spare. Fabio could have a family of fifty and they would never starve. But ready money—there wasn't much of that. "In England," the Count concluded, "you are rich. But we Italians . . ." He shook his head.

I spent the next quarter of an hour trying to persuade him that we were not all millionaires. But in vain. My statistics, based on somewhat imperfect memories of Mr and Mrs Sidney Webb, carried no conviction. In the end I gave it up.

The next morning Fabio appeared at the door of my hotel in a large, very old and very noisy Fiat. It was the family machine-of-all-work, bruised, scratched, and dirtied by years of service. Fabio drove it with a brilliant and easy recklessness. We rushed through the town, swerving from one side of the narrow street to the other, with a disregard for the rules of the road which, in a pedantic country like England, would have meant at the least a five-pound fine and an endorsed licence. But here the Carabiniers, walking gravely in couples under the arcades, let us pass without comment. Right or left—after all, what did it matter?

"Why do you keep the silencer out?" I shouted through the frightful clamour of the engine.

Fabio slightly shrugged his shoulders. "*È più allegro così,*" he answered.

I said no more. From a member of this hardy race which likes noise, which enjoys discomfort, a nerve-ridden Englishman could hardly hope to get much sympathy.

We were soon out of the town. Trailing behind us a seething white wake of dust and with the engine rattling off its explosions like a battery of machine-guns, we raced along the Fusina road. On either hand extended the cultivated plain. The road was bordered by ditches, and on the banks beyond, instead of hedges, stood rows of little pollards, with grape-laden vines festooned from tree to tree. White with the dust, tendrils, fruit, and leaves hung there like so much goldsmith's work sculptured in frosted metal, hung like the swags of fruit and foliage looped round the flanks of a great silver bowl. We hurried on. Soon, on our right hand, we had the Brenta, sunk deep between the banks of its canal. And now we were at Strà. Through gateways rich with fantastic stucco, down tunnels of undeciduous shade, we looked in a series of momentary glimpses into the heart of the park. And now for an instant the statues on the roof of the villa beckoned against the sky and were passed. On we went. To right and left, on either bank of the river, I got every now and then a glimpse of some enchanting mansion, gay and brilliant even in decay. Little baroque garden houses peeped at me over walls; and through great gates, at the end of powdery cypress avenues, half humorously, it seemed, the magniloquent and frivolous façades soared up in defiance of all the rules. I should have liked to do the journey slowly, to stop here and there, to look, to savour at leisure; but Fabio disdained to travel at anything less than fifty kilometres to the hour, and I had to be content with momentary and precarious glimpses. It was in these villas, I reflected, as we bumped along at the head of our desolation of white dust, that Casanova used to come and spend the summer; seducing the chamber-maids, taking advantage of terrified marchionesses in *calèches* during thunder-storms, bamboozling soft-witted old senators of Venice with his fortune-telling and black magic. Gorgeous and happy scoundrel! In spite of my professed detachment, I envied him. And, indeed, what was that famous detachment but a disguised expression of the envy which the successes and audacities of a Casanova must necessarily arouse in every timid and diffident mind? If I lived in splendid isolation, it was because I lacked the audacity to make war—even to make entangling alliances. I was absorbed in these pleasing self-condemnatory thoughts, when the car slowed down and came to a standstill in front of a huge imposing gate. Fabio hooted impatiently on his horn; there was a scurry of footsteps, the sound of bolts being drawn, and the gate swung open. At the end of a short drive, very large and grave, very chaste and austere, stood the house. It was considerably older than most of the other villas I had seen in glimpses on our way. There was no frivolousness in its façade, no irregular grandiloquence. A great block of stuccoed brick; a central portico approached by steps and topped with a massive pediment; a row of rigid statues on the balustrade above the cornice. It was correctly, coldly even, Palladian. Fabio brought the car to a halt in front of the porch. We got out. At the top of the steps stood a young woman with a red-headed child in her arms. It was the Countess with the son and heir.

The Countess impressed me very agreeably. She was slim and tall—two or three inches taller than her husband; with dark hair, drawn back from the forehead and twisted into a knot on the nape of her neck; dark eyes, vague, lustrous, and melancholy, like the eyes of a gentle animal; a skin brown and transparent like darkened amber. Her manner was gentle and unemphatic. She rarely gesticulated; I never heard her raise her voice. She spoke, indeed, very little. The old Count had told me that his daughter-in-law was religious, and from her appearance I could easily believe it. She looked at you with the calm, remote regard of one whose life mostly goes on behind the eyes.

Fabio kissed his wife and then, bending his face towards the child, he made a frightful grimace and roared like a lion. It was all done in affection; but the poor little creature shrank away, terrified. Fabio laughed and pinched its ear.

"Don't tease him," said the Countess gently. "You'll make him cry."

Fabio turned to me. "That's what comes of leaving a boy to be looked after by women. He cries at everything. Let's come in," he added. "At present we only use two or three rooms on the ground floor, and the kitchen in the basement. All the rest is deserted. I don't know how these old fellows managed to keep up their palaces. I can't." He shrugged his shoulders. Through a door on the right of the portico we passed into the house. "This is our drawing-room and dining-room combined."

It was a fine big room, nobly proportioned—a double cube, I guessed—with doorways of sculptured marble and a magnificent fireplace flanked by a pair of nymphs on whose bowed shoulders rested a sloping overmantel carved with coats of arms and festoons of foliage. Round the walls ran a frieze, painted in grisaille; in a graceful litter of cornucopias and panoplies, goddesses sumptuously reclined, cherubs wriggled and flew. The furniture was strangely mixed. Round a sixteenth-century dining-table that was a piece of Palladian architecture in wood, were ranged eight chairs in the Viennese secession style of 1905. A large chalet-shaped cuckoo clock from Bern hung on the wall between two cabinets of walnut, pilastered and pedimented to look like little temples, and with heroic statuettes in yellow boxwood, standing in niches between the pillars. And then the pictures on the walls, the cretonnes with which the arm-chairs were covered! Tactfully, however, I admired everything, new as well as old.

"And now," said the Count, "for the frescoes."

I followed him through one of the marble-framed doorways and found myself at once in the great central hall of the villa. The Count turned round to me. "There!" he said, smiling triumphantly with the air of one who has really succeeded in producing a rabbit out of an empty hat. And, indeed, the spectacle was sufficiently astonishing.

The walls of the enormous room were completely covered with frescoes which it did not need much critical judgment or knowledge to perceive were genuine Veroneses. The authorship was obvious, palpable. Who else could have painted those harmoniously undulating groups of figures set in their splendid architectural frame? Who else but Veronese could have combined such splendour with such coolness, so much extravagant opulence with such exquisite suavity?

"*È grandioso!*" I said to the Count.

And indeed it was. Grandiose; there was no other word. A rich triumphal arcade ran all round the room, four or five arches appearing on each wall. Through the arches one looked into a garden; and there, against a background of cypresses and statues and far-away blue mountains, companies of Venetian ladies and gentlemen gravely disported themselves. Under one arch they were making music; through another, one saw them sitting round a table, drinking one another's health in glasses of red wine, while a little blackamoor in a livery of green and yellow carried round the silver jug. In the next panel they were watching a fight between a monkey and a cat. On the opposite wall a poet was reading his verses to the assembled company, and next to him Veronese himself—the self-portrait was recognizable—stood at his easel, painting the picture of an opulent blonde in rose-coloured satin. At the feet of the artist lay his dog; two parrots and a monkey were sitting on the marble balustrade in the middle distance.

I gazed with delight. "What a marvellous thing to possess!" I exclaimed, fairly carried away by my enthusiasm. "I envy you."

The Count made a little grimace and laughed. "Shall we come and look at the Tiepolos?" he asked.

We passed through a couple of cheerful rooms by Carpioni—satyrs chasing nymphs through a romantic forest and, on the fringes of a seascape, a very eccentric rape of mermaids by centaurs—to step across a threshold into that brilliant universe, at once delicate and violently extravagant, wild and subtly orderly, which Tiepolo, in the last days of Italian painting, so masterfully and magically created. It was the story of Eros and Psyche, and the tale ran through three large rooms, spreading itself even on to the ceilings, where, in a pale sky dappled with white and golden clouds, the appropriate deities balanced themselves, diving or ascending through the empyrean with that air of being perfectly at home in their element which seems to belong, in nature, only to fishes and perhaps a few winged insects and birds.

Fabio had boasted to me that, in front of a picture, he could outstare any foreigner. But I was such a mortally long time admiring these dazzling phantasies that in the end he quite lost patience.

"I wanted to show you the farm before lunch," he said, looking at his watch. "There's only just time." I followed him reluctantly. We looked at the cows, the horses, the prize bull, the turkeys. We looked at the tall, thin haystacks, shaped like giant cigars set on end. We looked at the sacks of wheat in the barn. For lack of any better comment I told the Count that they reminded me of the sacks of wheat in English barns; he seemed delighted.

The farm buildings were set round an immense courtyard. We had explored three sides of this piazza; now we came to the fourth, which was occupied by a long, low building pierced with round archways and, I was surprised to see, completely empty.

"What's this?" I asked, as we entered.

"It *is* nothing," the Count replied. "But it might, some day, become . . . *chi sa*?" He stood there for a moment in silence, frowning pensively, with the expression of Napoleon on St Helena—dreaming of the future, regretting past opportunities for ever lost. His freckled face, ordinarily a lamp for brightness, became incongruously sombre. Then all at once he burst out—damning life, cursing fate, wishing to God he could get away and do something instead of wasting himself here. I listened, making every now and then a vague noise of sympathy. What could I do about it? And then, to my dismay, I found that I could do something about it, that I was expected to do something. I was being asked to help the Count to sell his frescoes. As an artist, it was obvious, I must be acquainted with rich patrons, museums, millionaires. I had seen the frescoes; I could honestly recommend them. And now there was this perfected process for transferring frescoes on to canvas. The walls could easily be peeled of their painting, the canvases rolled up and taken to Venice. And from there it would be the easiest thing in the world to smuggle them on board a ship and get away with them. As for prices—if he could get a million and a half of lire, so much the better; but he'd take a million, he'd even take three-quarters. And he'd give me ten per cent. commission. . . .

And afterwards, when he'd sold his frescoes, what would he do? To begin with—the Count smiled at me triumphantly—he'd turn this empty building in which we were now standing into an up-to-date cheese-factory. He could start the business handsomely on half a million, and then, using cheap female labour from the country round, he could be almost sure of making big profits at once. In a couple of years, he calculated, he'd be netting eighty or a hundred thousand a year from his cheeses. And then, ah then, he'd be independent, he'd be able to get away, he'd see the world. He'd go to Brazil and the Argentine. An enterprising man with capital could always do well out there. He'd go to New York, to London, to Berlin, to Paris. There was nothing he could not do.

But meanwhile the frescoes were still on the walls—beautiful, no doubt (for, the Count reminded me, he adored art), but futile; a huge capital frozen into the plaster, eating its head off, utterly useless. Whereas, with his cheese-factory . . .

Slowly we walked back towards the house.

I was in Venice again in the September of the following year, 1913. There were, I imagine, that autumn, more German honey-moon-couples, more parties of rucksacked Wander-Birds than there had ever been in Venice before. There were too many, in any case, for me; I packed my bag and took the train for Padua.

I had not originally intended to see young Tirabassi again. I didn't know, indeed, how pleased he would be to see me. For the frescoes, so far as I knew, at any rate, were still safely on the walls, the cheese-factory still remote in the future, in the imagination. I had written to him more than once, telling him that I was doing my best, but that at the moment, etcetera, etcetera. Not that I had ever held out much hope. I had made it clear from the first that my acquaintance among millionaires was limited, that I knew no directors of American museums, that I had nothing to do with any of the international picture dealers. But the Count's faith in me had remained, none the less, unshaken. It was the little Mexican, I believe, that inspired so much confidence. But now, after my letters, after all this lapse of time and nothing done, he might feel that I had let him down, deceived him somehow. That was why I took no steps to seek him out. But chance over-ruled my decision. On the third day of my stay in Padua, I ran into him in the street. Or rather he ran into me.

It was nearly six o'clock, and I had strolled down to the Piazza del Santo. At that hour, when the slanting light is full of colour and the shadows are long and profound, the great church, with its cupolas and turrets and campaniles, takes on an aspect more than ever fantastic and oriental. I had walked round the church, and now I was standing at the foot of Donatello's statue, looking up at the grim bronze man, the ponderously stepping beast, when I suddenly became aware that some one was standing very close behind me. I took a step to one side and turned round. It was Fabio. Wearing his famous expression of the sight-seeing parson, he was gazing up at the statue, his mouth open in a vacant and fish-like gape. I burst out laughing.

"Did I look like that?" I asked.

"Precisely." He laughed too. "I've been watching you for the last ten minutes, mooning round the church. You English! Really . . ." He shook his head.

Together we strolled up the Via del Santo, talking as we went.

"I'm sorry I wasn't able to do anything about the frescoes," I said. "But really . . ." I entered into explanations.

"Some day, perhaps." Fabio was still optimistic.

"And how's the Countess?"

"Oh, she's very well," said Fabio, "considering. You know she had another son three or four months after you came to see us."

"No?"

"She's expecting another now." Fabio spoke rather gloomily, I thought. More than ever I admired the old Count's sagacity. But I was sorry, for his son's sake, that he had not a wider field in which to exercise his talents.

"And your father?" I asked. "Shall we find him sitting at Pedrochi's, as usual?"

Fabio laughed. "We shall not," he said significantly. "He's flown."

"Flown?"

"Gone, vanished, disappeared."

"But where?"

"Who knows?" said Fabio. "My father is like the swallows; he comes and he goes. Every year. . . . But the migration isn't regular. Sometimes he goes away in the spring; sometimes it's the autumn, sometimes it's the summer. . . . One fine morning his man goes into his room to call him as usual, and he isn't there. Vanished. He might be dead. Oh, but he isn't." Fabio laughed. "Two or three months later, in he walks again, as though he were just coming back from a stroll in the Botanical Gardens. 'Good evening. Good evening.' " Fabio imitated the old Count's voice and manner, snuffing the air like a war-horse, twisting the ends of an imaginary white moustache. " 'How's your mother? How are the girls? How have the grapes done this year?' Snuff, snuff. 'How's Lucio? And who the devil has left all this rubbish lying about in my study?' " Fabio burst into an indignant roar that made the loiterers in the Via Roma turn, astonished, in our direction.

"And where does he go?" I asked.

"Nobody knows. My mother used to ask, once. But she soon gave it up. It was no good. 'Where have you been, Ascanio?' 'My dear, I'm afraid the olive crop is going to be very poor this year.' Snuff, snuff. And when she pressed him, he would fly into a temper and slam the doors. . . . What do you say to an aperitif?" Pedrochi's open doors invited. We entered, chose a retired table, and sat down.

"But what do you suppose the old gentleman does when he's away?"

"Ah!" And making the richly significant gesture I had so much admired in his father, the young Count laid his finger against his nose and slowly, solemnly winked his left eye.

"You mean . . .?"

Fabio nodded. "There's a little widow here in Padua." With his extended finger the young Count described in the air an undulating line. "Nice and plump. Black eyes. I've noticed that she generally seems to be out of town just at the time the old man does his migrations. But it may, of course, be a mere coincidence." The waiter brought us our vermouth. Pensively the young Count sipped. The gaiety went out of his open, lamp-like face. "And meanwhile," he went on slowly and in an altered voice, "I stay here, looking after the estate, so that the old man can go running round the world with his little pigeon—la sua colombella." (The expression struck me as particularly choice.) "Oh, it's funny, no doubt," the young Count went on. "But it isn't right. If I wasn't married, I'd go clean away and try my luck somewhere else. I'd leave him to look after everything himself. But with a wife and two children—three children soon—how can I take the risk? At any rate, there's plenty to eat as long as I stay here. My only hope," he added, after a little pause, "is in the frescoes."

Which implied, I reflected, that his only hope was in me; I felt sorry for him.

In the spring of 1914 I sent two rich Americans to look at Fabio's villa. Neither of them made any offer to buy the frescoes; it would have astonished me if they had. But Fabio was greatly encouraged by their arrival. "I feel," he wrote to me, "that a beginning has now been made. These Americans will go back to their country and tell their friends. Soon there will be a procession of millionaires coming to see the frescoes. Meanwhile, life is the same as ever. Rather worse, if anything. Our little daughter, whom we have christened Emilia, was born last month. My wife had a very bad time and is still far from well, which is very troublesome." (It seemed a curious adjective to use, in the circumstances. But coming from Fabio, I understood it; he was one of those exceedingly healthy people to whom any sort of illness is mysterious, unaccountable, and above all extraordinarily tiresome and irritating.) "The day before yesterday my father disappeared again. I have not yet had time to find out if the Colombella has also vanished. My brother, Lucio, has succeeded in getting a motor-bicycle out of him, which is more than I ever managed to do. But then I was never one for creeping diplomatically round and round a thing, as he can do. . . . I have been going very carefully into the cheese-factory business lately, and I am not sure that it might not be more profitable to set up a silk-weaving establishment instead. When you next come, I will go into details with you."

But it was a very long time before I saw Padua and the Count again. . . . The War put an end to my yearly visits to Italy, and for various reasons, even when it was over, I could not go south again as soon as I should have liked. Not till the autumn of 1921 did I embark again on the Venice express.

It was in an Italy not altogether familiar that I now found myself—an Italy full of violence and bloodshed. The Fascists and the Communists were still busily fighting. Roaring at the head of their dust-storms, the motor-lorries, loaded with cargoes of singing boys, careered across the country in search of adventure and lurking Bolshevism. One stood respectfully in the gutter while they passed; and through the flying dust, through the noise of the engine, a snatch of that singing would be blown back: "*Giovinezza, giovinezza, primavera di bellezza* . . ." (Youth, youth, springtime of beauty.) Where but in Italy would they have put such words to a political song? And then the proclamations, the manifestos, the denunciations, the appeals! Every hoarding and blank wall was plastered with them. Between the station and Pedrochi's I walked through a whole library of these things. "Citizens!" they would begin. "A heroic wind is to-day reviving the almost asphyxiated soul of our unhappy Italy, overcome by the poisonous fumes of Bolshevism and wallowing in ignoble abasement at the feet of the Nations." And they finished, for the most part, with references to Dante. I read them all with infinite pleasure.

I reached Pedrochi's at last. On the terrace, sitting in the very corner where I had seen him first, years before, was the old Count. He stared at me blankly when I saluted him, not recognizing me at all. I began to explain who I was; after a moment he cut me short, almost impatiently, protesting that he remembered now, perfectly well. I doubted very much whether he really did; but he was too proud to confess that he had forgotten. Meanwhile, he invited me to sit at his table.

At a first glance, from a distance, I fancied that the old Count had not aged a day since last I saw him. But I was wrong. From the street, I had only seen the rakish tilt of his hat, the bristling of his white moustache and imperial, the parted knees, the noble protrusion of the paunch. But now that I could look at him closely and at leisure, I saw that he was in fact a very different man. Under the tilted hat his face was unhealthily purple; the flesh sagged into pouches. In the whites of his eyes, discoloured and as though tarnished with age, the little broken veins showed red. And, lustreless, the eyes themselves seemed to look without interest at what they saw. His shoulders were bent as though under a weight, and when he lifted his cup to his lips his hand trembled so much that a drop of coffee splashed on to the table. He was an old man now, old and tired.

"How's Fabio?" I asked; since 1916 I had had no news of him.

"Oh, Fabio's well," the old Count answered, "Fabio's very well. He has six children now, you know." And the old gentleman nodded and smiled at me without a trace of malice. He seemed quite to have forgotten the reasons for which he had been at so much pains to select a good Catholic for a daughter-in-law. "Six," he repeated. "And then, you know, he did very well in the war. We Tirabassi have always been warriors." Full of pride, he went on to tell me of Fabio's exploits and sufferings. Twice wounded, special promotion on the field of battle, splendid decorations. He was a major now.

"And do his military duties still keep him in Padua?"

The old gentleman nodded, and suddenly there appeared on his face something like the old smile. "A little *combinazione* of mine," he said, and chuckled.

"And the estate?" I asked.

Oh, that was doing all right, everything considered. It had got rather out of hand during the war, while Fabio was at the front. And then, afterwards, there had been a lot of trouble with the peasants; but Fabio and his Fascists were putting all that to rights. "With Fabio on the spot," said the old gentleman, "I have no anxieties." And then he began to tell me, all over again, about Fabio's exploits in the war.

The next day I took the train to Strà, and after an hour agreeably spent in the villa and the park, I walked on at my leisure towards Dolo. It took me a long time to get there, for on this occasion I was able to stop and look for as long as I liked at all the charming things on the way. Casanova seemed, now, a good deal less enviable, I noticed, looking inwards on myself, than he had when last I passed this way. I was nine years older.

The gates were open; I walked in. There stood the house, as grave and ponderous as ever, but shabbier than when I saw it last. The shutters needed painting, and here and there the stucco was peeling off in scabs. I approached. From within the house came a cheerful noise of children's laughter and shouting. The family, I supposed, was playing hide-and-seek, or trains, or perhaps some topical game of Fascists and Communists. As I climbed the steps of the porch, I could hear the sound of small feet racing over the tiled floors; in the empty rooms footsteps and shouting strangely echoed. And then suddenly, from the sitting-room on the right, came the sound of Fabio's voice, furiously shouting, "Oh, for God's sake," it yelled, "keep those wretched children quiet." And then, petulantly, it complained, "How do you expect me to do accounts with this sort of thing going on?" There was at once a profound and as it were unnatural silence; then the sound of small feet tiptoeing away, some whispering, a little nervous laugh. I rang the bell.

It was the Countess who opened the door. She stood for a

moment hesitatingly, wondering who I was; then remembered, smiled, held out her hand. She had grown, I noticed, very thin, and with the wasting of her face, her eyes seemed to have become larger. Their expression was as gentle and serene as ever; she seemed to be looking at me from a distance.

"Fabio will be delighted to see you," she said, and she took me through the door on the right of the porch straight into the sitting-room. Fabio was sitting at the Palladian table in front of a heap of papers, biting the end of his pencil.

Even in his grey-green service uniform the young Count looked wonderfully brilliant, like a soldier on the stage. His face was still boyishly freckled, but the skin was deeply lined; he looked very much older than when I had seen him last—older than he really was. The open cheerfulness, the shining, lamp-like brightness were gone. On his snubby-featured face he wore a ludicrously incongruous expression of chronic melancholy. He brightened, it is true, for a moment when I appeared; I think he was genuinely glad to see me.

"*Caspita!*" he kept repeating. "*Caspita!*" (It was his favourite expression of astonishment, an odd, old-fashioned word.) "Who would have thought it? After all this time!"

"And all the eternity of the war as well," I said.

But when the first ebullition of surprise and pleasure subsided, the look of melancholy came back.

"It gives me the spleen," he said, "to see you again; still travelling about; free to go where you like. If you knew what life was like here . . ."

"Well, in any case," I said, feeling that I ought, for the Countess's sake, to make some sort of protest, "in any case the war's over, and you have escaped a real revolution. That's something."

"Oh, you're as bad as Laura," said the Count impatiently. He looked towards his wife, as though hoping that she would say something. But the Countess went on with her sewing without even looking up. The Count took my arm. "Come along," he said, and his tone was almost one of anger. "Let's take a turn outside." His wife's religious resignation, her patience, her serenity angered him, I could see, like a reprimand—tacit, indeed, and unintentionally given, but none the less galling.

Along the weed-grown paths of what had once, in the ancient

days of splendour, been the garden, slowly we walked towards the farm. A few ragged box-trees grew along the fringes of the paths; once there had been neat hedges. Poised over a dry basin a Triton blew his waterless conch. At the end of the vista a pair of rapes—Pluto and Proserpine, Apollo and Daphne—writhed desparately against the sky.

"I saw your father yesterday," I said. "He looks aged."

"And so he ought," said Fabio murderously. "He's sixty-nine."

I felt uncomfortably that the subject had become too serious for light conversation. I had wanted to ask after the Colombella; in the circumstances, I decided that it would be wiser to say nothing about her. I repressed my curiosity. We were walking now under the lea of the farm buildings.

"The cows look very healthy," I said politely, looking through an open doorway. In the twilight within, six grey rumps plastered with dry dung presented themselves in file; six long leather tails swished impatiently from side to side. Fabio made no comment; he only grunted.

"In any case," he went on slowly, after another silence, "he can't live much longer. I shall sell my share and clear off to South America, family or no family." It was a threat against his own destiny, a threat of which he must have known the vanity. He was deceiving himself to keep up his spirits.

"But I say," I exclaimed, taking another and better opportunity to change the conversation, "I see you have started a factory here after all." We had walked round to the farther side of the square. Through the windows of the long low building which, at my last visit, had stood untenanted, I saw the complicated shapes of machines, rows of them in a double line down the whole length of the building. "Looms? Then you decided against cheese? And the frescoes?" I turned questioningly towards the Count. I had a horrible fear that, when we got back to the house, I should find the great hall peeled of its Veroneses and a blank of plaster where once had been the history of Eros and Psyche.

"Oh, the frescoes are still there, what's left of them." And in spite of Fabio's long face, I was delighted at the news. "I persuaded my father to sell some of his house property in Padua, and we started this weaving business here two years ago. Just in time," Fabio added, "for the Communist revolution."

Poor Fabio, he had no luck. The peasants had seized his factory and had tried to possess themselves of his land. For three weeks he had lived at the villa in a state of siege, defending the place, with twenty Fascists to help him, against all the peasants of the countryside. The danger was over now; but the machines were broken, and in any case it was out of the question to start them again; feeling was still too high. And what, for Fabio, made it worse was the fact that his brother Lucio, who had also got a little capital out of the old man, had gone off to Bulgaria and invested it in a bootlace factory. It was the only bootlace factory in the country, and Lucio was making money hand over fist. Free as air he was, well off, with a lovely Turkish girl for a mistress. For Fabio, the Turkish girl was evidently the last straw. "*Una Turca, una vera Turca,*" he repeated, shaking his head. The female infidel symbolized in his eyes all that was exotic, irregular, undomestic; all that was not the family; all that was remote from Padua and the estate.

"And they were such beautiful machines," said Fabio, pausing for a moment to look in at the last of the long line of windows. "Whether to sell them, whether to wait till all this has blown over and have them put right and try to start again—I don't know." He shrugged his shoulders hopelessly. "Or just let things slide till the old man dies." We turned the corner of the square and began to walk back towards the house. "Sometimes," he added, after a silence, "I don't believe he ever will die."

The children were playing in the great hall of the Veroneses. The majestic double doors which gave on to the portico were ajar; through the opening we watched them for a moment without being seen. The family was formed up in order of battle. A red-headed boy of ten or eleven led the van, a brown boy followed. Then came three little girls, diminishing regularly in size like graded pearls; and finally a little toddling creature in blue linen crawlers. All six of them carried shouldered bamboos, and they were singing in ragged unison to a kind of trumpet call of three notes: "*All' armi i Fascisti; a morte i Communisti; a basso i Socialisti*"— over and over again. And as they sang they marched, round and round, earnestly, indefatigably. The huge empty room echoed like a swimming-bath. Remote under their triumphal arches, in their serene world of fantastic beauty, the silken ladies and gentlemen played their music, drank their wine; the poet declaimed, the painter poised his brush before the canvas; the monkeys clambered among the Roman ruins, the parrots dozed on the balustrades. "*All' armi i Fascisti, a morte i Communisti* . . ." I should have liked to stand there in silence, merely to see how long the children would continue their patriotic march. But Fabio had none of my scientific curiosity; or if he ever had, it had certainly been exhausted long before the last of his children was born. After indulging me for a moment with the spectacle, he pushed open the door and walked in. The children looked round and were immediately silent. What with his bad temper and his theory of education by teasing, they seemed to be thoroughly frightened of their father.

"Go on," he said, "go on." But they wouldn't; they obviously couldn't, in his terrifying presence. Unobtrusively they slipped away.

Fabio led me round the painted room. "Look here," he said, "and look here." In one of the walls of the great hall there were half a dozen bullet holes. A chip had been taken off one of the painted cornices; one lady was horribly wounded in the face; there were two or three holes in the landscape, and a monkey's tail was severed. "That's our friends, the peasants," Fabio explained.

In the Carpioni rooms all was still well; the satyrs still pursued their nymphs, and in the room of the centaurs and the mermaids, the men who were half horses still galloped as tumultuously as ever into the sea, to ravish the women who were half fish. But the tale of Eros and Psyche had suffered dreadfully. The exquisite panel in which Tiepolo had painted Psyche holding up the lamp to look at her mysterious lover was no more than a faint, mildewy smudge. And where once the indignant young god had flown upwards to rejoin his Olympian relatives (who still, fortunately, swam about intact among the clouds on the ceiling) there was nothing but the palest ghost of an ascending Cupid, while Psyche weeping on the earth below was now quite invisible.

"That's our friends the French," said Fabio. "They were quartered here in 1918, and they didn't trouble to shut the windows when it rained."

Poor Fabio! Everything was against him. I had no consolation to offer. That autumn I sent him an art critic and three more Americans. But nothing came of their visits. The fact was that he had too much to offer. A picture—that might easily have been disposed of. But what could one do with a whole houseful of paintings like this?

The months passed. About Easter time of the next year I had another letter from Fabio. The olive crop had been poor. The Countess was expecting another baby and was far from well. The two eldest children were down with measles, and the last but one had what the Italians call an "asinine cough." He expected all the children to catch both diseases in due course. He was very doubtful now if it would ever be worth while to restart his looms; the position of the silk trade was not so sound as it had been at the end of 1919. If only he had stuck to cheese, as he first intended! Lucio had just made fifty thousand lire by a lucky stroke of speculation. But the female infidel had run off with a Rumanian. The old Count was ageing rapidly; when Fabio saw him last, he had told the same anecdote three times in the space of ten minutes. With these two pieces of good news—they were for him, I imagine, the only bright spots in the surrounding gloom—Fabio closed his letter. I was left wondering why he troubled to write to me at all. It may be that he got a certain lacerating satisfaction by thus enumerating his troubles.

That August there was a musical festival in Salzburg. I had never been in Austria; the occasion seemed to me a good one. I went, and I enjoyed myself prodigiously. Salzburg at the moment is all in the movement. There are baroque churches in abundance; there are Italianate fountains; there are gardens and palaces that mimic in their extravagantly ponderous Teutonic way the gardens and palaces of Rome. And, choicest treasure of all, there is a tunnel, forty feet high, bored through a precipitous crag—a tunnel such as only a Prince Bishop of the seventeenth century could have dreamed of, having at either end an arch of triumph, with pilasters, broken pediments, statues, scutcheons, all carved out of the living rock—a masterpiece among tunnels, and in a town where everything, without being really good, is exquisitely "amusing," the most amusing feature of all. Ah, decidedly, Salzburg is in the movement.

One afternoon I took the funicular up to the castle. There is a beer-terrace under the walls of the fortress from which you get a view that is starred in Baedeker. Below you on one side lies the town, spread out in the curving valley, with a river running through it, like a small and German version of Florence. From the other side of the terrace you look out over a panorama that makes no pretence to Italianism; it is as sweetly and romantically German as an air out of Weber's *Freischütz*. There are mountains on the horizon, spiky and blue like mountains in a picture book; and in the foreground, extending to the very foot of the extremely improbable crag on which the castle and the beer-garden are perched, stretches a flat green plain — miles upon miles of juicy meadows dotted with minusculous cows, with here and there a neat toy farm, or, more rarely, a cluster of dolls' houses, with a spire going up glittering from the midst of them.

I was sitting with my blond beer in front of this delicious and slightly comical landscape, thinking comfortably of nothing in particular, when I heard behind me a rapturous voice exclaiming, "Bello, bello!" I looked round curiously—for it seemed to me somehow rather surprising to hear Italian spoken here—and saw one of those fine sumptuous women they admire so much in the South. She was a *bella grassa*, plump to the verge of over-ripeness and perilously near middle age; but still in her way exceedingly handsome. Her face had the proportions of an iceberg—one-fifth above water, four-fifths below. Ample and florid from the eyes downwards, it was almost foreheadless; the hair began immediately above the brows. The eyes themselves were dark, large, and, for my taste, at least, somewhat excessively tender in expression. I took her in in a moment and was about to look away again when her companion, who had been looking at the view on the other side, turned round. It was the old Count.

I was far more embarrassed, I believe, than he. I felt myself blushing, as our eyes met, as though it were I who had been travelling about the world with a Colombella and he who had caught me in the act. I did not know what to do—whether to smile and speak to him, or to turn away as though I had not recognized him, or to nod from a distance and then, discreetly, to disappear. But the old Count put an end to my irresolution by calling out my name in astonishment, by running up to me and seizing my hand. What a delight to see an old friend! Here of all places! In this God-forsaken country—though it was cheap enough, didn't I find? He would introduce me to a charming compatriot of his own, an Italian lady he had met yesterday in the train from Vienna.

I was made known to the Colombella, and we all sat down at my table. Speaking resolutely in Italian, the Count ordered two more beers. We talked. Or rather the Count talked; for the conversation was a monologue. He told us anecdotes of the Italy of fifty years ago; he gave us imitations of the queer characters he had known; he even, at one moment, imitated the braying of an ass—I forgot in what context; but the braying remains vividly in my memory. Snuffing the air between every sentence, he gave us his views on women. The Colombella screamed indignant protests, dissolved herself in laughter. The old Count twisted his moustaches, twinkling at her through the network of his wrinkles. Every now and then he turned in my direction and gave me a little wink.

I listened in astonishment. Was this the man who had told the same anecdote three times in ten minutes? I looked at the old Count. He was leaning towards the Colombella whispering something in her ear which made her laugh so much that she had to wipe the tears from her eyes. Turning away from her, he caught my eye; smiling, he shrugged his shoulders as though to say, "These women! What imbeciles, but how delicious, how indispensable!" Was this the tired old man I had seen a year ago sitting on Pedrochi's terrace? It seemed incredible.

"Well, good-bye, *a rivederci*." They had to get down into the town again. The funicular was waiting.

"I'm delighted to have seen you," said the old Count, shaking me affectionately by the hand.

"And so am I," I protested. "Particularly delighted to see you so well."

"Yes, I'm wonderfully well now," he said, blowing out his chest.

"And young," I went on. "Younger than I am! How have you done it?"

"Aha!" The old Count cocked his head on one side mysteriously.

More in joke than in earnest, "I believe you've been seeing Steinach in Vienna," I said. "Having a rejuvenating operation."

For all reply, the old Count raised the forefinger of his right hand, laying it first to his lips, then along the side of his nose, and as he did so he winked. Then clenching his fist, and with his thumb sticking rigidly up, he made a complicated gesture which would, I am sure, for an Italian, have been full of a profound and vital significance. To me, however, unfamiliar with the language of signs, the exact meaning was not entirely clear. But the Count offered no verbal explanation. Still without uttering a word, he raised his hat; then laying his finger once more to his lips, he turned and ran with an astonishing agility down the steep path towards the little carriage of the funicular, in which the Colombella had already taken her seat.

Hubert and Minnie

For Hubert Lapell this first love-affair was extremely important. "Important" was the word he had used himself when he was writing about it in his diary. It was an event in his life, a real event for a change. It marked, he felt, a genuine turning-point in his spiritual development.

"Voltaire," he wrote in his diary—and he wrote it a second time in one of his letters to Minnie—"Voltaire said that one died twice: once with the death of the whole body and once before, with the death of one's capacity to love. And in the same way one is born twice, the second time being on the occasion when one first falls in love. One is born, then, into a new world—a world of intenser feelings, heightened values, more penetrating insights." And so on.

In point of actual fact Hubert found this new world a little disappointing. The intenser feelings proved to be rather mild; not by any means up to literary standards.

> "*I tell thee I am mad*
> *In Cressid's love. Thou answer'st: she is fair,*
> *Pour'st in the open ulcer of my heart*
> *Her eyes, her hair, her cheek, her gait, her voice. . . .*"

No, it certainly wasn't quite that. In his diary, in his letters to Minnie, he painted, it is true, a series of brilliant and romantic landscapes of the new world. But they were composite imaginary landscapes in the manner of Salvator Rosa—richer, wilder, more picturesquely clear-obscure than the real thing. Hubert would seize with avidity on the least velleity of an unhappiness, a physical desire, a spiritual yearning, to work it up in his letters and journals into something substantially romantic. There were times, generally very late at night, when he succeeded in persuading himself that he was indeed the wildest, unhappiest, most passionate of lovers. But in the daytime he went about his business nourishing something like a grievance against love. The thing was a bit of a fraud; yes, really, he decided, rather a fraud. All the same, he supposed it was important.

For Minnie, however, love was no fraud at all. Almost from the first moment she had adored him. A common friend had brought him to one of her Wednesday evenings. "This is Mr Lapell; but he's too young to be called anything but Hubert." That was how he had been introduced. And, laughing, she had taken his hand and called him Hubert at once. He too had laughed, rather nervously. "My name's Minnie," she said. But he had been too shy to call her anything at all that evening. His brown hair was tufty and untidy, like a little boy's, and he had shy grey eyes that never looked at you for more than a glimpse at a time, but turned away almost at once, as though they were afraid. Quickly he glanced at you, eagerly—then away again; and his musical voice, with its sudden emphases, its quick modulations from high to low, seemed always to address itself to a ghost floating low down and a little to one side of the person to whom he was talking. Above the brows was a forehead beautifully domed, with a pensive wrinkle running up from between the eyes. In repose his full-lipped mouth pouted a little, as though he were expressing some chronic discontent with the world. And, of course, thought Minnie, the world wasn't beautiful enough for his idealism.

"But after all," he had said earnestly that first evening, "one has the world of thought to live in. That, at any rate, is simple and clear and beautiful. One can always live apart from the brutal scramble."

And from the depths of the arm-chair in which, fragile, tired, and in these rather "artistic" surroundings almost incongruously elegant, she was sitting, Helen Glamber laughed her clear little laugh. "I think, on the contrary," she said (Minnie remembered every incident of that first evening), "I think one ought to rush about and know thousands of people, and eat and drink enormously, and make love incessantly, and shout and laugh and knock people over the head." And having vented these Rabelaisian sentiments, Mrs Glamber dropped back with a sigh of fatigue, covering her eyes with a thin white hand; for she had a splitting headache, and the light hurt her.

"Really!" Minnie protested, laughing. She would have felt rather shocked if any one else had said that; but Helen Glamber was allowed to say anything.

Hubert reaffirmed his quietism. Elegant, weary, infinitely fragile, Mrs Glamber lay back in her arm-chair, listening. Or perhaps, under her covering hand, she was trying to go to sleep.

She had adored him at first sight. Now that she looked back she could see that it had been at first sight. Adored him protectively, maternally—for he was only twenty and very young, in spite of the wrinkle between his brows, and the long words, and the undergraduate's newly discovered knowledge; only twenty, and she was nearly twenty-nine. And she had fallen in love with his beauty, too. Ah, passionately.

Hubert, perceiving it later, was surprised and exceedingly flattered. This had never happened to him before. He enjoyed being worshipped, and since Minnie had fallen so violently in love with him, it seemed the most natural thing in the world for him to be in love with Minnie. True, if she had not started by adoring him, it would never have occurred to Hubert to fall in love with her. At their first meeting he had found her certainly very nice, but not particularly exciting. Afterwards, the manifest expression of her adoration had made him find her more interesting, and in the end he had fallen in love himself. But perhaps it was not to be wondered at if he found the process a little disappointing.

But still, he reflected on those secret occasions when he had to admit to himself that something was wrong with this passion, love without possession could never, surely, in the nature of things, be quite the genuine article. In his diary he recorded aptly those two quatrains of John Donne:

"So must pure lovers' souls descend
To affections and to faculties,
Which sense may reach and apprehend,
Else a great prince in prison lies.

To our bodies turn we then, that so
Weak men on love revealed may look;
Love's mysteries in souls do grow,
But yet the body is his book."

At their next meeting he recited them to Minnie. The conversation which followed, compounded as it was of philosophy and personal confidences, was exquisite. It really, Hubert felt, came up to literary standards.

The next morning Minnie rang up her friend Helen Glamber
and asked if she might come to tea that afternoon. She had
several things to talk to her about. Mrs. Glamber sighed as she
hung up the receiver. "Minnie's coming to tea," she called,
turning towards the open door.

From across the passage her husband's voice came back to her.
"Good Lord!" it said in a tone of far-away horror, of absent-
minded resignation; for John Glamber was deep in his work and
there was only a little of him left, so to speak, above the surface
to react to the bad news.

Helen Glamber sighed again, and propping herself more comfortably against her pillows she reached for her book. She knew
that far-away voice and what it meant. It meant that he wouldn't
answer if she went on with the conversation; only say "h'm" or
"m'yes." And if she persisted after that, it meant that he'd say,
plaintively, heart-breakingly, "Darling, you *must* let me get on
with my work." And at that moment she would so much have
liked to talk a little. Instead, she went on reading at the point
where she had broken off to answer Minnie's telephone call.

"By this time the flames had enveloped the gynaeceum.
Nineteen times did the heroic Patriarch of Alexandria venture
into the blazing fabric, from which he succeeded in rescuing all
but two of its lovely occupants, twenty-seven in number, all of
whom he caused to be transported at once to his own private
apartments. . . ."

It was one of those instructive books John liked her to read.
History, mystery, lesson, and law. But at the moment she didn't
feel much like history. She felt like talking. And that was out of
the question; absolutely out of it.

She put down her book and began to file her nails and think of
poor Minnie. Yes, poor Minnie. Why was it that one couldn't
help saying Good Lord! heart-feltly, when one heard she was
coming to tea? And why did one never have the heart to refuse to
let her come to tea? She was pathetic, but pathetic in such a boring way. There are some people you like being kind to, people
you want to help and befriend. People that look at you with the
eyes of sick monkeys. Your heart breaks when you see them. But
poor Minnie had none of the charms of a sick monkey. She was
just a great big healthy young woman of twenty-eight who ought
to have been married and the mother of children, and who

wasn't. She would have made such a good wife, such an admirably solicitous and careful mother. But it just happened that
none of the men she knew had ever wanted to marry her. And why
should they want to? When she came into a room, the light
seemed to grow perceptibly dimmer, the electric tension slackened
off. She brought no life with her; she absorbed what there was,
she was like so much blotting-paper. No wonder nobody wanted
to marry her. And yet, of course, it was the only thing. Particularly
as she was always falling in love herself. The only thing.

"John!" Mrs Glamber suddenly called. "Is it really true about
ferrets?"

"Ferrets?" the voice from across the passage repeated with a
remote irritation. "Is what true about ferrets?"

"That the females die if they're not mated."

"How on earth should I know?"

"But you generally know everything."

"But, my darling, really . . ." The voice was plaintive, full of
reproach.

Mrs Glamber clapped her hand over her mouth and only took
it off again to blow a kiss. "All right," she said very quickly.
"All right. Really. I'm sorry. I won't do it again. Really." She
blew another kiss towards the door.

"But ferrets . . ." repeated the voice.

"Sh—sh, sh—sh."

"Why ferrets?"

"Darling," said Mrs Glamber almost sternly, "you really must
go on with your work."

Minnie came to tea. She put the case—hypothetically at first,
as though it were the case of a third person; then, gaining courage,
she put it personally. It was her own case. Out of the depths of her
untroubled, pagan innocence, Helen Glamber brutally advised
her. "If you want to go to bed with the young man," she said,
"go to bed with him. The thing has no importance in itself. At
least not much. It's only important because it makes possible
more secret confidences, because it strengthens affection, makes
the man in a way dependent on you. And then, of course, it's the
natural thing. I'm all for nature except when it comes to painting
one's face. They say that ferrets . . ." But Minnie noticed that she
never finished the sentence. Appalled and fascinated, shocked and
yet convinced, she listened.

"My darling," said Mrs Glamber that evening when her husband came home—for he hadn't been able to face Minnie; he had gone to the Club for tea—"who was it that invented religion, and sin, and all that? And why?"

John laughed. "It was invented by Adam," he said, "for various little transcendental reasons which you would probably find it difficult to appreciate. But also for the very practical purpose of keeping Eve in order."

"Well, if you call complicating people's lives keeping them in order, then I dare say you're right." Mrs Glamber shook her head. "I find it all too obscure. At sixteen, yes. But one really ought to have grown out of that sort of thing by twenty. And at thirty—the woman's nearly thirty, you know—well, really . . ."

In the end, Minnie wrote to Hubert telling him that she had made up her mind. Hubert was staying in Hertfordshire with his friend Watchett. It was a big house, the food was good, one was very comfortable; and old Mr Watchett, moreover, had a very sound library. In the impenetrable shade of the Wellingtonias Hubert and Ted Watchett played croquet and discussed the best methods of cultivating the Me. You could do a good deal, they decided, with art—books, you know, and pictures and music. "Listen to Stravinsky's *Sacre*," said Ted Watchett, "and you're for ever excused from going to Tibet or the Gold Coast or any of those awful places. And then there's Dostoievsky instead of murder, and D. H. Lawrence as a substitute for sex."

"All the same," said Hubert, "one must have a *certain* amount of actual non-imaginative experience." He spoke earnestly, abstractedly; but Minnie's letter was in his pocket. "*Gnosce teipsum.* You can't really know yourself without coming into collision with events, can you?"

Next day, Ted's cousin, Phoebe, arrived. She had red hair and a milky skin, and was more or less on the musical comedy stage. "One foot on and one foot off." she explained. "The splits." And there and then she did them, the splits, on the drawing-room carpet. "It's quite easy," she said, laughing, and jumped up again with an easy grace that fairly took one's breath away. Ted didn't like her. "Tiresome girl," he said. "So silly, too. Consciously silly, silly on purpose, which makes it worse." And, it was true, she did like boasting about the amount of champagne she could put away without getting buffy, and the number of times she had exceeded the generous allowance and been "blind to the world." She liked talking about her admirers in terms which might make you suppose that they were all her accepted lovers. But then she had the justification of her vitality and her shining red hair.

"Vitality," Hubert wrote in his diary (he contemplated a distant date, after, or preferably before, his death, when these confessions and aphorisms would be published), "vitality can make claims on the world almost as imperiously as can beauty. Sometimes beauty and vitality meet in one person."

It was Hubert who arranged that they should stay at the mill. One of his friends had once been there with a reading party, and found the place comfortable, secluded, and admirably quiet. Quiet, that is to say, with the special quietness peculiar to mills. For the silence there was not the silence of night on a mountain; it was a silence made of continuous thunder. At nine o'clock every morning the mill-wheel began to turn, and its roaring never stopped all day. For the first moments the noise was terrifying, was almost unbearable. Then, after a little, one grew accustomed to it. The thunder became, by reason of its very unintermittence, a perfect silence, wonderfuly rich and profound.

At the back of the mill was a little garden hemmed in on three sides by the house, the outhouses, and a high brick wall, and open on the fourth towards the water. Looking over the parapet, Minnie watched it sliding past. It was like a brown snake with arrowy markings on its back; and it crawled, it glided, it slid along for ever. She sat there, waiting: her train, from London, had brought her here soon after lunch; Hubert, coming across country from the Watchetts, would hardly arrive before six. The water flowed beneath her eyes like time, like destiny, smoothly towards some new and violent event.

The immense noise that in this garden was silence enveloped her. Inured, her mind moved in it as though in its native element. From beyond the parapet came the coolness and the weedy smell of water. But if she turned back towards the garden, she breathed at once the hot perfume of sunlight beating on flowers and ripening fruit. In the afternoon sunlight all the world was ripe. The old red house lay there, ripe, like a dropped plum; the walls were riper than the fruits of the nectarine trees so tenderly and neatly crucified on their warm bricks. And that richer silence of un-remitting thunder seemed, as it were, the powdery bloom on a day that had come to exquisite maturity and was hanging, round as a peach and juicy with life and happiness, waiting in the sun-shine for the bite of eager teeth.

At the heart of this fruit-ripe world Minnie waited. The water flowed towards the wheel; smoothly, smoothly—then it fell, it broke itself to pieces on the turning wheel. And time was sliding onwards, quietly towards an event that would shatter all the smoothness of her life.

"If you really want to go to bed with the young man, go to bed with him." She could hear Helen's clear, shrill voice saying im-possible, brutal things. If any one else had said them, she would have run out of the room. But in Helen's mouth they seemed, somehow, so simple, so innocuous, and so true. And yet all that other people had said or implied—at home, at school, among the people she was used to meeting—seemed equally true.

But then, of course, there was love. Hubert had written a Shakespearean sonnet which began:

> *"Love hallows all whereon 'tis truly placed,*
> *Turns dross to gold with one touch of his dart,*
> *Makes matter mind, extremest passion chaste,*
> *And builds a temple in the lustful heart."*

She thought that very beautiful. And very true. It seemed to throw a bridge between Helen and the other people. Love, true love, made all the difference. It justified. Love—how much, how much she loved!

Time passed and the light grew richer as the sun declined out of the height of the sky. The day grew more and more deliciously ripe, swelling with unheard-of sweetness. Over its sun-flushed cheeks the thundery silence of the mill-wheel spread the softest, peachiest of blooms. Minnie sat on the parapet, waiting. Some-times she looked down at the sliding water, sometimes she turned her eyes towards the garden. Time flowed, but she was now no more afraid of that shattering event that thundered there, in the future. The ripe sweetness of the afternoon seemed to enter into her spirit, filling it to the brim. There was no more room for doubts, or fearful anticipations, or regrets. She was happy. Tenderly, with a tenderness she could not have expressed in words, only with the gentlest of light kisses, with fingers caressingly drawn through the ruffled hair, she thought of Hubert, her Hubert.

Hubert, Hubert. . . . And suddenly, startlingly, he was standing there at her side.

"Oh," she said, and for a moment she stared at him with round brown eyes, in which there was nothing but astonishment. Then the expression changed. "Hubert," she said softly.

Hubert took her hand and dropped it again; looked at her for an instant, then turned away. Leaning on the parapet, he stared down into the sliding water; his face was unsmiling. For a long time both were silent. Minnie remained where she was, sitting quite still, her eyes fixed on the young man's averted face. She was happy, happy, happy. The long day ripened and ripened, perfection after perfection.

"Minnie," said the young man suddenly, and with a loud abruptness, as though he had been a long time deciding himself to speak and had at last succeeded in bringing out the prepared and pent-up words, "I feel I've behaved very badly towards you. I never ought to have asked you to come here. It was wrong. I'm sorry."

"But I came because I wanted to," Minnie exclaimed.

Hubert glanced at her, then turned away his eyes and went on addressing a ghost that floated, it seemed, just above the face of the sliding water. "It was too much to ask. I shouldn't have done it. For a man it's different. But for a woman . . ."

"But, I tell you, I wanted to."

"It's too much."

"It's nothing," said Minnie, "because I love you." And leaning forward, she ran her fingers through his hair. Ah, tenderness that no words could express! "You silly boy," she whispered. "Did you think I didn't love you enough for that?"

Hubert did not look up. The water slid and slid away before his eyes; Minnie's fingers played in his hair, ran caressingly over the nape of his neck. He felt suddenly a positive hatred for this woman. Idiot! Why couldn't she take a hint? He didn't want her. And why on earth had he ever imagined that he did? All the way in the train he had been asking himself that question. Why? Why? And the question had asked itself still more urgently just now as, standing at the garden door, he had looked out between the apple tree and watched her, unobserved, through a long minute—watched her sitting there on the parapet, turning her vague brown eyes now at the water, now towards the garden, and smiling to herself with an expression that had seemed to him so dim and vacuous that he could almost have fancied her an imbecile.

And with Phoebe yesterday he had stood on the crest of the bare chalk down. Like a sea at their feet stretched the plain, and above the dim horizon towered heroic clouds. Fingers of the wind lifted the red locks of her hair. She stood as though poised, ready to leap off into the boisterous air. "How I should like to fly!" she said. "There's something particularly attractive about airmen, I always think." And she had gone running down the hill.

But Minnie, with her dull hair, her apple-red cheeks, and big, slow body, was like a peasant girl. How had he ever persuaded himself that he wanted her? And what made it much worse, of course, was that she adored him, embarrassingly, tiresomely, like a too affectionate spaniel that insists on tumbling about at your feet and licking your hand just when you want to sit quietly and concentrate on serious things.

Hubert moved away, out of reach of her caressing hand. He lifted towards her for a moment a pair of eyes that had become, as it were, opaque with a cold anger; then dropped them again.

"The sacrifice is too great," he said in a voice that sounded to him like somebody else's voice. He found it very difficult to say this sort of thing convincingly. "I can't ask it of you," the actor pursued. "I won't."

"But it isn't a sacrifice," Minnie protested. "It's a joy, it's happiness. Oh, can't you understand?"

Hubert did not answer. Motionless, his elbows on the parapet, he stared down into the water. Minnie looked at him, perplexed only, at first; but all at once she was seized with a nameless agonizing doubt that grew and grew within her, as the silence prolonged itself, like some dreadful cancer of the spirit, until it had eaten away all her happiness, until there was nothing left in her mind but doubt and apprehension.

"What is it?" she said at last. "Why are you so strange? What is it, Hubert? What is it?"

Leaning anxiously forward, she laid her two hands on either side of his averted face and turned it towards her. Blank and opaque with anger were the eyes. "What is it?" she repeated. "Hubert, what is it?"

Hubert disengaged himself. "It's no good," he said in a smothered voice. "No good at all. It was a mistake. I'm sorry. I think I'd better go away. The trap's still at the door.

And without waiting for her to say anything, without explaining himself any further, he turned and walked quickly away, almost ran, towards the house. Well, thank goodness, he said to himself, he was out of that. He hadn't done it very well, or handsomely, or courageously; but, at any rate, he was out of it. Poor Minnie! He felt sorry for her; but after all, what could he do about it? Poor Minnie! Still, it rather flattered his vanity to think that she would be mourning over him. And in any case, he reassured his conscience, she couldn't really mind very much. But on the other hand, his vanity reminded him, she did adore him. Oh, she absolutely worshipped . . .

The door closed behind him. Minnie was alone again in the garden. Ripe, ripe it lay there in the late sunshine. Half of it was in shadow now; but the rest of it, in the coloured evening light, seemed to have come to the final and absolute perfection of maturity. Bloomy with thundery silence, the choicest fruit of all time hung there, deliciously sweet, sweet to the core; hung flushed and beautiful on the brink of darkness.

Minnie sat there quite still, wondering what had happened. Had he gone, had he really gone? The door closed behind him with a bang, and almost as though the sound were a signal prearranged, a man walked out from the mill on to the dam and closed the sluice. And all at once the wheel was still. Apocalyptically there was silence; the silence of soundlessness took the place of that other silence that was uninterrupted sound. Gulfs opened endlessly out around her; she was alone. Across the void of soundlessness a belated bee trailed its thin buzzing; the sparrows chirped, and from across the water came the sound of voices and far-away laughter. And as though woken from a sleep, Minnie looked up and listened, fearfully, turning her head from side to side.

Fard

THEY had been quarrelling now for nearly three-quarters of an hour. Muted and inarticulate, the voices floated down the corridor, from the other end of the flat. Stooping over her sewing, Sophie wondered, without much curiosity, what it was all about this time. It was Madame's voice that she heard most often. Shrill with anger and indignant with tears, it burst out in gusts, in gushes. Monsieur was more self-controlled, and his deeper voice was too softly pitched to penetrate easily the closed doors and to carry along the passage. To Sophie, in her cold little room, the quarrel sounded, most of the time, like a series of monologues by Madame, interrupted by strange and ominous silences. But every now and then Monsieur seemed to lose his temper outright, and then there was no silence between the gusts, but a harsh, deep, angry shout. Madame kept up her loud shrillness continuously and without flagging; her voice had, even in anger, a curious, level monotony. But Monsieur spoke now loudly, now softly, with emphases and modulations and sudden outbursts, so that his contributions to the squabble, when they were audible, sounded like a series of separate explosions. Bow, wow, wow-wow-wow, wow— a dog barking rather slowly.

After a time Sophie paid no more heed to the noise of quarrelling. She was mending one of Madame's camisoles, and the work required all her attention. She felt very tired; her body ached all over. It had been a hard day; so had yesterday, so had the day before. Every day was a hard day, and she wasn't so young as she had been. Two years more and she'd be fifty. Every day had been a hard day ever since she could remember. She thought of the sacks of potatoes she used to carry when she was a little girl in the country. Slowly, slowly she was walking along the dusty road with the sack over her shoulder. Ten steps more; she could manage that. Only it never was the end; one always had to begin again.

She looked up from her sewing, moved her head from side to side, blinked. She had begun to see lights and spots of colour dancing before her eyes; it often happened to her now. A sort of yellowish bright worm was wriggling up towards the right-hand corner of her field of vision; and though it was always moving upwards, upwards, it was always there in the same place. And there were stars of red and green that snapped and brightened and faded all round the worm. They moved between her and her sewing; they were there when she shut her eyes. After a moment she went on with her work; Madame wanted her camisole most particularly to-morrow morning. But it was difficult to see round the worm.

There was suddenly a great increase of noise from the other end of the corridor. A door had opened; words articulated themselves.

". . . bien tort, mon ami, si tu crois que je suis ton esclave. Je ferai ce que je voudrai."

"Moi aussi." Monsieur uttered a harsh, dangerous laugh. There was the sound of heavy footsteps in the passage, a rattling in the umbrella stand; then the front door banged.

Sophie looked down again at her work. Oh, the worm, the coloured stars, the aching fatigue in all her limbs! If one could only spend a whole day in bed—in a huge bed, feathery, warm and soft, all the day long . . .

The ringing of the bell startled her. It always made her jump, that furious wasp-like buzzer. She got up, put her work down on the table, smoothed her apron, set straight her cap, and stepped out into the corridor. Once more the bell buzzed furiously. Madame was impatient.

"At last, Sophie. I thought you were never coming."

Sophie said nothing; there was nothing to say. Madame was standing in front of the open wardrobe. A bundle of dresses hung over her arm, and there were more of them lying in a heap on the bed.

"Une beauté à la Rubens," her husband used to call her when he was in an amorous mood. He liked these massive, splendid, great women. None of your flexible drain-pipes for him. "Hélène Fourmont" was his pet name for her.

"Some day," Madame used to tell her friends, "some day I really must go to the Louvre and see my portrait. By Rubens, you know. It's extraordinary that one should have lived all one's life in Paris and never have seen the Louvre. Don't you think so?"

She was superb to-night. Her cheeks were flushed; her blue

eyes shone with an unusual brilliance between their long lashes; her short, red-brown hair had broken wildly loose.

"To-morrow, Sophie," she said dramatically, "we start for Rome. To-morrow morning." She unhooked another dress from the wardrobe as she spoke, and threw it on to the bed. With the movement her dressing-gown flew open, and there was a vision of ornate underclothing and white exuberant flesh. "We must pack at once."

"For how long, Madame?"

"A fortnight, three months—how should I know?"

"It makes a difference, Madame."

"The important thing is to get away. I shall not return to this house, after what has been said to me to-night, till I am humbly asked to."

"We had better take the large trunk, then, Madame; I will go and fetch it."

The air in the box-room was sickly with the smell of dust and leather. The big trunk was jammed in a far corner. She had to bend and strain at it in order to pull it out. The worm and the coloured stars flickered before her eyes; she felt dizzy when she straightened herself up. "I'll help you to pack, Sophie," said Madame, when the servant returned, dragging the heavy trunk after her. What a death's-head the old woman looked nowadays! She hated having old, ugly people near her. But Sophie was so efficient; it would be madness to get rid of her.

"Madame need not trouble." There would be no end to it, Sophie knew, if Madame started opening drawers and throwing things about. "Madame had much better go to bed. It's late."

No, no. She wouldn't be able to sleep. She was to such a degree enervated. These men . . . What an embeastment! One was not their slave. One would not be treated in this way.

Sophie was packing. A whole day in bed, in a huge, soft bed, like Madame's. One would doze, one would wake up for a moment, one would doze again.

"His latest game," Madame was saying indignantly, "is to tell me he hasn't got any money. I'm not to buy any clothes, he says. Too grotesque. I can't go about naked, can I?" She threw out her hands. "And as for saying he can't afford, that's simply nonsense. He can, perfectly well. Only he's mean, mean, horribly mean. And if he'd only do a little honest work, for a change, instead of writing silly verses and publishing them at his own expense, he'd have plenty and to spare." She walked up and down the room. "Besides," she went on, "there's his old father. What's he for, I should like to know? 'You must be proud of having a poet for a husband,' he says." She made her voice quaver like an old man's. "It's all I can do not to laugh in his face. 'And what beautiful verses Hégésippe writes about you! What passion, what fire!' " Thinking of the old man, she grimaced, wobbled her head, shook her finger, doddered on her legs. "And when one reflects that poor Hégésippe is bald, and dyes the few hairs he has left." She laughed. "As for the passion he talks so much about in his beastly verses," she laughed—"that's all pure invention. But, my good Sophie, what are you thinking of? Why are you packing that hideous old green dress?"

Sophie pulled out the dress without saying anything. Why did the woman choose this night to look so terribly ill? She had a yellow face and blue teeth. Madame shuddered; it was too horrible. She ought to send her to bed. But, after all, the work had to be done. What could one do about it? She felt more than ever aggrieved.

"Life is terrible." Sighing, she sat down heavily on the edge of the bed. The buoyant springs rocked her gently once or twice before they settled to rest. "To be married to a man like this. I shall soon be getting old and fat. And never once unfaithful. But look how he treats me." She got up again and began to wander aimlessly about the room. "I won't stand it, though," she burst out. She had halted in front of the long mirror, and was admiring her own splendid tragic figure. No one would believe, to look at her, that she was over thirty. Behind the beautiful tragedian she could see in the glass a thin, miserable, old creature, with a yellow face and blue teeth, crouching over the trunk. Really, it was too disagreeable. Sophie looked like one of those beggar women one sees on a cold morning, standing in the gutter. Does one hurry past, trying not to look at them? Or does one stop, open one's purse, and give them one's copper and nickel—even as much as a two-franc note, if one has no change? But whatever one did, one always felt uncomfortable, one always felt apologetic for one's furs. That was what came of walking. If one had a car—but that was another of Hégésippe's meannesses—one wouldn't, rolling along behind closed windows, have to be conscious of them at all. She turned away from the glass.

"I won't stand it," she said, trying not to think of the beggar women, of blue teeth in a yellow face; "I won't stand it." She dropped into a chair.

But think of a lover with a yellow face and blue, uneven teeth! She closed her eyes, shuddered at the thought. It would be enough to make one sick. She felt impelled to take another look: Sophie's eyes were the colour of greenish lead, quite without life. What was one to do about it? The woman's face was a reproach, an accusation. And besides, the sight of it was making her feel positively ill. She had never been so profoundly enervated.

Sophie rose slowly and with difficulty from her knees; an expression of pain crossed her face. Slowly she walked to the chest of drawers, slowly counted out six pairs of silk stockings. She turned back towards the trunk. The woman was a walking corpse!

"Life is terrible," Madame repeated with conviction, "terrible, terrible, terrible."

She ought to send the woman to bed. But she would never be able to get her packing done by herself. And it was so important to get off to-morrow morning. She had told Hégésippe she would go, and he had simply laughed; he hadn't believed it. She must give him a lesson this time. In Rome she would see Luigino. Such a charming boy, and a marquis, too. Perhaps . . . But she could think of nothing but Sophie's face; the leaden eyes, the bluish teeth, the yellow, wrinkled skin.

"Sophie," she said suddenly; it was with difficulty that she prevented herself screaming, "look on my dressing-table. You'll see a box of rouge, the Dorin number twenty-four. Put a little on your cheeks. And there's a stick of lip salve in the right-hand drawer."

She kept her eyes resolutely shut while Sophie got up—with what a horrible creaking of the joints!—walked over to the dressing-table, and stood there, rustling faintly, through what seemed an eternity. What a life, my God, what a life! Slow footsteps trailed back again. She opened her eyes. Oh, that was far better, far better.

"Thank you, Sophie. You look much less tired now." She got up briskly. "And now we must hurry." Full of energy, she ran to the wardrobe. "Goodness me," she exclaimed, throwing up her hands, "you've forgotten to put in my blue evening dress. How could you be so stupid, Sophie?"

The Portrait

"PICTURES," said Mr Bigger; "you want to see some pictures? Well, we have a very interesting mixed exhibition of modern stuff in our galleries at the moment. French and English, you know."

The customer held up his hand, shook his head. "No, no. Nothing modern for me," he declared, in his pleasant northern English. "I want real pictures, old pictures. Rembrandt and Sir Joshua Reynolds and that sort of thing."

"Perfectly." Mr Bigger nodded. "Old Masters. Oh, of course we deal in the old as well as the modern."

"The fact is," said the other, "that I've just bought a rather large house—a Manor House," he added, in impressive tones.

Mr Bigger smiled; there was an ingenuousness about this simple-minded fellow which was most engaging. He wondered how the man had made his money. "A Manor House." The way he had said it was really charming. Here was a man who had worked his way up from serfdom to the lordship of a manor, from the broad base of the feudal pyramid to the narrow summit. His own history and all the history of classes had been implicit in that awed proud emphasis on the "Manor". But the stranger was running on; Mr Bigger could not allow his thoughts to wander farther. "In a house of this style," he was saying, "and with a position like mine to keep up, one must have a few pictures. Old Masters, you know; Rembrandts and What's-his-names."

"Of course," said Mr Bigger, "an Old Master is a symbol of social superiority."

"That's just it," cried the other, beaming; "you've said just what I wanted to say."

Mr Bigger bowed and smiled. It was delightful to find some one who took one's little ironies as sober seriousness.

"Of course, we should only need Old Masters downstairs, in the reception-room. It would be too much of a good thing to have them in the bedrooms too."

"Altogether too much of a good thing," Mr Bigger assented.

"As a matter of fact," the Lord of the Manor went on, "my daughter—she does a bit of sketching. And very pretty it is. I'm having some of her things framed to hang in the bedrooms. It's useful having an artist in the family. Saves you buying pictures. But, of course, we must have something old downstairs."

"I think I have exactly what you want." Mr Bigger got up and rang the bell. "My daughter does a little sketching"—he pictured a large, blonde, barmaidish personage, thirty-one and not yet married, running a bit to seed. His secretary appeared at the door. "Bring me the Venetian portrait, Miss Pratt, the one in the back room. You know which I mean."

"You're very snug in here," said the Lord of the Manor. "Business good, I hope."

Mr Bigger sighed. "The slump," he said. "We art dealers feel it worse than any one."

"Ah, the slump." The Lord of the Manor chuckled. "I foresaw it all the time. Some people seemed to think the good times were going to last for ever. What fools! I sold out of everything at the crest of the wave. That's why I can buy pictures now."

Mr. Bigger laughed too. This was the right sort of customer. "Wish I'd had anything to sell out during the boom," he said.

The Lord of the Manor laughed till the tears rolled down his cheeks. He was still laughing when Miss Pratt re-entered the room. She carried a picture, shieldwise, in her two hands, before her.

"Put it on the easel, Miss Pratt," said Mr Bigger. "Now," he turned to the Lord of the Manor, "what do you think of that?"

The picture that stood on the easel before them was a half-length portrait. Plump-faced, white-skinned, high-bosomed in her deeply scalloped dress of blue silk, the subject of the picture seemed a typical Italian lady of the middle eighteenth century. A little complacent smile curved the pouting lips, and in one hand she held a black mask, as though she had just taken it off after a day of carnival.

"Very nice," said the Lord of the Manor; but he added doubtfully, "It isn't very like Rembrandt, is it? It's all so clear and bright. Generally in Old Masters you can never see anything at all, they're so dark and foggy."

"Very true," said Mr Bigger. "But not all Old Masters are like Rembrandt."

"I suppose not." The Lord of the Manor seemed hardly to be convinced.

"This is eighteenth-century Venetian. Their colour was always luminous. Giangolini was the painter. He died young, you know. Not more than half a dozen of his pictures are known. And this is one."

The Lord of the Manor nodded. He could appreciate the value of rarity.

"One notices at a first glance the influence of Longhi," Mr Bigger went on airily. "And there is something of the morbidezza of Rosalba in the painting of the face."

The Lord of the Manor was looking uncomfortably from Mr Bigger to the picture and from the picture to Mr Bigger. There is nothing so embarrassing as to be talked at by some one possessing more knowledge than you do. Mr Bigger pressed his advantage. "Curious," he went on, "that one sees nothing of Tiepolo's manner in this. Don't you think so?"

The Lord of the Manor nodded. His face wore a gloomy expression. The corners of his baby's mouth drooped. One almost expected him to burst into tears.

"It's pleasant," said Mr Bigger, relenting at last, "to talk to somebody who really knows about painting. So few people do."

"Well, I can't say I've ever gone into the subject very deeply," said the Lord of the Manor modestly. "But I know what I like when I see it." His face brightened again, as he felt himself on safer ground.

"A natural instinct," said Mr Bigger. "That's a very precious gift. I could see by your face that you had it; I could see that the moment you came into the gallery."

The Lord of the Manor was delighted. "Really, now," he said. He felt himself growing larger, more important. "Really." He cocked his head critically on one side. "Yes. I must say I think that's a very fine bit of painting. Very fine. But the fact is, I should rather have liked a more historical piece, if you know what I mean. Something more ancestor-like, you know. A portrait of somebody with a story—like Anne Boleyn, or Nell Gwynn, or the Duke of Wellington, or some one like that."

"But, my dear sir, I was just going to tell you. This picture has a story." Mr Bigger leaned forward and tapped the Lord of the Manor on the knee. His eyes twinkled with benevolent and amused brightness under his bushy eyebrows. There was a knowing kindliness in his smile. "A most remarkable story is connected with the painting of that picture."

"You don't say so?" The Lord of the Manor raised his eyebrows.

Mr Bigger leaned back in his chair. "The lady you see there," he said, indicating the portrait with a wave of the hand, "was the wife of the fourth Earl Hurtmore. The family is now extinct. The ninth Earl died only last year. I got this picture when the house was sold up. It's sad to see the passing of these old ancestral homes." Mr Bigger sighed. The Lord of the Manor looked solemn, as though he were in church. There was a moment's silence; then Mr Bigger went on in a changed tone. "From his portraits, which I have seen, the fourth Earl seems to have been a long-faced, gloomy, grey-looking fellow. One can never imagine him young; he was the sort of man who looks permanently fifty. His chief interests in life were music and Roman antiquities. There's one portrait of him holding an ivory flute in one hand and resting the other on a fragment of Roman carving. He spent at least half his life travelling in Italy, looking for antiques and listening to music. When he was about fifty-five, he suddenly decided that it was about time to get married. This was the lady of his choice." Mr Bigger pointed to the picture. "His money and his title must have made up for many deficiencies. One can't imagine, from her appearance, that Lady Hurtmore took a great deal of interest in Roman antiquities. Nor, I should think, did she care much for the science and history of music. She liked clothes, she liked society, she liked gambling, she liked flirting, she liked enjoying herself. It doesn't seem that the newly wedded couple got on too well. But still, they avoided an open breach. A year after the marriage Lord Hurtmore decided to pay another visit to Italy. They reached Venice in the early autumn. For Lord Hurtmore, Venice meant unlimited music. It meant Galuppi's daily concerts at the orphanage of the Misericordia. It meant Piccini at Santa Maria. It meant new operas at the San Moise; it meant delicious cantatas at a hundred churches. It meant private concerts of amateurs; it meant Porpora and the finest singers in Europe; it meant Tartini and the greatest violinists. For Lady Hurtmore, Venice meant something rather different. It meant gambling at the Ridotto, masked balls, gay supper-parties—all the delights of the most amusing city in the world. Living their separate lives, both might have been happy here in Venice almost indefinitely. But one day Lord Hurtmore had the disastrous idea of having his wife's portrait painted. Young Giangolini was re-commended to him as the promising, the coming painter. Lady Hurtmore began her sittings. Giangolini was handsome and dashing, Giangolini was young. He had an amorous technique as perfect as his artistic technique. Lady Hurtmore would have been more than human if she had been able to resist him. She was not more than human."

"None of us are, eh?" The Lord of the Manor dug his finger into Mr Bigger's ribs and laughed.

Politely, Mr Bigger joined in his mirth; when it had subsided, he went on. "In the end they decided to run away together across the border. They would live at Vienna—live on the Hurtmore family jewels, which the lady would be careful to pack in her suit-case. They were worth upwards of twenty thousand, the Hurt-more jewels; and in Vienna, under Maria-Theresa, one could live handsomely on the interest of twenty thousand.

"The arrangements were easily made. Giangolini had a friend who did everything for them—got them passports under an assumed name, hired horses to be in waiting on the mainland, placed his gondola at their disposal. They decided to flee on the day of the last sitting. The day came. Lord Hurtmore, according to his usual custom, brought his wife to Giangolini's studio in a gondola, left her there, perched on the high-backed model's throne, and went off again to listen to Galuppi's concert at the Misericordia. It was the time of full carnival. Even in broad daylight people went about in masks. Lady Hurtmore wore one of black silk—you see her holding it, there, in the portrait. Her husband, though he was no reveller and disapproved of carnival junketings, preferred to conform to the grotesque fashion of his neighbours rather than attract attention to himself by not conforming.

"The long black cloak, the huge three-cornered black hat, the long-nosed mask of white paper were the ordinary attire of every Venetian gentleman in these carnival weeks. Lord Hurtmore did not care to be conspicuous; he wore the same. There must have been something richly absurd and incongruous in the spectacle of this grave and solemn-faced English milord dressed in the clown's uniform of a gay Venetian masker. 'Pantaloon in the clothes of Pulcinella,' was how the lovers described him to one another; the old dotard of the eternal comedy dressed up as the clown. Well, this morning, as I have said, Lord Hurtmore came as usual in his hired gondola, bringing his lady with him. And she in her turn was bringing, under the folds of her capacious cloak, a little leather box wherein, snug on their silken bed, reposed the Hurtmore jewels. Seated in the dark little cabin of the gondola they watched the churches, the richly fretted palazzi, the high mean houses gliding past them. From under his Punch's mask Lord Hurtmore's voice spoke gravely, slowly, imperturbably.

"'The learned Father Martini,' he said, 'has promised to do me the honour of coming to dine with us to-morrow. I doubt if any man knows more of musical history than he. I will ask you to be at pains to do him special honour.'

"'You may be sure I will, my lord.' She could hardly contain the laughing excitement that bubbled up within her. To-morrow at dinner-time she would be far away—over the frontier, beyond Gorizia, galloping along the Vienna road. Poor old Pantaloon! But no, she wasn't in the least sorry for him. After all, he had his music, he had his odds and ends of broken marble. Under her cloak she clutched the jewel-case more tightly. How intoxicatingly amusing her secret was!"

Mr Bigger clasped his hands and pressed them dramatically over his heart. He was enjoying himself. He turned his long, foxy nose towards the Lord of the Manor, and smiled benevolently. The Lord of the Manor for his part was all attention.

"Well?" he inquired.

Mr Bigger unclasped his hands, and let them fall on to his knees.

"Well," he said, "the gondola draws up at Giangolini's door, Lord Hurtmore helps his wife out, leads her up to the painter's great room on the first floor, commits her into his charge with his usual polite formula, and then goes off to hear Galuppi's morning concert at the Misericordia. The lovers have a good two hours to make their final preparations.

"Old Pantaloon safely out of sight, up pops the painter's useful friend, masked and cloaked like every one else in the streets and on the canals of this carnival Venice. There follow embracements and handshakings and laughter all round; everything has been so marvellously successful, not a suspicion roused. From under Lady Hurtmore's cloak comes the jewel-case. She opens it, and there are loud Italian exclamations of astonishment and admiration.

The brilliants, the pearls, the great Hurtmore emeralds, the ruby clasps, the diamond ear-rings—all these bright, glittering things are lovingly examined, knowingly handled. Fifty thousand sequins at the least is the estimate of the useful friend. The two lovers throw themselves ecstatically into one another's arms.

"The useful friend interrupts them; there are still a few last things to be done. They must go and sign for their passports at the Ministry of Police. Oh, a mere formality; but still it has to be done. He will go out at the same time and sell one of the lady's diamonds to provide the necessary funds for the journey."

Mr Bigger paused to light a cigarette. He blew a cloud of smoke, and went on.

"So they set out, all in their masks and capes, the useful friend in one direction, the painter and his mistress in another. Ah, love in Venice!" Mr Bigger turned up his eyes in ecstasy. "Have you ever been in Venice and in love, sir?" he inquired of the Lord of the Manor.

"Never farther than Dieppe," said the Lord of the Manor, shaking his head.

"Ah, then you've missed one of life's great experiences. You can never fully and completely understand what must have been the sensations of little Lady Hurtmore and the artist as they glided down the long canals, gazing at one another through the eyeholes of their masks. Sometimes, perhaps, they kissed—though it would have been difficult to do that without unmasking, and there was always the danger that some one might have recognized their naked faces through the windows of their little cabin. No, on the whole," Mr Bigger concluded reflectively, "I expect they confined themselves to looking at one another. But in Venice, drowsing along the canals, one can almost be satisfied with looking—just looking."

He caressed the air with his hand and let his voice droop away into silence. He took two or three puffs at his cigarette without saying anything. When he went on, his voice was very quiet and even.

"About half an hour after they had gone, a gondola drew up at Giangolini's door and a man in a paper mask, wrapped in a black cloak and wearing on his head the inevitable three-cornered hat, got out and went upstairs to the painter's room. It was empty. The portrait smiled sweetly and a little fatuously from the easel.

But no painter stood before it and the model's throne was untenanted. The long-nosed mask looked about the room with an
expressionless curiosity. The wandering glance came to rest at
last on the jewel-case that stood where the lovers had carelessly
left it, open on the table. Deep-set and darkly shadowed behind
the grotesque mask, the eyes dwelt long and fixedly on this object.
Long-nosed Pulcinella seemed to be wrapped in meditation.

"A few minutes later there was the sound of footsteps on the
stairs, of two voices laughing together. The masker turned away
to look out of the window. Behind him the door opened noisily;
drunk with excitement, with gay, laughable irresponsibility, the
lovers burst in.

"'Aha, *caro amico!* Back already. What luck with the diamond?'

"The cloaked figure at the window did not stir; Giangolini
rattled gaily on. There had been no trouble whatever about the
signatures, no questions asked; he had the passports in his pocket.
They could start at once.

"Lady Hurtmore suddenly began to laugh uncontrollably; she
couldn't stop.

"'What's the matter?' asked Giangolini, laughing too.

"'I was thinking,' she gasped between the paroxysms of her
mirth, 'I was thinking of old Pantaloon sitting at the Misericordia,
solemn as an owl, listening'—she almost choked, and the words
came out shrill and forced as though she were speaking through
tears—'listening to old Galuppi's boring old cantatas.'

"The man at the window turned round. 'Unfortunately,
madam,' he said, 'the learned maestro was indisposed this morning. There was no concert.' He took off his mask. 'And so I took
the liberty of returning earlier than usual.' The long, grey, unsmiling face of Lord Hurtmore confronted them.

"The lovers stared at him for a moment speechlessly. Lady
Hurtmore put her hand to her heart; it had given a fearful jump,
and she felt a horrible sensation in the pit of her stomach. Poor
Giangolini had gone as white as his paper mask. Even in these
days of *cicisbei*, of official gentlemen friends, there were cases on
record of outraged and jealous husbands resorting to homicide.
He was unarmed, but goodness only knew what weapons of
destruction were concealed under that enigmatic black cloak.
But Lord Hurtmore did nothing brutal or undignified. Gravely
and calmly, as he did everything, he walked over to the table,

picked up the jewel-case, closed it with the greatest care, and saying, 'My box, I think,' put it in his pocket and walked out of the room. The lovers were left looking questioningly at one another.

There was a silence.

"What happened then?" asked the Lord of the Manor.

"The anti-climax," Mr Bigger replied, shaking his head mournfully. "Giangolini had bargained to elope with fifty thousand sequins. Lady Hurtmore didn't, on reflection, much relish the idea of love in a cottage. Woman's place, she decided at last, is the home—with the family jewels. But would Lord Hurtmore see the matter in precisely the same light? That was the question, the alarming, disquieting question. She decided to go and see for herself.

"She got back just in time for dinner. 'His Illustrissimous Excellency is waiting in the dining-room,' said the major-domo. The tall doors were flung open before her; she swam in majestically, chin held high—but with what a terror in her soul! Her husband was standing by the fireplace. He advanced to meet her.

"'I was expecting you, madam,' he said, and led her to her place.

"That was the only reference he ever made to the incident. In the afternoon he sent a servant to fetch the portrait from the painter's studio. It formed part of their baggage when, a month later, they set out for England. The story has been passed down with the picture from one generation to the next. I had it from an old friend of the family when I bought the portrait last year."

Mr Bigger threw his cigarette end into the grate. He flattered himself that he had told that tale very well.

'Very interesting,' said the Lord of the Manor, "very interesting indeed. Quite historical, isn't it? One could hardly do better with Nell Gwynn or Anne Boleyn, could one?"

Mr Bigger smiled vaguely, distantly. He was thinking of Venice —the Russian countess staying in his pension, the tufted tree in the courtyard outside his bedroom, that strong, hot scent she used (it made you catch your breath when you first smelt it), and there was the bathing on the Lido, and the gondola, and the dome of the Salute against the hazy sky, looking just as it looked when Guardi painted it. How enormously long ago and far away it all seemed now! He was hardly more than a boy then; it had been his first great adventure. He woke up with a start from his reverie.

The Lord of the Manor was speaking. "How much, now, would you want for that picture?" he asked. His tone was detached, off-hand; he was a rare one for bargaining.

"Well," said Mr Bigger, quitting with reluctance the Russian countess, the paradisiacal Venice of five-and-twenty years ago, "I've asked as much as a thousand for less important works than this. But I don't mind letting this go to you for seven-fifty."

The Lord of the Manor whistled. "Seven-fifty?" he repeated. "It's too much."

"But, my dear sir," Mr Bigger protested, "think what you'd have to pay for a Rembrandt of this size and quality—twenty thousand at least. Seven hundred and fifty isn't at all too much. On the contrary, it's very little considering the importance of the picture you're getting. You have a good enough judgment to see that this is a very fine work of art."

"Oh, I'm not denying that," said the Lord of the Manor. "All I say is that seven-fifty's a lot of money. Whe-ew! I'm glad my daughter does sketching. Think if I'd had to furnish the bedrooms with pictures at seven-fifty a time!" He laughed.

Mr Bigger smiled. "You must also remember," he said, "that you're making a very good investment. Late Venetians are going up. If I had any capital to spare——" The door opened and Miss Pratt's blonde and frizzy head popped in.

"Mr Crowley wants to know if he can see you, Mr Bigger."

Mr Bigger frowned. "Tell him to wait," he said irritably. He coughed and turned back to the Lord of the Manor. "If I had any capital to spare, I'd put it all into late Venetians. Every penny."

He wondered, as he said the words, how often he had told people that he'd put all his capital, if he had any, into primitives cubism, nigger sculpture, Japanese prints. . . .

In the end the Lord of the Manor wrote him a cheque for six hundred and eighty.

"You might let me have a typewritten copy of the story," he said, as he put on his hat. "It would be a good tale to tell one's guests at dinner, don't you think? I'd like to have the details quite correct."

"Oh, of course, of course," said Mr Bigger, "the details are most important."

He ushered the little round man to the door. "Good morning. Good morning." He was gone.

A tall, pale youth with side whiskers appeared in the doorway. His eyes were dark and melancholy; his expression, his general appearance, were romantic and at the same time a little pitiable. It was young Crowley, the painter.

"Sorry to have kept you waiting," said Mr Bigger. "What did you want to see me for?"

Mr Crowley looked embarrassed, he hesitated. How he hated having to do this sort of thing! "The fact is," he said at last, "I'm horribly short of money. I wondered if perhaps you wouldn't mind—if it would be convenient to you—to pay me for that thing I did for you the other day. I'm awfully sorry to bother you like this."

"Not at all, my dear fellow." Mr Bigger felt sorry for this wretched creature who didn't know how to look after himself. Poor young Crowley was as helpless as a baby. "How much did we settle it was to be?"

"Twenty pounds, I think it was," said Mr Crowley timidly.

Mr Bigger took out his pocket-book. "We'll make it twenty-five," he said.

"Oh no, really, I couldn't. Thanks very much." Mr Crowley blushed like a girl. "I suppose you wouldn't like to have a show of some of my landscapes, would you?" he asked, emboldened by Mr Bigger's air of benevolence.

"No, no. Nothing of your own." Mr Bigger shook his head inexorably.

"There's no money in modern stuff. But I'll take any number of those sham Old Masters of yours." He drummed with his fingers on Lady Hurtmore's sleekly painted shoulder. "Try another Venetian," he added. "This one was a great success."

Young Archimedes

IT was the view which finally made us take the place. True, the house had its disadvantages. It was a long way out of town and had no telephone. The rent was unduly high, the drainage system poor. On windy nights, when the ill-fitting panes were rattling so furiously in the window-frames that you could fancy yourself in an hotel omnibus, the electric light, for some mysterious reason, used invariably to go out and leave you in the noisy dark. There was a splendid bathroom; but the electric pump, which was supposed to send up water from the rain-water tanks in the terrace, did not work. Punctually every autumn the drinking well ran dry. And our landlady was a liar and a cheat.

But these are the little disadvantages of every hired house, all over the world. For Italy they were not really at all serious. I have seen plenty of houses which had them all and a hundred others, without possessing the compensating advantages of ours—the southward facing garden and terrace for the winter and spring, the large cool rooms against the midsummer heat, the hilltop air and freedom from mosquitoes, and finally the view.

And what a view it was! Or rather, what a succession of views. For it was different every day; and without stirring from the house one had the impression of an incessant change of scene: all the delights of travel without its fatigues. There were autumn days when all the valleys were filled with mist and the crests of Apennines rose darkly out of a flat white lake. There were days when the mist invaded even our hilltop and we were enveloped in a soft vapour in which the mist-coloured olive trees, that sloped away below our windows towards the valley, disappeared as though into their own spiritual essence; and the only firm and definite things in the small, dim world within which we found ourselves confined were the two tall black cypresses growing on a little projecting terrace a hundred feet down the hill. Black, sharp, and solid, they stood there, twin pillars of Hercules at the extremity of the known universe; and beyond them there was only pale cloud and round them only the cloudy olive trees.

These were the wintry days; but there were days of spring and

autumn, days unchangingly cloudless, or—more lovely still—
made various by the huge floating shapes of vapour that, snowy
above the far-away snow-capped mountains, gradually un-
folded, against the pale bright blue, enormous heroic gestures.
And in the height of the sky the bellying draperies, the swans, the
aerial marbles, hewed and left unfinished by gods grown tired of
creation almost before they had begun, drifted sleeping along the
wind, changing form as they moved. And the sun would come
and go behind them; and now the town in the valley would fade
and almost vanish in the shadow, and now, like an immense
fretted jewel between the hills, it would glow as though by its
own light. And looking across the nearer tributary valley that
wound from below our crest down towards the Arno, looking over
the low dark shoulder of hill on whose extreme promontory stood
the towered church of San Miniato, one saw the huge dome airily
hanging on its ribs of masonry, the square campanile, the sharp
spire of Santa Croce, and the canopied tower of the Signoria,
rising above the intricate maze of houses, distinct and brilliant,
like small treasures carved out of precious stones. For a moment
only, and then their light would fade away once more, and the
travelling beam would pick out, among the indigo hills beyond, a
single golden crest.

There were days when the air was wet with passed or with
approaching rain, and all the distances seemed miraculously near
and clear. The olive trees detached themselves one from another
on the distant slopes; the far-away villages were lovely and
pathetic like the most exquisite small toys. There were days in
summer-time, days of impending thunder when, bright and sunlit
against huge bellying masses of black and purple, the hills and
the white houses shone as it were precariously, in a dying
splendour, on the brink of some fearful calamity.

How the hills changed and varied! Every day and every hour
of the day, almost, they were different. There would be moments
when, looking across the plain of Florence, one would see only a
dark blue silhouette against the sky. The scene had no depth; there
was only a hanging curtain painted flatly with the symbols of
mountains. And then, suddenly almost, with the passing of a
cloud, or when the sun had declined to a certain level in the sky,
the flat scene transformed itself; and where there had been only a
painted curtain, now there were ranges behind ranges of hills,

graduated tone after tone from brown, or grey, or a green gold to far-away blue. Shapes that a moment before had been fused together indiscriminately into a single mass, now came apart into their constituents. Fiesole, which had seemed only a spur of Monte Morello, now revealed itself as the jutting headland of another system of hills, divided from the nearest bastions of its greater neighbour by a deep and shadowy valley.

At noon, during the heats of summer, the landscape became dim, powdery, vague, and almost colourless under the midday sun; the hills disappeared into the trembling fringes of the sky. But as the afternoon wore on the landscape emerged again, it dropped its anonymity, it climbed back out of nothingness into form and life. And its life, as the sun sank and slowly sank through the long afternoon, grew richer, grew more intense with every moment. The level light, with its attendant long, dark shadows, laid bare, so to speak, the anatomy of the land; the hills —each western escarpment shining, and each slope averted from the sunlight profoundly shadowed—became massive, jutty, and solid. Little folds and dimples in the seemingly even ground revealed themselves. Eastward from our hilltop, across the plain of the Ema, a great bluff cast its ever-increasing shadow; in the surrounding brightness of the valley a whole town lay eclipsed within it. And as the sun expired on the horizon, the further hills flushed in its warm light, till their illumined flanks were the colour of tawny roses; but the valleys were already filled with the blue mist of evening. And it mounted, mounted; the fire went out of the western windows of the populous slopes; only the crests were still alight, and at last they too were all extinct. The mountains faded and fused together again into a flat painting of mountains against the pale evening sky. In a little while it was night; and if the moon were full, a ghost of the dead scene still haunted the horizons.

Changeful in its beauty, this wide landscape always preserved a quality of humanness and domestication which made it, to my mind at any rate, the best of all landscapes to live with. Day by day one travelled through its different beauties; but the journey, like our ancestors' Grand Tour, was always a journey through civilization. For all its mountains, its steep slopes and deep valleys, the Tuscan scene is dominated by its inhabitants. They have cultivated every rood of ground that can be cultivated; their houses are thickly scattered even over the hills, and the valleys are populous. Solitary on the hilltop, one is not alone in a wilderness. Man's traces are across the country, and already—one feels it with satisfaction as one looks out across it—for centuries, for thousands of years, it has been his, submissive, tamed, and humanized. The wide, blank moorlands, the sands, the forests of innumerable trees—these are places for occasional visitation, healthful to the spirit which submits itself to them for not too long. But fiendish influences as well as divine haunt these total solitudes. The vegetative life of plants and things is alien and hostile to the human. Men cannot live at ease except where they have mastered their surroundings and where their accumulated lives outnumber and outweigh the vegetative lives about them. Stripped of its dark woods, planted, terraced, and tilled almost to the mountains' tops, the Tuscan landscape is humanized and safe. Sometimes upon those who live in the midst of it there comes a longing for some place that is solitary, inhuman, lifeless, or peopled only with alien life. But the longing is soon satisfied, and one is glad to return to the civilized and submissive scene.

I found that house on the hilltop the ideal dwelling-place. For there, safe in the midst of a humanized landscape, one was yet alone; one could be as solitary as one liked. Neighbours whom one never sees at close quarters are the ideal and perfect neighbours.

Our nearest neighbours, in terms of physical proximity, lived very near. We had two sets of them, as a matter of fact, almost in the same house with us. One was the peasant family, who lived in a long, low building, part dwelling-house, part stables, storerooms and cowsheds, adjoining the villa. Our other neighbours—intermittent neighbours, however, for they only ventured out of town every now and then, during the most flawless weather—were the owners of the villa, who had reserved for themselves the smaller wing of the huge L-shaped house—a mere dozen rooms or so—leaving the remaining eighteen or twenty to us.

They were a curious couple, our proprietors. An old husband, grey, listless, tottering, seventy at least; and a signora of about forty, short, very plump, with tiny fat hands and feet and a pair of very large, very dark black eyes, which she used with all the skill of a born comedian. Her vitality, if you could have harnessed it and made it do some useful work, would have supplied a whole town with electric light. The physicists talk of deriving energy from the atom; they would be more profitably employed nearer home—in discovering some way of tapping those enormous stores of vital energy which accumulate in unemployed women of sanguine temperament and which, in the present imperfect state of social and scientific organization, vent themselves in ways that are generally so deplorable: in interfering with other people's affairs, in working up emotional scenes, in thinking about love and making it, and in bothering men till they cannot get on with their work.

Signora Bondi got rid of her superfluous energy, among other ways, by "doing in" her tenants. The old gentleman, who was a retired merchant with a reputation for the most perfect rectitude, was allowed to have no dealings with us. When we came to see the house, it was the wife who showed us round. It was she who, with a lavish display of charm, with irresistible rollings of the eyes, expatiated on the merits of the place, sang the praises of the electric pump, glorified the bathroom (considering which, she insisted, the rent was remarkably moderate), and when we suggested calling in a surveyor to look over the house, earnestly begged us, as though our well-being were her only consideration, not to waste our money unnecessarily in doing anything so superfluous. "After all," she said, "we are honest people. I wouldn't dream of letting you the house except in perfect condition. Have confidence." And she looked at me with an appealing, pained expression in her magnificent eyes, as though begging me not to insult her by my coarse suspiciousness. And leaving us no time to pursue the subject of surveyors any further, she began assuring us that our little boy was the most beautiful angel she had ever seen. By the time our interview with Signora Bondi was at an end, we had definitely decided to take the house.

"Charming woman," I said, as we left the house. But I think that Elizabeth was not quite so certain of it as I.

Then the pump episode began.

On the evening of our arrival in the house we switched on the electricity. The pump made a very professional whirring noise; but no water came out of the taps in the bathroom. We looked at one another doubtfully.

"Charming woman?" Elizabeth raised her eyebrows.

We asked for interviews; but somehow the old gentleman could never see us, and the Signora was invariably out or indisposed.

We left notes; they were never answered. In the end, we found that the only method of communicating with our landlords, who were living in the same house with us, was to go down into Florence and send a registered express letter to them. For this they had to sign two separate receipts and even, if we chose to pay forty centimes more, a third incriminating document, which was then returned to us. There could be no pretending, as there always was with ordinary letters or notes, that the communication had never been received. We began at last to get answers to our complaints. The Signora, who wrote all the letters, started by telling us that, naturally, the pump didn't work, as the cisterns were empty, owing to the long drought. I had to walk three miles to the post office in order to register my letter reminding her that there had been a violent thunderstorm only last Wednesday, and that the tanks were consequently more than half full. The answer came back: bath water had not been guaranteed in the contract; and if I wanted it, why hadn't I had the pump looked at before I took the house? Another walk into town to ask the Signora next door whether she remembered her adjurations to us to have confidence in her, and to inform her that the existence in a house of a bathroom was in itself an implicit guarantee of bath water. The reply to that was that the Signora couldn't continue to have communications with people who wrote so rudely to her. After that I put the matter into the hands of a lawyer. Two months later the pump was actually replaced. But we had to serve a writ on the lady before she gave in. And the costs were considerable.

One day, towards the end of the episode, I met the old gentleman in the road, taking his big maremman dog for a walk—or being taken, rather, for a walk by the dog. For where the dog pulled the old gentleman had perforce to follow. And when it stopped to smell, or scratch the ground, or leave against a gatepost its visiting-card or an offensive challenge, patiently, at his end of the leash, the old man had to wait. I passed him standing at the side of the road, a few hundred yards below our house. The dog was sniffing at the roots of one of the twin cypresses which grew one on either side of the entry to a farm; I heard the beast growling indignantly to itself, as though it scented an intolerable insult. Old Signor Bondi, leashed to his dog, was waiting. The knees inside the tubular grey trousers were slightly bent.

Leaning on his cane, he stood gazing mournfully and vacantly at the view. The whites of his old eyes were discoloured, like ancient billiard balls. In the grey, deeply wrinkled face, his nose was dyspeptically red. His white moustache, ragged and yellowing at the fringes, drooped in a melancholy curve. In his black tie he wore a very large diamond; perhaps that was what Signora Bondi had found so attractive about him.

I took off my hat as I approached. The old man stared at me absently, and it was only when I was already almost past him that he recollected who I was.

"Wait," he called after me, "wait!" And he hastened down the road in pursuit. Taken utterly by surprise and at a disadvantage—for it was engaged in retorting to the affront imprinted on the cypress roots—the dog permitted itself to be jerked after him. Too much astonished to be anything but obedient, it followed its master. "Wait!"

I waited.

"My dear sir," said the old gentleman, catching me by the lapel of my coat and blowing most disagreeably in my face, "I want to apologize." He looked around him, as though afraid that even here he might be overheard. "I want to apologize," he went on, "about that wretched pump business. I assure you that, if it had been only my affair, I'd have put the thing right as soon as you asked. You were quite right: a bathroom is an implicit guarantee of bath water. I saw from the first that we should have no chance if it came to court. And besides, I think one ought to treat one's tenants as handsomely as one can afford to. But my wife"—he lowered his voice—"the fact is that she likes this sort of thing, even when she knows that she's in the wrong and must lose. And besides, she hoped, I dare say, that you'd get tired of asking and have the job done yourself. I told her from the first that we ought to give in; but she wouldn't listen. You see, she enjoys it. Still, now she sees that it must be done. In the course of the next two or three days you'll be having your bath water. But I thought I'd just like to tell you how . . ." But the Maremmano, which had recovered by this time from its surprise of a moment since, suddenly bounded, growling, up the road. The old gentleman tried to hold the beast, strained at the leash, tottered unsteadily, then gave way and allowed himself to be dragged off. ". . . how sorry I am," he went on, as he receded from me, "that this little misunderstanding . . ." But it was no use. "Good-bye." He smiled politely, made a little deprecating gesture, as though he had suddenly remembered a pressing engagement, and had no time to explain what it was. "Good-bye." He took off his hat and abandoned himself completely to the dog.

A week later the water really did begin to flow, and the day after our first bath Signora Bondi, dressed in dove-grey satin and wearing all her pearls, came to call.

"Is it peace now?" she asked, with a charming frankness, as she shook hands.

We assured her that, so far as we were concerned, it certainly was.

"But why *did* you write me such dreadfully rude letters?" she said, turning on me a reproachful glance that ought to have moved the most ruthless malefactor to contrition. "And then that writ. How *could* you? To a lady . . ."

I mumbled something about the pump and our wanting baths.

"But how could you expect me to listen to you while you were in that mood? Why didn't you set about it differently—politely, charmingly?" She smiled at me and dropped her fluttering eyelids.

I thought it best to change the conversation. It is disagreeable, when one is in the right, to be made to appear in the wrong.

A few weeks later we had a letter—duly registered and by express messenger—in which the Signora asked us whether we proposed to renew our lease (which was only for six months), and notifying us that, if we did, the rent would be raised 25 per cent., in consideration of the improvements which had been carried out. We thought ourselves lucky, at the end of much bargaining, to get the lease renewed for a whole year with an increase in the rent of only 15 per cent.

It was chiefly for the sake of the view that we put up with these intolerable extortions. But we had found other reasons, after a few days' residence, for liking the house. Of these the most cogent was that, in the peasant's youngest child, we had discovered what seemed the perfect playfellow for our own small boy. Between little Guido—for that was his name—and the youngest of his brothers and sisters there was a gap of six or seven years. His two elder brothers worked with their father in the fields; since the time of the mother's death, two or three years before we knew them, the eldest sister had ruled the house, and the younger, who had just left school, helped her and in between-whiles kept an eye on Guido, who by this time, however, needed very little looking after; for he was between six and seven years old and as precocious, self-assured, and responsible as the children of the poor, left as they are to themselves almost from the time they can walk, generally are.

Though fully two and a half years older than little Robin—and at that age thirty months are crammed with half a lifetime's experience—Guido took no undue advantage of his superior intelligence and strength. I have never seen a child more patient, tolerant, and untyrannical. He never laughed at Robin for his clumsy efforts to imitate his own prodigious feats; he did not tease or bully, but helped his small companion when he was in difficulties and explained when he could not understand. In return, Robin adored him, regarded him as the model and perfect Big Boy, and slavishly imitated him in every way he could.

These attempts of Robin's to imitate his companion were often exceedingly ludicrous. For by an obscure psychological law, words and actions in themselves quite serious become comic as soon as they are copied; and the more accurately, if the imitation is a deliberate parody, the funnier—for an overloaded imitation of some one we know does not make us laugh so much as one that is almost indistinguishably like the original. The bad imitation is only ludicrous when it is a piece of sincere and earnest flattery which does not quite come off. Robin's imitations were mostly of this kind. His heroic and unsuccessful attempts to perform the feats of strength and skill, which Guido could do with ease, were exquisitely comic. And his careful, long-drawn imitations of Guido's habits and mannerisms were no less amusing. Most ludicrous of all, because most earnestly undertaken and most incongruous in the imitator, were Robin's impersonations of Guido in the pensive mood. Guido was a thoughtful child, given to brooding and sudden abstractions. One would find him sitting in a corner by himself, chin in hand, elbow on knee, plunged, to all appearances, in the profoundest meditation. And sometimes, even in the midst of his play, he would suddenly break off, to stand, his hands behind his back, frowning and staring at the ground. When this happened, Robin became overawed and a little disquieted. In a puzzled silence he looked at his companion.

"Guido," he would say softly, "Guido." But Guido was generally too much preoccupied to answer; and Robin, not venturing to insist, would creep near him, and throwing himself as nearly as possible into Guido's attitude—standing Napoleonically, his hands clasped behind him, or sitting in the posture of Michelangelo's Lorenzo the Magnificent—would try to meditate too. Every few seconds he would turn his bright blue eyes towards the elder child to see whether he was doing it quite right. But at the end of a minute he began to grow impatient; meditation wasn't his strong point. "Guido," he called again and, louder, "Guido!" And he would take him by the hand and try to pull him away. Sometimes Guido roused himself from his reverie and went back to the interrupted game. Sometimes he paid no attention. Melancholy, perplexed, Robin had to take himself off to play by himself. And Guido would go on sitting or standing there, quite still; and his eyes, if one looked into them, were beautiful in their grave and pensive calm.

They were large eyes, set far apart and, what was strange in a dark-haired Italian child, of a luminous pale blue-grey colour. They were not always grave and calm, as in these pensive moments. When he was playing, when he talked or laughed, they lit up; and the surface of those clear, pale lakes of thought seemed, as it were, to be shaken into brilliant sun-flashing ripples. Above those eyes was a beautiful forehead, high and steep and domed in a curve that was like the subtle curve of a rose petal. The nose was straight, t..e chin small and rather pointed, the mouth drooped a little sadly at the corners.

I have a snapshot of the two children sitting together on the parapet of the terrace. Guido sits almost facing the camera, but looking a little to one side and downwards; his hands are crossed in his lap and his expression, his attitude are thoughtful, grave, and meditative. It is Guido in one of those moods of abstraction into which he would pass even at the height of laughter and play —quite suddenly and completely, as though he had all at once taken it into his head to go away and had left the silent and beautiful body behind, like an empty house, to wait for his return. And by his side sits little Robin, turning to look up at him, his face half averted from the camera, but the curve of his cheek showing that he is laughing; one little raised hand is caught at the top of a gesture, the other clutches at Guido's sleeve, as though

he were urging him to come away and play. And the legs dangling from the parapet have been seen by the blinking instrument
in the midst of an impatient wriggle; he is on the point of slipping
down and running off to play hide-and-seek in the garden. All the
essential characteristics of both the children are in that little
snapshot.

"If Robin were not Robin," Elizabeth used to say, "I could
almost wish he were Guido."

And even at that time, when I took no particular interest in the
child, I agreed with her. Guido seemed to me one of the most
charming little boys I had ever seen.

We were not alone in admiring him. Signora Bondi when, in
those cordial intervals between our quarrels, she came to call, was
constantly speaking of him. "Such a beautiful, beautiful child!"
she would exclaim with enthusiasm. "It's really a waste that he
should belong to peasants who can't afford to dress him properly.
If he were mine, I should put him into black velvet; or little
white knickers and a white knitted silk jersey with a red line at the
collar and cuffs; or perhaps a white sailor suit would be pretty.
And in winter a little fur coat, with a squirrel skin cap, and
possibly Russian boots . . ." Her imagination was running away
with her. "And I'd let his hair grow, like a page's, and have it just
curled up a little at the tips. And a straight fringe across his forehead. Every one would turn round and stare after us if I took
him out with me in Via Tornabuoni."

What you want, I should have liked to tell her, is not a child;
it's a clock-work doll or a performing monkey. But I did not say
so—partly because I could not think of the Italian for a clock-
work doll and partly because I did not want to risk having the
rent raised another 15 per cent.

"Ah, if only I had a little boy like that!" She sighed and
modestly dropped her eyelids. "I adore children. I sometimes
think of adopting one—that is, if my husband would allow it."

I thought of the poor old gentleman being dragged along at
the heels of his big white dog and inwardly smiled.

"But I don't know if he would," the Signora was continuing,
"I don't know if he would." She was silent for a moment, as
though considering a new idea.

A few days later, when we were sitting in the garden after
luncheon, drinking our coffee, Guido's father, instead of passing

with a nod and the usual cheerful good-day, halted in front of us and began to talk. He was a fine handsome man, not very tall, but well proportioned, quick and elastic in his movements, and full of life. He had a thin brown face, featured like a Roman's and lit by a pair of the most intelligent-looking grey eyes I ever saw. They exhibited almost too much intelligence when, as not infrequently happened, he was trying, with an assumption of perfect frankness and a childlike innocence, to take one in or get something out of one. Delighting in itself, the intelligence shone there mischievously. The face might be ingenuous, impassive, almost imbecile in its expression; but the eyes on these occasions gave him completely away. One knew, when they glittered like that, that one would have to be careful.

To-day, however, there was no dangerous light in them. He wanted nothing out of us, nothing of any value—only advice, which is a commodity, he knew, that most people are only too happy to part with. But he wanted advice on what was, for us, rather a delicate subject: on Signora Bondi. Carlo had often complained to us about her. The old man is good, he told us, very good and kind indeed. Which meant, I dare say, among other things, that he could easily be swindled. But his wife . . . Well, the woman was a beast. And he would tell us stories of her insatiable rapacity: she was always claiming more than the half of the produce which, by the laws of the métayage system, was the proprietor's due. He complained of her suspiciousness: she was for ever accusing him of sharp practices, of downright stealing—him, he struck his breast, the soul of honesty. He complained of her short-sighted avarice: she wouldn't spend enough on manure, wouldn't buy him another cow, wouldn't have electric light installed in the stables. And we had sympathized, but cautiously, without expressing too strong an opinion on the subject. The Italians are wonderfully non-committal in their speech; they will give nothing away to an interested person until they are quite certain that it is right and necessary and, above all, safe to do so. We had lived long enough among them to imitate their caution. What we said to Carlo would be sure, sooner or later, to get back to Signora Bondi. There was nothing to be gained by unnecessarily embittering our relations with the lady—only another 15 per cent., very likely, to be lost.

To-day he wasn't so much complaining as feeling perplexed.

The Signora had sent for him, it seemed, and asked him how he would like it if she were to make an offer—it was all very hypo-thetical in the cautious Italian style—to adopt little Guido. Carlo's first instinct had been to say that he wouldn't like it at all. But an answer like that would have been too coarsely committal. He had preferred to say that he would think about it. And now he was asking for our advice.

Do what you think best, was what in effect we replied. But we gave it distantly but distinctly to be understood that we didn't think that Signora Bondi would make a very good foster-mother for the child. And Carlo was inclined to agree. Besides, he was very fond of the boy.

"But the thing is," he concluded rather gloomily, "that if she has really set her heart on getting hold of the child, there's nothing she won't do to get him—nothing."

He too, I could see, would have liked the physicists to start on unemployed childless women of sanguine temperament before they tried to tackle the atom. Still, I reflected, as I watched him striding away along the terrace, singing powerfully from a brazen gullet as he went, there was force there, there was life enough in those elastic limbs, behind those bright grey eyes, to put up a good fight even against the accumulated vital energies of Signora Bondi.

It was a few days after this that my gramophone and two or three boxes of records arrived from England. They were a great comfort to us on the hilltop, providing as they did the only thing in which that spiritually fertile solitude—otherwise a perfect Swiss Family Robinson's island—was lacking: music. There is not much music to be heard nowadays in Florence. The times when Dr Burney could tour through Italy, listening to an unend-ing succession of new operas, symphonies, quartets, cantatas, are gone. Gone are the days when a learned musician, inferior only to the Reverend Father Martini of Bologna, could admire what the peasants sang and the strolling players thrummed and scraped on their instruments. I have travelled for weeks through the peninsula and hardly heard a note that was not "Salome" or the Fascists' song. Rich in nothing else that makes life agreeable or even supportable, the northern metropolises are rich in music. That is perhaps the only inducement that a reasonable man can find for living there. The other attractions—organized gaiety, people, miscellaneous conversation, the social pleasures—what are those, after all, but an expense of spirit that buys nothing in return? And then the cold, the darkness, the mouldering dirt, the damp and squalor. . . . No, where there is no necessity that retains, music can be the only inducement. And that, thanks to the ingenious Edison, can now be taken about in a box and unpacked in whatever solitude one chooses to visit. One can live at Benin, or Nuneaton, or Tozeur in the Sahara, and still hear Mozart quartets, and selections from the Well-Tempered Clavichord, and the Fifth Symphony, and the Brahms clarinet quintet, and motets by Palestrina.

Carlo, who had gone down to the station with his mule and cart to fetch the packing-case, was vastly interested in the machine.

"One will hear some music again," he said, as he watched me unpacking the gramophone and the disks. "It is difficult to do much oneself."

Still, I reflected, he managed to do a good deal. On warm nights we used to hear him, where he sat at the door of his house, playing his guitar and softly singing; the eldest boy shrilled out the melody on the mandoline, and sometimes the whole family would join in, and the darkness would be filled with their passionate, throaty singing. Piedigrotta songs they mostly sang; and the voices drooped slurringly from note to note, lazily climbed or jerked themselves with sudden sobbing emphases from one tone to another. At a distance and under the stars the effect was not unpleasing.

"Before the war," he went on, "in normal times" (and Carlo had a hope, even a belief, that the normal times were coming back and that life would soon be as cheap and easy as it had been in the days before the flood), "I used to go and listen to the operas at the Politeama. Ah, they were magnificent. But it costs five lire now to get in."

"Too much," I agreed.

"Have you got *Trovatore*?" he asked.

I shook my head.

"*Rigoletto?*"

"I'm afraid not."

"*Bohème? Fanciulla del West? Pagliacci?*"

I had to go on disappointing him.

"Not even *Norma?* Or the *Barbiere?*"

I put on Battistini in "La ci darem" out of *Don Giovanni*. He agreed that the singing was good; but I could see that he didn't much like the music. Why not? He found it difficult to explain. "It's not like *Pagliacci*," he said at last.

"Not palpitating?" I suggested, using a word with which I was sure he would be familiar; for it occurs in every Italian political speech and patriotic leading article.

"Not palpitating," he agreed.

And I reflected that it is precisely by the difference between *Pagliacci* and *Don Giovanni*, between the palpitating and the non-palpitating, that modern musical taste is separated from the old. The corruption of the best, I thought, is the worst. Beethoven taught music to palpitate with his intellectual and spiritual passion. It has gone on palpitating ever since, but with the passion of inferior men. Indirectly, I thought, Beethoven is responsible for *Parsifal*, *Pagliacci*, and the *Poem of Fire*; still more indirectly for *Samson and Delilah* and "Ivy, cling to me." Mozart's melodies may be brilliant, memorable, infectious; but they don't palpitate, don't catch you between wind and water, don't send the listener off into erotic ecstasies.

Carlo and his elder children found my gramophone, I am afraid, rather a disappointment. They were too polite, however, to say so openly; they merely ceased, after the first day or two, to take any interest in the machine and the music it played. They preferred the guitar and their own singing.

Guido, on the other hand, was immensely interested. And he liked, not the cheerful dance tunes, to whose sharp rhythms our little Robin loved to go stamping round and round the room, pretending that he was a whole regiment of soldiers, but the genuine stuff. The first record he heard, I remember, was that of the slow movement of Bach's Concerto in D Minor for two violins. That was the disk I put on the turn-table as soon as Carlo had left me. It seemed to me, so to speak, the most musical piece of music with which I could refresh my long-parched mind—the coolest and clearest of all draughts. The movement had just got under way and was beginning to unfold its pure and melancholy beauties in accordance with the laws of the most exacting intellectual logic, when the two children, Guido in front and little Robin breathlessly following, came clattering into the room from the loggia.

Guido came to a halt in front of the gramophone and stood there, motionless, listening. His pale blue-grey eyes opened themselves wide; making a little nervous gesture that I had often noticed in him before, he plucked at his lower lip with his thumb and forefinger. He must have taken a deep breath; for I noticed that, after listening for a few seconds, he sharply expired and drew in a fresh gulp of air. For an instant he looked at me—a questioning, astonished, rapturous look—gave a little laugh that ended in a kind of nervous shudder, and turned back towards the source of the incredible sounds. Slavishly imitating his elder comrade, Robin had also taken up his stand in front of the gramophone, and in exactly the same position, glancing at Guido from time to time to make sure that he was doing everything, down to plucking at his lip, in the correct way. But after a minute or so he became bored.

"Soldiers," he said, turning to me; "I want soldiers. Like in London." He remembered the rag-time and the jolly marches round and round the room.

I put my fingers to my lips. "Afterwards," I whispered.

Robin managed to remain silent and still for perhaps another twenty seconds. Then he seized Guido by the arm, shouting, "Vieni, Guido! Soldiers. Soldati. Vieni giuocare soldati."

It was then, for the first time, that I saw Guido impatient. "Vai!" he whispered angrily, slapped at Robin's clutching hand and pushed him roughly away. And he leaned a little closer to the instrument, as though to make up by yet intenser listening for what the interruption had caused him to miss.

Robin looked at him, astonished. Such a thing had never happened before. Then he burst out crying and came to me for consolation.

When the quarrel was made up—and Guido was sincerely repentant, was as nice as he knew how to be when the music had stopped and his mind was free to think of Robin once more—I asked him how he liked the music. He said he thought it was beautiful. But *bello* in Italian is too vague a word, too easily and frequently uttered, to mean very much.

"What did you like best?" I insisted. For he had seemed to enjoy it so much that I was curious to find out what had really impressed him.

He was silent for a moment, pensively frowning. "Well," he

said at last, "I liked the bit that went like this." And he hummed a long phrase. "And then there's the other thing singing at the same time—but what are those things," he interrupted himself, "that sing like that?"

"They're called violins," I said.

"Violins." He nodded. "Well, the other violin goes like this." He hummed again. "Why can't one sing both at once? And what is in that box? What makes it make that noise?" The child poured out his questions.

I answered him as best I could, showing him the little spirals on the disk, the needle, the diaphragm. I told him to remember how the string of the guitar trembled when one plucked it; sound is a shaking in the air, I told him, and I tried to explain how those shakings get printed on the black disk. Guido listened to me very gravely, nodding from time to time. I had the impression that he understood perfectly well everything I was saying.

By this time, however, poor Robin was so dreadfully bored that in pity for him I had to send the two children out into the garden to play. Guido went obediently; but I could see that he would have preferred to stay indoors and listen to more music. A little while later, when I looked out, he was hiding in the dark recesses of the big bay tree, roaring like a lion, and Robin, laughing, but a little nervously, as though he were afraid that the horrible noise might possibly turn out, after all, to be the roaring of a real lion, was beating the bush with a stick, and shouting, "Come out, come out! I want to shoot you."

After lunch, when Robin had gone upstairs for his afternoon sleep, he reappeared. "May I listen to the music now?" he asked. And for an hour he sat there in front of the instrument, his head cocked slightly on one side, listening while I put on one disk after another.

Thenceforward he came every afternoon. Very soon he knew all my library of records, had his preferences and dislikes, and could ask for what he wanted by humming the principal theme.

"I don't like that one," he said of Strauss's "Till Eulenspiegel." "It's like what we sing in our house. Not really like, you know. But somehow rather like, all the same. You understand?" He looked at us perplexedly and appealingly, as though begging us to understand what he meant and so save him from going on explaining. We nodded. Guido went on. "And then," he said, "the end doesn't seem to come properly out of the beginning. It's not like the one you played the first time." He hummed a bar or two from the slow movement of Bach's D Minor Concerto.

"It isn't," I suggested, "like saying: All little boys like playing. Guido is a little boy. Therefore Guido likes playing."

He frowned. "Yes, perhaps that's it," he said at last. "The one you played first is more like that. But, you know," he added, with an excessive regard for truth, "I don't like playing as much as Robin does."

Wagner was among his dislikes; so was Debussy. When I played the record of one of Debussy's Arabesques, he said, "Why does he say the same thing over and over again? He ought to say something new, or go on, or make the thing grow. Can't he think of anything different?" But he was less censorious about the "Après-midi d'un Faune." "The things have beautiful voices," he said.

Mozart overwhelmed him with delight. The duet from *Don Giovanni*, which his father had found insufficiently palpitating, enchanted Guido. But he preferred the quartets and the orchestral pieces.

"I like music," he said, "better than singing."

Most people, I reflected, like singing better than music; are more interested in the executant than in what he executes, and find the impersonal orchestra less moving than the soloist. The touch of the pianist is the human touch, and the soprano's high C is the personal note. It is for the sake of his touch, that note, that audiences fill the concert halls.

Guido, however, preferred music. True, he liked "La ci darem"; he liked "Deh vieni alla finestra"; he thought "Che soave zefiretto" so lovely that almost all our concerts had to begin with it. But he preferred the other things. The *Figaro* overture was one of his favourites. There is a passage not far from the beginning of the piece, where the first violins suddenly go rocketing up into the heights of loveliness; as the music approached that point, I used always to see a smile developing and gradually brightening on Guido's face, and when, punctually, the thing happened, he clapped his hands and laughed aloud with pleasure.

On the other side of the same disk, it happened, was recorded Beethoven's *Egmont* overture. He liked that almost better than *Figaro*.

"It has more voices," he explained. And I was delighted by the acuteness of the criticism; for it is precisely in the richness of its orchestration that *Egmont* goes beyond *Figaro*.

But what stirred him almost more than anything was the *Coriolan* overture. The third movement of the Fifth Symphony, the second movement of the Seventh, the slow movement of the Emperor Concerto—all these things ran it pretty close. But none excited him so much as *Coriolan*. One day he made me play it three or four times in succession; then he put it away.

"I don't think I want to hear that any more," he said.

"Why not?"

"It's too . . . too . . ." he hesitated, "too big," he said at last. "I don't really understand it. Play me the one that goes like this." He hummed the phrase from the D Minor Concerto.

"Do you like that one better?" I asked.

He shook his head. "No, it's not that exactly. But it's easier."

"Easier?" It seemed to me rather a queer word to apply to Bach.

"I understand it better."

One afternoon, while we were in the middle of our concert, Signora Bondi was ushered in. She began at once to be overwhelmingly affectionate towards the child; kissed him, patted his head, paid him the most outrageous compliments on his appearance. Guido edged away from her.

"And do you like music?" she asked.

The child nodded.

"I think he has a gift," I said. "At any rate, he has a wonderful ear and a power of listening and criticizing such as I've never met with in a child of that age. We're thinking of hiring a piano for him to learn on."

A moment later I was cursing myself for my undue frankness in praising the boy. For Signora Bondi began immediately to protest that, if she could have the upbringing of the child, she would give him the best masters, bring out his talent, make an accomplished maestro of him—and, on the way, an infant prodigy. And at that moment, I am sure, she saw herself sitting maternally, in pearls and black satin, in the lea of the huge Steinway, while an angelic Guido, dressed like little Lord Fauntleroy, rattled out Liszt and Chopin, to the loud delight of a thronged auditorium. She saw the bouquets and all the elaborate floral tributes, heard the clapping and the few well-chosen words with which the veteran maestri, touched almost to tears, would hail the coming of the little genius. It became more than ever important for her to acquire the child.

"You've sent her away fairly ravening," said Elizabeth, when Signora Bondi had gone. "Better tell her next time that you made a mistake, and that the boy's got no musical talent whatever."

In due course, the piano arrived. After giving him the minimum of preliminary instruction, I let Guido loose on it. He began by picking out for himself the melodies he had heard, reconstructing the harmonies in which they were embedded. After a few lessons, he understood the rudiments of musical notation and could read a simple passage at sight, albeit very slowly. The whole process of reading was still strange to him; he had picked up his letters somehow, but nobody had yet taught him to read whole words and sentences.

I took occasion, next time I saw Signora Bondi, to assure her that Guido had disappointed me. There was nothing in his musical talent, really. She professed to be very sorry to hear it; but I could see that she didn't for a moment believe me. Probably she thought that we were after the child too, and wanted to bag the infant prodigy for ourselves, before she could get in her claim, thus depriving her of what she regarded almost as her feudal right. For, after all, weren't they her peasants? If any one was to profit by adopting the child it ought to be herself.

Tactfully, diplomatically, she renewed her negotiations with Carlo. The boy, she put it to him, had genius. It was the foreign gentleman who had told her so, and he was the sort of man, clearly, who knew about such things. If Carlo would let her adopt the child, she'd have him trained. He'd become a great maestro and get engagements in the Argentine and the United States, in Paris and London. He'd earn millions and millions. Think of Caruso, for example. Part of the millions, she explained, would of course come to Carlo. But before they began to roll in, those millions, the boy would have to be trained. But training was very expensive. In his own interest, as well as in that of his son, he ought to let her take charge of the child. Carlo said he would think it over, and again applied to us for advice. We suggested that it would be best in any case to wait a little and see what progress the boy made.

He made, in spite of my assertions to Signora Bondi, excellent progress. Every afternoon, while Robin was asleep, he came for his concert and his lesson. He was getting along famously with his reading; his small fingers were acquiring strength and agility. But what to me was more interesting was that he had begun to make up little pieces on his own account. A few of them I took down as he played them and I have them still. Most of them, strangely enough, as I thought then, are canons. He had a passion for canons. When I explained to him the principles of the form he was enchanted.

"It is beautiful," he said, with admiration. "Beautiful, beautiful. And so easy!"

Again the word surprised me. The canon is not, after all, so conspicuously simple. Thenceforward he spent most of his time at the piano in working out little canons for his own amusement. They were often remarkably ingenious. But in the invention of other kinds of music he did not show himself so fertile as I had hoped. He composed and harmonized one or two solemn little airs like hymn tunes, with a few sprightlier pieces in the spirit of the military march. They were extraordinary, of course, as being the inventions of a child. But a great many children can do extraordinary things; we are all geniuses up to the age of ten. But I had hoped that Guido was a child who was going to be a genius at forty; in which case what was extraordinary for an ordinary child was not extraordinary enough for him. "He's hardly a Mozart," we agreed, as we played his little pieces over. I felt, it must be confessed, almost aggrieved. Anything less than a Mozart, it seemed to me, was hardly worth thinking about.

He was not a Mozart. No. But he was somebody, as I was to find out, quite as extraordinary. It was one morning in the early summer that I made the discovery. I was sitting in the warm shade of our westward-facing balcony, working. Guido and Robin were playing in the little enclosed garden below. Absorbed in my work, it was only, I suppose, after the silence had prolonged itself a considerable time that I became aware that the children were making remarkably little noise. There was no shouting, no running about; only a quiet talking. Knowing by experience that when children are quiet it generally means that they are absorbed in some delicious mischief, I got up from my chair and looked over the balustrade to see what they were doing. I expected to

catch them dabbling in water, making a bonfire, covering themselves with tar. But what I actually saw was Guido, with a burnt
stick in his hand, demonstrating on the smooth paving-stones of
the path, that the square on the hypotenuse of a right-angled
triangle is equal to the sum of the squares on the other two sides.

Kneeling on the floor, he was drawing with the point of his
blackened stick on the flagstones. And Robin, kneeling imitatively
beside him, was growing, I could see, rather impatient with this
very slow game.

"Guido," he said. But Guido paid no attention. Pensively
frowning, he went on with his diagram. "Guido!" The younger
child bent down and then craned round his neck so as to look up
into Guido's face. "Why don't you draw a train?"

"Afterwards," said Guido. "But I just want to show you this
first. It's *so* beautiful," he added cajolingly.

"But I want a train," Robin persisted.

"In a moment. Do just wait a moment." The tone was almost
imploring. Robin armed himself with renewed patience. A
minute later Guido had finished both his diagrams.

"There!" he said triumphantly, and straightened himself up to
look at them. "Now I'll explain."

And he proceeded to prove the theorem of Pythagoras—not in
Euclid's way, but by the simpler and more satisfying method
which was, in all probability, employed by Pythagoras himself.
He had drawn a square and dissected it, by a pair of crossed per-
pendiculars, into two squares and two equal rectangles. The
equal rectangles he divided up by their diagonals into four equal
right-angled triangles. The two squares are then seen to be the
squares on the two sides of any one of these triangles other than
the hypotenuse. So much for the first diagram. In the next he
took the four right-angled triangles into which the rectangles had
been divided and rearranged them round the original square so
that their right angles filled the corners of the square, the hypo-
tenuses looked inwards, and the greater and less sides of the
triangles were in continuation along the sides of the square (which
are each equal to the sum of these sides). In this way the original
square is redissected into four right-angled triangles and the
square on the hypotenuse. The four triangles are equal to the two
rectangles of the original dissection. Therefore the square on the
hypotenuse is equal to the sum of the two squares—the squares on

the other two sides—into which, with the rectangles, the original square was first dissected.

In very untechnical language, but clearly and with a relentless logic, Guido expounded his proof. Robin listened, with an expression on his bright, freckled face of perfect incomprehension. "Treno," he repeated from time to time. "Treno. Make a train."

"In a moment," Guido implored. "Wait a moment. But do just look at this. *Do*." He coaxed and cajoled. "It's so beautiful. It's so easy."

So easy. . . . The theorem of Pythagoras seemed to explain for me Guido's musical predilections. It was not an infant Mozart we had been cherishing; it was a little Archimedes with, like most of his kind, an incidental musical twist.

"Treno, treno!" shouted Robin, growing more and more restless as the exposition went on. And when Guido insisted on going on with his proof, he lost his temper. "Cattivo Guido," he shouted, and began to hit out at him with his fists.

"All right," said Guido resignedly. "I'll make a train." And with his stick of charcoal he began to scribble on the stones.

I looked on for a moment in silence. It was not a very good train. Guido might be able to invent for himself and prove the theorem of Pythagoras; but he was not much of a draughtsman.

"Guido!" I called. The two children turned and looked up. "Who taught you to draw those squares?" It was conceivable, of course, that somebody might have taught him.

"Nobody." He shook his head. Then, rather anxiously, as though he were afraid there might be something wrong about drawing squares, he went on to apologize and explain. "You see," he said, "it seemed to me so beautiful. Because those squares"—he pointed at the two small squares in the first figure—"are just as big as this one." And, indicating the square on the hypotenuse in the second diagram, he looked up at me with a deprecating smile.

I nodded. "Yes, it's very beautiful," I said—"it's very beautiful indeed."

An expression of delighted relief appeared on his face; he laughed with pleasure. "You see, it's like this," he went on, eager to initiate me into the glorious secret he had discovered. "You cut these two long squares"—he meant the rectangles—"into two slices. And then there are four slices, all just the same, because, because—oh, I ought to have said that before—because these long squares are the same, because those lines, you see . . ."

"But I want a train," protested Robin.

Leaning on the rail of the balcony, I watched the children below. I thought of the extraordinary thing I had just seen and of what it meant.

I thought of the vast differences between human beings. We classify men by the colour of their eyes and hair, the shape of their skulls. Would it not be more sensible to divide them up into intellectual species? There would be even wider gulfs between the extreme mental types than between a Bushman and a Scandinavian. This child, I thought, when he grows up, will be to me, intellectually, what a man is to a dog. And there are other men and women who are, perhaps, almost as dogs to me.

Perhaps the men of genius are the only true men. In all the history of the race there have been only a few thousand real men. And the rest of us—what are we? Teachable animals. Without the help of the real men, we should have found out almost nothing at all. Almost all the ideas with which we are familiar could never have occurred to minds like ours. Plant the seeds there and they will grow; but our minds could never spontaneously have generated them.

There have been whole nations of dogs, I thought; whole epochs in which no Man was born. From the dull Egyptians the Greeks took crude experience and rules of thumb and made sciences. More than a thousand years passed before Archimedes had a comparable successor. There has been only one Buddha, one Jesus, only one Bach that we know of, one Michelangelo.

Is it by a mere chance, I wondered, that a Man is born from time to time? What causes a whole constellation of them to come contemporaneously into being and from out of a single people? Taine thought that Leonardo, Michelangelo, and Raphael were born when they were because the time was ripe for great painters and the Italian scene congenial. In the mouth of a rationalizing nineteenth-century Frenchman the doctrine is strangely mystical; it may be none the less true for that. But what of those born out of time? Blake, for example. What of those?

This child, I thought, has had the fortune to be born at a time when he will be able to make good use of his capacities. He will find the most elaborate analytical methods lying ready to his hand; he will have a prodigious experience behind him. Suppose him born while Stone Henge was building; he might have spent a lifetime discovering the rudiments, guessing darkly where now he might have had a chance of proving. Born at the time of the Norman Conquest, he would have had to wrestle with all the preliminary difficulties created by an inadequate symbolism; it would have taken him long years, for example, to learn the art of dividing MMMCCCCLXXXVIII by MCMXIX. In five years, nowadays, he will learn what it took generations of Men to discover.

And I thought of the fate of all the Men born so hopelessly out of time that they could achieve little or nothing of value. Beethoven born in Greece, I thought, would have had to be content to play thin melodies on the flute or lyre; in those intellectual surroundings it would hardly have been possible for him to imagine the nature of harmony.

From drawing trains, the children in the garden below had gone on to playing trains. They were trotting round and round; with blown round cheeks and pouting mouth, like the cherubic symbol of a wind, Robin puff-puffed, and Guido. holding the skirt of his smock, shuffled behind him, tooting. They ran forward, backed, stopped at imaginary stations, shunted, roared over bridges, crashed through tunnels, met with occasional collisions and derailments. The young Archimedes seemed to be just as happy as the little tow-headed barbarian. A few minutes ago he had been busy with the theorem of Pythagoras. Now, tooting indefatigably along imaginary rails, he was perfectly content to shuffle backwards and forwards among the flower-beds, between the pillars of the loggia, in and out of the dark tunnels of the laurel tree. The fact that one is going to be Archimedes does not prevent one from being an ordinary cheerful child meanwhile. I thought of this strange talent distinct and separate from the rest of the mind, independent, almost, of experience. The typical child-prodigies are musical and mathematical; the other talents ripen slowly under the influence of emotional experience and growth. Till he was thirty Balzac gave proof of nothing but ineptitude; but at four the young Mozart was already a musician, and some of Pascal's most brilliant work was done before he was out of his teens.

In the weeks that followed, I alternated the daily piano lessons with lessons in mathematics. Hints rather than lessons they were; for I only made suggestions, indicated methods, and left the child himself to work out the ideas in detail. Thus I introduced him to algebra by showing him another proof of the theorem of Pythagoras. In this proof one drops a perpendicular from the right angle on to the hypotenuse, and arguing from the fact that the two triangles thus created are similar to one another and to the original triangle, and that the proportions which their corresponding sides bear to one another are therefore equal, one can show in algebraical form that c^2+d^2 (the squares on the other two sides) are equal to a^2+b^2 (the squares on the two segments of the hypotenuse) $+2ab$; which last, it is easy to show geometrically, is equal to $(a+b)^2$, or the square on the hypotenuse. Guido was as much enchanted by the rudiments of algebra as he would have been if I had given him an engine worked by steam, with a methylated spirit lamp to heat the boiler; more enchanted, perhaps—for the engine would have got broken, and, remaining always itself, would in any case have lost its charm, while the rudiments of algebra continued to grow and blossom in his mind with an unfailing luxuriance. Every day he made the discovery of something which seemed to him exquisitely beautiful; the new toy was inexhaustible in its potentialities.

In the intervals of applying algebra to the second book of Euclid, we experimented with circles; we stuck bamboos into the parched earth, measured their shadows at different hours of the day, and drew exciting conclusions from our observations. Sometimes, for fun, we cut and folded sheets of paper so as to make cubes and pyramids. One afternoon Guido arrived carrying carefully between his small and rather grubby hands a flimsy dodecahedron.

"È tanto bello!" he said, as he showed us his paper crystal; and when I asked him how he had managed to make it, he merely smiled and said it had been so easy. I looked at Elizabeth and laughed. But it would have been more symbolically to the point, I felt, if I had gone down on all fours, wagged the spiritual outgrowth of my os coccyx, and barked my astonished admiration.

It was an uncommonly hot summer. By the beginning of July our little Robin, unaccustomed to these high temperatures, began to look pale and tired; he was listless, had lost his appetite and energy. The doctor advised mountain air. We decided to spend the next ten or twelve weeks in Switzerland. My parting gift to Guido was the first six books of Euclid in Italian. He turned over the pages, looking ecstatically at the figures.

"If only I knew how to read properly," he said "I'm so stupid. But now I shall really try to learn."

From our hotel near Grindelwald we sent the child, in Robin's name, various post cards of cows, Alp-horns, Swiss chalets, edelweiss, and the like. We received no answers to these cards; but then we did not expect answers. Guido could not write, and there was no reason why his father or his sisters should take the trouble to write for him. No news, we took it, was good news. And then one day, early in September, there arrived at the hotel a strange letter. The manager had it stuck up on the glass-fronted notice-board in the hall, so that all the guests might see it, and whoever conscientiously thought that it belonged to him might claim it. Passing the board on the way into lunch, Elizabeth stopped to look at it.

"But it must be from Guido," she said.

I came and looked at the envelope over her shoulder. It was unstamped and black with postmarks. Traced out in pencil, the big uncertain capital letters sprawled across its face. In the first line was written: AL BABBO DI ROBIN, and there followed a travestied version of the name of the hotel and the place. Round the address bewildered postal officials had scrawled suggested emendations. The letter had wandered for a fortnight at least, back and forth across the face of Europe.

"Al Babbo di Robin. To Robin's father." I laughed. "Pretty smart of the postmen to have got it here at all." I went to the manager's office, set forth the justice of my claim to the letter and, having paid the fifty-centime surcharge for the missing stamp, had the case unlocked and the letter given me. We went in to lunch.

"The writing's magnificent," we agreed, laughing, as we examined the address at close quarters. "Thanks to Euclid," I added. "That's what comes of pandering to the ruling passion."

But when I opened the envelope and looked at its contents I no longer laughed. The letter was brief and almost telegraphical in style. "SONO DALLA PADRONA," it ran, "NON MI PIACE HA RUBATO IL MIO LIBRO NON VOGLIO SUONARE PIU VOGLIO TORNARE A CASA VENGA SUBITO GUIDO."

"What is it?"

I handed Elizabeth the letter. "That blasted woman's got hold of him," I said.

Busts of men in Homburg hats, angels bathed in marble tears extinguishing torches, statues of little girls, cherubs, veiled figures, allegories and ruthlessrealisms—the strangest and most diverse idols beckoned and gesticulated as we passed. Printed indelibly on tin and embedded in the living rock, the brown photographs looked out, under glass, from the humbler crosses, headstones, and broken pillars. Dead ladies in the cubistic geometrical fashions of thirty years ago—two cones of black satin meeting point to point at the waist, and the arms; a sphere to the elbow, a polished cylinder below—smiled mournfully out of their marble frames; the smiling faces, the white hands, were the only recognizably human things that emerged from the solid geometry of their clothes. Men with black moustaches, men with white beards, young clean-shaven men, stared or averted their gaze to show a Roman profile. Children in their stiff best opened wide their eyes, smiled hopefully in anticipation of the little bird that was to issue from the camera's muzzle, smiled sceptically in the knowledge that it wouldn't, smiled laboriously and obediently because they had been told to. In spiky Gothic cottages of marble the richer dead privately reposed; through grilled doors one caught a glimpse of pale Inconsolables weeping, of distraught Geniuses guarding the secret of the tomb. The less prosperous sections of the majority slept in communities, close-crowded but elegantly housed under smooth continuous marble floors, whose every flagstone was the mouth of a separate grave.

These continental cemeteries, I thought, as Carlo and I made our way among the dead, are more frightful than ours, because these people pay more attention to their dead than we do. That primordial cult of corpses, that tender solicitude for their material well-being, which led the ancients to house their dead in stone, while they themselves lived between wattles and under thatch, still lingers here; persists, I thought, more vigorously than with us. There are a hundred gesticulating statues here for every one in an English graveyard. There are more family vaults, more "luxuriously appointed" (as they say of liners and hotels) than one would find at home. And embedded in every tombstone there are photographs to remind the powdered bones within what form they will have to resume on the Day of Judgment; beside each are little hanging lamps to burn optimistically on All Soul's Day. To the Man who built the Pyramids they are nearer, I thought, than we.

"If I had known," Carlo kept repeating, "if only I had known." His voice came to me through my reflections as though from a distance. "At the time he didn't mind at all. How should I have known that he would take it so much to heart afterwards? And she deceived me, she lied to me."

I assured him yet once more that it wasn't his fault. Though, of course, it was, in part. It was mine too, in part; I ought to have thought of the possibility and somehow guarded against it. And he shouldn't have let the child go, even temporarily and on trial, even though the woman was bringing pressure to bear on him. And the pressure had been considerable. They had worked on the same holding for more than a hundred years, the men of Carlo's family; and now she had made the old man threaten to turn him out. It would be a dreadful thing to leave the place; and besides, another place wasn't so easy to find. It was made quite plain, however, that he could stay if he let her have the child. Only for a little to begin with; just to see how he got on. There would be no compulsion whatever on him to stay if he didn't like it. And it would be all to Guido's advantage; and to his father's, too, in the end. All that the Englishman had said about his not being such a good musician as he had thought at first was obviously untrue—mere jealousy and little-mindedness: the man wanted to take credit for Guido himself, that was all. And the boy, it was obvious, would learn nothing from him. What he needed was a real good professional master.

All the energy that, if the physicists had known their business, would have been driving dynamos, went into this campaign. It began the moment we were out of the house, intensively. She would have more chance of success, the Signora doubtless thought, if we weren't there. And besides, it was essential to take the opportunity when it offered itself and get hold of the child before we could make our bid—for it was obvious to her that we wanted Guido just as much as she did.

Day after day she renewed the assault. At the end of a week she sent her husband to complain about the state of the vines: they were in a shocking condition; he had decided, or very nearly decided, to give Carlo notice. Meekly, shamefacedly, in obedience to higher orders, the old gentleman uttered his threats. Next day Signora Bondi returned to the attack. The padrone, she declared, had been in a towering passion; but she'd do her best, her very best, to mollify him. And after a significant pause she went on to talk about Guido.

In the end Carlo gave in. The woman was too persistent and she held too many trump cards. The child could go and stay with her for a month or two on trial. After that, if he really expressed a desire to remain with her, she could formally adopt him.

At the idea of going for a holiday to the seaside—and it was to the seaside, Signora Bondi told him, that they were going—Guido was pleased and excited. He had heard a lot about the sea from Robin. "Tanta acqua!" It had sounded almost too good to be true. And now he was actually to go and see this marvel. It was very cheerfully that he parted from his family.

But after the holiday by the sea was over, and Signora Bondi had brought him back to her town house in Florence, he began to be homesick. The Signora, it was true, treated him exceedingly kindly, bought him new clothes, took him out to tea in the Via Tornabuoni and filled him up with cakes, iced strawberryade, whipped cream, and chocolates. But she made him practise the piano more than he liked, and what was worse, she took away his Euclid, on the score that he wasted too much time with it. And when he said that he wanted to go home, she put him off with promises and excuses and downright lies. She told him that she couldn't take him at once, but that next week, if he were good and worked hard at his piano meanwhile, next week . . . And when the time came she told him that his father didn't want him back. And she redoubled her petting, gave him expensive presents, and stuffed him with yet unhealthier foods. To no purpose. Guido didn't like his new life, didn't want to practise scales, pined for his book, and longed to be back with his brothers and sisters. Signora Bondi, meanwhile, continued to hope that time and chocolates would eventually make the child hers; and to keep his family at a distance, she wrote to Carlo every few days letters which still purported to come from the seaside (she took the trouble to send them to a friend, who posted them back again to Florence), and in which she painted the most charming picture of Guido's happiness.

It was then that Guido wrote his letter to me. Abandoned, as he supposed, by his family—for that they shouldn't take the trouble to come to see him when they were so near was only to be explained on the hypothesis that they really had given him up —he must have looked to me as his last and only hope. And the letter, with its fantastic address, had been nearly a fortnight on its way. A fortnight—it must have seemed hundreds of years; and as the centuries succeeded one another, gradually, no doubt, the poor child became convinced that I too had abandoned him. There was no hope left.

"Here we are," said Carlo.

I looked up and found myself confronted by an enormous monument. In a kind of grotto hollowed in the flanks of a monolith of grey sandstone, Sacred Love, in bronze, was embracing a funerary urn. And in bronze letters riveted into the stone was a long legend to the effect that the inconsolable Ernesto Bondi had raised this monument to the memory of his beloved wife, Annunziata, as a token of his undying love for one whom, snatched from him by a premature death, he hoped very soon to join beneath this stone. The first Signora Bondi had died in 1912. I thought of the old man leashed to his white dog; he must always, I reflected, have been a most uxorious husband.

"They buried him here."

We stood there for a long time in silence. I felt the tears coming into my eyes as I thought of the poor child lying there underground. I thought of those luminous grave eyes, and the curve of that beautiful forehead, the droop of the melancholy mouth, of the expression of delight which illumined his face when he learned of some new idea that pleased him, when he heard a piece of music that he liked. And this beautiful small being was dead; and the spirit that inhabited this form, the amazing spirit, that too had been destroyed almost before it had begun to exist.

And the unhappiness that must have preceded the final act, the child's despair, the conviction of his utter abandonment— those were terrible to think of, terrible.

"I think we had better come away now," I said at last, and touched Carlo on the arm. He was standing there like a blind man, his eyes shut, his face slightly lifted towards the light; from between his closed eyelids the tears welled out, hung for a moment, and trickled down his cheeks. His lips trembled and I could see that he was making an effort to keep them still. "Come away," I repeated.

The face which had been still in its sorrow, was suddenly convulsed; he opened his eyes, and through the tears they were bright with a violent anger. "I shall kill her," he said, "I shall kill her. When I think of him throwing himself out, falling through the air . . ." With his two hands he made a violent gesture, bringing them down from over his head and arresting them with a sudden jerk when they were on a level with his breast. "And then crash." He shuddered. "She's as much responsible as though she had pushed him down herself. I shall kill her." He clenched his teeth.

To be angry is easier than to be sad, less painful. It is comforting to think of revenge. "Don't talk like that," I said. "It's no good. It's stupid. And what would be the point?" He had had those fits before, when grief became too painful and he had tried to escape from it. Anger had been the easiest way of escape. I had had, before this, to persuade him back into the harder path of grief. "It's stupid to talk like that," I repeated, and I led him away through the ghastly labyrinth of tombs, where death seemed more terrible even than it is.

By the time we had left the cemetery, and were walking down from San Miniato towards the Piazzale Michelangelo below, he had become calmer. His anger had subsided again into the sorrow from which it had derived all its strength and its bitterness. In the Piazzale we halted for a moment to look down at the city in the valley below us. It was a day of floating clouds—great shapes, white, golden, and grey; and between them patches of a thin, transparent blue. Its lantern level, almost, with our eyes, the dome of the cathedral revealed itself in all its grandiose lightness, its vastness and aerial strength. On the innumerable brown and rosy roofs of the city the afternoon sunlight lay softly, sumptuously, and the towers were as though varnished and enamelled with an old gold. I thought of all the Men who had lived here and left the visible traces of their spirit and conceived extraordinary things. I thought of the dead child.

Half-holiday

I

IT was Saturday afternoon and fine. In the hazy spring sunlight London was beautiful, like a city of the imagination. The lights were golden, the shadows blue and violet. Incorrigibly hopeful, the sooty trees in the Park were breaking into leaf; and the new green was unbelievably fresh and light and aerial, as though the tiny leaves had been cut out of the central emerald stripe of a rainbow. The miracle, to all who walked in the Park that afternoon, was manifest. What had been dead now lived; soot was budding into rainbow green. Yes, it was manifest. And, moreover, those who perceived this thaumaturgical change from death to life were themselves changed. There was something contagious about the vernal miracle. Loving more, the loitering couples under the trees were happier—or much more acutely miserable. Stout men took off their hats, and while the sun kissed their bald heads, made good resolutions—about whisky, about the pretty typist at the office, about early rising. Accosted by spring-intoxicated boys, young girls consented, in the teeth of all their upbringing and their alarm, to go for walks. Middle-aged gentlemen, strolling homewards through the Park, suddenly felt their crusted, business-grimy hearts burgeoning, like these trees, with kindness and generosity. They thought of their wives, thought of them with a sudden gush of affection, in spite of twenty years of marriage. "Must stop on the way back," they said to themselves, "and buy the missus a little present." What should it be? A box of candied fruits? She liked candied fruits. Or a pot of azaleas? Or . . . And then they remembered that it was Saturday afternoon. The shops would all be shut. And probably, they thought, sighing, the missus's heart would also be shut; for the missus had not walked under the budding trees. Such is life, they reflected, looking sadly at the boats on the glittering Serpentine, at the playing children, at the lovers sitting, hand in hand, on the green grass. Such is life; when the heart is open, the shops are generally shut. But they resolved nevertheless to try, in future, to control their tempers.

On Peter Brett, as on every one else who came within their range of influence, this bright spring sunlight and the new-budded trees profoundly worked. They made him feel, all at once, more lonely, more heart-broken than he had ever felt before. By contrast with the brightness around him, his soul seemed darker. The trees had broken into leaf; but he remained dead. The lovers walked in couples; he walked alone. In spite of the spring, in spite of the sunshine, in spite of the fact that to-day was Saturday and that to-morrow would be Sunday—or rather because of all these things which should have made him happy and which did make other people happy—he loitered through the miracle of Hyde Park feeling deeply miserable.

As usual, he turned for comfort to his imagination. For example, a lovely young creature would slip on a loose stone just in front of him and twist her ankle. Grown larger than life and handsomer, Peter would rush forward to administer first aid. He would take her in a taxi (for which he had money to pay) to her home—in Grosvenor Square. She turned out to be a peer's daughter. They loved each other. . . .

Or else he rescued a child that had fallen into the Round Pond and so earned the eternal gratitude, and more than the gratitude, of its rich young widowed mother. Yes, widowed; Peter always definitely specified her widowhood. His intentions were strictly honourable. He was still very young and had been well brought up.

Or else there was no preliminary accident. He just saw a young girl sitting on a bench by herself, looking very lonely and sad. Boldly, yet courteously, he approached, he took off his hat, he smiled. "I can see that you're lonely," he said; and he spoke elegantly and with ease, without a trace of his Lancashire accent, without so much as a hint of that dreadful stammer which, in real life, made speech such a torment to him. "I can see that you're lonely. So am I. May I sit down beside you?" She smiled, and he sat down. And then he told her that he was an orphan and that all he had was a married sister who lived in Rochdale. And she said, "I'm an orphan too." And that was a great bond between them. And they told one another how miserable they were. And she began to cry. And then he said, "Don't cry. You've got me." And at that she cheered up a little. And then they went to the pictures together. And finally, he supposed, they got married. But that part of the story was a little dim.

But of course, as a matter of fact, no accidents ever did happen and he never had the courage to tell any one how lonely he was; and his stammer was something awful; and he was small, he wore spectacles, and nearly always had pimples on his face; and his dark grey suit was growing very shabby and rather short in the sleeves; and his boots, though carefully blacked, looked just as cheap as they really were.

It was the boots which killed his imaginings this afternoon. Walking with downcast eyes, pensively, he was trying to decide what he should say to the peer's lovely young daughter in the taxi on the way to Grosvenor Square, when he suddenly became aware of his alternately striding boots, blackly obtruding themselves through the transparent phantoms of his inner life. How ugly they were! And how sadly unlike those elegant and sumptuously shining boots which encase the feet of the rich! They had been ugly enough when they were new; age had rendered them positively repulsive. No boot-trees had corrected the effects of walking, and the uppers, just above the toe-caps, were deeply and hideously wrinkled. Through the polish he could see a network of innumerable little cracks in the parched and shoddy leather. On the outer side of the left boot the toe-cap had come unstitched and had been coarsely sewn up again; the scar was only too visible. Worn by much lacing and unlacing, the eyeholes had lost their black enamel and revealed themselves obtrusively in their brassy nakedness.

Oh, they were horrible, his boots; they were disgusting! But they'd have to last him a long time yet. Peter began to re-make the calculations he had so often and often made before. If he spent three-halfpence less every day on his lunch; if, during the fine weather he were to walk to the office every morning instead of taking the bus. . . . But however carefully and however often he made his calculations, twenty-seven and sixpence a week always remained twenty-seven and six. Boots were dear; and when he had saved up enough to buy a new pair, there was still the question of his suit. And, to make matters worse, it was spring; the leaves were coming out, the sun shone, and among the amorous couples he walked alone. Reality was too much for him to-day; he could not escape. The boots pursued him whenever he tried to flee, and dragged him back to the contemplation of his misery.

II

The two young women turned out of the crowded walk along the edge of the Serpentine, and struck uphill by a smaller path in the direction of Watts's statue. Peter followed them. An exquisite perfume lingered in the air behind them. He breathed it greedily and his heart began to beat with unaccustomed violence. They seemed to him marvellous and hardly human beings. They were all that was lovely and unattainable. He had met them walking down there, by the Serpentine, had been overwhelmed by that glimpse of a luxurious and arrogant beauty, had turned immediately and followed them. Why? He hardly knew himself. Merely in order that he might be near them; and perhaps with the fantastic, irrepressible hope that something might happen, some miracle, that should project him into their lives.

Greedily he sniffed their delicate perfume; with a kind of desperation, as though his life depended on it, he looked at them, he studied them. Both were tall. One of them wore a grey cloth coat, trimmed with dark grey fur. The other's coat was all of fur; a dozen or two of ruddily golden foxes had been killed in order that she might be warm among the chilly shadows of this spring afternoon. One of them wore grey and the other buff-coloured stockings. One walked on grey kid, the other on serpent's leather. Their hats were small and close-fitting. A small black French bull-dog accompanied them running now at their heels, now in front of them. The dog's collar was trimmed with brindled wolf's fur that stuck out like a ruff round its black head.

Peter walked so close behind them that, when they were out of the crowd, he could hear snatches of their talk. One had a cooing voice; the other spoke rather huskily.

"Such a divine man," the husky voice was saying, "such a really divine man!"

"So Elizabeth told me," said the cooing one.

"Such a perfect party, too," Husky went on. "He kept us laughing the whole evening. Everybody got rather buffy, too. When it was time to go, I said I'd walk and trust to luck to find a taxi on the way. Whereupon he invited me to come and look for a taxi in his heart. He said there were so many there, and all of them disengaged."

They both laughed. The chatter of a party of children who had come up from behind and were passing at this moment prevented Peter from hearing what was said next. Inwardly he cursed the children. Beastly little devils—they were making him lose his revelation. And what a revelation! Of how strange, unfamiliar and gaudy a life! Peter's dreams had always been idyllic and pastoral. Even with the peer's daughter he meant to live in the country, quietly and domestically. The world in which there are perfect parties where everybody gets rather buffy and divine men invite young goddesses to look for taxis in their hearts was utterly unknown to him. He had had a glimpse of it now; it fascinated him by its exotic and tropical strangeness. His whole ambition was now to enter this gorgeous world, to involve himself, somehow and at all costs, in the lives of these young goddesses. Suppose, now, they were both simultaneously to trip over that projecting root and twist their ankles. Suppose . . . But they both stepped over it in safety. And then, all at once, he saw a hope—in the bulldog.

The dog had left the path to sniff at the base of an elm tree growing a few yards away on the right. It had sniffed, it had growled, it had left a challenging souvenir of its visit and was now indignantly kicking up earth and twigs with its hinder paws against the tree, when a yellow Irish terrier trotted up and began in its turn to sniff, first at the tree, then at the bulldog. The bulldog stopped its scrabbling in the dirt and sniffed at the terrier. Cautiously, the two beasts walked round one another, sniffing and growling as they went. Peter watched them for a moment with a vague and languid curiosity. His mind was elsewhere; he hardly saw the two dogs. Then, in an illuminating flash, it occurred to him that they might begin to fight. If they fought, he was a made man. He would rush in and separate them, heroically. He might even be bitten. But that didn't matter. Indeed, it would be all the better. A bite would be another claim on the goddesses' gratitude. Ardently, he hoped that the dogs would fight. The awful thing would be if the goddesses or the owners of the yellow terrier were to notice and interfere before the fight could begin. "Oh God," he fervently prayed, "don't let them call the dogs away from each other now. But let the dogs fight. For Jesus Christ's sake. Amen." Peter had been piously brought up.

The children had passed. The voices of the goddesses once more became audible.

". . . Such a fearful bore," the cooing one was saying. "I can never move a step without finding him there. And nothing penetrates his hide. I've told him that I hate Jews, that I think he's ugly and stupid and tactless and impertinent and boring. But it doesn't seem to make the slightest difference."

"You should make him useful, at any rate," said Husky.

"Oh, I do," affirmed Coo.

"Well, that's something."

"Something," Coo admitted. "But not much."

There was a pause. "Oh, God," prayed Peter, "don't let them see."

"If only," began Coo meditatively, "if only men would understand that . . ." A fearful noise of growling and barking violently interrupted her. The two young women turned in the direction from which the sound came.

"Pongo!" they shouted in chorus, anxiously and commandingly. And again, more urgently, "Pongo!"

But their cries were unavailing. Pongo and the yellow terrier were already fighting too furiously to pay any attention.

"Pongo! Pongo!"

And, "Benny!" the little girl and her stout nurse to whom the yellow terrier belonged as unavailing shouted. "Benny, come here!"

The moment had come, the passionately anticipated, the richly pregnant moment. Exultantly, Peter threw himself on the dogs. "Get away, you brute," he shouted, kicking the Irish terrier. For the terrier was the enemy, the French bulldog—*their* French bulldog—the friend whom he had come, like one of the Olympian gods in the Iliad, to assist. "Get away!" In his excitement, he forgot that he had a stammer. The letter G was always a difficult one for him; but he managed on this occasion to shout "Get away" without a trace of hesitation. He grabbed at the dogs by their stumpy tails, by the scruffs of their necks, and tried to drag them apart. From time to time he kicked the yellow terrier. But it was the bulldog which bit him. Stupider even than Ajax, the bulldog had failed to understand that the immortal was fighting on his side. But Peter felt no resentment and, in the heat of the moment, hardly any pain. The blood came oozing out of a row of jagged holes in his left hand.

"Ooh!" cried Coo, as though it were her hand that had been bitten.

"Be careful," anxiously admonished Husky. "Be careful."

The sound of their voices nerved him to further efforts. He kicked and he tugged still harder; and at last, for a fraction of a second, he managed to part the angry beasts. For a fraction of a second neither dog had any portion of the other's anatomy in his mouth. Peter seized the opportunity, and catching the French bulldog by the loose skin at the back of his neck, he lifted him, still furiously snapping, growling and struggling, into the air. The yellow terrier stood in front of him, barking and every now and then leaping up in a frantic effort to snap the dangling black paws of his enemy. But Peter, with the gesture of Perseus raising on high the severed head of the Gorgon, lifted the writhing Pongo out of danger to the highest stretch of his arm. The yellow dog he kept off with his foot; and the nurse and the little girl, who had by this time somewhat recovered their presence of mind, approached the furious animal from behind and succeeded at last in hooking the leash to his collar. His four rigidly planted paws skidding over the grass, the yellow terrier was dragged away by main force, still barking, though feebly—for he was being half strangled by his efforts to escape. Suspended six feet above the ground by the leathery black scruff of his neck, Pongo vainly writhed.

Peter turned and approached the goddesses. Husky had narrow eyes and a sad mouth; it was a thin, tragic-looking face. Coo was rounder, pinker and whiter, bluer-eyed. Peter looked from one to the other and could not decide which was the more beautiful.

He lowered the writhing Pongo. "Here's your dog," was what he wanted to say. But the loveliness of these radiant creatures suddenly brought back all his self-consciousness and with his self-consciousness his stammer. "Here's your . . ." he began; but could not bring out the dog. D, for Peter, was always a difficult letter.

For all common words beginning with a difficult letter Peter had a number of easier synonyms in readiness. Thus, he always called cats "pussies", not out of any affectation of childishness, but because p was more pronounceable than the impossible c. Coal he had to render in the vaguer form of "fuel." Dirt, with him, was always "muck." In the discovery of synonyms he had become almost as ingenious as those Anglo-Saxon poets who using alliteration instead of rhyme, were compelled, in their efforts to make (shall we say) the sea begin with the same letter as its waves or its billows, to call it the "whale-road" or the "bath of the swans". But Peter, who could not permit himself the full poetic licence of his Saxon ancestors, was reduced sometimes to spelling the most difficult words to which there happened to be no convenient and prosaic equivalent. Thus, he was never quite sure whether he should call a cup a mug or a c, u, p. And since "ovum" seemed to be the only synonym for egg, he was always reduced to talking of e, g, g's.

At the present moment, it was the miserable little word "dog" that was holding up. Peter had several synonyms for dog. P being a slightly easier letter than d, he could, when not too nervous, say "pup." Or if the p's weren't coming easily, he could call the animal, rather facetiously and mock-heroically, a "hound". But the presence of the two goddesses was so unnerving, that Peter found it as hopelessly impossible to pronounce a p or an h as a d. He hesitated painfully, trying to bring out in turn, first dog, then pup, then hound. His face became very red. He was in an agony.

"Here's your whelp," he managed to say at last. The word, he was conscious, was a little too Shakespearean for ordinary conversation. But it was the only one which came.

"Thank you most awfully," said Coo.

"You were splendid, really splendid," said Husky. "But I'm afraid you're hurt."

"Oh, it's n-nothing," Peter declared. And twisting his handkerchief round the bitten hand, he thrust it into his pocket.

Coo, meanwhile, had fastened the end of her leash to Pongo's collar. "You can put him down now," she said.

Peter did as he was told. The little black dog immediately bounded forward in the direction of his reluctantly retreating enemy. He came to the end of his tether with a jerk that brought him up on to his hind legs and kept him, barking, in the position of a rampant lion on a coat of arms.

"But are you sure it's nothing?" Husky insisted. "Let me look at it."

Obediently, Peter pulled off the handkerchief and held out his hand. It seemed to him that all was happening as he had hoped. Then he noticed with horror that the nails were dirty. If only, if only he had thought of washing before he went out! What would they think of him? Blushing, he tried to withdraw his hand. But Husky held it.

"Wait," she said. And then added: "It's a nasty bite."

"Horrid," affirmed Coo, who had also bent over it. "I'm so awfully sorry that my stupid dog should have . . ."

"You ought to go straight to a chemist," said Husky, interrupting her, "and get him to disinfect it and tie it up."

She lifted her eyes from his hand and looked into his face.

"A chemist," echoed Coo, and also looked up.

Peter looked from one to the other, dazzled equally by the wide-open blue eyes and the narrowed, secret eyes of green. He smiled at them vaguely and vaguely shook his head. Unobtrusively he wrapped up his hand in his handkerchief and thrust it away, out of sight.

"It's n-nothing," he said.

"But you must," insisted Husky.

"You must," cried Coo.

"N-nothing," he repeated. He didn't want to go to a chemist. He wanted to stay with the goddesses.

Coo turned to Husky. "Qu'est-ce qu'on donne à ce petit bonhomme?" she asked, speaking very quickly and in a low voice.

Husky shrugged her shoulders and made a little grimace suggestive of uncertainty. "Il serait offensé, peut-être," she suggested.

"Tu crois?"

Husky stole a rapid glance at the subject of their discussion, taking him in critically from his cheap felt hat to his cheap boots, from his pale spotty face to his rather dirty hands, from his steel-framed spectacles to his leather watch-guard. Peter saw that she was looking at him and smiled at her with shy, vague rapture. How beautiful she was! He wondered what they had been whispering about together. Perhaps they were debating whether they should ask him to tea. And no sooner had the idea occurred to him than he was sure of it. Miraculously, things were happening just as they happened in his dreams. He wondered if he would have the face to tell them—this first time—that they could look for taxis in his heart.

Husky turned back to her companion. Once more she shrugged her shoulders. "Vraiment, je ne sais pas," she whispered.

"Si on lui donnait une livre?" suggested Coo.

Husky nodded. "Comme tu voudras." And while the other turned away to fumble unobtrusively in her purse, she addressed herself to Peter.

"You were awfully brave," she said, smiling.

Peter could only shake his head, blush and lower his eyes from before that steady, self-assured, cool gaze. He longed to look at her; but when it came to the point, he simply could not keep his eyes steadily fixed on those unwavering eyes of hers.

"Perhaps you're used to dogs," she went on. "Have you got one of your own?"

"N-no," Peter managed to say.

"Ah, well, that makes it all the braver," said Husky. Then, noticing that Coo had found the money she had been looking for, she took the boy's hand and shook it, heartily. "Well, good-bye," she said, smiling more exquisitely than ever. "We're so awfully grateful to you. Most awfully," she repeated. And as she did so, she wondered why she used that word "awfully" so often. Ordinarily she hardly ever used it. It had seemed suitable somehow, when she was talking with this creature. She was always very hearty and emphatic and schoolboyishly slangy when she was with the lower classes.

"G-g-g . . ." began Peter. Could they be going, he wondered in an agony, suddenly waking out of his comfortable and rosy dream. Really going, without asking him to tea or giving him their addresses? He wanted to implore them to stop a little longer, to let him see them again. But he knew that he wouldn't be able to utter the necessary words. In the face of Husky's good-bye he felt like a man who sees some fearful catastrophe impending and can do nothing to arrest it. "G-g . . ." he feebly stuttered. But he found himself shaking hands with the other one before he had got to the end of that fatal good-bye.

"You were really splendid," said Coo, as she shook his hand. "Really splendid. And you simply must go to a chemist and have the bite disinfected at once. Good-bye, and thank you very, very much." As she spoke these last words she slipped a neatly folded one-pound note into his palm and with her two hands shut his fingers over it. "Thank you *so* much," she repeated.

Violently blushing, Peter shook his head. "N-n . . .," he began, and tried to make her take the note back.

But she only smiled more sweetly. "Yes, yes," she insisted.

"Please." And without waiting to hear any more, she turned and ran lightly after Husky, who had walked on, up the path, leading the reluctant Pongo, who still barked and strained heraldically at his leash.

"Well, that's all right," she said, as she came up with her companion.

"He accepted it?" asked Husky.

"Yes, yes." She nodded. Then changing her tone, "Let me see," she went on, "what were we saying when this wretched dog interrupted us?"

"N-no," Peter managed to say at last. But she had already turned and was hurrying away. He took a couple of strides in pursuit; then checked himself. It was no good. It would only lead to further humiliation if he tried to explain. Why, they might even think, while he was standing there, straining to bring out his words, that he had run after them to ask for more. They might slip another pound into his hand and hurry away still faster. He watched them till they were out of sight, over the brow of the hill; then turned back towards the Serpentine.

In his imagination he re-acted the scene, not as it had really happened, but as it ought to have happened. When Coo slipped the note into his hand he smiled and courteously returned it, saying: "I'm afraid you've made a mistake. A quite justifiable mistake, I admit. For I look poor, and indeed I am poor. But I am a gentleman, you know. My father was a doctor in Rochdale. My mother was a doctor's daughter. I went to a good school till my people died. They died when I was sixteen, within a few months of one another. So I had to go to work before I'd finished my schooling. But you see that I can't take your money." And then, becoming more gallant, personal and confidential, he went on: "I separated those beastly dogs because I wanted to do someing for you and your friend. Because I thought you so beautiful and wonderful. So that even if I weren't a gentleman, I wouldn't take your money." Coo was deeply touched by this little speech. She shook him by the hand and told him how sorry she was. And he put her at her ease by assuring her that her mistake had been perfectly comprehensible. And then she asked if he'd care to come along with them and take a cup of tea. And from this point onwards Peter's imaginings became vaguer and rosier, till he was dreaming the old familiar dream of the peer's daughter, the grateful widow and the lonely orphan; only there happened to be two goddesses this time, and their faces, instead of being dim creations of fancy, were real and definite.

But he knew, even in the midst of his dreaming, that things hadn't happened like this. He knew that she had gone before he could say anything; and that even if he had run after them and tried to make his speech of explanation, he could never have done it. For example, he would have had to say that his father was a "medico," not a doctor (m being an easier letter than d). And when it came to telling them that his people had died, he would have had to say that they had "perished"—which would sound facetious, as though he were trying to make a joke of it. No, no, the truth must be faced. He had taken the money and they had gone away thinking that he was just some sort of a street loafer, who had risked a bite for the sake of a good tip. They hadn't even dreamed of treating him as an equal. As for asking him to tea and making him their friend . . .

But his fancy was still busy. It struck him that it had been quite unnecessary to make any explanation. He might simply have forced the note back into her hand, without saying a word. Why hadn't he done it? He had to excuse himself for his remissness. She had slipped away too quickly; that was the reason.

Or what if he had walked on ahead of them and ostentatiously given the money to the first street-boy he happened to meet? A good idea, that. Unfortunately it had not occurred to him at the time.

All that afternoon Peter walked and walked, thinking of what had happened, imagining creditable and satisfying alternatives. But all the time he knew that these alternatives were only fanciful. Sometimes the recollection of his humiliation was so vivid that it made him physically wince and shudder.

The light began to fail. In the grey and violet twilight the lovers pressed closer together as they walked, more frankly clasped one another beneath the trees. Strings of yellow lamps blossomed in the increasing darkness. High up in the pale sky overhead, a quarter of the moon made itself visible. He felt unhappier and lonelier than ever.

His bitten hand was by this time extremely painful. He left the Park and walked along Oxford Street till he found a chemist.

When his hand had been disinfected and bandaged he went into a tea-shop and ordered a poached e, g, g, a roll, and a mug of mocha, which he had to translate for the benefit of the uncomprehending waitress as a c, u, p of c, o, f, f, e, e.

"You seem to think I'm a loafer or a tout." That's what he ought to have said to her, indignantly and proudly. "You've insulted me. If you were a man, I'd knock you down. Take your dirty money." But then, he reflected, he could hardly have expected them to become his friends, after that. On second thoughts, he decided that indignation would have been no good.

"Hurt your hand?" asked the waitress sympathetically, as she set down his egg and his mug of mocha.

Peter nodded. "B-bitten by a d-d . . . by a h-h-hound." The word burst out at last, explosively.

Remembered shame made him blush as he spoke. Yes, they had taken him for a tout, they had treated him as though he didn't really exist, as though he were just an instrument whose services you hired and to which, when the bill had been paid, you gave no further thought. The remembrance of humiliation was so vivid, the realization of it so profound and complete, that it affected not only his mind but his body too. His heart beat with unusual rapidity and violence; he felt sick. It was with the greatest difficulty that he managed to eat his egg and drink his mug of mocha.

Still remembering the painful reality, still feverishly constructing his fanciful alternatives to it, Peter left the tea-shop and, though he was very tired, resumed his aimless walking. He walked along Oxford Street as far as the Circus, turned down Regent Street, halted on Piccadilly to look at the epileptically twitching sky-signs, walked up Shaftesbury Avenue, and turning southwards made his way through by-streets towards the Strand.

In a street near Covent Garden a woman brushed against him. "Cheer up, dearie," she said. "Don't look so glum."

Peter looked at her in astonishment. Was it possible that she should have been speaking to him? A woman—was it possible? He knew, of course, that she was what people called a bad woman. But the fact that she should have spoken to him seemed none the less extraordinary; and he did not connect it, somehow, with her "badness".

"Come along with me," she wheedled.

Peter nodded. He could not believe it was true. She took his arm.

"You got money?" she asked anxiously.

He nodded again.

"You look as though you'd been to a funeral," said the woman.

"I'm l-lonely," he explained. He felt ready to weep. He even longed to weep—to weep and to be comforted. His voice trembled as he spoke.

"Lonely? That's funny. A nice-looking boy like you 's got no call to be lonely." She laughed significantly and without mirth.

Her bedroom was dimly and pinkly lighted. A smell of cheap scent and unwashed underlinen haunted the air.

"Wait a tick," she said, and disappeared through a door into an inner room.

He sat there, waiting. A minute later she returned, wearing a kimono and bedroom slippers. She sat on his knees, threw her arms round his neck and began to kiss him. "Lovey," she said in her cracked voice, "lovey." Her eyes were hard and cold. Her breath smelt of spirits. Seen at close range she was indescribably horrible.

Peter saw her, it seemed to him for the first time—saw and completely realized her. He averted his face. Remembering the peer's daughter who had sprained her ankle, the lonely orphan, the widow whose child had tumbled into the Round Pond; remembering Coo and Husky, he untwined her arms, he pushed her away from him, he sprang to his feet.

"S-sorry," he said. "I must g-g . . . I'd forg-gotten something. I . . ." He picked up his hat and moved towards the door.

The woman ran after him and caught him by the arm. "You young devil, you," she screamed. Her abuse was horrible and filthy. "Asking a girl and then trying to sneak away without paying. Oh, no you don't, no you don't. You . . ."

And the abuse began again.

Peter dipped his hand into his pocket, and pulled out Coo's neatly folded note. "L-let me g-go," he said as he gave it her.

While she was suspiciously unfolding it, he hurried away, slamming the door behind him, and ran down the dark stairs, into the street.

The Monocle

THE drawing-room was on the first floor. The indistinct, inarticulate noise of many voices floated down the stairs, like the roaring of a distant train. Gregory took off his greatcoat and handed it to the parlour-maid.

"Don't trouble to show me up," he said. "I know the way."

Always so considerate! And yet, for some reason, servants would never do anything for him; they despised and disliked him.

"Don't bother," he insisted.

The parlour-maid, who was young, with high colours and yellow hair, looked at him, he thought, with silent contempt and walked away. In all probability, he reflected, she had never meant to show him up. He felt humiliated—yet once more.

A mirror hung at the bottom of the stairs. He peered at his image, gave his hair a pat, his tie a straightening touch. His face was smooth and egg-shaped; he had regular features, pale hair and a very small mouth, with cupid's bow effects in the upper lip. A curate's face. Secretly, he thought himself handsome and was always astonished that more people were not of his opinion.

Gregory mounted the stairs, polishing his monocle as he went. The volume of sound increased. At the landing, where the staircase turned, he could see the open door of the drawing-room. At first he could see only the upper quarter of the tall doorway and, through it, a patch of ceiling; but with every step he saw more—a strip of wall below the cornice, a picture, the heads of people, their whole bodies, their legs and feet. At the penultimate step, he inserted his monocle and replaced his handkerchief in his pocket. Squaring his shoulders, he marched in—almost militarily, he flattered himself. His hostess was standing near the window, at the other side of the room. He advanced towards her, already, though she had not yet seen him, mechanically smiling his greetings. The room was crowded, hot, and misty with cigarette smoke. The noise was almost palpable; Gregory felt as though he were pushing his way laboriously through some denser element. Neck-deep, he waded through noise, still holding preciously above the flood his smile. He presented it, intact, to his hostess.

"Good evening, Hermione."

"Ah, Gregory. How delightful! Good evening."

"I adore your dress," said Gregory, conscientiously following the advice of the enviably successful friend who had told him that one should never neglect to pay a compliment, however manifestly insincere. It wasn't a bad dress, for that matter. But, of course, poor dear Hermione contrived to ruin anything she put on. She was quite malignantly ungraceful and ugly—on purpose, it always seemed to Gregory. "Too lovely," he cooed in his rather high voice.

Hermione smiled with pleasure. "I'm so glad," she began. But before she could get any further, a loud voice, nasally chanting, interrupted her.

"Behold the monster Polypheme, behold the monster Polypheme," it quoted, musically, from *Acis and Galatea*.

Gregory flushed. A large hand slapped him in the middle of the back, below the shoulder blades. His body emitted the drum-like thud of a patted retriever.

"Well, Polypheme"; the voice had ceased to sing and was conversational—"well, Polypheme, how are you?"

"Very well, thanks," Gregory replied, without looking round. It was that drunken South African brute, Paxton. "Very well, thanks, Silenus," he added.

Paxton had called him Polypheme because of his monocle: Polypheme, the one-eyed, wheel-eyed Cyclops. Tit for mythological tat. In future, he would always call Paxton Silenus.

"Bravo!" shouted Paxton. Gregory winced and gasped under a second, heartier slap. "Pretty high-class, this party. Eh, Hermione? Pretty cultured, what? It isn't every day that a hostess can hear her guests shooting Greco-Roman witticisms at one another. I congratulate you, Hermione." He put his arm round her waist. "I congratulate you on us."

Hermione disengaged herself. "Don't be a bore, Paxton," she said impatiently.

Paxton laughed theatrically. "Ha, ha!" A villain's laugh on the melodrama stage. And it was not his laughter only that was theatrical; his whole person parodied the old-time tragedian. The steep aquiline profile, the deeply sunken eyes, the black hair worn rather long—they were characteristic. "A thousand apologies": he spoke with an ironical courtesy. "The poor colonial forgets himself. Boozy and ill-mannered boor!"

"Idiot!" said Hermione, and moved away.

Gregory made a movement to follow her, but Paxton caught him by the sleeve. "Tell me," he inquired earnestly, "why *do* you wear a monocle, Polypheme?"

"Well, if you really want to know," Gregory answered stiffly, "for the simple reason that I happen to be short-sighted and astigmatic in the left eye and not in the right."

"Short-sighted and astigmatic?" the other repeated in tones of affected astonishment. "Short-sighted and astigmatic? God forgive me—and I thought it was because you wanted to look like a duke on the musical-comedy stage."

Gregory's laugh was meant to be one of frankly amazed amusement. That any one should have imagined such a thing! Incredible, comical! But a note of embarrassment and discomfort sounded through the amusement. For in reality, of course, Paxton was so devilishly nearly right. Conscious, only too acutely, of his nullity, his provincialism, his lack of successful arrogance, he had made the oculist's diagnosis an excuse for trying to look smarter, more insolent, and impressive. In vain. His eyeglass had done nothing to increase his self-confidence. He was never at ease when he wore it. Monocle-wearers, he decided, are like poets: born, not made. Cambridge had not eradicated the midland grammar-school boy. Cultured, with literary leanings, he was always aware of being the wealthy boot manufacturer's heir. He could not get used to his monocle. Most of the time, in spite of the oculist's recommendations, it dangled at the end of its string, a pendulum when he walked and involving itself messily, when he ate, in soup and tea, in marmalade and the butter. It was only occasionally, in specially favourable circumstances, that Gregory adjusted it to his eye; more rarely still that he kept it, once adjusted, more than a few minutes, a few seconds even, without raising his eyebrow and letting it fall again. And how seldom circumstances *were* favourable to Gregory's eyeglass! Sometimes his environment was too sordid for it, sometimes too smart. To wear a monocle in the presence of the poor, the miserable, the analphabetic is too triumphantly pointed a comment on their lot. Moreover, the poor and the analphabetic have a most deplorable habit of laughing derisively at such symbols of superior caste. Gregory was not laughter-proof; he lacked the lordly confidence and unawareness of nature's monocle-wearers. He did not know how to ignore the poor, to treat them, if it were absolutely necessary to have dealings with them, as machines or domestic animals. He had seen too much of them in the days when his father was alive and had compelled him to take a practical interest in the business. It was the same lack of confidence that made him almost as chary of fixing his eyeglass in the presence of the rich. With them, he never felt quite sure that he had a right to his monocle. He felt himself a parvenu to monocularity. And then there were the intelligent. Their company, too, was most unfavourable to the eyeglass. Eyeglassed, how could one talk of serious things? "Mozart," you might say, for example, "Mozart is so pure, so spiritually beautiful." It was unthinkable to speak those words with a disk of crystal screwed into your left eye-socket. No, the environment was only too rarely favourable. Still, benignant circumstances did sometimes present themselves. Hermione's half-Bohemian parties, for example. But he had reckoned without Paxton.

Amused, amazed, he laughed. As though by accident, the monocle dropped from his eye. "Oh, put it back," cried Paxton, "put it back, I implore you," and himself caught the glass, where it dangled over Gregory's stomach, and tried to replace it.

Gregory stepped back; with one hand he pushed away his persecutor, with the other he tried to snatch the monocle from between his fingers. Paxton would not let it go.

"I implore you," Paxton kept repeating.

"Give it me at once," said Gregory, furiously, but in a low voice, so that people should not look round and see the grotesque cause of the quarrel. He had never been so outrageously made a fool of.

Paxton gave it him at last. "Forgive me," he said, with mock penitence. "Forgive a poor drunken colonial who doesn't know what's done in the best society and what isn't. You must remember I'm only a boozer, just a poor, hard-working drunkard. You know those registration forms they give you in French hotels? Name, date of birth and so on. You know?"

Gregory nodded, with dignity.

"Well, when it comes to profession, I always write 'ivrogne'. That is, when I'm sober enough to remember the French word. If I'm too far gone, I just put 'Drunkard.' They all know English, nowadays."

"Oh," said Gregory coldly.

"It's a capital profession," Paxton confided. "It permits you to do whatever you like—any damned thing that comes into your head. Throw your arms round any woman you fancy, tell her the most gross and fantastic impertinences, insult the men, laugh in people's faces—everything's permitted to the poor drunkard, particularly if he's only a poor colonial and doesn't know any better. *Verb. sap.* Take the hint from me, old boy. Drop the monocle. It's no damned good. Be a boozer; you'll have much more fun. Which reminds me that I must go and find some more drink at all costs. I'm getting sober."

He disappeared into the crowd. Relieved, Gregory looked round in search of familiar faces. As he looked, he polished his monocle, took the opportunity to wipe his forehead, then put the glass to his eye.

"Excuse me." He oozed his way insinuatingly between the close-set chairs, passed like a slug ("Excuse me") between the all but contiguous backs of two standing groups. "Excuse me." He had seen acquaintances over there, by the fireplace: Ransom and Mary Haig and Miss Camperdown. He joined in their conversation: they were talking about Mrs Mandragore.

All the old familiar stories about that famous lion-huntress were being repeated. He himself repeated two or three, with suitable pantomime, perfected by a hundred tellings. In the middle of a grimace, at the top of an elaborate gesture, he suddenly saw himself grimacing, gesticulating, he suddenly heard the cadences of his voice repeating, by heart, the old phrases. Why does one come to parties, why on earth? Always the same boring people, the same dull scandal, and one's own same parlour tricks. Each time. But he smirked, he mimed, he fluted and bellowed his story through to the end. His auditors even laughed; it was a success. But Gregory felt ashamed of himself. Ransom began telling the story of Mrs Mandragore and the Maharajah of Pataliapur. He groaned in the spirit. Why? he asked himself, why, why, why? Behind him, they were talking politics. Still pretending to smile at the Mandragore fable, he listened.

"It's the beginning of the end," the politician was saying, prophesying destructions in a loud and cheerful voice.

"'Dear Maharajah,'" Ransom imitated the Mandragore's intense voice, her aimed and yearning gestures, "'if you knew how I *adore* the East.'"

"Our unique position was due to the fact that we started the industrial system before any one else. Now, when the rest of the world has followed our example, we find it's a disadvantage to have started first. All our equipment is old-fash——"

"Gregory," called Mary Haig, "what's your story about the Unknown Soldier?"

"Unknown Soldier?" said Gregory vaguely, trying to catch what was being said behind him.

"The latest arrivals have the latest machinery. It's obvious. We . . ."

"You know the one. The Mandragore's party; you know."

"Oh, when she asked us all to tea to meet the Mother of the Unknown Soldier."

". . . like Italy," the politician was saying in his loud, jolly voice. "In future, we shall always have one or two millions more population than we can employ. Living on the State."

One or two millions. He thought of the Derby. Perhaps there might be a hundred thousand in that crowd. Ten Derbies, twenty Derbies, all half-starved, walking through the streets with brass bands and banners. He let his monocle fall. Must send five pounds to the London Hospital, he thought. Four thousand eight hundred a year. Thirteen pounds a day. Less taxes, of course. Taxes were terrible. Monstrous, sir, monstrous. He tried to feel as indignant about taxes as those old gentlemen who get red in the face when they talk about them. But somehow, he couldn't manage to do it. And after all, taxes were no excuse, no justification. He felt all at once profoundly depressed. Still, he tried to comfort himself, not more than twenty or twenty-five out of the two million could live on his income. Twenty-five out of two millions—it was absurd, derisory! But he was not consoled.

"And the odd thing is," Ransom was still talking about the Mandragore, "she isn't really in the least interested in her lions. She'll begin telling you about what Anatole France said to her and then forget in the middle, out of pure boredom, what she's talking about."

Oh, God, God, thought Gregory. How often had he heard Ransom making the same reflections on the Mandragore's psychology! How often! He'd be bringing out that bit about the chimpanzees in half a moment. God help us!

"Have you ever watched the chimpanzees at the Zoo?" said

Ransom. "The way they pick up a straw or a banana skin and examine it for a few seconds with a passionate attention." He went through a simian pantomine. "Then, suddenly, get utterly bored, let the thing drop from their fingers and look round vaguely in search of something else. They always remind me of the Mandragore and her guests. The way she begins, earnestly, as though you were the only person in the world; then all at once . . ."

Gregory could bear it no longer. He mumbled something to Miss Camperdown about having seen somebody he must talk to, and disappeared, "Excuse me," slug-like, through the crowd. Oh, the misery, the appalling gloom of it all! In a corner, he found young Crane and two or three other men with tumblers in their hands.

"Ah, Crane," he said, "for God's sake tell me where you got that drink."

That golden fluid—it seemed the only hope. Crane pointed in the direction of the archway leading into the back drawing-room. He raised his glass without speaking, drank, and winked at Gregory over the top of it. He had a face that looked like an accident. Gregory oozed on through the crowd. "Excuse me," he said aloud; but inwardly he was saying, "God help us."

At the further end of the back drawing-room was a table with bottles and glasses. The professional drunkard was sitting on a sofa near by, glass in hand, making personal remarks to himself about all the people who came within earshot.

"Christ!" he was saying, as Gregory came up to the table. "Christ! Look at that!" *That* was the gaunt Mrs Labadie in cloth of gold and pearls. "Christ!" She had pounced on a shy young man entrenched behind the table.

"Tell me, Mr Foley," she began, approaching her horse-like face very close to that of the young man and speaking appealingly, "you who know *all* about mathematics, tell me . . ."

"Is it possible?" exclaimed the professional drunkard. "In England's green and pleasant land? Ha, ha, ha!" He laughed his melodramatic laugh.

Pretentious fool, thought Gregory. How romantic he thinks himself! The laughing philosopher, what? Drunk because the world isn't good enough for him. Quite the little Faust.

"And Polypheme too," Paxton soliloquized on, "funny little

Polypheme!" He laughed again. "The heir to all the ages. Christ!"

With dignity, Gregory poured himself out some whisky and filled up the glass from the siphon—with dignity, with conscious grace and precision, as though he were acting the part of a man who helps himself to whisky and soda on the stage. He took a sip; then elaborately acted the part of one who takes out his handkerchief and blows his nose.

"Don't they make one believe in birth control, all these people," continued the professional drunkard. "If only their parents could have had a few intimate words with Stopes! Heigh ho!" He uttered a stylized Shakespearean sigh.

Buffoon, thought Gregory. And the worst is that if one called him one, he'd pretend that he'd said so himself, all the time And so he has, of course, just to be on the safe side. But in reality, it's obvious, the man thinks of himself as a sort of Musset or up-to-date Byron. A beautiful soul, darkened and embittered by experience. Ugh!

Still pretending to be unaware of the professional boozer's proximity, Gregory went through the actions of the man who sips.

"How *clear* you make it!" Mrs Labadie was saying, point blank, into the young mathematician's face. She smiled at him; the horse, thought Gregory, has a terribly human expression.

"Well," said the young mathematician nervously, "now we come on to Riemann."

"Riemann!" Mrs Labadie repeated, with a kind of ecstasy. "Riemann!" as though the geometrician's soul were in his name.

Gregory wished that there were somebody to talk to, somebody who would relieve him of the necessity of acting the part of unaware indifference before the scrutinizing eyes of Paxton. He leaned against the wall in the attitude of one who falls, all of a sudden, into a brown study. Blankly and pensively, he stared at a point on the opposite wall, high up, just below the ceiling. People must be wondering, he reflected, what he was thinking about. And what was he thinking about? Himself. Vanity, vanity. Oh, the gloom, the misery of it all!

"Polypheme!"

He pretended not to hear.

"Polypheme!" It was a shout this time.

Gregory slightly overacted the part of one who is suddenly

aroused from profoundest meditation. He started; blinking, a little dazed, he turned his head.

"Ah, Paxton," he said. "Silenus! I hadn't noticed that you were there."

"Hadn't you?" said the professional drunkard. "That was damned clever of you. What were you thinking about so picturesquely there?"

"Oh, nothing," said Gregory, smiling with the modest confusion of the Thinker, caught in the act.

"Just what I imagined," said Paxton. "Nothing. Nothing at all. Jesus Christ!" he added, for himself.

Gregory's smile was rather sickly. He averted his face and passed once more into meditation. It seemed, in the circumstances, the best thing he could do. Dreamily, as though unconscious of what he was doing, he emptied his glass.

"Crippen!" he heard the professional drunkard muttering. "It's like a funeral. Joyless, joyless."

"Well, Gregory."

Gregory did another of his graceful starts, his dazed blinkings. He had been afraid, for a moment, that Spiller was going to respect his meditation and not speak to him. That would have been very embarrassing.

"Spiller!" he exclaimed with delight and astonishment. "My dear chap." He shook him heartily by the hand.

Square-faced, with a wide mouth and an immense forehead, framed in copious and curly hair, Spiller looked like a Victorian celebrity. His friends declared that he might actually have been a Georgian celebrity but for the fact that he preferred talking to writing.

"Just up for the day," explained Spiller. "I couldn't stand another hour of the bloody country. Working all day. No company but my own. I find I bore myself to death." He helped himself to whisky.

"Jesus! The great man! Ha, ha!" The professional drunkard covered his face with his hands and shuddered violently.

"Do you mean to say you came specially for this?" asked Gregory, waving his hand to indicate the party at large.

"Not specially. Incidentally. I heard that Hermione was giving a party, so I dropped in."

"Why *does* one go to parties?" said Gregory, unconsciously

assuming something of the embittered Byronic manner of the professional drunkard.

"To satisfy the cravings of the herd instinct." Spiller replied to the rhetorical question without hesitation and with a pontifical air of infallibility. "Just as one pursues women to satisfy the cravings of the reproductive instinct." Spiller had an impressive way of making everything he said sound very scientific; it all seemed to come straight from the horse's mouth, so to speak. Vague-minded Gregory found him most stimulating.

"You mean, one goes to parties just in order to be in a crowd?"

"Precisely," Spiller replied. "Just to feel the warmth of the herd around one and sniff the smell of one's fellow-humans." He snuffed the thick, hot air.

"I suppose you must be right," said Gregory. "It's certainly very hard to think of any other reason."

He looked round the room as though searching for other reasons. And surprisingly, he found one: Molly Voles. He had not seen her before; she must have only just arrived.

"I've got a capital idea for a new paper," began Spiller.

"Have you?" Gregory did not show much curiosity. How beautiful her neck was, and those thin arms!

"Art, literature, and science," Spiller continued. "The idea's a really modern one. It's to bring science into touch with the arts and so into touch with life. Life, art, science—all three would gain. You see the notion?"

"Yes," said Gregory, "I see." He was looking at Molly, hoping to catch her eye. He caught it at last, that cool and steady grey eye. She smiled and nodded.

"You like the idea?" asked Spiller.

"I think it's splendid," answered Gregory with a sudden warmth that astonished his interlocutor.

Spiller's large severe face shone with pleasure. "Oh, I'm glad," he said, "I'm very glad indeed that you like it so much."

"I think it's splendid," said Gregory extravagantly. "Simply splendid." She had seemed really glad to see him, he thought.

"I was thinking," Spiller pursued, with a rather elaborate casualness of manner, "I was thinking you might like to help me start the thing. One could float it comfortably with a thousand pounds of capital."

The enthusiasm faded out of Gregory's face: it became blank

in its clerical roundness. He shook his head. "If I had a thousand pounds," he said regretfully. Damn the man! he was thinking. Setting me a trap like that.

"If," repeated Spiller. "But, my dear fellow!" He laughed. "And besides, it's a safe six per cent. investment. I can collect an extraordinarily strong set of contributors, you know."

Gregory shook his head once more. "Alas," he said, "alas!"

"And what's more," insisted Spiller, "you'd be a benefactor of society."

"Impossible." Gregory was firm; he planted his feet like a donkey and would not be moved. Money was the one thing he never had a difficulty in being firm about.

"But come," said Spiller, "come. What's a thousand pounds to a millionaire like you? You've got—how much *have* you got?"

Gregory stared him glassily in the eyes.

"Twelve hundred a year," he said. "Say fourteen hundred." He could see that Spiller didn't believe him. Damn the man! Not that he really expected him to believe; but still . . . "And then there are one's taxes," he added plaintively, "and one's contributions to charities." He remembered that fiver he was going to send to the London Hospital. "The London Hospital, for example —always short of money." He shook his head sadly. "Quite impossible, I'm afraid." He thought of all the unemployed; ten Derby crowds, half starved, with banners and brass bands. He felt himself blushing. Damn the man! He was furious with Spiller.

Two voices sounded simultaneously in his ears: the professional drunkard's and another, a woman's—Molly's.

"The succubus!" groaned the professional drunkard. 'Il ne manquait que ça!"

"Impossible?" said Molly's voice, unexpectedly repeating his latest word. "What's impossible?"

"Well——" said Gregory, embarrassed, and hesitated.

It was Spiller who explained.

"Why, of course Gregory can put up a thousand pounds," said Molly, when she had learned what was the subject at issue. She looked at him indignantly, contemptuously, as though reproaching him for his avarice.

"You know better than I, then," said Gregory, trying to take the airy jocular line about the matter. He remembered what the enviably successful friend had told him about compliments. "How lovely you look in that white dress, Molly!" he added, and tempered the jocularity of his smile with a glance that was meant to be at once insolent and tender. "Too lovely," he repeated, and put up his monocle to look at her.

"Thank you," she said, looking back at him unwaveringly. Her eyes were calm and bright. Against that firm and penetrating regard his jocularity, his attempt at insolent tenderness, punctured and crumpled up. He averted his eyes, he let fall his eyeglass. It was a weapon he did not dare or know how to use—it made him look ridiculous. He was like horse-faced Mrs Labadie flirting coquettishly with her fan.

"I'd like to discuss the question in any case," he said to Spiller, glad of any excuse to escape from those eyes. "But I assure you I really can't. . . . Not the whole thousand, at any rate," he added, feeling despairingly that he had been forced against his will to surrender.

"Molly!" shouted the professional drunkard.

Obediently she went and sat down beside him on the sofa.

"Well, Tom," she said, and laid her hand on his knee. "How are you?"

"As I always am, when you're anywhere about," answered the professional drunkard tragically: "insane." He put his arm round her shoulders and leaned towards her. "Utterly insane."

"I'd rather we didn't sit like this, you know." She smiled at him; they looked at one another closely. Then Paxton withdrew his arm and leaned back in his corner of the sofa.

Looking at them, Gregory was suddenly convinced that they were lovers. We needs must love the lowest when we see it. All Molly's lovers were like that: ruffians.

He turned to Spiller. "Shouldn't we go back to my rooms?" he suggested, interrupting him in the midst of a long explanatory discourse about the projected paper. "It'll be quieter there and less stuffy." Molly and Paxton, Molly and that drunken brute. Was it possible? It was certain: he had no doubts. "Let's get out of this beastly place quickly," he added.

"All right," Spiller agreed. "One last lashing of whisky to support us on the way." He reached for the bottle.

Gregory drank nearly half a tumbler, undiluted. A few yards down the street, he realized that he was rather tipsy.

"I think I must have a very feebly developed herd instinct," he said. "How I hate these crowds!" Molly and Silenus-Paxton! He imagined their loves. And he had thought that she had been glad to see him, when first he caught her eye.

They emerged into Bedford Square. The gardens were as darkly mysterious as a piece of country woodland. Woodland without, whisky within, combined to make Gregory's melancholy vocal. *Che farò senz' Euridice?* he softly sang.

"You can do without her very well," said Spiller, replying to the quotation. "That's the swindle and stupidity of love. Each time you feel convinced that it's something immensely significant and everlasting: you feel infinitely. Each time. Three weeks later you're beginning to find her boring; or somebody else rolls the eye and the infinite emotions are transferred and you're off on another eternal week-end. It's a sort of practical joke. Very stupid and disagreeable. But then nature's humour isn't ours."

"You think it's a joke, that infinite feeling?" asked Gregory indignantly. "I don't. I believe that it represents something real, outside ourselves, something in the structure of the universe."

"A different universe with every mistress, eh?"

"But if it occurs only once in a lifetime?" asked Gregory in a maudlin voice. He longed to tell his companion how unhappy he felt about Molly, how much unhappier than anybody had ever felt before.

"It doesn't," said Spiller.

"But if I say it does?" Gregory hiccoughed.

"That's only due to lack of opportunities, Spiller replied in his most decisively scientific, *ex cathedra* manner.

"I don't agree with you," was all that Gregory could say, feebly. He decided not to mention his unhappiness. Spiller might not be a sympathetic listener. Coarse old devil!

"Personally," Spiller continued, "I've long ago ceased trying to make sense of it. I just accept these infinite emotions for what they are—very stimulating and exciting while they last—and don't attempt to rationalize or explain them. It's the only sane and scientific way of treating the facts."

There was a silence. They had emerged into the brilliance of the Tottenham Court Road. The polished roadway reflected the arc lamps. The entrances to the cinema palaces were caverns of glaring yellow light. A pair of buses roared past.

"They're dangerous, those infinite emotions," Spiller went on, "very dangerous. I once came within an inch of getting married on the strength of one of them. It began on a steamer. You know what steamers are. The extraordinary aphrodisiac effects sea voyaging has on people who aren't used to it, especially women! They really ought to be studied by some competent physiologist. Of course, it may be simply the result of idleness, high feeding and constant proximity—though I doubt if you'd get the same results in similar circumstances on land. Perhaps the total change of environment, from earth to water, undermines the usual terrestrial prejudices. Perhaps the very shortness of the voyage helps—the sense that it's so soon coming to an end that rosebuds must be gathered and hay made while the sun shines. Who knows?" He shrugged his shoulders. "But in any case, it's most extraordinary. Well, it began, as I say, on a steamer."

Gregory listened. A few minutes since the trees of Bedford Square had waved in the darkness of his boozily maudlin soul. The lights, the noise, the movement of the Tottenham Court Road were now behind his eyes as well as before them. He listened, grinning. The story lasted well into the Charing Cross Road.

By the time it had come to an end, Gregory was feeling in an entirely jolly and jaunty mood. He had associated himself with Spiller; Spiller's adventures were his. He guffawed with laughter, he readjusted his monocle, which had been dangling all this time at the end of its string, which had been tinkling at every step against the buttons of his waistcoat. (A broken heart, it must be obvious to any one who has the slightest sensibility, cannot possibly wear an eyeglass.) He too was a bit of a dog, now. He hiccoughed; a certain suspicion of queasiness tempered his jollity, but it was no more than the faintest suspicion. Yes, yes; he too knew all about life on steamers, even though the longest of his sea voyages had only been from Newhaven to Dieppe.

When they reached Cambridge Circus, the theatres were just disgorging their audiences. The pavements were crowded; the air was full of noise and the perfume of women. Overhead, the sky-signs winced and twitched. The theatre vestibules brightly glared. It was an inaristocratic and vulgar luxury, to which Gregory had no difficulty in feeling himself superior. Through his Cyclopean monocle, he gazed inquiringly at every woman they passed. He felt wonderfully reckless (the queasiness was the merest suspicion of an unpleasant sensation), wonderfully jolly and—yes, that was curious—large: larger than life. As for Molly Voles, he'd teach her.

"Lovely creature, that," he said, indicating a cloak of pink silk and gold, a close-cropped golden head.

Spiller nodded, indifferently. "About that paper of ours," he said thoughtfully. "I was thinking that we might start off with a series of articles on the metaphysical basis of science, the reasons, historical and philosophical, that we have for assuming that scientific truth is true."

"H'm," said Gregory.

"And concurrently a series on the meaning and point of art. Start right from the beginning in both cases. Quite a good idea, don't you think?"

"Quite," said Gregory. One of his monocular glances had been received with a smile of invitation; she was ugly, unfortunately, and obviously professional. Haughtily he glared past her, as though she were not there.

"But whether Tolstoy was right," Spiller was meditatively saying, "I never feel sure. Is it true, what he says, that the function of art is the conveyance of emotion? In part, I should say, but not exclusively, not exclusively." He shook his large head.

"I seem to be getting tipsier," said Gregory, more to himself than to his companion. He still walked correctly, but he was conscious, too conscious, of the fact. And the suspicion of queasiness was becoming well founded.

Spiller did not hear or, hearing, ignored the remark. "For me," he continued, "the main function of art is to impart knowledge. The artist knows more than the rest of us. He is born knowing more about his soul than we know of ours, and more about the relations existing between his soul and the cosmos. He anticipates what will be common knowledge in a higher state of development. Most of our moderns are primitives compared with the most advanced of the dead."

"Quite," said Gregory, not listening. His thoughts were elsewhere, with his eyes.

"Moreover," Spiller went on, "he can say what he knows, and say it in such a way that our own rudimentary, incoherent, unrealized knowledge of what he talks about falls into a kind of pattern—like iron filings under the influence of the magnet."

There were three of them—ravishingly, provocatively young—standing in a group at the pavement's edge. They chattered, they stared with bright derisive eyes at the passers-by, they commented in audible whispers, they burst into irrepressible shrill laughter. Spiller and Gregory approached, were spied by one of the three, who nudged her fellows.

"Oh, Lord!"

They giggled, they laughed aloud, they were contorted with mockery.

"Look at old Golliwog!" That was for Spiller, who walked bareheaded, his large grey hat in his hand.

"And the nut!" Another yell for the monocle.

"It's that magnetic power," said Spiller, quite unaware of the lovely derision of which he was the object, "that power of organizing mental chaos into a pattern, which makes a truth uttered poetically, in art, more valuable than a truth uttered scientifically, in prose."

Playfully reproving, Gregory wagged a finger at the mockers. There was a yet more piercing yell. The two men passed; smilingly Gregory looked back. He felt jauntier and jollier than ever; but the suspicion was ripening to a certainty.

"For instance," said Spiller, "I may know well enough that all men are mortal. But this knowledge is organized and given a form, it is even actually increased and deepened, when Shakespeare talks about all our yesterdays having lighted fools the way to dusty death."

Gregory was trying to think of an excuse for giving his companion the slip and turning back to dally with the three. He would love them all, simultaneously.

La touffe échevelée
De baisers que les dieux gardaient si bien mêlée.

The Mallarméan phrase came back to him, imposing on his vague desires (old man Spiller was quite right, old imbecile!) the most elegant of forms. Spiller's words came to him as though from a great distance.

"And the *Coriolan* overture is a piece of new knowledge, as well as a composer of existing chaotic knowledge."

He would suggest dropping in at the Monico, pretext a call of nature, slip out and never return. Old imbecile, maundering on like that! Not but what it mightn't have been quite interesting, at the right moment. But now . . . And he thought, no doubt, that he was going to tap him, Gregory, for a thousand pounds! Gregory could have laughed aloud. But his derision was tinged with an uneasy consciousness that his tipsiness had definitely taken a new and disquieting form.

"Some of Cézanne's landscapes," he heard Spiller saying.

Suddenly, from a shadowed doorway a few yards down the street in front of them, there emerged, slowly, tremulously, a thing: a bundle of black tatters that moved on a pair of old squashed boots, that was topped by a broken, dog's-eared hat. It had a face, clay-coloured and emaciated. It had hands, in one of which it held a little tray with match-boxes. It opened its mouth, from which two or three of the discoloured teeth were missing; it sang, all but inaudibly. Gregory thought he recognized "Nearer, my God, to Thee." They approached.

"Certain frescoes of Giotto, certain early Greek sculptures," Spiller went on with his interminable catalogue.

The thing looked at them, Gregory looked at the thing. Their eyes met. Gregory expanded his left eye-socket. The monocle dropped to the end of its silken tether. He felt in his right-hand trouser pocket, the pocket where he kept his silver, for a sixpence, a shilling even. The pocket contained only four half-crowns. Half a crown? He hesitated, drew one of the coins half-way to the surface, then let it fall again with a chink. He dipped his left hand into his other trouser pocket, he withdrew it, full. Into the proffered tray he dropped three pennies and a halfpenny.

"No, I don't want any matches," he said.

Gratitude interrupted the hymn. Gregory had never felt so much ashamed in his life. His monocle tinkled against the buttons of his waistcoat. Deliberately, he placed one foot before the other, walking with correctness, but as though on a tight-rope. Yet another insult to the thing. He wished to God he were sober. He wished to God he hadn't desired with such precision that "dishevelled tuft of kisses". Threepence-halfpenny! But he could still run back and give half a crown, two half-crowns. He could still run back. Step by step, as though on the tight-rope, he advanced, keeping step with Spiller. Four steps, five steps . . . eleven steps, twelve steps, thirteen steps. Oh, the unluckiness! Eighteen steps, nineteen. . . . Too late; it would be ridiculous to turn back now, it would be too conspicuously silly. Twenty-three, twenty-four steps. The suspicion was a certainty of queasiness, a growing certainty.

"At the same time," Spiller was saying, "I really don't see how the vast majority of scientific truths and hypotheses can ever become the subject of art. I don't see how they can be given poetic, emotive significance without losing their precision. How could you render the electro-magnetic theory of light, for example, in a moving literary form? It simply can't be done."

"Oh, for God's sake," shouted Gregory with a sudden outburst of fury, "for God's sake, shut up! How can you go on talking and talking away like this?" He hiccoughed again, more profoundly and menacingly than before.

"But why on earth not?" asked Spiller with a mild astonishment.

"Talking about art and science and poetry," said Gregory tragically, almost with tears in his eyes, "when there are two million people in England on the brink of starvation. Two million." He meant the repetition to be impressive, but he hiccoughed yet once more; he was feeling definitely rather sick. "Living in stinking hovels," he went on, *decrescendo*, "promiscuously, herded together, like animals. Worse than animals."

They had halted; they confronted one another.

"How can you?" repeated Gregory, trying to reproduce the generous indignation of a moment since. But anticipations of nausea were creeping up from his stomach, like a miasma from a marsh, filling his mind, driving out from it every thought, every emotion except the horrid apprehension of being sick.

Spiller's large face suddenly lost its monumental, Victorian celebrity's appearance; it seemed to fall to pieces. The mouth opened, the eyes puckered up, the forehead broke into wrinkles and the deep lines running from either side of the nose to the corners of the mouth expanded and contracted wildly, like a pair of demented glove-stretchers. An immense sound came out of him. His great body was shaken with gigantic laughter.

Patiently—patience was all that was left him, patience and a fading hope—Gregory waited for the paroxysm to subside. He had made a fool of himself; he was being derided. But he was past caring.

Spiller so far recovered as to be able to speak. "You're wonderful, my dear Gregory," he said, gasping. The tears stood in his eyes. "Really superb." He took him affectionately by the arm and, still laughing, walked on. Gregory perforce walked too; he had no choice.

"If you don't mind," he said after a few steps, "I think we'll take a taxi."

"What, to Jermyn Street?" said Spiller.

"I think we'd better," Gregory insisted.

Climbing into the vehicle, he managed to entangle his monocle in the handle of the door. The string snapped: the glass dropped on the floor of the cab. Spiller picked it up and returned it to him.

"Thank you," said Gregory, and put it out of harm's way into a waistcoat pocket.

Fairy Godmother

AT 17 Purlieu Villas it was a fairy godmother's arrival. The enormous Daimler—it looked larger than the house itself—rolled whispering up the street, dark blue and discreetly lustrous. ("Like stars on the sea"—the darkly glittering Daimler always reminded Susan of the Hebrew Melodies—"when the blue wave rolls nightly on deep Galilee.") Between lace curtains eyes followed its passage; it was rarely that forty horses passed these suburban windows. At the gate of Number Seventeen the portent came to a halt. The chauffeur jumped down and opened the door. The fairy godmother emerged.

Mrs Escobar was tall and slender, so abnormally so, that, fashionably dressed, she looked like a fashion-plate—fabulously elegant, beyond all reality.

She was wearing black to-day—a black suit very thinly piped at the cuffs and collar, at the pockets and along the seams of the skirt, with red. A high muslin stock encased her neck and from it depended an elaborate frill, which projected from between the lapels of her coat like the idly waving fin of a tropical fish. Her shoes were red; there was a touch of red in the garnishing of her gloves, another in her hat.

She stepped out of the car and, turning back towards the open door, "Well, Susan," she said, "you don't seem to be in any hurry to get out."

Susan, who was bending down to pick up the parcels scattered on the floor of the car, looked up.

"I'm just coming," she said.

She reached hurriedly for the bunch of white roses and the terrine of *foie gras*. Reaching, she dropped the box containing the chocolate cake.

Mrs Escobar laughed. "You old goose," she said, and a charming mockery set her voice deeply vibrating. "Come out and let Robbins take the things. You'll take them, Robbins," she added in a different tone, turning to the chauffeur, "you'll take them, won't you?"

She looked at him intimately; her smile was appealing, almost languishing.

"Won't you, Robbins?" she repeated, as though she were asking the most immense of personal favours.

That was Mrs Escobar's way. She liked to endow every relationship, the most casual, the most business-like or formal, with a certain intimate, heart-to-heart quality. She talked to shop assistants about their sweethearts, smiled at servants as though she wanted to make them her confidants or even her lovers, discussed philosophy with the plumber, gave chocolates to district messenger boys and even, when they were particularly cherubic, maternally kissed them. She wanted to "get into touch with people," as she called it, to finger and tweak their souls and squeeze the secrets out of their hearts. She wanted everybody to be aware of her, to like and adore her at first sight. Which did not prevent her from flying into rages with the shop assistants who could not provide her immediately with precisely the thing she wanted, from violently abusing the servants when they failed to answer the bell with a sufficient promptitude, from calling the dilatory plumber a thief and a liar, from dismissing the messenger boy who brought a present from the wrong admirer, not only chocolateless and unkissed, but without even a tip.

"Won't you?" And her look seemed to add, "for *my* sake." Her eyes were long and narrow. The lower lid described an almost straight horizontal line, the upper a gradual curve. Between the lids, a pair of pale blue irises rolled their lights expressively this way and that.

The chauffeur was young and new to his post. He blushed, he averted his eyes. "Oh yes, m'm, of course," he said, and touched his cap.

Susan abandoned the chocolate cake and the *foie gras* and stepped out. Her arms were full of parcels and flowers.

"You look like a little Mother Christmas," said Mrs Escobar, playfully affectionate. "Let me take something." She selected the bunch of white roses, leaving to Susan the bag of oranges, the cold roast chicken, the tongue and the teddy bear.

Robbins opened the gate; they stepped into the little garden.

"Where's Ruth?" said Mrs Escobar. "Isn't she expecting us?" Her voice expressed disappointment and implied reproof.

Evidently, she had expected to be met at the gate and escorted across the garden.

"I suppose she couldn't leave Baby," said Susan, looking anxiously at Mrs Escobar over the top of her heaped-up parcels. "One can never be certain of being able to do what one wants when one's got children, can one?" Still, she wished that Ruth had turned up at the gate. It would be dreadful if Mrs Escobar were to think her negligent or ungrateful. "Oh, Ruth, do come!" she said to herself, and she wished so hard that she found herself clenching her fists and contracting the muscles of her stomach.

The fists and the abdominal muscles did their work, for the door of the house suddenly burst open and Ruth came running down the steps, carrying Baby on her arm.

"I'm so sorry, Mrs Escobar," she began. "But, you see, Baby was just . . ."

Mrs Escobar did not allow her to finish her sentence. Momentarily clouded, her face lit up again. She smiled, ravishingly. Her eyelids came still closer together; little lines radiated out from them, a halo of charming humour. "Here's little Mother Christmas," she said, pointing at Susan. "Loaded with goodness knows what! And a few poor flowers from me." She raised the roses to her lips, kissed them and touched Ruth's cheek with the half-opened flowers. "And how's this delicious person?" She took the child's little hand and kissed it. The child looked at her with large, grave eyes—candid and, by reason of their candour, profoundly critical, like the eyes of an angel on the day of judgment.

"How do you do," he said in his solemn, childish voice.

"Sweet pet!" said Mrs Escobar and paid no further attention to him. She was not much interested in children. "And you, my dear?" she asked, addressing herself to Ruth. She kissed her. She kissed her on the lips.

"Very well, thanks, Mrs Escobar."

Mrs Escobar scrutinized her at arm's-length one hand on Ruth's shoulder. "You certainly look well, my dear child," she said. "And prettier than ever." She thrust the great sheaf of roses into the crook of the young mother's unoccupied arm. "What a sweet little Madonna!" she exclaimed, and, turning to Susan, "Did you ever see anything more charming?" she asked. Susan smiled and nodded, rather awkwardly; after all, Ruth was

her elder sister. "And so absurdly, *absurdly* young!" Mrs Escobar
went on. "Why, it's positively a *détournement de mineur*, your being
married and having a baby. Do you know, my dear, you really
look younger than Susan. It's a scandal."

Embarrassed by Mrs Escobar's point-blank praises, Ruth
blushed. And it was not modesty alone that brought the blood to
her cheeks. This insistence on the youthfulness of her appearance
humiliated her. For it was mostly due, this air of childishness, to
her clothes. She made her own frocks—rather "artistic" little
affairs in brightly coloured linens or large checks—made them in
the only way she knew how or had time to make them: straight
up and down, with a yoke and no sleeves, to be worn over a shirt.
Monotonously schoolgirlish! But what can you do, if you can't
afford to buy decent clothes? And her bobbed hair was dreadfully
schoolgirlish too. She knew it. But again, what could she do about
that? Let it grow? It would be such a trouble to keep tidy, and she
had so little time. Have it shingled? But she would need to get it
waved as well, and it would always have to be kept trimmed by a
good hairdresser. All that meant money. Money, money, money!

No, if she looked so preposterously young, that was simply
because she was poor. Susan was a baby, five years her junior.
But she looked more grown-up. She looked grown-up, because she
was properly dressed in frocks from a real dressmaker. Grown-up
clothes, though she was only seventeen. And her cropped brown
hair was beautifully waved. Mrs Escobar gave Susan everything
she wanted. Every blessed thing.

Suddenly she found herself hating and despising this enviably
happy sister of hers. After all, what was she? Just a little pet lap-
dog in Mrs Escobar's house. Just a doll; Mrs Escobar amused
herself by dressing her up, playing with her, making her say
"Mama". It was a despicable position, despicable. But even as
she thought of Susan's contemptibleness, she was complaining to
the fates which had not permitted her to share Susan's beatitude.
Why should Susan have everything, when she . . .?

But then, all at once, she remembered Baby. She turned her
head impulsively and kissed the child's round, peach-pink cheek.
The skin was smooth, soft and cool, like the petal of a flower.
Thinking of Baby made her think of Jim. She imagined how he
would kiss her when he came back from work. And this evening,
while she sewed, he would read aloud from Gibbon's *Decline and*

Fall. How she adored him, when he sat there in his spectacles, reading! And the curious way he pronounced the word "Persians" —not "Pershuns," but "Perzyans." The thought of the Perzyans made her violently wish that he were there beside her, so that she could throw her arms round his neck and kiss him. Perzyans, Perzyans—she repeated the word to herself. Oh, *how* she adored him!

With a sudden outburst of affection, intensified at once by repentance for her odious thoughts and the recollection of Jim, she turned to her sister.

"Well, Sue," she said. They kissed over the cold roast chicken and the tongue.

Mrs Escobar looked at the two sisters and, looking, was filled with pleasure. How charming they were, she thought; how fresh and young and pretty! She felt proud of them. For after all, were they not in some sort her own invention? A couple of young girls, nicely brought up, luxuriously even; then suddenly orphaned and left without a penny. They might simply have sunk, disappeared and never been heard of again. But Mrs Escobar, who had known their mother, came to the rescue. They were to come and live with her, poor children! and she would be their mother. A little ungratefully, as it always seemed to her, Ruth had preferred to accept young Jim Waterton's offer of a premature and hazardous marriage. Waterton had no money, of course; he was only a boy, with all his career to make. But Ruth had made her choice, deliberately. They had been married nearly five years now. Mrs Escobar had been a little hurt. Still, she had periodically paid her fairy godmother's visits to Purlieu Villas; she had stood plain human godmother to the baby. Susan, meanwhile, who was only thirteen when her father died, had grown up under Mrs Escobar's care. She was rising eighteen now, and charming.

"The greatest pleasure in the world," Mrs Escobar was fond of saying, "is being kind to other people." Particularly, she might have added, when the other people are young and ravishing little creatures who worship you.

"Dear children," she said, and, coming between them, she put an arm round either's waist. She felt all at once deeply and beautifully moved—much as she felt when she heard the Sermon on the Mount or the story of the woman taken in adultery read out in church. "Dear children." Her rich voice trembled a little, the tears came into her eyes. She pressed the two girls more closely to her. Interlaced, they walked along the path towards the door of the house. Robbins followed at a respectful distance, carrying the *foie gras* and the chocolate cake.

II

"But why isn't it a train?" asked Baby.

"But it's such a lovely bear."

"Such a beautiful . . . ." Susan insisted.

The faces of the sisters expressed an embarrassed anxiety. Who could have foreseen it? Baby hated the teddy bear. He wanted a train, and nothing but a train. And Mrs Escobar had chosen the bear herself. It was a most special bear, comic in a rather artistic way, don't you know; made of black plush, with very large eyes of white leather and boot-buttons.

"And see how it rolls," wheedled Ruth. She gave the animal a push; it rolled across the floor. "On wheels," she added. Baby had a weakness for wheels.

Susan reached out and drew the bear back again. "And when you pull this string," she explained, "it roars." She pulled the string. The bear squeaked hoarsely.

"But I want a train," insisted the child. "With rails and tunnels and signals." He called them siggernals.

"Another time, my darling," said Ruth. "Now go and give your bear a big kiss. Poor Teddy! He's so sad."

The child's lips trembled, his face became distorted with grief, he began to cry. "I want siggernals," he said. "Why doesn't she bring me siggernals?" He pointed accusingly at Mrs Escobar.

"Poor pet," said Mrs Escobar. "He shall have his siggernals."

"No, no," implored Ruth. "He really adores his bear, you know. It's just a foolish idea he's got into his head."

"Poor *little* pet," Mrs Escobar repeated. But how badly brought up the child was, she thought. So spoiled, and *blasé* already. She had taken such trouble about the bear. A real work of art. Ruth ought to be told, for her own good and the child's. But she was so touchy. How silly it was of people to be touchy about this sort of thing! Perhaps the best thing would be to talk to Susan about it and let her talk to Ruth quietly, when they were alone together.

Ruth tried to make a diversion. "Look at this lovely book Mrs

Escobar has brought you." She held up a brand new copy of Lear's *Book of Nonsense*. "Look." She turned over the pages invitingly before the child's eyes.

"Don't want to look," Baby replied, determined to be a martyr. In the end, however, he could not resist the pictures. "What's that?" he asked, sulkily, still trying to pretend that he wasn't interested.

"Would you like me to read you one of these lovely poems?" asked Mrs Escobar, heaping coals of fire on the despiser of the bear.

"Oh yes," cried Ruth with an anxious eagerness. "Yes, please."

"Please," repeated Susan.

Baby said nothing, but when his mother wanted to hand the book to Mrs Escobar, he tried to resist. . . . "It's my book," he said in a voice of loud and angry complaint.

"Hush," said Ruth, and stroked his head soothingly. He relinquished the book.

"Which shall it be?" asked Mrs Escobar, turning over the pages of the volume. "'The Yonghy-Bonghy-Bo'? Or 'The Pobble who has no Toes'? Or 'The Dong'? Or 'The Owl and the Pussy Cat'? Which?" She looked up, smiling inquiringly.

"'The Pobble,'" suggested Susan.

"I think 'The Owl and the Pussy Cat' would be the best to begin with," said Ruth. "It's easier to understand than the others. You'd like to hear about the Pussy, wouldn't you, darling?"

The child nodded, unenthusiastically.

"Sweet pet!" said Mrs Escobar. "He shall have his Pussy. I love it too." She found her place in the book, "'The Owl and the Pussy Cat,'" she announced in a voice more richly and cooingly vibrant than the ordinary. Mrs Escobar had studied elocution with the best teachers, and was fond of acting, for charity. She had been unforgettable as Tosca in aid of the Hoxton Children's Hospital. And then there was her orthopaedic Portia, her tuberculous Mrs Tanqueray (or was Mrs. Tanqueray for the incurables?).

"What's a owl?" asked Baby.

Interrupted, Mrs Escobar began a preliminary reading of the poem to herself; her lips moved as she read.

"An owl's a kind of big funny bird," his mother answered and put her arm round him. She hoped he'd keep quieter if she held him like this.

"Do nowls bite?"

"Owls, darling, not nowls."

"Do they bite?"

"Only when people tease them."

"Why do people tease them?"

"Sh-sh!" said Ruth. "Now you must listen. Mrs Escobar's going to read you a lovely story about an owl and a pussy."

Mrs Escobar, meanwhile, had been studying her poem. "Too charming!" she said, to nobody in particular, smiling as she spoke with eyes and lips. "Such poetry, really, though it is nonsense. After all, what is poetry but nonsense? Divine nonsense." Susan nodded her agreement. "Shall I begin?" Mrs Escobar inquired.

"Oh, do," said Ruth, without ceasing to caress the child's silky hair. He was calmer now.

Mrs Escobar began:—

"'The aul and the pooseh-cut went to sea
In a beautiful (after a little pause and with intensity) *pea-grreen*
    boat.
They took some honey and (the rich voice rose a tone and sank)
    plenty of money,
Wrapped (little pause) up (little pause) in a five-pound note.'"

"What's a five-pound note?" asked Baby.

Ruth pressed her hand more heavily on the head, as though to squeeze down his rising curiosity. "Sh-sh!" she said.

Ignoring the interruption, Mrs Escobar went on, after a brief dramatic silence, to the second stanza.

"'The aul looked up to the starrs above (her voice thrilled
    deeply with the passion of the tropical and amorous night)
And sang to a small (little pause) guitarr. . .'"

"Mummy, what's a guit . . .?"

"Hush, pet, hush." She could almost feel the child's questioning spirit oozing out between her confining fingers.

With a green flash of emeralds, a many-coloured glitter of brilliants, Mrs Escobar laid her long white hand on her heart and raised her eyes towards imaginary constellations.

"'Oh lovely poosseh, oh poosseh my love,
What a (from high, the voice dropped emphatically) *beau*tiful poosseh you are, you are,
What a *beau*tiful poosseh you are!'"

"But, mummy, do owls like cats?"
"Don't talk, darling."
"But you told me cats eat birds."
"Not this cat, my pet."
"But you said so, mummy . . ."
Mrs Escobar began the next stanza.

"'Said the cut to the aul, You elegant faul,
How charrmingly sweet you sing (Mrs Escobar's voice became languishing).
Come, let us be murried; too long have we turried.
But *what* (pause; Mrs Escobar made a despairing gesture, luminous with rings) shall we do (pause) for the (her voice rose to the question) rring, the rring?
But *what* shall we do for the rring?

"'So they sailed away for a yeerr and a day
To the lund where the bong-tree grows. . . .'"

"What's a bongtrygroze, mummy?"
Mrs Escobar slightly raised her voice so as to cover the childish interruption and went on with her recitation.

"'And there (pause) in a wood (pause) a *Pig*-gywig stood,
With a rring. . . .'"
'But, mummy . . ."

"'With a rring (Mrs Escobar repeated still more loudly, describing in the air, as she did so, a flashing circle) at the end of his nose, his nose. . . .'"

"Mummy!" The child was furious with impatience; he shook

his mother's arm. "Why don't you say? What is a bongtrygroze?"
"You must wait, my pet.'

Susan put her finger to her lips. "Sh-sh!" Oh, how she wished
that he would be good! What would Mrs Escobar think? And her
reading was so beautiful.

"'With a rring (Mrs Escobar described a still larger circle) at
the end of his nose'"

"It's a kind of tree," whispered Ruth.

"'Deerr peeg, arre you willing to sell for one shilling
Your rring? Said the Peeggy, I will.
So they took it a-way and were murried next day
By the turrkey who lives on the hill (the dreamy note in Mrs
Escobar's voice made the turkey's hill sound wonderfully
blue, romantic and remote),
By the turrkey who lived on the hill.

"'They dined on mince and slices of quince,
Which they ate with a runcible spoon,
And . . .'"
"What's runcible?"
"Hush, darling."

"'. . . hand in hand (the voice became cooingly tender, bloomy
like a peach with velvety sentiment) by the edge . . .'"

"But why do you say sh-sh, like that?" the little boy shouted.
He was so angry, that he began to hit his mother with his fists.

The interruption was so scandalous, that Mrs Escobar was
forced to take notice of it. She contented herself with frowning
and laying her finger on her lips.

"'. . . by the edge of the sand (all the ocean was in Mrs Escobar's
voice),
They danced (how gay and yet how exquisitely, how nuptially
tender!) by the light (she spoke very slowly; she allowed her
hand, which she had lifted, to come gradually down, like a
tired bird, on to her knee) of the moo-oon.'"

If any one could have heard those final words, he would have heard interstellar space, and the mystery of planetary motion, and Don Juan's serenade, and Juliet's balcony. If any one could have heard them. But the scream which Baby uttered was so piercingly loud, that they were quite inaudible.

III

"I think you ought to talk to Ruth seriously one day," said Mrs Escobar, on the way back from Purlieu Villas, "about Baby. I don't think she really brings him up at all well. He's spoiled."

The accusation was couched in general terms. But Susan began at once to apologize for what she felt sure was Baby's particular offence.

"Of course," she said, "the trouble was that there were so many words in the poem he didn't understand."

Mrs Escobar was annoyed at having been too well understood.

"The poem?" she repeated, as though she didn't understand what Susan was talking about. "Oh, I didn't mean that. I thought he was so good, considering, while I was reading. Didn't you?"

Susan blushed, guiltily. "I thought he interrupted rather a lot," she said.

Mrs Escobar laughed indulgently. "But what can you expect of a little child like that?" she said. "No, no; I was thinking of his behaviour in general. At tea, for example. . . . You really ought to talk to Ruth about it."

Susan promised that she would.

Changing the subject, Mrs Escobar began to talk about Sydney Fell, who was coming to dinner that evening. Such a darling creature! She liked him more and more. He had a most beautiful mouth; so refined and sensitive, and yet at the same time so strong, so sensual. And he was so witty and such an accomplished amorist. Susan listened in misery and silence.

"Don't you think so?" Mrs Escobar kept asking insistently. "Don't you think he's delightful?"

Susan suddenly burst out. "I hate him," she said, and began to cry.

"You hate him?" said Mrs Escobar. "But why? Why? You're not jealous, are you?" She laughed.

Susan shook her head.

"You are!" Mrs Escobar insisted. "You are!"

Susan continued obstinately to shake her head. But Mrs Escobar knew that she had got her revenge.

"You silly, silly child," she said in a voice in which there were treasures of affection. She put her arm round the girl's shoulders, drew her gently and tenderly towards her and began to kiss her wet face. Susan abandoned herself to her happiness.

Chawdron

FROM behind the outspread *Times* I broke a silence. "Your friend Chawdron's dead, I see."

"Dead?" repeated Tilney, half incredulously. "Chawdron dead?"

"'Suddenly, of heart failure,'" I went on, reading from the obituary, "'at his residence in St James's Square.'"

"Yes, his heart . . ." He spoke meditatively. "How old was he? Sixty?"

"Fifty-nine. I didn't realize the ruffian had been rich for so long. '. . . the extraordinary business instinct, coupled with a truly Scottish doggedness and determination, which raised him, before he was thirty-five, from obscurity and comparative poverty to the height of opulence.' Don't you wish you could write like that? My father lost a quarter of a century's savings in one of his companies."

"Served him right for saving!" said Tilney with a sudden savagery. Surprised, I looked at him over the top of my paper. On his gnarled and ruddy face was an expression of angry gloom. The news had evidently depressed him. Besides, he was always ill-tempered at breakfast. My poor father was paying. "What sort of jam is that by you?" he asked fiercely.

"Strawberry."

"Then I'll have some marmalade."

I passed him the marmalade and, ignoring his bad temper, "When the Old Man," I continued, "and along with him, of course, most of the other shareholders, had sold out at about eighty per cent. dead loss, Chawdron did a little quiet conjuring and the price whizzed up again. But by that time he was the owner of practically all the stock."

"I'm always on the side of the ruffians," said Tilney. "On principle."

"Oh, so am I. All the same, I do regret those twelve thousand pounds."

Tilney said nothing. I returned to the obituary.

"What do they say about the New Guinea Oil Company scandal?" he asked after a silence.

"Very little; and the touch is beautifully light. The findings of the Royal Commission were on the whole favourable, though it was generally considered at the time that Mr Chawdron had acted somewhat inconsiderately.'"

Tilney laughed. "'Inconsiderately' is good. I wish I made fourteen hundred thousand pounds each time I was inconsiderate."

"Was that what he made out of the New Guinea Oil business?"

"So he told me, and I don't think he exaggerated. He never lied for pleasure. Out of business hours he was remarkably honest."

"You must have known him very well."

"Intimately," said Tilney, and, pushing away his plate, he began to fill his pipe.

"I envy you. What a specimen for one's collection! But didn't you get rather bored with living inside the museum, so to speak, behind the menagerie bars? Being intimate with a specimen—it must be trying."

"Not if the specimen's immensely rich," Tilney answered. "You see, I'm partial to Napoleon brandy and Corona Coronas; parasitism has its rewards. And if you're skilful, it needn't have too many penalties. It's possible to be a high-souled louse, an independent tapeworm. But Napoleon brandy and Coronas weren't the only attractions Chawdron possessed for me. I have a disinterested, scientific curiosity about the enormously wealthy. A man with an income of more than fifty thousand a year is such a fantastic and improbable being. Chawdron was specially interesting because he'd *made* all his money—mainly dishonestly; that was the fascinating thing. He was a large-scale, Napoleonic crook. And, by God, he looked it! Did you know him by sight?"

I shook my head.

"Like an illustration to Lombroso. A criminal type. But intelligently criminal, not brutally. He wasn't brutal."

"I thought he was supposed to look like a chimpanzee," I put in.

"He did," said Tilney. "But, after all, a chimpanzee isn't brutal-looking. What you're struck by in a chimpanzee is its all-but-human appearance. So very intelligent, so nearly a man.

Chawdron's face had just that look. But with a difference. The chimpanzee looks gentle and virtuous and quite without humour. Whereas Chawdron's intelligent all-but-humanity was sly and, underneath the twinkling jocularity, quite ruthless. Oh, a strange, interesting creature! I got a lot of fun out of my study of him. But in the end, of course, he did bore me. Bored me to death. He was so drearily uneducated. Didn't know the most obvious things, couldn't understand a generalization. And then quite disgustingly without taste, without aesthetic sense or understanding. Metaphysically and artistically a cretin."

"The obituarist doesn't seem to be of your opinion." I turned again to *The Times*. "Where is it now? Ah! 'A remarkable writer was lost when Chawdron took up finance. Not entirely lost, however; for the brilliant *Autobiography*, published in 1921, remains as a lasting memorial to his talents as a stylist and narrator.' What do you say to that?" I asked, looking up at Tilney.

He smiled enigmatically. "It's quite true."

"I never read the book, I confess. Is it any good?"

"It's damned good." His smile mocked, incomprehensibly.

"Are you pulling my leg?"

"No, it was really and genuinely good."

"Then he can hardly have been such an artistic cretin as you make out."

"Can't he?" Tilney echoed and, after a little pause, suddenly laughed aloud. "But he *was* a cretin," he continued on a little gush of confidingness that seemed to sweep away the barriers of his willed discretion, "and the book *was* good. For the excellent reason that he didn't write it. I wrote it."

"You?" I looked at him, wondering if he were joking. But his face, after the quick illumination of laughter, had gone serious, almost gloomy. A curious face, I reflected. Handsome in its way, intelligent, aware, yet with something rather sinister about it, almost repulsive. The superficial charm and good humour of the man seemed to overlie a fundamental hardness, an uncaringness, a hostility even. Too much good living, moreover, had left its marks on that face. It was patchily red and lumpy. The fine features had become rather gross. There was a coarseness mingled with the native refinement. Did I like Tilney or did I not? I never rightly knew. And perhaps the question was irre-

levant. Perhaps Tilney was one of those men who are not meant
to be liked or disliked as men—only as performers. I liked his
conversation, I was amused, interested, instructed by what he
said. To ask myself if I also liked what he *was*—this was, no
doubt, beside the point.

Tilney got up from the table and began to walk up and down
the room, his pipe between his teeth, smoking. "Poor Chawdron's
dead now, so there's no reason . . ." He left the sentence unfinished, and for a few seconds was silent. Standing by the
window, he looked out through the rain-blurred glass on to the
greens and wet greys of the Kentish landscape. "England looks
like the vegetables at a Bloomsbury boarding-house dinner," he
said slowly. "Horrible! Why do we live in this horrible country?
Ugh!" He shuddered and turned away. There was another
silence. The door opened and the maid came in to clear the
breakfast table. I say "the maid"; but the brief impersonal term
is inaccurate. Inaccurate, because wholly inadequate to describe
Hawtrey. What came in, when the door opened, was personified
efficiency, was a dragon, was stony ugliness, was a pillar of
society, was the Ten Commandments on legs. Tilney, who did
not know her, did not share my terror of the domestic monster.
Unaware of the intense disapproval which I could feel her
silently radiating (it was after ten; Tilney's slug-a-bed habits had
thrown out of gear the whole of her morning's routine) he continued to walk up and down, while Hawtrey busied herself round
the table. Suddenly he laughed. "Chawdron's *Autobiography* was
the only one of my books I ever made any money out of," he said.
I listened apprehensively, lest he should say anything which
might shock or offend the dragon. "He turned over all the
royalties to me," Tilney went on. "I made the best part of three
thousand pounds out of his *Autobiography*. Not to mention the five
hundred he gave me for writing it." (Was it quite delicate, I
wondered, to talk of such large sums of money in front of one so
incomparably more virtuous than ourselves and so much poorer?
Fortunately, Tilney changed the subject.) "You ought to read it,"
he said. "I'm really quite offended that you haven't. All that
lower middle-class childhood in Peebles—it's really masterly."
("Lower middle-class"—I shuddered. Hawtrey's father had
owned a shop; but he had had misfortunes.) "It's *Clayhanger* and
L'Education Sentimentale and *David Copperfield* all rolled into one.

Really superb. And the first adventurings into the world of finance were pure Balzac—magnificent." He laughed again, this time without bitterness, amusedly; he was warming to his subject. "I even put in a Rastignac soliloquy from the top of the dome of St Paul's, made him shake his fist at the City. Poor old Chawdron! he was thrilled. 'If only I'd known what an interesting life I'd had,' he used to say to me. 'Known while the life was going on.'" (I looked at Hawtrey to see if she was resenting the references to an interesting life. But her face was closed; she worked as though she were deaf.) "'You wouldn't have lived it,' I told him. 'You must leave the discovery of the excitingness to the artists.'" He was silent again. Hawtrey laid the last spoon on the tray and moved towards the door. Thank heaven! "Yes, the artist," Tilney went on in a tone that had gone melancholy again. "I really was one, you know." (The departing Hawtrey must have heard that damning confession. But then, I reflected, she always did know that I and my friends were a bad lot.) "Really *am* one," he insisted. "*Qualis artifex!* But *pereo, pereo.* Somehow, I've never done anything but perish all my life. Perish, perish, perish. Out of laziness and because there always seemed so much time. But I'm going to be forty-eight next June. Forty-eight! There isn't any time. And the laziness is such a habit. So's the talking. It's so easy to talk. And so amusing. At any rate for oneself."

"For other people too," I said; and the compliment was sincere. I might be uncertain whether or no I liked Tilney. But I genuinely liked his performance as a talker. Sometimes, perhaps, that performance was a little too professional. But, after all, an artist must be a professional.

"It's what comes of being mostly Irish," Tilney went on. "Talking's the national vice. Like opium-smoking with the Chinese!" (Hawtrey re-entered silently to sweep up the crumbs and fold the table-cloth.) "If you only knew the number of masterpieces I've allowed to evaporate at dinner tables, over the cigars and the whisky!" (Two things of which, I knew, the Pillar of Society virtuously disapproved.) "A whole library. I might have been—what? Well, I suppose I might have been a frightful old bore," he answered himself with a forced self-mockery. "'The Complete Works of Edmund Tilney, in Thirty-Eight Volumes, post octavo.' I dare say the world ought to be grateful to me for sparing it *that*. All the same, I get a bit depressed when I look over the back numbers of the *Thursday Review* and read those measly little weekly articles of mine. *Parturiunt montes . . .*"

"But they're good articles," I protested. If I had been more truthful, I would have said that they were sometimes good—when he took the trouble to make them good. Sometimes, on the contrary . . .

"*Merci, cher maître!*" he answered ironically. "But hardly more perennial than brass, you must admit. Monuments of wood pulp. It's depressing being a failure. Particularly if it's your fault, if you might have been something else."

I mumbled something. But what was there to say? Except as a professional talker, Tilney *had* been a failure. He had great talents and he was a literary journalist who sometimes wrote a good article. He had reason to feel depressed.

"And the absurd, ironical thing," he continued, "is that the one really good piece of work I ever did is another man's autobiography. I could never prove my authorship even if I wanted to. Old Chawdron was very careful to destroy all the evidences of the crime. The business arrangements were all verbal. No documents of any kind. And the manuscript, *my* manuscript—he bought it off me. It's burnt."

I laughed. "He took no risks with you." Thank heaven! The dragon was preparing to leave the room for good.

"None whatever," said Tilney. "He was going to be quite sure of wearing his laurel wreath. There was to be no other claimant. And at the time, of course, I didn't care two pins. I took the high line about reputation. Good art—and Chawdron's *Autobiography* was good art, a really first-rate novel—good art is its own reward." (Hawtrey's comment on this was almost to slam the door as she departed.) "You know the style of thing? And in this case it was more than its own reward. There was money in it. Five hundred down and all the royalties. And I was horribly short of money at the moment. If I hadn't been, I'd never have written the book. Perhaps that's been one of my disadvantages—a small independent income and not very extravagant tastes. I happened to be in love with a very expensive young woman at the time when Chawdron made his offer. You can't go dancing and drinking champagne on five hundred a year. Chawdron's cheque was timely. And there I was, committed to writing his memoirs for him. A bore, of course. But luckily the young woman jilted me soon afterwards; so I had time to waste. And Chawdron was a ruthless taskmaster. And besides, I really enjoyed it once I got started. It really was its own reward. But now—now that the book's written and the money's spent and I'm soon going to be fifty, instead of forty as it was then—now, I must say, I'd rather like to have at least one good book to my credit. I'd like to be known as the author of that admirable novel, *The Autobiography of Benjamin Chawdron*, but, alas, I shan't be." He sighed . "It's Benjamin Chawdron, not Edmund Tilney, who'll have his little niche in the literary histories. Not that I care much for literary history. But I do rather care, I must confess, for the present anticipations of the niche. The drawing-room reputation, the mentions in the newspapers, the deference of the young, the sympathetic curiosity of the women. All the by-products of successful authorship. But there, I sold them to Chawdron. For a good price. I can't complain. Still, I *do* complain. Have you got any pipe tobacco? I've run out of mine."

I gave him my pouch. "If I had the energy," he went on, as he refilled his pipe, "or if I were desperately hard up, which, thank heaven and at the same time alas! I'm not at the moment, I could make another book out of Chawdron. Another and a better one. Better," he began explaining, and then interrupted himself to suck at the flame of the match he had lighted, "because . . . so much more . . . malicious." He threw the match away. "You can't write a good book without being malicious. In the *Autobiography* I made a hero of Chawdron. I was paid to; besides, it was Chawdron himself who provided me with my documents. In this other book he'd be the villain. Or in other words, he'd be himself as others saw him, not as he saw himself. Which is, incidentally, the only valid difference between the virtuous and the wicked that *I*'ve ever been able to detect. When you yourself indulge in any of the deadly sins, you're always justified—they're never deadly. But when any one else indulges, you're very properly indignant. Old Rousseau had the courage to say that he was the most virtuous man in the world. The rest of us only silently believe it. But to return to Chawdron. What I'd like to do now is to write his biography, not his autobiography. And the biography of a rather different aspect of the man. Not about the man of action, the captain of industry, the Napoleon of finance and so forth. But about the domestic, the private, the sentimental Chawdron."

"*The Times* had its word about that," said I; and picking up the paper once more, I read: "'Under a disconcertingly brusque and even harsh manner Mr Chawdron concealed the kindliest of natures. A stranger meeting him for the first time was often repelled by a certain superficial roughness. It was only to his intimates that he revealed'—guess what!—'the heart of gold beneath.'"

"Heart of gold!" Tilney took his pipe out of his mouth to laugh.

"And he also, I see, had 'a deep religious sense.'" I laid the paper down.

"Deep? It was bottomless."

"Extraordinary," I reflected aloud, "the way they *all* have hearts of gold and religious senses. Every single one, from the rough old man of science to the tough old business man and the gruff old statesman."

"Hearts of gold!" Tilney repeated. "But gold's much too hard. Hearts of putty, hearts of vaseline, hearts of hog-wash. That's more like it. Hearts of hog-wash. The tougher and bluffer and gruffer they are outside, the softer they are within. It's a law of nature. I've never come across an exception. Chawdron was the rule incarnate. Which is precisely what I want to show in this other, potential book of mine—the ruthless Napoleon of finance paying for his ruthlessness and his Napoleonism by dissolving internally into hog-wash. For that's what happened to him: he dissolved into hog-wash. Like the Strange Case of Mr Valdemar in Edgar Allan Poe. I saw it with my own eyes. It's a terrifying spectacle. And the more terrifying when you realize that, but for the grace of God, there goes yourself—and still more so when you begin to doubt of the grace of God, when you see that there in fact you *do* go. Yes, you and I, my boy. For it isn't only the tough old business men who have the hearts of hog-wash. It's also, as you yourself remarked just now, the gruff old scientists, the rough old scholars, the bluff old admirals and bishops and all the other pillars of Christian society. It's everybody, in a word, who has made himself too hard in the head or the carapace; everybody who aspires to be non-human—whether angel or machine it doesn't matter. Super-humanity is as bad as sub-humanity, is the same thing finally. Which shows how careful one should be if one's an intellectual. Even the mildest sort of intellectual. Like me, for example. I'm not one of your genuine ascetic scholars. God forbid! But I'm decidedly high-brow, and I'm literary; I'm even what the newspapers call a 'thinker'. I suffer from a passion for ideas. Always have, from boyhood onwards. With what results? That I've never been attracted by any woman who wasn't a bitch."

I laughed. But Tilney held up his hand in a gesture of protest. "It's a serious matter," he said. "It's disastrous, even. Nothing but bitches. Imagine!"

"I'm imagining," I said. "But where do the books and the ideas come in? *Post* isn't necessarily *propter*."

"It's *propter* in this case all right. Thanks to the books and the ideas, I never learnt how to deal with real situations, with solid people and things. Personal relationships—I've never been able to manage them effectively. Only ideas. With ideas I'm at home. With the *idea* of personal relationships. for example. People think I'm an excellent psychologist. And I suppose I am. Spectatorially. But I'm a bad experiencer. I've lived most of my life posthumously, if you see what I mean; in reflections and conversations after the fact. As though my existence were a novel or a text-book of psychology or a biography, like any of the others on the library shelves. An awful situation. That was why I've always liked the bitches so much, always been so grateful to them—because they were the only women I ever contrived to have a non-posthumous, contemporary, concrete relation with. The only ones." He smoked for a moment in silence.

"But why the only ones?" I asked.

"Why?" repeated Tilney. "But isn't it rather obvious? For the shy man, that is to say the man who doesn't know how to deal with real situations and people, bitches are the only possible lovers, because they're the only women who are prepared to come to meet him, the only ones who'll make the advances he doesn't know how to make."

I nodded. "Shy men have cause to be drawn to bitches: I see that. But why should the bitches be drawn to the shy men? What's their inducement to make those convenient advances? That's what I don't see."

"Oh, of course they don't make them unless the shy man's

attractive," Tilney answered. "But in my case the bitches always were attracted. Always. And, quite frankly, they were right. I was tolerably picturesque, I had that professional Irish charm, I could talk, I was several hundred times more intelligent than any of the young men they were likely to know. And then, I fancy, my very shyness was an asset. You see, it didn't really look like shyness. It exteriorized itself as a kind of god-like impersonality and remoteness—most exciting for such women. I had the charm in their eyes of Mount Everest or the North Pole—something difficult and unconquered that aroused the record-breaking instincts in them. And at the same time my shy remoteness made me seem somehow superior; and, as you know, few pleasures can be compared with the sport of dragging down superiority and proving that it's no better than oneself. My air of disinterested remoteness has always had a *succès fou* with the bitches. They all adore me because I'm so 'different.' 'But you're different, Edmund, you're different,'" he fluted in falsetto. "The bitches! Under their sentimentalities, their one desire, of course, was to reduce me as quickly as possible to the most ignoble un-difference. . . ."

"And were they successful?" I asked.

"Oh, always. Naturally. It's not because a man's shy and bookish that he isn't a *porco di prim' ordine*. Indeed, the more shyly bookish, the more likely he is to be secretly porkish. Or if not a *porco*, at least an *asino*, an *oca*, a *vitello*. It's the rule, as I said just now; the law of nature. There's no escaping."

I laughed. "I wonder which of the animals I am?"

Tilney shook his head. "I'm not a zoologist. At least," he added, "not when I'm talking to the specimen under discussion. Ask your own conscience."

"And Chawdron?" I wanted to hear more about Chawdron. "Did Chawdron grunt, or bray, or moo?"

"A little of each. And if earwigs made a noise . . . No, not earwigs. Worse than that. Chawdron was an extreme case, and the extreme cases are right outside the animal kingdom."

"What are they, then? Vegetables?"

"No, no. Worse than vegetables. They're spiritual. Angels, that's what they are: putrefied angels. It's only in the earlier stages of the degeneration that they bleat and bray. After that they twang the harp and flap their wings. Pigs' wings, of course. They're

Angels in pigs' clothing. Hearts of hog-wash. Did I ever tell you about Chawdron and Charlotte Salmon?"

"The 'cellist?"

He nodded. "What a woman!"

"And her playing! So clotted, so sagging, so greasy . . ." I fumbled for the apt description.

"So terribly Jewish, in a word," said Tilney. "That retching emotionalism, that sea-sickish spirituality—purely Hebraic. If only there were a few more Aryans in the world of music! The tears come into my eyes whenever I see a blonde beast at the piano. But that's by the way. I was going to tell you about Charlotte. You know her, of course?"

"Do I not!"

"Well, it was Charlotte who first revealed to me poor Chawdron's heart of hog-wash. Mine too, indirectly. It was one evening at old Cryle's. Chawdron was there, and Charlotte, and myself, and I forget who else. People from all the worlds, anyhow. Cryle, as you know, has a foot in each. He thinks it's his mission to bring them together. He's the match-maker between God and Mammon. In this case he must have imagined that he'd really brought off the marriage. Chawdron was Mammon all right; and though you and I would be chary of labelling Charlotte as God, old Cryle, I'm sure, had no doubts. After all, she plays the 'cello; she's an Artist. What more can you want?"

"What indeed!"

"I must say, I admired Charlotte that evening," he went on. "She knew so exactly the line to take with Chawdron; which was the more surprising as with me she's never quite pulled it off. She tries the siren on me, very dashing and at the same time extremely mysterious. Her line is to answer my most ordinary remarks with something absolutely incomprehensible, but obviously very significant. If I ask her, for example: 'Are you going to the Derby this year?' she'll smile a really Etruscan smile and answer: 'No, I'm too busy watching the boat-race in my own heart.' Well, then, obviously it's my cue to be terribly intrigued. 'Fascinating Sphinx,' I ought to say, 'tell me more about your visceral boat-race,' or words to that effect. Whereupon it would almost certainly turn out that I was rowing stroke in the winning boat. But I'm afraid I can't bring myself to do what's expected of me. I just say: 'What a pity! I was making up a party to go to

Epsom'—and hastily walk away. No doubt, if she was less blackly Semitic I'd be passionately interested in her boat-race. But as it is, her manœuvre doesn't come off. She hadn't yet been able to think of a better one. With Chawdron, however, she discovered the correct strategy from the first moment. No siren, no mystery for him. His heart was too golden and hog-washy for that. Besides, he was fifty. It's the age when clergymen first begin to be preoccupied with the underclothing of little schoolgirls in trains, the age when eminent archaeologists start taking a really passionate interest in the Scout movement. Under Chawdron's criminal mask Charlotte detected the pig-like angel, the sentimental Pickwickian child-lover with a taste for the *détournement de mineurs*. Charlotte's a practical woman: a child was needed, she immediately became the child. And what a child! I've never seen anything like it. Such prattling! Such innocent big eyes! Such merry, merry laughter! Such a wonderfully ingenuous way of saying extremely *risqué* things without knowing (sweet innocent) what they meant! I looked on and listened—staggered. Horrified too. The performance was really frightful. Suffer little children . . . But when the little child's twenty-eight and tough for her age— ah, no; of such is the kingdom of hell. For me, at any rate. But Chawdron was enchanted. Really did seem to imagine he'd got hold of something below the age of consent. I looked at him in amazement. Was it possible he should be taken in? The acting was so bad, so incredibly unconvincing. Sarah Bernhardt at seventy playing L'Aiglon looked more genuinely like a child than our tough little Charlotte. But Chawdron didn't see it. This man who had lived by his wits, and not merely lived, but made a gigantic fortune by them:—was it possible that the most brilliant financier of the age should be so fabulously stupid? 'Youth's infectious,' he said to me after dinner, when the women had gone out. And then —you should have seen the smile on his face: beatific, lubrically tender—'She's like a jolly little kitten, don't you think?' But what I thought of was the New Guinea Oil Company. How was it possible? And then suddenly I perceived that it wasn't merely possible; it was absolutely necessary. Just because he'd made fourteen hundred thousand pounds out of the New Guinea Oil scandal, it was inevitable that he should mistake a jolly little tarantula like Charlotte for a jolly little kitten. Inevitable. Just as it was inevitable that I should be bowled over by every bitch that came my way. Chawdron had spent his life thinking of oil and stock markets and flotations. I'd spent mine reading the Best that has been Thought or Said. Neither of us had had the time or energy to live—completely and intensely live, as a human being ought to, on every plane of existence. So he was taken in by the pseudo-kitten, while I succumbed to the only too genuine bitch. Succumbed, what was worse, with full knowledge. For I was never really taken in. I always knew that the bitches were bitches and not milk-white hinds. And now I also know why I was captivated by them. But that, of course, didn't prevent me from continuing to be captivated by them. *Experientia* doesn't, in spite of Mrs Micawber's Papa. Nor does knowledge." He paused to relight his pipe.

"What does, then?" I asked.

Tilney shrugged his shoulders. "Nothing does, once you've gone off the normal instinctive rails."

"I wonder if they really exist, those rails?"

"So do I, sometimes," he confessed. "But I piously believe."

"Rousseau and Shelley piously believed too. But has anybody ever seen a Natural Man? Those Noble Savages . . . Read Malinowsky about them; read Frazer; read . . ."

"Oh, I have, I have. And of course the savage isn't noble. Primitives are horrible. I know. But then the Natural Man isn't Primitive Man. He isn't the raw material of humanity; he's the finished product. The Natural Man is a manufactured article—no, not manufactured; rather, a work of art. What's wrong with people like Chawdron is that they're such bad works of art. Unnatural because inartistic. Ary Scheffer instead of Manet. But with this difference. An Ary Scheffer is statically bad; it doesn't get worse with the passage of time. Whereas an inartistic human being degenerates, dynamically. Once he's started badly, he becomes more and more inartistic. It needs a moral earthquake to arrest the process. Mere flea-bites, like experience or knowledge, are quite unavailing. *Experientia* doesn't. If it did, I should never have succumbed as I did, never have got into financial straits, and therefore never have written Chawdron's autobiography, never have had an opportunity for collecting the intimate and discreditable materials for the biography that, alas, I shall never write. No, no; experience didn't save me from falling a victim yet once more. And to such a ruinously expensive specimen. Not that she was mercenary," he put in parenthetically. "She was too well off to need to be. So well off, however, that the mere cost of feeding and amusing her in the style she was accustomed to being fed and amused in was utterly beyond my means. Of course she never realized it. People who are born with more than five thousand a year can't be expected to realize. She'd have been terribly upset if she had; for she had a heart of gold— like all the rest of us." He laughed mournfully. "Poor Sybil! I expect you remember her."

The name evoked for me a pale-eyed, pale-haired ghost. "What an astonishingly lovely creature she was!"

"Was, was," he echoed. "*Fuit*. Lovely and fatal. The agonies she made me suffer! But she was as fatal to herself as to other people. Poor Sybil! I could cry when I think of that inevitable course of hers, that predestined trajectory." With a stretched forefinger he traced in the air a curve that rose and fell away again. "She had just passed the crest when I knew her. The descending branch of the curve was horribly steep. What depths awaited her! That horrible little East-Side Jew she even went to the trouble of marrying! And after the Jew, the Mexican Indian. And meanwhile a little champagne had become rather a lot of champagne, rather a lot of brandy; and the occasional Good Times came to be incessant, a necessity, but so boring, such a dismal routine, so terribly exhausting. I didn't see her for four years after our final quarrel; and then (you've no idea how painful it was) I suddenly found myself shaking hands with a *momento mori*. So worn and ill and tired, so terribly old. Old at thirty-four. And the last time I'd seen her, she'd been radiant. Eighteen months later she was dead; but not before the Indian had given place to a Chinaman and the brandy to cocaine. It was all inevitable, of course, all perfectly foreseeable. Nemesis had functioned with exemplary regularity. Which only made it worse. Nemesis is all right for strangers and casual acquaintances. But for oneself, for the people one likes—ah, no! *We* ought to be allowed to sow without reaping. But we mayn't. I sowed books and reaped Sybil. Sybil sowed me (not to mention the others) and reaped Mexicans, cocaine, death. Inevitable, but an outrage, an insulting denial of one's uniqueness and difference. Whereas when people like Chawdron sow New Guinea Oil and reap kittenish Charlottes, one's delighted; the punctuality of fate seems admirable."

"I never knew that Charlotte had been reaped by Chawdron," I put in. "The harvesting must have been done with extraordinary discretion. Charlotte's usually so fond of publicity, even in these matters. I should never have expected her . . ."

"But the reaping was very brief and partial," Tilney explained.

That surprised me even more. "Charlotte who's always so determined and clinging! And with Chawdron's millions to cling to. . . ."

"Oh, it wasn't her fault that it went no further. She had every intention of being reaped and permanently garnered. But she had arranged to go to America for two months on a concert tour. It would have been troublesome to break the contract; Chawdron seemed thoroughly infatuated; two months are soon passed. So she went. Full of confidence. But when she came back, Chawdron was otherwise occupied."

"Another kitten?"

"A kitten? Poor Charlotte was a grey-whiskered old tigress by comparison. She even came to me in her despair. No enigmatic subtleties this time; she'd forgotten she was the Sphinx. 'I think you ought to warn Mr Chawdron against that woman,' she told me. 'He ought to be made to realize that she's exploiting him. It's outrageous.' She was full of righteous indignation. Not unnaturally. Even got angry with me because I wouldn't do anything. 'But he wants to be exploited,' I told her. 'It's his only joy in life.' Which was perfectly true. But I couldn't resist being a little malicious. 'What makes you want to spoil his fun?' I asked. She got quite red in the face. 'Because I think it's disgusting.'" Tilney made his voice indignantly shrill. "'It really shocks me to see a man like Mr Chawdron being made a fool of in that way.' Poor Charlotte! Her feelings did her credit. But they were quite unavailing. Chawdron went on being made a fool of, in spite of her moral indignation. Charlotte had to retreat. The enemy was impregnably entrenched."

"But who was she—the enemy?"

"The unlikeliest *femme fatale* you ever saw. Little; rather ugly; sickly—yes, genuinely sickly, I think, though she did a good deal of pathetic malingering too; altogether too much the lady—refined; you know the type. A governess; not the modern breezy, athletic sort of governess—the genteel, Jane Eyre, daughter-of-clergyman kind. Her only visible merit was that she was young. About twenty-five, I suppose."

"But how on earth did they meet? Millionaires and governesses . . ."

"A pure miracle," said Tilney. "Chawdron himself detected the hand of Providence. That was the deep religious sense coming in. 'If it hadn't been for *both* my secretaries falling ill on the same day,' he said to me solemnly (and you've no idea how ridiculous he looked when he was being solemn—the saintly forger, the burglar in the pulpit), 'if it hadn't been for that—and after all, how unlikely it is that both one's secretaries should fall ill at the same moment; what a *fateful* thing to happen!—I should never have got to know my little Fairy.' And you must imagine the last words pronounced with a reverent and beautiful smile—indescribably incongruous on that crook's mug of his. 'My little Fairy' (her real name, incidentally, was Maggie Spindell), 'my little Fairy!' " Tilney seraphically smiled and rolled up his eyes. "You can't imagine the expression. St Charles Borromeo in the act of breaking into the till."

"Painted by Carlo Dolci," I suggested.

"With the assistance of Rowlandson. Do you begin to get it?"

I nodded. "But the secretaries?" I was anxious to hear the story.

"They had orders to deal summarily with all begging letters, all communications from madmen, inventors, misunderstood genuises, and, finally, women. The job was a heavy one, I can tell you. You've no idea what a rich man's post-bag is like. Fantastic. Well, as I say, Providence had given both private secretaries the 'flu. Chawdron happened to have nothing better to do that morning (Providence again); so he started opening his own correspondence. The third letter he opened was from the Fairy. It bowled him over."

"What was in it?"

Tilney shrugged his shoulders. "He never showed it me. But from what I gathered, she wrote about God and the Universe in general and her soul in particular, not to mention *his* soul. Having no taste, and being wholly without education, Chawdron was tremendously impressed by her philosophical rigmarole. It appealed to that deep religious sense! Indeed, he was so much impressed that he immediately wrote giving her an appointment. She came, saw, and conquered. 'Providential, my dear boy, providential.' And of course he was right. Only I'd have de-christened the power and called it Nemesis. Miss Spindell was the instrument of Nemesis; she was Ate in the fancy dress that Chawdron's way of life had caused him to find irresistible. She was the finally ripened fruit of sowings in New Guinea Oil and the like."

"But if your account's correct," I put in, "delicious fruit—that is, *his* taste. Being exploited by kittens was his only joy; you said it yourself. Nemesis was rewarding him for his offences, not punishing."

Tilney paused in his striding up and down the room, meditatively knitted his brows and, taking his pipe out of his mouth, rubbed the side of his nose with the hot bowl. "Yes," he said slowly, "that's an important point. I've had it vaguely in my head before now; but now you've put it clearly. From the point of view of the offender, the punishments of Nemesis may actually look like rewards. Yes, it's quite true."

"In which case your Nemesis isn't much use as a policewoman."

He held up his hand. "But Nemesis isn't a policewoman. Nemesis isn't moral. At least she's only incidentally moral, more or less by accident. Nemesis is something like gravitation, in-different. All that she does is to guarantee that you shall reap what you sow. And if you sow self-stultification, as Chawdron did with his excessive interest in money, you reap grotesque humiliation. But as you're already reduced by your offences to a sub-human condition, you won't notice that the grotesque humiliation is a humiliation. There's your explanation why Nemesis sometimes seems to reward. What she brings is a humil-iation only in the absolute sense—for the ideal and complete human being; or at any rate, in practice, for the nearly complete, the approaching-the-ideal human being. For the sub-human specimen it may seem a triumph, a consummation, a fulfilment of the heart's desire. But then, you must remember, the desiring heart is a heart of hog-wash. . . ."

"Moral," I concluded: "Live sub-humanly and Nemesis may bring you happiness."

"Precisely. But *what* happiness!"

I shrugged my shoulders.

"But after all, for the relativist, one sort of happiness is as good as another. You're taking the God's-eye view."

"The Greek's-eye view," he corrected.

"As you like. But anyhow, from the Chawdron's-eye view the happiness is perfect. Therefore we ought to make ourselves like Chawdron."

Tilney nodded. "Yes," he said, "you need to be a bit of a platonist to see that the punishments *are* punishments. And of course if there *were* another life . . . Or better still, metempsychosis: there are some unbelievably disgusting insects. . . . But even from the merely utilitarian point of view Chawdronism is dangerous. Socially dangerous. A society constructed by and for men can't work if all its components are emotionally sub-men. When the majority of hearts have turned to hog-wash, something catastrophic must happen. So that Nemesis turns out to be a police-woman after all. I hope you're satisfied."

"Perfectly."

"You always did have a very discreditable respect for law and order and morality," he complained.

"They must exist . . ."

"I don't know why," he interrupted me.

"In order that you and I may be immoral in comfort," I explained. "Law and order exist to make the world safe for lawless and disorderly individualists."

"Not to mention ruffians like Chawdron. From whom, by the way, we seem to have wandered. Where was I?"

"You'd just got to his providential introduction to the Fairy."

"Yes, yes. Well, as I said, she came, saw, conquered. Three days later she was installed in the house. He made her his librarian."

"*And* his mistress, I suppose."

Tilney raised his shoulders and threw out his hands in a questioning gesture. "Ah," he said, "that's the question. There you're touching the heart of the mystery."

"But you don't mean to tell me . . ."

"I don't mean to tell you anything, for the good reason that I don't know. I only guess."

"And what do you guess?"

"Sometimes one thing and sometimes another. The Fairy was genuinely enigmatic. None of poor Charlotte's fabricated sphinxishness; a real mystery. With the Fairy anything was possible."

"But not with Chawdron surely. In these matters, wasn't he . . . well, all too human?"

"No, only sub-human. Which is rather different. The Fairy roused in him all his sub-human spirituality and religiosity. Whereas with Charlotte it was the no less sub-human passion for the *détournement de mineurs* that came to the surface."

I objected. "That's too crude and schematic to be good psychology. Emotional states aren't so definite and clear-cut as that. There isn't one compartment for spirituality and another, watertight, for the *détournement de mineurs*. There's an overlapping, a fusion, a mixture."

"You're probably right," said Tilney. "And, indeed, one of my conjectures was precisely of such a fusion. You know the sort of thing: discourses insensibly giving place to amorous action— though 'action' seems too strong a word to describe what I have in mind. Something ever so softly senile and girlish. Positively spiritual contacts. The loves of the angels—so angelic that, when it was all over, one wouldn't be quite sure whether there had been any interruption in the mystical conversation or not. Which would justify the Fairy in her righteous indignation when she heard of any one's venturing to suppose that she was anything more than Chawdron's librarian. She could almost honestly believe she wasn't. 'I think people are too horrid,' she used to say to me on these occasions. 'I think they're simply disgusting. Can't they even believe in the possibility of purity?' Angry she was, outraged, hurt. And the emotion seemed absolutely real. Which was such a rare occurrence in the Fairy's life—at any rate, so it seemed to me—that I was forced to believe it had a genuine cause."

"Aren't we all genuinely angry when we hear that our acquaintances say the same sort of things about us as we say about them?"

"Of course; and the truer the gossip, the angrier we are. But the Fairy was angry because the gossip was untrue. She insisted on that—and insisted so genuinely (this is the point I was trying to make) that I couldn't help believing she had some justification. Either nothing had happened, or else something so softly and slimily angelic that it slipped past the attention, escaped notice, counted for nothing."

"But after all," I protested, "it's not because one looks truthful that one's telling the truth."

"No. But then you didn't know the Fairy. She hardly ever looked or sounded truthful. There was hardly anything she said that didn't strike me as being in one way or another a manifest lie. So that when she did seem to be telling the truth (and it was incredible how rarely that happened), I was always impressed. I couldn't help thinking there must be a reason. That's why I attach such importance to the really heart-felt way she got angry when doubts were cast on the purity of her relations with Chawdron. I believe that they really were pure, or else, more probably, that the impurity was such a little one, so to speak, that she could honestly regard it as non-existent. You'd have had the same impression too, if you'd heard her. The genuineness of the anger, the outraged protest, was obvious. And then suddenly she remembered that she was a Christian, practically a saint; she'd start forgiving her enemies. 'One's sorry for them,' she'd say, 'because they don't know any better. Poor people! ignorant of all the finer feelings, all the more beautiful relationships.' I can't tell you how awful the word 'beautiful' was in her mouth! Really blood-curdling. Be-yütiful. Very long-drawn-out, with the oo sound thinned and refined into German u-modified. Be-yütiful. Ugh!" He shuddered. "It made one want to kill her. But then the whole tone of these Christian sentiments made one want to kill her. When she forgave the poor misguided people who couldn't see the be-yüty of her relations with Chawdron you were horrified, you felt sick, you went cold all over. For the whole thing was such a lie, so utterly and bottomlessly false. After the genuine anger against the scandalmongers, the falseness rang even falser than usual. Obvious, unmistakable, painful—like an untuned piano, like a cuckoo in June. Chawdron was deaf to it, of course; just didn't hear the falseness. If you have a deep religious sense, I suppose you don't notice those things. 'I think she has the most beautiful character I've ever met with in a human being,' he used to tell me. ('Beautiful' again, you notice. Chawdron caught the trick from her. But in his mouth it was merely funny, not gruesome.) 'The most beautiful character'—and then his beatific smile. Grotesque! It was just the same as with Charlotte; he swallowed her whole. Charlotte played the jolly kitten and he accepted her as the jolly kitten. The Fairy's ambition was to be regarded as a sanctified Christian kitten; and duly, as a Christian kitten, a confirmed, communicant, Catholic, canonized Kitten, he did regard her. Incredible; but, there! if you spend all your wits and energies knowing about oil, you can't be expected to know much about anything else. You can't be expected to know the difference between tarantulas and kittens, for example; nor the difference between St Catherine of Siena and a little liar like Maggie Spindell."

"But did she know she was lying?" I asked. "Was she consciously a hypocrite?"

Tilney repeated his gesture of uncertainty. *"Chi lo sa?"* he said. "That's the finally unanswerable question. It takes us back to where we were just now with Chawdron—to the borderland between biography and autobiography. Which is more real: you as you see yourself, or you as others see you? you in your intentions and motives, or you in the product of your intentions? you in your actions, or you in the results of your actions? And anyhow, what *are* your intentions and motives? And who is the 'you' who has intentions? So that when you ask if the Fairy was a conscious liar and hypocrite, I just have to say that I don't know. Nobody knows. Not even the Fairy herself. For, after all, there were several Fairies. There was one that wanted to be fed and looked after and given money and perhaps married one day, if Chawdron's wife happened to die."

"I didn't know he had a wife," I interrupted in some astonishment.

"Mad," Tilney telegraphically explained. "Been in an asylum for the last twenty-five years. I'd have gone mad too, if I'd been married to Chawdron. But that didn't prevent the Fairy from aspiring to be the second Mrs C. Money is always money. Well, there was *that* Fairy—the adventuress, the Darwinian specimen struggling for existence. But there was also a Fairy that genuinely wanted to be Christian and saintly. A spiritual Fairy. And if the spirituality happened to pay with tired business men like Chawdron—well, obviously, *tant mieux.*"

"But the falseness you spoke of, the lying, the hypocrisy?"

"Mere inefficiency," Tilney answered. "Just bad acting. For, when all's said and done, what is hypocrisy but bad acting? It differs from saintliness as a performance by Lucien Guitry differed from a performance by his son. One's artistically good and the other isn't."

I laughed. "You forget I'm a moralist; at least, you said I was. These aesthetic heresies . . ."

"Not heresies; just obvious statements of the facts. For what is the practice of morality? It's just pretending to be somebody that by nature you aren't. It's acting the part of a saint, or a hero, or a respectable citizen. What's the highest ethical ideal in Christianity? It's expressed in A Kempis's formula—'The Imitation of Christ.' So that the organized Churches turn out to be nothing but vast and elaborate Academies of Dramatic Art. And every school's a school of acting. Every family's a family of Crummleses. Every human being is brought up as a mummer. All education, aside from merely intellectual education, is just a series of rehearsals for the part of Jesus or Podsnap or Alexander the Great, or whoever the local favourite may be. A virtuous man is one who's learned his part thoroughly and acts it competently and convincingly. The saint and the hero are great actors; they're Kembles and Siddonses—people with a genius for representing heroic characters not their own; or people with the luck to be born so like the heroic ideal that they can just step straight into the part without rehearsal. The wicked are those who either can't or won't learn to act. Imagine a scene-shifter, slightly drunk, dressed in his overalls and smoking a pipe; he comes reeling on to the stage in the middle of the trial scene in the *Merchant of Venice*, shouts down Portia, gives Antonio a kick in the stern, knocks over a few Magnificos and pulls off Shylock's false beard. That's a criminal. As for a hypocrite—he's either a criminal interrupter disguised, temporarily and for his own purposes, as an actor (that's Tartuffe); or else (and I think this is the commoner type) he's just a bad actor. By nature, like all the rest of us, he's a criminal interrupter; but he accepts the teaching of the local Academies of Dramatic Art and admits that man's highest duty is to act star parts to applauding houses. But he is wholly without talent. When he's thinking of his noble part, he mouths and rants and gesticulates, till you feel really ashamed as you watch him— ashamed for yourself, for him, for the human species. 'Methinks the lady, or gentleman, doth protest too much,' is what you say. And these protestations seem even more excessive when, a few moments later, you observe that the protester has forgotten altogether that he's playing a part and is behaving like the interrupting criminal that it's his nature to be. But he himself is so little the mummer, so utterly without a talent for convincing representation, that he simply doesn't notice his own interruptions; or if he notices them, does so only slightly and with the conviction that nobody else will notice them. In other words, most hypocrites are more or less unconscious hypocrites. The Fairy, I'm sure, was one of them. She was simply not aware of being an adventuress with an eye on Chawdron's millions. What she was conscious of was her rôle—the rôle of St Catherine of Siena. She believed in her acting; she was ambitious to be a high-class West-End artiste. But, unfortunately, she was without talent. She played her part so unnaturally, with such grotesque exaggerations, that a normally sensitive person could only shudder at the shameful spectacle. It was a performance that only the spiritually deaf and blind could be convinced by. And, thanks to his preoccupations with New Guinea Oil, Chawdron *was* spiritually deaf and blind. His deep religious sense was the deep religious sense of a sub-man. When she paraded the canonized kitten, I felt sea-sick; but Chawdron thought she had the most be-yütiful character he'd ever met with in a human being. And not only did he think she had the most beautiful character; he also, which was almost funnier, thought she had the finest mind. It was her metaphysical conversation that impressed him. She'd read a few snippets from Spinoza and Plato and some little book on the Christian mystics and a fair amount of that flabby theosophical literature that's so popular in Garden Suburbs and among retired colonels and ladies of a certain age; so she could talk about the cosmos very profoundly. And, by God, she was profound! I used to lose my temper sometimes, it was such drivel, so dreadfully illiterate. But Chawdron listened reverently, fairly goggling with rapture and faith and admiration. He believed every word. When you're totally, uneducated and have amassed an enormous fortune by legal swindling, you can afford to believe in the illusoriness of matter, the non-existence of evil, the oneness of all diversity and the spirituality of everything. All his life he'd kept up his childhood's Presbyterianism—most piously. And now he grafted the Fairy's rigmarole on to the Catechism, or whatever it is that Presbyterians learn in infancy. He didn't see that there was any contradiction between the two metaphysics, just as he'd never seen that there was any incongruity in his being both a good Presbyterian and a consummate swindler. He had acted the Presbyterian part only on Sundays and when he was ill, never in business hours. Religion had never been permitted to invade the sanctities of private life. But with the advance of middle age his mind grew flabbier; the effects of a misspent life began to make themselves felt. And at the same time his retirement from business removed almost all the external distractions. His deep religious sense had more chance to express itself. He could wallow in sentimentality and silliness undisturbed. The Fairy made her providential appearance and showed him which were the softest emotional and intellectual muck-heaps to wallow on. He was grateful—loyally, but a little ludicrously. I shall never forget, for example, the time he talked about the Fairy's genius. We'd been dining at his house, he and I and the Fairy. A terrible dinner, with the Fairy, as a mixture between St Catherine of Siena and Mahatma Gandhi, explaining why she was a vegetarian and an ascetic. She had that awful genteel middle-class food complex which makes table manners at Lyons' Corner Houses so appallingly good—that haunting fear of being low or vulgar which causes people to eat as though they weren't eating. They never take a large mouthful, and only masticate with their front teeth, like rabbits. And they never touch anything with their fingers. I've actually seen a woman eating cherries with a knife and fork at one of those places. Most extraordinary and most repulsive. Well, the Fairy had that complex—it's a matter of class—but it was rationalized, with her, in terms of *ahimsa* and ascetic Christianity. Well, she'd been chattering the whole evening about the spirit of love and its incompatibility with a meat diet, and the necessity of mortifying the body for the sake of the soul, and about Buddha and St Francis and mystical ecstasies and, above all, herself. Drove me almost crazy with irritation, not to mention the fact that she really began putting me off my food with her rhapsodies of pious horror and disgust. I was thankful when at last she left us in peace to our brandy and cigars. But Chawdron leaned across the table towards me, spiritually beaming from every inch of that forger's face of his. 'Isn't she wonderful?' he said. 'Isn't she simply *wonderful*,' 'Wonderful,' I agreed. And then, very solemnly, wagging his finger at me, 'I've known three great intellects in my time,' he said, 'three minds of genius—Lord Northcliffe, Mr John

Morley, and this little girl. Those three.' And he leant back in his chair and nodded at me almost fiercely, as though challenging me to deny it."

"And did you accept the challenge?" I asked, laughing.

Tilney shook his head. "I just helped myself to another nip of his 1820 brandy; it was the only retort a rational man could make."

"And did the Fairy share Chawdron's opinion about her mind?"

"Oh, I think so," said Tilney, "I think so. She had a great conceit of herself. Like all these spiritual people. An inordinate conceit. She played the superior rôle very badly and inconsistently. But all the same she was convinced of her superiority. Inevitably; for, you see, she had an enormous capacity for auto-suggestion. What she told herself three times became true. For example, I used at first to think there was some hocus-pocus about her asceticism. She ate so absurdly little in public and at meals that I fancied she must do a little tucking-in privately in between whiles. But later I came to the conclusion that I'd maligned her By dint of constantly telling herself and other people that eating was unspiritual and gross, not to mention impolite and lower-class, she'd genuinely succeeded, I believe, in making food disgust her. She'd got to a point where she really couldn't eat more than a very little. Which was one of the causes of her sickliness. She was just under-nourished. But under-nourishment was only *one* of the causes. She was also diplomatically sick. She threatened to die as statesmen threaten to mobilize, in order to get what she wanted. Blackmail, in fact. Not for money; she was curiously disinterested in many ways. What she wanted was his interest, was power over him, was self-assertion. She had headaches for the same reason as a baby howls. If you give in to the baby and do what it wants, it'll howl again, it'll make a habit of howling. Chawdron was one of the weak-minded sort of parents. When the Fairy had one of her famous headaches, he was terribly disturbed. The way he fluttered round the sick-room with ice and hot-water bottles and eau-de-Cologne! *The Times* obituarist would have wept to see him; such a touching exhibition of the heart of gold! The result was that the Fairy used to have a headache every three or four days. It was absolutely intolerable."

"But were they purely imaginary, these headaches?"

Tilney shrugged his shoulders. "Yes and no. There was certainly a physiological basis. The woman did have pains in her head from time to time. It was only to be expected; she was run down, through not eating enough; she didn't take sufficient exercise, so she had chronic constipation; chronic constipation probably set up a slight chronic inflammation of the ovaries; and she certainly suffered from eye-strain—you could tell that from the beautifully vague, spiritual look in her eyes, the look that comes from un-corrected myopia. There were, as you see, plenty of physiological reasons for her headaches. Her body made her a present, so to speak, of the pain. Her mind then proceeded to work up this raw material. Into what remarkable forms! Touched by her imagina-tion, the headaches became mystic, transcendental. It was infinity in a grain of sand and eternity in an intestinal stasis. Regularly every Tuesday and Friday she died—died with a beautiful Christian resignation, a martyr's fortitude. Chawdron used to come down from the sick-room with tears in his eyes. He'd never seen such patience, such courage, such grit. There were few men she wouldn't put to shame. She was a wonderful example. And so on. And I dare say it was all quite true. She started by malinger-ing a little, by pretending that the headaches were worse than they were. But her imagination was too lively for her; it got beyond her control. Her pretendings gradually came true and she really did suffer martyrdom each time; she really did very nearly die. And then she got into the habit of being a martyr, and the attacks came on regularly; imagination stimulated the normal activities of inflamed ovaries and poisoned intestines; the pain made its appearance and at once became the raw material of a mystic, spiritual martyrdom taking place on a higher plane. Anyhow, it was all very complicated and obscure. And, obviously, if the Fairy herself had given you an account of her existence at this time, it would have sounded like St Lawrence's reminiscences of life on the grill. Or rather it would have sounded like the in-sincere fabrication of such reminiscences. For the Fairy, as I've said before, was without talent, and sincerity and saintliness are matters of talent. Hypocrisy and insincerity are the products of native incompetence. Those who are guilty of them are people without skill in the arts of behaviour and self-expression. The Fairy's talk would have sounded utterly false to you. But for her it was all genuine. She really suffered, really died, really was good and resigned and courageous. Just as the paranoiac is really Napoleon Bonaparte and the young man with *dementia præcox* is really being spied on and persecuted by a gang of fiendishly ingenious enemies. If *I* were to tell the story from *her* point of view, it would sound really beautiful—not be-yütiful, mind you; but truly and genuinely beautiful; for the good reason that *I* have a gift of expression, which the poor Fairy hadn't. So that, for all but emotional cretins like Chawdron, she was obviously a hypocrite and a liar. Also a bit of a pathological case. For that capacity for auto-suggestion really was rather pathological. She could make things come *too* true. Not merely diseases and martyrdoms and saintliness, but also historical facts, or rather historical not-facts. She authenticated the not-facts by simply repeating that they had happened. For example, she wanted people to believe—she wanted to believe herself—that she had been intimate with Chawdron for years and years, from childhood, from the time of her birth. The fact that he had known her since she was 'so high' would explain and justfy her present relationship with him. The scandalmongers would have no excuse for talking. So she proceeded bit by bit to fabricate a lifelong intimacy, even a bit of an actual kinship, with her Uncle Benny. I told you that that was what she called him, didn't I? That nickname had its significance; it planted him at once in the table of consanguinity and so disinfected their relations, so to speak, automatically made them innocent."

"Or incestuous," I added.

"Or incestuous. Quite. But she didn't consider the D'Annunzio-esque refinements. When she gave him that name, she promoted Chawdron to the rank of a dear old kinsman, or at least a dear old family friend. Sometimes she even called him 'Nunky Benny,' so as to show that she had known him from the cradle—had lisped of nunkies, for the nunkies came. But that wasn't enough. The evidence had to be fuller, more circumstantial. So she invented it —romps with Nunky in the hay, visits to the pantomime with him, a whole outfit of childish memories."

"But what about Chawdron?" I asked. "Did he share the invented memories?"

Tilney nodded. "But for him, of course, they *were* invented. Other people, however, accepted them as facts. Her reminiscences were so detailed and circumstantial that, unless you *knew* she was

a liar, you simply had to accept them. With Chawdron himself
she couldn't, of course, pretend that she'd known him, literally
and historically, all those years. Not at first, in any case. The
lifelong intimacy started by being figurative and spiritual. 'I feel
as though I'd known my Uncle Benny ever since I was a tiny
baby,' she said to me in his presence, quite soon after she'd first
got to know him; and as always, on such occasions, she made her
voice even more whiningly babyish than usual. Dreadful that voice
was—so whiny-piny, so falsely sweet. 'Ever since I was a teeny,
tiny baby. Don't you feel like that, Uncle Benny?' And Chawdron
heartily agreed; of course he felt like that. From that time forward
she began to expatiate on the incidents which ought to have
occurred in that far-off childhood with darling Nunky. They were
the same incidents, of course, as those which she actually remembered when she was talking to strangers and he wasn't there.
She made him give her old photographs of himself—visions of
him in high collars and frock-coats, in queer-looking Norfolk
jackets, in a top-hat sitting in a Victoria. They helped her to make
her fancies real. With their aid and the aid of his reminiscences
she constructed a whole life in common with him. 'Do you remember, Uncle Benny, the time we went to Cowes on your yacht
and I fell into the sea?' she'd ask. And Chawdron, who thoroughly
entered into the game, would answer: 'Of course I remember.
And when we'd fished you out, we had to wrap you in hot
blankets and give you warm rum and milk. And you got quite
drunk.' 'Was I funny when I was drunk, Uncle Benny?' And
Chawdron would rather lamely and ponderously invent a few
quaintnesses which were then incorporated in the history. So that
on a future occasion the Fairy could begin: 'Nunky Benny, do
you remember those ridiculous things I said when you made me
drunk with rum and hot milk that time I fell into the sea at
Cowes?' And so on. Chawdron loved the game, thought it simply
too sweet and whimsical and touching—positively like something
out of Barrie or A. A. Milne—and was never tired of playing it.
As for the Fairy—for her it wasn't a game at all. The not-facts had
been repeated till they became facts. 'But, come, Miss Spindell,' I
said to her once, when she'd been telling me—*me!*—about some
adventure she'd had with Uncle Benny when she was a toddler,
'come, come, Miss Spindell' (I always called her that, though she
longed to be my Fairy as well as Chawdron's, and would have

called me Uncle Ted if I'd given her the smallest encouragement; but I took a firm line; she was always Miss Spindell for me), 'come,' I said, 'you seem to forget that it's only just over a year since you saw Mr Chawdron for the first time.' She looked at me quite blankly for a moment without saying anything. 'You can't seriously expect me to forget too,' I added. Poor Fairy! The blankness suddenly gave place to a painful, blushing embarrassment. 'Oh, of course,' she began, and laughed nervously. 'It's as though I'd known him for ever. My imagination . . .' She tailed off into silence, and a minute later made an excuse to leave me. I could see she was upset, physically upset, as though she'd been woken up too suddenly out of a sound sleep, jolted out of one world into another moving in a different direction. But when I saw her the next day, she seemed to be quite herself again. She had suggested herself back into the dream world; from the other end of the table, at lunch, I heard her talking to an American business acquaintance of Chawdron's about the fun she and Uncle Benny used to have on his grouse moor in Scotland. But from that time forth, I noticed, she never talked to me about her apocryphal childhood again. A curious incident; it made me look at her hypocrisy in another light. It was then I began to realize that the lie in her soul was mainly an unconscious lie, the product of pathology and a lack of talent. Mainly; but sometimes, on the contrary, the lie was only too conscious and deliberate. The most extraordinary of them was the lie at the bottom of the great Affair of the Stigmata."

"The stigmata?" I echoed. "A pious lie, then."

"Pious." He nodded. "That was how she justified it to herself. Though, of course, in her eyes, all her lies were pious lies. Pious, because they served *her* purposes and she was a saint; her cause was sacred. And afterwards, of course, when she'd treated the lies to her process of imaginative disinfection, they ceased to be lies and fluttered away as snow-white pious truths. But to start with they were undoubtedly pious lies, even for her. The Affair of the Stigmata made that quite clear. I caught her in the act. It all began with a boil that developed on Chawdron's foot."

"Curious place to have a boil."

"Not common," he agreed. "I once had one there myself, when I was a boy. Most unpleasant, I can assure you. Well, the same thing happened to Chawdron. He and I were down at his country place, playing golf and in the intervals concocting the *Autobiography*. We'd settle down with brandy and cigars and I'd gently question him. Left to himself, he was apt to wander and become incoherent and unchronological. I had to canalize his narrative, so to speak. Remarkably frank he was. I learned some curious things about the business world, I can tell you. Needless to say, they're not in the *Autobiography*. I'm reserving them for the *Life*. Which means, alas, that nobody will ever know them. Well, as I say, we were down there in the country for a long week-end, Friday to Tuesday. The Fairy had stayed in London. Periodically she took her librarianship very seriously and protested that she simply had to get on with the catalogue. 'I have my duties,' she said when Chawdron suggested that she should come down to the country with us. 'You must let me get on with my duties. I don't think one ought to be just frivolous; do you, Uncle Benny? Besides, I really love my work.' God, how she enraged me with that whiney-piney talk! But Chawdron, of course, was touched and enchanted. 'What an extraordinary little person she is!' he said to me as we left the house together. Even more extraordinary than you suppose, I thought. He went on rhapsodizing as far as Watford. But in a way, I could see, when we arrived, in a way he was quite pleased she hadn't come. It was a relief to him to be having a little masculine holiday. She had the wit to see that he needed these refreshments from time to time. Well, we duly played our golf, with the result that by Sunday morning poor Chawdron's boil, which had been a negligible little spot on the Friday, had swollen up with the chafing and the exercise into a massive red hemisphere that made walking an agony. Unpleasant, no doubt; but nothing, for any ordinary person, to get seriously upset about. Chawdron, however, wasn't an ordinary person where boils were concerned. He had a carbuncle-complex, a boilophobia. Excusably, perhaps; for it seems that his brother had died of some awful kind of gangrene that had started, to all appearances harmlessly, in a spot on his cheek. Chawdron couldn't develop a pimple without imagining that he'd caught his brother's disease. This affair on his foot scared him out of his wits. He saw the bone infected, the whole leg rotting away, amputations, death. I offered what comfort and encouragement I could and sent for the local doctor. He came at once and turned out to be a young man, very determined and efficient and confidence-inspiring. The boil was anaesthetized, lanced, cleaned out, tied up. Chawdron was promised there'd be no complications. And there weren't. The thing healed up quite normally. Chawdron decided to go back to town on the Tuesday, as he'd arranged. 'I wouldn't like to disappoint Fairy,' he explained. 'She'd be so sad if I didn't come back when I'd promised. Besides, she might be nervous. You've no idea what an intuition that little girl has—almost uncanny, like second sight. She'd guess something was wrong and be upset; and you know how bad it is for her to be upset.' I did indeed; those mystic headaches of hers were the bane of my life. No, no, I agreed. She mustn't be upset. So it was decided that the Fairy should be kept in blissful ignorance of the boil until Chawdron had actually arrived. But the question then arose: how should he arrive? We had gone down into the country in Chawdron's Bugatti. He had a weakness for speed. But it wasn't the car for an invalid. It was arranged that the chauffeur should drive the Bugatti up to town and come back with the Rolls. In the unlikely event of his seeing Miss Spindell, he was not to tell her why he had been sent to town. Those were his orders. The man went and duly returned with the Rolls. Chawdron was installed, almost as though he were in an ambulance, and we rolled majestically up to London. What a home-coming! In anticipation of the sympathy he would get from the Fairy, Chawdron began to have a slight relapse as we approached the house. 'I feel it throbbing,' he assured me; and when he got out of the car, what a limp! As though he'd lost a leg at Gallipoli. Really heroic. The butler had to support him up to the drawing-room. He was lowered on to the sofa. 'Is Miss Spindell in her room?' The butler thought so. 'Then ask her to come down here at once.' The man went out; Chawdron closed his eyes—wearily, like a very sick man. He was preparing to get all the sympathy he could and, I could see, luxuriously relishing it in advance. 'Still throbbing?' I asked, rather irreverently. He nodded, without opening his eyes. 'Still throbbing.' The manner was grave and sepulchral. I had to make an effort not to laugh. There was a silence; we waited. And then the door opened. The Fairy appeared. But a maimed Fairy. One foot in a high-heeled shoe, the other in a slipper. Such a limp! 'Another leg lost at Gallipoli,' thought I. When he heard the door open, Chawdron shut his eyes tighter than ever and turned his face to the wall, or at any rate the back of the sofa. I could see that this rather embarrassed the Fairy. Her entrance had been dramatic; she had meant him to see her disablement at once; hadn't counted on finding a death-bed scene. She had hastily to ir ɔrovise another piece of stage business, a new set of lines; the scene she had prepared wouldn't do. Which was the more embarrassing for her as I was there, looking on—a very cool spectator, as she knew; not in the least a Maggie Spindell fan. She hesitated a second near the door, hoping Chawdron would look round; but he kept his eyes resolutely shut and his face averted. He'd evidently decided to play the moribund part for all it was worth. So, after one rather nervous glance at me, she limped across the room to the sofa. 'Uncle Benny!' He gave a great start, as though he hadn't known she was there. 'Is that you, Fairy?' This was *pianissimo, con espressione*. Then, *molto agitato* from the Fairy: 'What is it, Nunky Benny? What is it? Oh, tell me.' She was close enough now to lay a hand on his shoulder. 'Tell me.' He turned his face towards her—the tenderly transfigured burglar. His heart overflowed—'Fairy!'—a slop of hog-wash. 'But what's the matter, Nunky Benny?' 'Nothing, Fairy.' The tone implied that it was a heroic under-statement in the manner of Sir Philip Sidney. 'Only my foot.' 'Your foot!' The Fairy registered such astonishment that we both fairly jumped. 'Something wrong with your foot?' 'Yes, why not?' Chawdron was rather annoyed; he wasn't getting the kind of sympathy he'd looked forward to. She turned to me. 'But when did it happen, Mr Tilney?' I was breezy. 'A nasty boil,' I explained. 'Walking round the course did it no good. It had to be lanced on Sunday.' 'At about half-past eleven on Sunday morning?' 'Yes, I suppose it was about half-past eleven,' I said, thinking the question was an odd one. 'It was just half-past eleven when *this* happened,' she said dramatically, pointing to her slippered foot. 'What's "this"?' asked Chawdron crossly. He was thoroughly annoyed at being swindled out of sympathy. I took pity on the Fairy; things seemed to be going so badly for her. I could see that she had prepared a coup and that it hadn't come off. 'Miss Spindell also seems to have hurt her foot,' I explained. 'You didn't see how she limped.' 'How did you hurt it?' asked Chawdron. He was still very grumpy. 'I was sitting quietly in the library, working at the catalogue,' she began: and I guessed, by the way the phrases came rolling out, that she was at last being able to make use of the material she had prepared, 'when suddenly, almost exactly at half-past eleven (I remember looking at the clock), I felt a terrible pain in my foot. As though some one were driving a sharp, sharp knife into it. It was so intense that I nearly fainted.' She paused for a moment, expecting appropriate comment. But Chawdron wouldn't make it. So I put in a polite 'Dear me, most extraordinary!' with which she had to be content. 'When I got up,' she continued, 'I could hardly stand, my foot hurt me so; and I've been limping ever since. And the most extraordinary thing is that there's a red mark on my foot, like a scar.' Another expectant pause. But still no word from Chawdron. He sat there with his mouth tight shut, and the lines that divided his cheeks from that wide simian upper lip of his were as though engraved in stone. The Fairy looked at him and saw that he had taken hopelessly the wrong line. Was it too late to remedy the mistake? She put the new plan of campaign into immediate execution. 'But you poor Nunky Benny!' she began, in the sort of tone in which you'd talk to a sick dog. 'How selfish of me to talk about my ailments, when you're lying there with your poor foot bandaged up!' The dog began to wag his tail at once. The beatific look returned to his face. He took her hand. I couldn't stand it. 'I think I'd better be going,' I said; and I went."

"But the foot?" I asked. "The stabbing pain at exactly half-past eleven?"

"You may well ask. As Chawdron himself remarked, when next I saw him, 'There are more things in heaven and earth, Horatio, than are dreamt of in your philosophy.'" Tilney laughed. "The Fairy had triumphed. After he'd had his dose of mother love and Christian charity and kittenish sympathy, he'd been ready, I suppose, to listen to *her* story. The stabbing pain at eleven-thirty, the red scar. Strange, mysterious, unaccountable. He discussed it all with me, very gravely and judiciously. We talked of spiritualism and telepathy. We distinguished carefully between the miraculous and the super-normal. 'As you know,' he told me, 'I've been a good Presbyterian all my life, and as such have been inclined to dismiss as mere fabrications all the stories of the Romish saints. I never believed in the story of St Francis's stigmata, for example. But now I accept it!' Solemn and tremendous pause. 'Now I *know* it's true.' I just bowed my head in silence. But the next time I saw M'Crae, the chauffeur, I asked a few questions. Yes, he *had* seen Miss Spindell that day he drove the Bugatti up to London and came back with the Rolls. He'd gone into the secretaries' office to see if there were any letters to take down for Mr Chawdron, and Miss Spindell had run into him as he came out. She'd asked him what he was doing in London and he hadn't been able to think of anything to answer, in spite of Mr Chawdron's orders, except the truth. It had been on his conscience ever since; he hoped it hadn't done any harm. 'On the contrary,' I assured him, and that I certainly wouldn't tell Mr Chawdron. Which I never did. I thought . . . But good heavens!" he interrupted himself; "what's this?" It was Hawtrey, who had come in to lay the table for lunch. She ignored us, actively. It was not only as though we didn't exist; it was as though we also had no right to exist. Tilney took out his watch. "Twenty past one. God almighty! Do you mean to say I've been talking here the whole morning since breakfast?"

"So it appears," I answered.

He groaned. "You see," he said, "you see what it is to have a gift of the gab. A whole precious morning utterly wasted."

"Not for me," I said.

He shrugged his shoulders. "Perhaps not. But then for you the story was new and curious. Whereas for me it's known, it's stale."

"But for Shakespeare so was the story of Othello, even before he started to write it."

"Yes, but he *wrote*, he didn't talk. There was something to show for the time he'd spent. His Othello didn't just disappear into thin air, like my poor Chawdron." He sighed and was silent. Stone-faced and grim, Hawtrey went rustling starchily round the table; there was a clinking of steel and silver as she laid the places. I waited till she had left the room before I spoke again. When one's servants are more respectable than one is oneself (and nowadays they generally are), one cannot be too careful.

"And how did it end?" I asked.

"How did it end?" he repeated in a voice that had suddenly gone flat and dull; he was bored with his story, wanted to think of something else. "It ended, so far as I was concerned, with my finishing the *Autobiography* and getting tired of its subject. I gradually faded out of Chawdron's existence. Like the Cheshire Cat."

"And the Fairy?"

"Faded out of life about a year after the Affair of the Stigmata. She retired to her mystic death-bed once too often. Her pretending came true at last; it was always the risk with her. She really did die."

The door opened; Hawtrey re-entered the room, carrying a dish.

"And Chawdron, I suppose, was inconsolable?" Inconsolability is, happily, a respectable subject.

Tilney nodded. "Took to spiritualism, of course. Nemesis again."

Hawtrey raised the lid of the dish; a smell of fried soles escaped into the air. "Luncheon is served," she said. with what seemed to me an ill-concealed contempt and disapproval.

"Luncheon is served," Tilney echoes, moving towards his place. He sat down and opened his napkin. "One meal after another, punctuality, day after day, day after day. Such a life. Which would be tolerable enough if something ever got done between meals. But in my case nothing does. Meal after meal, and between meals a vacuum, a kind of . . ." Hawtrey, who had been offering him the *sauce tartare* for the past several seconds, here gave him the discreetest nudge. Tilney turned his head. "Ah, thank you," he said, and helped himself.

The Rest Cure

SHE was a tiny woman, dark-haired and with grey-blue eyes, very large and arresting in a small pale face. A little girl's face, with small, delicate features, but worn—prematurely; for Mrs Tarwin was only twenty-eight; and the big, wide-open eyes were restless and unquietly bright. "Moira's got nerves," her husband would explain when people inquired why she wasn't with him. Nerves that couldn't stand the strain of London or New York. She had to take things quietly in Florence. A sort of rest cure. "Poor darling!" he would add in a voice that had suddenly become furry with sentiment; and he would illuminate his ordinarily rather blankly intelligent face with one of those lightning smiles of his—so wistful and tender and charming. Almost too charming, one felt uncomfortably. He turned on the charm and the wistfulness like electricity. Click! his face was briefly illumined. And then, click! the light went out again and he was once more the blankly intelligent research student. Cancer was his subject.

Poor Moira! Those nerves of her! She was full of caprices and obsessions. For example, when she leased the villa on the slopes of Bello Sguardo, she wanted to be allowed to cut down the cypresses at the end of the garden. "So terribly like a cemetery," she kept repeating to old Signori Bargioni. Old Bargioni was charming, but firm. He had no intention of sacrificing his cypresses. They gave the finishing touch of perfection to the loveliest view in all Florence; from the best bedroom window you saw the dome and Giotto's tower framed between their dark columns. Inexhaustibly loquacious, he tried to persuade her that cypresses weren't really at all funereal. For the Etruscans, on the contrary (he invented this little piece of archaeology on the spur of the moment), the cypress was a symbol of joy; the feasts of the vernal equinox concluded with dances round the sacred tree. Boecklin, it was true, had planted cypresses on his Island of the Dead. But then Boecklin, after all . . . And if she really found the trees depressing, she could plant nasturtiums to climb up them. Or roses. Roses, which the Greeks . . .

"All right, all right," said Moira Tarwin hastily. "Let's leave the cypresses."

That voice, that endless flow of culture and foreign English! Old Bargioni was really terrible. She would have screamed if she had had to listen a moment longer. She yielded in mere self-defence.

"*E la Tarwinnè?*" questioned Signora Bargioni when her husband came home.

He shrugged his shoulders. "*Una donnina piuttosto sciocca,*" was his verdict.

Rather silly. Old Bargioni was not the only man who had thought so. But he was one of the not so many who regarded her silliness as a fault. Most of the men who knew her were charmed by it; they adored while they smiled. In conjunction with that tiny stature, those eyes, that delicate childish face, her silliness inspired avuncular devotions and protective loves. She had a faculty for making men feel, by contrast, agreeably large, superior and intelligent. And as luck, or perhaps as ill luck, would have it, Moira had passed her life among men who were really intelligent and what is called superior. Old Sir Watney Croker, her grandfather, with whom she had lived ever since she was five (for her father and mother had both died young), was one of the most eminent physicians of his day. His early monograph on duodenal ulcers remains even now the classical work on the subject. Between one duodenal ulcer and another Sir Watney found leisure to adore and indulge and spoil his little granddaughter. Along with fly-fishing and metaphysics she was his hobby. Time passed; Moira grew up, chronologically; but Sir Watney went on treating her as a spoilt child, went on being enchanted by her birdy chirrupings and ingenuousness and impertinent *enfant-terrible-isms*. He encouraged, he almost compelled her to preserve her childishness. Keeping her a baby in spite of her age amused him. He loved her babyish and could only love her so. All those duodenal ulcers—perhaps they had done something to his sensibility, warped it a little, kept it somehow stunted and un-adult, like Moira herself. In the depths of his unspecialized, unprofessional being Sir Watney was a bit of a baby himself. Too much preoccupation with the duodenum had prevented this neglected instinctive part of him from fully growing up. Like gravitates to like; old baby Watney loved the baby in Moira and wanted to keep the young woman permanently childish. Most of his friends shared Sir Watney's tastes. Doctors, judges, professors, civil servants—every member of Sir Watney's circle was professionally eminent, a veteran specialist. To be asked to one of his dinner parties was a privilege. On these august occasions Moira had always, from the age of seventeen, been present, the only woman at the table. Not really a woman, Sir Watney explained; a child. The veteran specialists were all her indulgent uncles. The more childish she was, the better they liked her. Moira gave them pet names. Professor Stagg, for example, the neo-Hegelian, was Uncle Bonzo; Mr Justice Gidley was Giddy Goat. And so on. When they teased, she answered back impertinently. How they laughed! When they started to discuss the Absolute or Britain's Industrial Future, she interjected some deliciously irrelevant remark that made them laugh even more heartily. Exquisite! And the next day the story would be told to colleagues in the law-courts or the hospital, to cronies at the Athenæum. In learned and professional circles Moira enjoyed a real celebrity. In the end she had ceased not only to be a woman; she had almost ceased to be a child. She was hardly more than their mascot.

At half-past nine she left the dining-room, and the talk would come back to ulcers and Reality and Emergent Evolution.

"One would like to keep her as a pet," John Tarwin had said as the door closed behind her on that first occasion he dined at Sir Watney's.

Professor Broadwater agreed. There was a little silence. It was Tarwin who broke it.

"What's your feeling," he asked, leaning forward with that expression of blank intelligence on his eager, sharp-featured face, "what's *your* feeling about the validity of experiments with artificially grafted tumours as opposed to natural tumours?"

Tarwin was only thirty-three and looked even younger among Sir Watney's veterans. He had already done good work, Sir Watney explained to his assembled guests before the young man's arrival, and might be expected to do much more. An interesting fellow too. Had been all over the place—tropical Africa, India, North and South America. Well off. Not tied to an academic job to earn his living. Had worked here in London, in Germany, at the Rockefeller Institute in New York, in Japan. Enviable opportunities. A great deal to be said for a private income. "Ah, here you are, Tarwin. Good evening. No, not at all late. This is Mr Justice Gidley, Professor Broadwater, Professor Stagg and—bless me! I hadn't noticed you, Moira; you're really too ultra-microscopic—my granddaughter." Tarwin smiled down at her. She was really ravishing.

Well, now they had been married five years, Moira was thinking, as she powdered her face in front of the looking-glass. Tonino was coming to tea; she had been changing her frock. Through the window behind the mirror one looked down between the cypress trees on to Florence—a jumble of brown roofs, and above them, in the midst, the marble tower and the huge, up-leaping, airy dome. Five years. It was John's photograph in the leather travelling-frame that made her think of their marriage. Why did she keep it there on the dressing-table? Force of habit, she supposed. It wasn't as though the photograph reminded her of days that had been particularly happy. On the contrary. There was something, she now felt, slightly dishonest about keeping it there. Pretending to love him when she didn't. . . . She looked at it again. The profile was sharp and eager. The keen young research student intently focused on a tumour. She really liked him better as a research student than when he was having a soul, or being a poet or a lover. It seemed a dreadful thing to say—but there it was: the research student was of better quality than the human being.

She had always known it—or, rather, not known, felt it. The human being had always made her rather uncomfortable. The more human, the more uncomfortable. She oughtn't ever to have married him, of course. But he asked so persistently; and then he had so much vitality; everybody spoke so well of him; she rather liked his looks; and he seemed to lead such a jolly life, travelling about the world; and she was tired of being a mascot for her grandfather's veterans. There were any number of such little reasons. Added together, she had fancied they would be the equivalent of the one big, cogent reason. But they weren't; she had made a mistake.

Yes, the more human, the more uncomfortable. The disturbing way he turned on the beautiful illumination of his smile! Turned it on suddenly, only to switch it off again with as little warning when something really serious, like cancer or philosophy, had to be discussed. And then his voice, when he was talking

about Nature, or Love, or God, or something of that sort—furry
with feeling! The quite unnecessarily moved and tremulous way
he said Good-bye! "Like a Landseer dog," she told him once,
before they were married, laughing and giving a ludicrous
imitation of his too heart-felt "Good-bye, Moira." The mockery
hurt him. John prided himself as much on his soul and his feelings
as upon his intellect; as much on his appreciation of Nature and
his poetical love-longings as upon his knowledge of tumours.
Goethe was his favourite literary and historical character. Poet
and man of science, deep thinker and ardent lover, artist in
thought and in life—John saw himself in the rich part. He made
her read *Faust* and *Wilhelm Meister*. Moira did her best to feign
the enthusiasm she did not feel. Privately she thought Goethe a
humbug.

"I oughtn't to have married him," she said to her image in the
glass, and shook her head.

John was the pet-fancier as well as the loving educator. There
were times when Moira's childishnesses delighted him as much as
they had delighted Sir Watney and his veterans, when he laughed
at every naïveté or impertinence she uttered, as though it were a
piece of the most exquisite wit; and not only laughed, but drew
public attention to it, led her on into fresh infantilities and repeated the stories of her exploits to any one who was prepared to
listen to them. He was less enthusiastic, however, when Moira
had been childish at his expense, when her silliness had in any
way compromised *his* dignity or interests. On these occasions he
lost his temper, called her a fool, told her she ought to be ashamed
of herself. After which, controlling himself, he would become
grave, paternal, pedagogic. Moira would be made to feel,
miserably, that she wasn't worthy of him. And finally he switched
on the smile and made it all up with caresses that left her like a
stone.

"And to think," she reflected, putting away her powder-puff,
"to think of my spending all that time and energy trying to keep
up with him."

All those scientific papers she had read, those outlines of
medicine and physiology, those text-books of something or other
(she couldn't even remember the name of the science), to say
nothing of all that dreary stuff by Goethe! And then all the going
out when she had a headache or was tired! All the meeting of

people who bored her, but who were really, according to John, so interesting and important! All the travelling, the terribly strenuous sight-seeing, the calling on distinguished foreigners and their generally less distinguished wives! It was difficult for her to keep up even physically—her legs were so short and John was always in such a hurry. Mentally, in spite of all her efforts, she was always a hundred miles behind.

"Awful!" she said aloud.

Her whole marriage had really been awful. From that awful honeymoon at Capri, when he had made her walk too far, too fast, uphill, only to read her extracts from Wordsworth when they reached the *Aussichtspunkt*; when he had talked to her about love and made it, much too frequently, and told her the Latin names of the plants and butterflies—from that awful honeymoon to the time when, four months ago, her nerves had gone all to pieces and the doctor had said that she must take things quietly, apart from John. Awful! The life had nearly killed her. And it wasn't (she had come at last to realize), it wasn't really a life at all. It was just a galvanic activity, like the twitching of a dead frog's leg when you touch the nerve with an electrified wire. Not life, just galvanized death.

She remembered the last of their quarrels, just before the doctor had told her to go away. John had been sitting at her feet, with his head against her knee. And his head was beginning to go bald! She could hardly bear to look at those long hairs plastered across the scalp. And because he was tired with all that microscope work, tired and at the same time (not having made love to her, thank goodness! for more than a fortnight) amorous, as she could tell by the look in his eyes, he was being very sentimental and talking in his furriest voice about Love and Beauty and the necessity for being like Goethe. Talking till she felt like screaming aloud. And at last she could bear it no longer.

"For goodness sake, John," she said in a voice that was on the shrill verge of being out of control, "be quiet!"

"What *is* the matter?" He looked up at her questioningly, pained.

"Talking like that!" She was indignant. "But you've never loved anybody, outside yourself. Nor felt the beauty of anything. Any more than that old humbug Goethe. You know what you *ought* to feel when there's a woman about, or a landscape; you

know what the best people feel. And you deliberately set yourself
to feel the same, out of your head."

John was wounded to the quick of his vanity. "How can you
say that?"

"Because it's true, it's true. You only live out of your head. And
it's a bald head too," she added, and began to laugh, uncontrollably.

What a scene there had been! She went on laughing all the
time he raged at her; she couldn't stop.

"You're hysterical," he said at last; and then he calmed down.
The poor child was ill. With an effort he switched on the expression of paternal tenderness and went to fetch the sal volatile.

One last dab at her lips, and there! she was ready. She went
downstairs to the drawing-room, to find that Tonino had already
arrived—he was always early—and was waiting. He rose as she
entered, bowed over her outstretched hand and kissed it. Moira
was always charmed by his florid, rather excessive Southern good
manners. John was always too busy being the keen research
student or the furry-voiced poet to have good manners. He didn't
think politeness particularly important. It was the same with
clothes. He was chronically ill-dressed. Tonino, on the other hand,
was a model of dapper elegance. That pale grey suit, that
lavender-coloured tie, those piebald shoes of white kid and patent
leather—marvellous!

One of the pleasures or dangers of foreign travel is that you
lose class-consciousness. At home you can never, with the best
will in the world, forget it. Habit has rendered your own people
as immediately legible as your own language. A word, a gesture
are sufficient; your man is placed. But in foreign parts your
fellows are unreadable. The less obvious products of upbringing
—all the subtler refinements, the finer shades of vulgarity—
escape your notice. The accent, the inflexion of voice, the
vocabulary, the gestures tell you nothing. Between the duke and
the insurance clerk, the profiteer and the country gentleman,
your inexperienced eye and ear detect no difference. For Moira,
Tonino seemed the characteristic flower of Italian gentility. She
knew, of course, that he wasn't well off; but then, plenty of the
nicest people are poor. She saw in him the equivalent of one of
those younger sons of impoverished English squires—the sort of
young man who advertises for work in the Agony Column of *The*

Times. "Public School education, sporting tastes; would accept any well-paid position of trust and confidence." She would have been pained, indignant, and surprised to hear old Bargioni describing him, after their first meeting, as *"il tipo del parrucchiere napoletano"*—the typical Neapolitan barber. Signora Bargioni shook her head over the approaching scandal and was secretly delighted.

As a matter of actual fact Tonino was not a barber. He was the son of a capitalist—on a rather small scale, no doubt; but still a genuine capitalist. Vasari senior owned a restaurant at Pozzuoli and was ambitious to start a hotel. Tonino had been sent to study the tourist industry with a family friend who was the manager of one of the best establishments in Florence. When he had learnt all the secrets, he was to return to Pozzuoli and be the managing director of the rejuvenated boarding-house which his father was modestly proposing to rechristen the Grand Hotel Ritz-Carlton. Meanwhile, he was an underworked lounger in Florence. He had made Mrs Tarwin's acquaintance romantically, on the highway. Driving, as was her custom, alone, Moira had run over a nail. A puncture. Nothing is easier than changing wheels—nothing, that is to say, if you have sufficient muscular strength to undo the nuts which hold the punctured wheel to its axle. Moira had not. When Tonino came upon her, ten minutes after the mishap, she was sitting on the running-board of the car, flushed and dishevelled with her efforts, and in tears.

"Una signora forestiera." At the café that evening Tonino recounted his adventure with a certain rather fatuous self-satisfaction. In the small bourgeoisie in which he had been brought up, a Foreign Lady was an almost fabulous creature, a being of legendary wealth, eccentricity, independence. *"Inglese,"* he specified. *"Giovane,"* and *"bella, bellissima."* His auditors were incredulous; beauty, for some reason, is not common among the specimens of English womanhood seen in foreign parts. *"Ricca,"* he added. That sounded less intrinsically improbable; foreign ladies were all rich, almost by definition. Juicily, and with unction, Tonino described the car she drove, the luxurious villa she inhabited.

Acquaintance had ripened quickly into friendship. This was the fourth or fifth time in a fortnight that he had come to the house.

"A few poor flowers," said the young man in a tone of soft, ingratiating apology; and he brought forward his left hand, which he had been hiding behind his back. It held a bouquet of white roses.

"But how kind of you!" she cried in her bad Italian. "How lovely!" John never brought flowers to any one; he regarded that sort of thing as rather nonsensical. She smiled at Tonino over the blossoms. "Thank you a thousand times."

Making a deprecating gesture, he returned her smile. His teeth flashed pearly and even. His large eyes were bright, dark, liquid, and rather expressionless, like a gazelle's. He was exceedingly good-looking. "White roses for the white rose," he said.

Moira laughed. The compliment was ridiculous; but it pleased her all the same.

Paying compliments was not the only thing Tonino could do. He knew how to be useful. When, a few days later, Moira decided to have the rather dingy hall and dining-room redistempered, he was invaluable. It was he who haggled with the decorator, he who made scenes when there were delays, he who interpreted Moira's rather special notions about colours to the workmen, he who superintended their activities.

"If it hadn't been for you," said Moira gratefully, when the work was finished, "I'd have been hopelessly swindled and they wouldn't have done anything properly."

It was such a comfort, she reflected, having a man about the place who didn't always have something more important to do and think about; a man who could spend his time being useful and a help. Such a comfort! And such a change! When she was with John, it was she who had to do all the tiresome, practical things. John always had his work, and his work took precedence of everything, including her convenience. Tonino was just an ordinary man, with nothing in the least superhuman about either himself or his functions. It was a great relief.

Little by little Moira came to rely on him for everything. He made himself universally useful. The fuses blew out; it was Tonino who replaced them. The hornets nested in the drawing-room chimney; heroically Tonino stank them out with sulphur. But his speciality was domestic economy. Brought up in a restaurant, he knew everything there was to be known about food and drink and prices. When the meat was unsatisfactory, he went to the butcher and threw the tough beefsteak in his teeth, almost literally. He beat down the extortionate charges of the green-grocer. With a man at the fish market he made a friendly arrange-ment whereby Moira was to have the pick of the soles and the red mullet. He bought her wine for her, her oil—wholesale, in huge glass demijohns; and Moira, who since Sir Watney's death could have afforded to drink nothing cheaper than Pol Roger 1911 and do her cooking in imported yak's butter, exulted with him in long domestic conversations over economies of a farthing a quart or a shilling or two on a hundredweight. For Tonino the price and the quality of victuals and drink were matters of gravest importance. To secure a flask of Chianti for five lire ninety instead of six lire was, in his eyes, a real victory; and the victory became a triumph if it could be proved that the Chianti was fully three years old and had an alcohol content of more than fourteen per cent. By nature Moira was neither greedy nor avaricious. Her upbringing had confirmed her in her natural tendencies. She had the dis-interestedness of those who have never known a shortage of cash; and her abstemious indifference to the pleasures of the table had never been tempered by the housewife's pre-occupation with other people's appetites and digestions. Never; for Sir Watney had kept a professional housekeeper, and with John Tarwin, who anyhow hardly noticed what he ate, and thought that women ought to spend their time doing more important and intellectual things than presiding over kitchens, she had lived for the greater part of their married life in hotels or service flats, or else in furnished rooms and in a chronic state of picnic. Tonino revealed to her the world of markets and the kitchen. Still accustomed to thinking, with John, that ordinary domestic life wasn't good enough, she laughed at first at his earnest preoccupation with meat and halfpence. But after a little she began to be infected by his almost religious enthusiasm for housekeeping; she began to discover that meat and halfpence were interesting after all, that they were real and important—much more real and important, for example, than reading Goethe when one found him a bore and a humbug. Tenderly brooded over by the most competent of solicitors and brokers, the late Sir Watney's fortune was bring-ing in a steady five per cent. free of tax. But in Tonino's company Moira could forget her bank balance. Descending from the financial Sinai on which she had been lifted so high above the common earth, she discovered, with him, the preoccupations of poverty. They were curiously interesting and exciting.

"The prices they ask for fish in Florence!" said Tonino, after a silence, when he had exhausted the subject of white rosse. "When I think how little we pay for octopus at Naples! It's scandalous."

"Scandalous!" echoed Moira with an indignation as genuine as his own. They talked, interminably.

Next day the sky was no longer blue, but opaquely white. There was no sunshine, only a diffused glare that threw no shadows. The landscape lay utterly lifeless under the dead and fishy stare of heaven. It was very hot, there was no wind, the air was hardly breathable and as though woolly. Moira woke up with a headache, and her nerves seemed to have an uneasy life of their own, apart from hers. Like caged birds they were, fluttering and starting and twittering at every alarm; and her aching, tired body was their aviary. Quite against her own wish and intention she found herself in a temper with the maid and saying the unkindest things. She had to give her a pair of stockings to make up for it. When she was dressed, she wanted to write some letters; but her fountain-pen made a stain on her fingers and she was so furious that she threw the beastly thing out of the window. It broke to pieces on the flagstones below. She had nothing to write with; it was too exasperating. She washed the ink off her hands and took out her embroidery frame. But her fingers were all thumbs. And then she pricked herself with the needle. Oh, so painfully! The tears came into her eyes; she began to cry. And having begun, she couldn't stop. Assunta came in five minutes later and found her sobbing. "But what is it, signora?" she asked, made most affectionately solicitous by the gift of the stockings. Moria shook her head. "Go away," she said brokenly. The girl was insistent. "Go away," Moira repeated. How could she explain what was the matter when the only thing that had happened was that she had pricked her finger? Nothing was the matter. And yet everything was the matter, everything.

The everything that was the matter resolved itself finally into the weather. Even in the best of health Moira had always been painfully conscious of the approach of thunder. Her jangled nerves were more than ordinarily sensitive. The tears and furies and despairs of this horrible day had a purely meteorological cause. But they were none the less violent and agonizing for that. The hours passed dismally. Thickened by huge black clouds, the twilight came on in a sultry and expectant silence, and it was prematurely night. The reflection of distant lightnings, flashing far away below the horizon, illuminated the eastern sky. The peaks and ridges of the Apennines stood out black against the momentary pale expanses of silvered vapour and disappeared again in silence; the attentive hush was still unbroken. With a kind of sinking apprehension—for she was terrified of storms— Moira sat at her window, watching the black hills leap out against the silver and die again, leap out and die. The flashes brightened; and then, for the first time, she heard the approaching thunder, far off and faint like the whisper of the sea in a shell. Moira shuddered. The clock in the hall struck nine, and, as though the sound were a signal prearranged, a gust of wind suddenly shook the magnolia tree that stood at the crossing of the paths in the garden below. Its long stiff leaves rattled together like scales of horn. There was another flash. In the brief white glare she could see the two funereal cypresses writhing and tossing as though in the desperate agitation of pain. And then all at once the storm burst catastrophically, it seemed directly overhead. At the savage violence of that icy downpour Moira shrank back and shut the window. A streak of white fire zig-zagged fearfully just behind the cypresses. The immediate thunder was like the splitting and fall of a solid vault. Moira rushed away from the window and threw herself on the bed. She covered her face with her hands. Through the continuous roaring of the rain the thunder crashed and reverberated, crashed again and sent the fragments of sound rolling unevenly in all directions through the night. The whole house trembled. In the window-frames the shaken glasses rattled like the panes of an old omnibus rolling across the cobbles.

"Oh God, oh God," Moira kept repeating. In the enormous tumult her voice was small and, as it were, naked, utterly abject.

"But it's too stupid to be frightened." She remembered John's voice, his brightly encouraging, superior manner. "The chances are thousands to one against your being struck. And anyhow, hiding your head won't prevent the lightning from . . ."

How she hated him for being so reasonable and right! "Oh God!" There was another. "God, God, God. . . ."

And then suddenly a terrible thing happened; the light went out. Through her closed eyelids she saw no longer the red of translucent blood, but utter blackness. Uncovering her face, she opened her eyes and anxiously looked round—on blackness again. She fumbled for the switch by her bed, found it, turned and turned; the darkness remained impenetrable.

"Assunta!" she called.

And all at once the square of the window was a suddenly uncovered picture of the garden, seen against a background of mauve-white sky and shining, down-pouring rain.

"Assunta!" Her voice was drowned in a crash that seemed to have exploded in the very roof. "Assunta, Assunta!" In a panic she stumbled across the grave-dark room to the door. Another flash revealed the handle. She opened. "Assunta!"

Her voice was hollow above the black gulf of the stairs. The thunder exploded again above her. With a crash and a tinkle of broken glass one of the windows in her room burst open. A blast of cold wind lifted her hair. A flight of papers rose from her writing-table and whirled with crackling wings through the darkness. One touched her cheek like a living thing and was gone. She screamed aloud. The door slammed behind her. She ran down the stairs in terror, as though the fiend were at her heels. In the hall she met Assunta and the cook coming towards her, lighting matches as they came.

"Assunta, the lights!" She clutched the girl's arm.

Only the thunder answered. When the noise subsided, Assunta explained that the fuses had all blown out and that there wasn't a candle in the house. Not a single candle, and only one more box of matches.

"But then we shall be left in the dark," said Moira hysterically.

Through the three blackly reflecting windows of the hall three separate pictures of the streaming garden revealed themselves and vanished. The old Venetian mirrors on the walls blinked for an instant into life, like dead eyes briefly opened.

"In the dark," she repeated with an almost mad insistence.

"Aie!" cried Assunta, and dropped the match that had begun to burn her fingers. The thunder fell on them out of a darkness made denser and more hopeless by the loss of light.

When the telephone bell rang, Tonino was sitting in the

managerial room of his hotel, playing cards with the proprietor's two sons and another friend. "Some one to speak to you, Signor Tonino," said the under-porter, looking in. "A lady." He grinned significantly.

Tonino put on a dignified air and left the room. When he returned a few minutes later, he held his hat on one hand and was buttoning up his rain-coat with the other.

"Sorry," he said. "I've got to go out."

"Go out?" exclaimed the others incredulously. Beyond the shuttered windows the storm roared like a cataract and savagely exploded. "But where?" they asked. "Why? Are you mad?"

Tonino shrugged his shoulders, as though it were nothing to go out into a tornado, as though he were used to it. The *signora forestiera*, he explained, hating them for their inquisitiveness; the Tarwin—she had asked him to go up to Bello Sguardo at once. The fuses . . . not a candle in the house . . . utterly in the dark . . . very agitated . . . nerves. . . .

"But on a night like this. . . . But you're not the electrician." The two sons of the proprietor spoke in chorus. They felt, indignantly, that Tonino was letting himself be exploited.

But the third young man leaned back in his chair and laughed. "*Vai, caro, vai,*" he said, and then, shaking his finger at Tonino knowingly, "*Ma fatti pagare per il tuo lavoro,*" he added. "Get yourself paid for your trouble." Berto was notoriously the lady-killer, the tried specialist in amorous strategy, the acknowledged expert. "Take the opportunity." The others joined in his rather unpleasant laughter. Tonino also grinned and nodded.

The taxi rushed splashing through the wet deserted streets like a travelling fountain. Tonino sat in the darkness of the cab ruminating Berto's advice. She was pretty, certainly. But somehow—why was it?—it had hardly occurred to him to think of her as a possible mistress. He had been politely gallant with her—on principle almost, and by force of habit—but without really wanting to succeed; and when she had shown herself unresponsive, he hadn't cared. But perhaps he ought to have cared, perhaps he ought to have tried harder. In Berto's world it was a sporting duty to do one's best to seduce every woman one could. The most admirable man was the man with the greatest number of women to his credit. Really lovely, Tonino went on to himself, trying to work up an enthusiasm for the sport. It would be a triumph to be proud of. The more so as she was a foreigner. And very rich. He thought with inward satisfaction of that big car, of the house, the servants, the silver. *"Certo,"* he said to himself complacently, *"mi vuol bene."* She liked him; there was no doubt of it. Meditatively he stroked his smooth face; the muscles stirred a little under his fingers. He was smiling to himself in the darkness; naïvely, an ingenuous prostitute's smile. *"Moira,"* he said aloud. *"Moira. Strano, quel nome. Piuttosto ridicolo."*

It was Moira who opened the door for him. She had been standing at the window, looking out, waiting and waiting.

"Tonino!" She held out both her hands to him; she had never felt so glad to see any one.

The sky went momentarily whitish-mauve behind him as he stood there in the open doorway. The skirts of his rain-coat fluttered in the wind; a wet gust blew past him, chilling her face. The sky went black again. He slammed the door behind him. They were in utter darkness.

"Tonino, it was too sweet of you to have come. Really too . . ."

The thunder that interrupted her was like the end of the world. Moira shuddered. "Oh God!" she whimpered; and then suddenly she was pressing her face against his waistcoat and crying, and Tonino was holding her and stroking her hair. The next flash showed him the position of the sofa. In the ensuing darkness he carried her across the room, sat down and began to kiss her tear-wet face. She lay quite still in his arms, relaxed, like a frightened child that has at last found comfort. Tonino held her, kissing her softly again and again. *"Ti amo, Moira,"* he whispered. And it was true. Holding her, touching her in the dark, he did love her. *"Ti amo."* How profoundly! *"Ti voglio un bene immenso,"* he went on, with a passion, a deep warm tenderness born almost suddenly of darkness and soft blind contact. Heavy and warm with life, she lay pressed against him. Her body curved and was solid under his hands, her cheeks were rounded and cool, her eyelids round and tremulous and tear-wet, her mouth so soft, so soft under his touching lips. *"Ti amo, ti amo."* He was breathless with love, and it was as though there were a hollowness at the centre of his being, a void of desiring tenderness that longed to be filled, that could only be filled by her, an emptiness that drew her towards him, into him, that drank her as an empty vessel eagerly drinks the water. Still, with closed eyes, quite still she lay there in his arms, suffering herself to be drunk up by his tenderness, to be drawn into the yearning vacancy of his heart, happy in being passive, in yielding herself to his soft insistent passion.

"*Fatti pagare, fatti pagare.*" The memory of Berto's words transformed him suddenly from a lover into an amorous sportsman with a reputation to keep up and records to break. "*Fatti pagare.*" He risked a more intimate caress. But Moira winced so shudderingly at the touch that he desisted, ashamed of himself.

"*Ebbene,*" asked Berto when, an hour later, he returned, "did you mend the fuses?"

"Yes, I mended the fuses."

"And did you get yourself paid?"

Tonino smiled an amorous sportsman's smile. "A little on account," he answered, and at once disliked himself for having spoken the words, disliked the others for laughing at them. Why did he go out of his way to spoil something which had been so beautiful? Pretexting a headache, he went upstairs to his bedroom. The storm had passed on, the moon was shining now out of a clear sky. He opened the window and looked out. A river of ink and quick-silver, the Arno flowed whispering past. In the street below the puddles shone like living eyes. The ghost of Caruso was singing from a gramophone, far away on the other side of the water. "*Stretti, stretti, nell' estasì d'amor. . . .*" Tonino was profoundly moved.

The sky was blue next morning, the sunlight glittered on the shiny leaves of the magnolia tree, the air was demurely windless. Sitting at her dressing-table, Moira looked out and wondered incredulously if such things as storms were possible. But the plants were broken and prostrate in their beds; the paths were strewn with scattered leaves and petals. In spite of the soft air and the sunlight, last night's horrors had been more than a bad dream. Moira sighed and began to brush her hair. Set in its leather frame, John Tarwin's profile confronted her, brightly focused on imaginary tumours. Her eyes fixed on it, Moira went on mechanically brushing her hair. Then, suddenly, interrupting the rhythm of her movements, she got up, took the leather frame and, walking across the room, threw it up, out of sight, on to the top of the high wardrobe. There! She returned to her seat and, filled with a kind of frightened elation, went on with her interrupted brushing.

When she was dressed, she drove down to the town and spent

an hour at Settepassi's, the jewellers. When she left, she was bowed out on to the Lungarno like a princess.

"No, don't smoke those," she said to Tonino that afternoon as he reached for a cigarette in the silver box that stood on the drawing-room mantelpiece. "I've got a few of those Egyptian ones you like. Got them specially for you." And, smiling, she handed him a little parcel.

Tonino thanked her profusely—too profusely, as was his custom. But when he had stripped away the paper and saw the polished gold of a large cigarette-case, he could only look at her in an embarrassed and inquiring amazement.

"Don't you think it's rather pretty?" she asked.

"Marvellous! But is it . . ." He hesitated. "Is it for me?"

Moira laughed with pleasure at his embarrassment. She had never seen him embarrassed before. He was always the self-possessed young man of the world, secure and impregnable within his armour of Southern good manners. She admired that elegant carapace. But it amused her for once to take him without it, to see him at a loss, blushing and stammering like a little boy. It amused and it pleased her; she liked him all the more for being the little boy as well as the polished and socially competent young man.

"For me?" she mimicked, laughing. "Do you like it?" Her tone changed; she became grave. "I wanted you to have something to remind you of last night." Tonino took her hands and silently kissed them. She had received him with such off-handed gaiety, so nonchalantly, as though nothing had happened, that the tender references to last night's happenings (so carefully prepared as he walked up the hill) had remained unspoken. He had been afraid of saying the wrong thing and offending her. But now the spell was broken—and by Moira herself. "One oughtn't to forget one's good actions," Moira went on, abandoning him her hands. "Each time you take a cigarette out of this case, will you remember how kind and good you were to a silly ridiculous little fool?"

Tonino had had time to recover his manners. "I shall remember the most adorable, the most beautiful . . ." Still holding her hands, he looked at her for a moment in silence, eloquently. Moira smiled back at him. "Moira!" And she was in his arms. She shut her eyes and was passive in the strong circle of his arms, soft and passive against his firm body. "I love you, Moira." The breath of his whispering was warm on her cheek. "*Ti amo.*" And suddenly his lips were on hers again, violently, impatiently kissing. Between the kisses his whispered words came passionate to her ears. "*Ti amo pazzamente . . . piccina . . . tesoro . . . amore . . . cuore . . .*" Uttered in Italian, his love seemed somehow specially strong and deep. Things described in a strange language themselves take on a certain strangeness. "*Amami, Moira, amami. Mi am un po?*" He was insistent. "A little, Moira—do you love me a little?"

She opened her eyes and looked at him. Then, with a quick movement, she took his face between her two hands, drew it down and kissed him on the mouth. "Yes," she whispered, "I love you." And then, gently, she pushed him away. Tonino wanted to kiss her again. But Moira shook her head and slipped away from him. "No, no," she said with a kind of peremptory entreaty. "Don't spoil it all now."

The days passed, hot and golden. Summer approached. The nightingales sang unseen in the cool of the evening.

"*L'usignuolo,*" Moira whispered softly to herself as she listened to the singing. "*L'usignuolo.*" Even the nightingales were subtly better in Italian. The sun had set. They were sitting in the little summer-house at the end of the garden, looking out over the darkening landscape. The white-walled farms and villas on the slope below stood out almost startlingly clear against the twilight of the olive trees, as though charged with some strange and novel significance. Moira sighed. "I'm so happy," she said; Tonino took her hand. "Ridiculously happy." For, after all, she was thinking, it *was* rather ridiculous to be so happy for no valid reason. John Tarwin had taught her to imagine that one could only be happy when one was doing something "interesting" (as he put it), or associating with people who were "worth while." Tonino was nobody in particular, thank goodness! And going for picnics wasn't exactly "interesting" in John's sense of the word; nor was talking about the respective merits of different brands of car; nor teaching him to drive; nor going shopping; nor discussing the problem of new curtains for the drawing-room; nor, for that matter, sitting in the summer-house and saying nothing. In spite of which, or because of which, she was happy with an unprecedented happiness. "Ridiculously happy," she repeated.

Tonino kissed her hand. "So am I," he said. And he was not

merely being polite. In his own way he was genuinely happy with her. People envied him sitting in that magnificent yellow car at her side. She was so pretty and elegant, so foreign too; he was proud to be seen about with her. And then the cigarette-case, the gold-mounted, agate-handled cane she had given him for his birthday. . . . Besides, he was really very fond of her, really, in an obscure way, in love with her. It was not for nothing that he had held and caressed her in the darkness of that night of thunder. Something of that deep and passionate tenderness, born suddenly of the night and their warm sightless contact, still remained in him—still remained even after the physical longings she then inspired had been vicariously satisfied. (And under Berto's knowing guidance they *had* been satisfied, frequently.) If it hadn't been for Berto's satirical comments on the still platonic nature of his attachment, he would have been perfectly content.

"*Alle donne,*" Berto sententiously generalized, "*piace sempre la violenza*. They long to be raped. You don't know how to make love, my poor boy." And he would hold up his own achievements as examples to be followed. For Berto, love was a kind of salacious vengeance on women for the crime of their purity.

Spurred on by his friend's mockeries, Tonino made another attempt to exact full payment for his mending of the fuses on the night of the storm. But his face was so soundly slapped, and the tone in which Moira threatened never to see him again unless he behaved himself was so convincingly stern, that he did not renew his attack. He contented himself with looking sad and complaining of her cruelty. But in spite of his occasionally long face, he was happy with her. Happy like a fireside cat. The car, the house, her elegant foreign prettiness, the marvellous presents she gave him, kept him happily purring.

The days passed and the weeks. Moira would have liked life to flow on like this forever, a gay bright stream with occasional reaches of calm sentimentality but never dangerously deep or turbulent, without fall or whirl or rapid. She wanted her existence to remain for ever what it was at this moment—a kind of game with a pleasant and emotionally exciting companion, a playing at living and loving. If only this happy play-time could last for ever!

It was John Tarwin who decreed that it should not. "ATTEND-ING CYTOLOGICAL CONGRESS ROME WILL STOP FEW DAYS ON WAY

ARRIVING THURSDAY LOVE JOHN." That was the text of the telegram Moira found awaiting her on her return to the villa one
evening. She read it and felt suddenly depressed and appre-
hensive. Why did he want to come? He would spoil everything.
The bright evening went dead before her eyes; the happiness
with which she had been brimming when she returned with
Tonino from that marvellous drive among the Apennines was
drained out of her. Her gloom retrospectively darkened the blue
and golden beauty of the mountains, put out the bright flowers,
dimmed the day's laughter and talk. "Why does he want to
come?" Miserably and resentfully, she wondered. "And what's
going to happen, what's going to happen?" She felt cold and
rather breathless and almost sick with the questioning
apprehension.

John's face, when he saw her standing there at the station, lit
up instantaneously with all its hundred-candle-power tenderness
and charm.

"My darling!" His voice was furry and tremulous. He leaned
towards her; stiffening, Moira suffered herself to be kissed. His
nails, she noticed disgustedly, were dirty.

The prospect of a meal alone with John had appalled her; she
had asked Tonino to dinner. Besides, she wanted John to meet
him. To have kept Tonino's existence a secret from John would
have been to admit that there was something wrong in her
relations with him. And there wasn't. She wanted John to meet
him just like that, naturally, as a matter of course. Whether he'd
like Tonino when he'd met him was another question. Moira had
her doubts. They were justified by the event. John had begun by
protesting when he heard that she had invited a guest. Their first
evening—how could she? The voice trembled—fur in a breeze.
She had to listen to outpourings of sentiment. But finally, when
dinner-time arrived, he switched off the pathos and became once
more the research student. Brightly inquiring, blankly intelligent,
John cross-questioned his guest about all the interesting and important things that were happening in Italy. What was the real
political situation? How did the new educational system work?
What did people think of the reformed penal code? On all these
matters Tonino was, of course, far less well-informed than his
interrogator. The Italy he knew was the Italy of his friends and
his family, of shops and cafés and girls and the daily fight for

money. All that historical, impersonal Italy, of which John so intelligently read in the high-class reviews, was utterly unknown to him. His answers to John's questions were childishly silly. Moira sat listening, dumb with misery.

"What *do* you find in that fellow?" her husband asked, when Tonino had taken his leave. "He struck me as quite particularly uninteresting."

Moira did not answer. There was a silence. John suddenly switched on his tenderly, protectively, yearningly marital smile. "Time to go to bed, my sweetheart," he said. Moira looked up at him and saw in his eyes that expression she knew so well and dreaded. "My sweetheart," he repeated, and the Landseer dog was also amorous. He put his arms round her and bent to kiss her face. Moira shuddered—but helplessly, dumbly, not knowing how to escape. He led her away.

When John had left her, she lay awake far into the night, remembering his ardours and his sentimentalities with a horror that the passage of time seemed actually to increase. Sleep came at last to deliver her.

Being an archaeologist, old Signor Bargioni was decidedly "interesting."

"But he bores me to death," said Moira when, next day, her husband suggested that they should go and see him. "That voice! And the way he goes on and on! And that beard! And his wife!"

John flushed with anger. "Don't be childish," he snapped out, forgetting how much he enjoyed her childishness when it didn't interfere with his amusements or his business. "After all," he insisted, "there's probably no man living who knows more about Tuscany in the Dark Ages."

Nevertheless, in spite of darkest Tuscany, John had to pay his call without her. He spent a most improving hour, chatting about Romanesque architecture and the Lombard kings. But just before he left, the conversation somehow took another turn; casually, as though by chance, Tonino's name was mentioned. It was the signora who had insisted that it should be mentioned. Ignorance, her husband protested, is bliss. But Signora Bargioni loved scandal, and being middle-aged, ugly, envious, and malicious, was full of righteous indignation against the young wife and of hypocritical sympathy for the possibly injured husband. Poor Tarwin, she insisted—he ought to be warned. And so, tactfully, without seeming to say anything in particular, the old man dropped his hints.

Walking back to Bello Sguardo, John was uneasily pensive. It was not that he imagined that Moira had been, or was likely to prove, unfaithful. Such things really didn't happen to oneself. Moira obviously liked the uninteresting young man; but, after all and in spite of her childishness, Moira was a civilized human being, She had been too well brought up to do anything stupid. Besides, he reflected, remembering the previous evening, remembering all the years of their marriage, she had no temperament; she didn't know what passion was, she was utterly without sensuality. Her native childishness would reinforce her principles. Infants may be relied on to be pure; but not (and this was what troubled John Tarwin) worldly-wise. Moira wouldn't allow herself to be made love to; but she might easily let herself be swindled. Old Bargioni had been very discreet and non-committal; but it was obvious that he regarded this young fellow as an adventurer, out for what he could get. John frowned as he walked, and bit his lip.

He came home to find Moira and Tonino superintending the fitting of the new cretonne covers for the drawing-room chairs.

"Carefully, carefully," Moira was saying to the upholsterer as he came in. She turned at the sound of his footsteps. A cloud seemed to obscure the brightness of her face when she saw him; but she made an effort to keep up her gaiety. "Come and look, John," she called. "It's like getting a very fat old lady into a very tight dress. Too ridiculous!"

But John did not smile with her; his face was a mask of stony gravity. He stalked up to the chair, nodded curtly to Tonino, curtly to the upholsterer, and stood there watching the work as though he were a stranger, a hostile stranger at that. The sight of Moira and Tonino laughing and talking together had roused in him a sudden and violent fury. "Disgusting little adventurer," he said to himself ferociously behind his mask.

"It's a pretty stuff, don't you think?" said Moira. He only grunted.

"Very modern too," added Tonino. "The shops are very modern here," he went on, speaking with all the rather touchy insistence on up-to-dateness which characterizes the inhabitants of an under-bathroomed and over-monumented country.

"Indeed?" said John sarcastically.

Moira frowned. "You've no idea how helpful Tonino has been," she said with a certain warmth.

Effusively Tonino began to deny that she had any obligation towards him. John Tarwin interrupted him. "Oh, I've no doubt he was helpful," he said in the same sarcastic tone and with a little smile of contempt.

There was an uncomfortable silence. Then Tonino took his leave. The moment he was gone, Moira turned on her husband. Her face was pale, her lips trembled. "How dare you speak to one of my friends like that?" she asked in a voice unsteady with anger.

John flared up. "Because I wanted to get rid of the fellow," he answered; and the mask was off, his face was nakedly furious. "It's disgusting to see a man like that hanging round the house. An adventurer. Exploiting your silliness. Sponging on you."

"Tonino doesn't sponge on me. And anyhow, what do you know about it?"

He shrugged his shoulders. "One hears things."

"Oh, it's those old beasts, is it?" She hated the Bargionis, *hated* them. "Instead of being grateful to Tonino for helping me! Which is more than you've ever done, John. You, with your beastly tumours and your rotten old *Faust!*" The contempt in her voice was blasting. "Just leaving me to sink or swim. And when somebody comes along and is just humanly decent to me, you insult him. And you fly into a rage of jealousy because I'm normally grateful to him."

John had had time to readjust his mask. "I don't fly into any sort of rage," he said, bottling his anger and speaking slowly and coldly. "I just don't want you to be preyed upon by handsome, black-haired young pimps from the slums of Naples."

"John!"

"Even if the preying *is* done platonically," he went on. "Which I'm sure it is. But I don't want to have even a platonic pimp about." He spoke coldly, slowly, with the deliberate intention of hurting her as much as he could. "How much has he got out of you so far?"

Moira did not answer, but turned and hurried from the room.

Tonino had just got to the bottom of the hill, when a loud insistent hooting made him turn round. A big yellow car was close at his heels.

"Moira!" he called in astonishment. The car came to a halt beside him.

"Get in," she commanded almost fiercely, as though she were angry with him. He did as he was told.

"But where did you think of going?" he asked.

"I don't know. Anywhere. Let's take the Bologna road, into the mountains."

"But you've got no hat," he objected, "no coat."

She only laughed and, throwing the car into gear, drove off at full speed. John spent his evening in solitude. He began by reproaching himself. "I oughtn't to have spoken so brutally," he thought, when he heard of Moira's precipitate departure. What tender, charming things he would say, when she came back, to make up for his hard words! And then, when she'd made peace, he would talk to her gently, paternally about the dangers of having bad friends. Even the anticipation of what he would say to her caused his face to light up with a beautiful smile. But when, three-quarters of an hour after dinner-time, he sat down to a lonely and overcooked meal, his mood had changed. "If she wants to sulk," he said to himself, "why, let her sulk." And as the hours passed, his heart grew harder. Midnight struck. His anger began to be tempered by a certain apprehension. Could anything have happened to her? He was anxious. But all the same he went to bed, on principle, firmly. Twenty minutes later he heard Moira's step on the stairs and then the closing of her door. She was back; nothing had happened; perversely, he felt all the more exasperated with her for being safe. Would she come and say good-night? He waited.

Absently, meanwhile, mechanically, Moira had undressed. She was thinking of all that had happened in the eternity since she had left the house. That marvellous sunset in the mountains! Every westward slope was rosily gilded; below them lay a gulf of blue shadow. They had stood in silence, gazing. "Kiss me, Tonino," she had suddenly whispered, and the touch of his lips had sent a kind of delicious apprehension fluttering under her skin. She pressed herself against him; his body was firm and solid with her clasp. She could feel the throb of his heart against her cheek, like something separately alive. Beat, beat, beat—and the throbbing life was not the life of the Tonino she knew, the Tonino who laughed and paid compliments and brought flowers;

it was the life of some mysterious and separate power. A power with which the familiar individual Tonino happened to be connected, but almost irrelevantly. She shuddered a little. Mysterious and terrifying. But the terror was somehow attractive, like a dark precipice that allures. "Kiss me, Tonino, kiss me." The light faded; the hills died away into featureless flat shapes against the sky. "I'm cold," she said at last, shivering. "Let's go." They dined at a little inn, high up between the two passes. When they drove away, it was night. He put his arm round her and kissed her neck, at the nape, where the cropped hair was harsh against his mouth. "You'll make me drive into the ditch," she laughed. But there was no laughter for Tonino. "Moira, Moira," he repeated; and there was something like agony in his voice. "Moira." And finally, at his suffering entreaty, she stopped the car. They got out. Under the chestnut trees, what utter darkness!

Moira slipped off her last garment and, naked before the mirror, looked at her image. It seemed the same as ever, her pale body; but in reality it was different, it was new, it had only just been born.

John still waited, but his wife did not come. "All right, then," he said to himself, with a spiteful little anger that disguised itself as a god-like and impersonal serenity of justice; "let her sulk if she wants to. She only punishes herself." He turned out the light and composed himself to sleep. Next morning he left for Rome and the Cytological Congress without saying good-bye; that would teach her. But "thank goodness!" was Moira's first reflection when she heard that he had gone. And then, suddenly, she felt rather sorry for him. Poor John! Like a dead frog, galvanized; twitching, but never alive. He was pathetic really. She was so rich in happiness, that she could afford to be sorry for him. And in a way she was even grateful to him. If he hadn't come, if he hadn't behaved so unforgivably, nothing would have happened between Tonino and herself. Poor John! But all the same he was hopeless.

Day followed bright serene day. But Moira's life no longer flowed like the clear and shallow stream it had been before John's coming. It was turbulent now, there were depths and darknesses. And love was no longer a game with a pleasant companion; it was violent, all-absorbing, even rather terrible. Tonino became for her a kind of obsession. She was haunted by him—by his face, by his white teeth and his dark hair, by his hands and limbs and body. She wanted to be with him, to feel his nearness, to touch him. She would spend whole hours stroking his hair, ruffling it up, rearranging it fantastically, on end, like a golliwog's, or with hanging fringes, or with the locks twisted up into horns. And when she had contrived some specially ludicrous effect, she clapped her hands and laughed, laughed, till the tears ran down her cheeks. "If you could see yourself now!" she cried. Offended by her laughter, "You play with me as though I were a doll," Tonino would protest with a rather ludicrous expression of angry dignity. The laughter would go out of Moira's face and, with a seriousness that was fierce, almost cruel, she would lean forward and kiss him, silently, violently, again and again.

Absent, he was still unescapably with her, like a guilty conscience. Her solitudes were endless meditations on the theme of him. Sometimes the longing for his tangible presence was too achingly painful to be borne. Disobeying all his injunctions, breaking all her promises, she would telephone for him to come to her, she would drive off in search of him. Once, at about midnight, Tonino was called down from his room at the hotel by a message that a lady wanted to speak to him. He found her sitting in the car. "But I couldn't help it, I simply couldn't help it," she cried, to excuse herself and mollify his anger. Tonino refused to be propitiated. Coming like this in the middle of the night! It was madness, it was scandalous! She sat there, listening, pale and with trembling lips and the tears in her eyes. He was silent at last. "But if you knew, Tonino," she whispered, "if you only knew . . ." She took his hand and kissed it, humbly.

Berto, when he heard the good news (for Tonino proudly told him at once), was curious to know whether the *signora forestiera* was as cold as Northern ladies were proverbially supposed to be. "*Macchè!*" Tonino protested vigorously. On the contrary. For a long time the two young sportsmen discussed the question of amorous temperatures, discussed it technically, professionally.

Tonino's raptures were not so extravagant as Moira's. So far as he was concerned, this sort of thing had happened before. Passion with Moira was not diminished by satisfaction, but rather, since the satisfaction was for her so novel, so intrinsically apocalyptic, increased. But that which caused her passion to increase produced in his a waning. He had got what he wanted; his night-begotten, touch-born longing for her (dulled in the interval and diminished by all the sporting love-hunts undertaken with Berto) had been fulfilled. She was no longer the desired and unobtainable, but the possessed, the known. By her surrender she had lowered herself to the level of all the other women he had ever made love to; she was just another item in the sportsman's grand total.

His attitude towards her underwent a change. Familiarity began to blunt his courtesy; his manner became offhandedly marital. When he saw her after an absence, *"Ebbene, tesoro,"* he would say in a genially unromantic tone, and pat her once or twice on the back or shoulder, as one might pat a horse. He permitted her to run her own errands and even his. Moira was happy to be his servant. Her love for him was, in one at least of its aspects, almost abject. She was dog-like in her devotion. Tonino found her adoration very agreeable so long as it expressed itself in fetching and carrying, in falling in with his suggestions, and in making him presents. "But you mustn't, my darling, you shouldn't," he protested each time she gave him something. Nevertheless, he accepted a pearl tie-pin, a pair of diamond and enamel links, a half-hunter on a gold and platinum chain. But Moira's devotion expressed itself also in other ways. Love demands as much as it gives. She wanted so much—his heart, his physical presence, his caresses, his confidences, his time, his fidelity. She was tyrannous in her adoring abjection. She pestered him with devotion, Tonino was bored and irritated by her excessive love. The omniscient Berto, to whom he carried his troubles, advised him to take a strong line. Women, he pronounced, must be kept in their places, firmly. They love one all the better if they are a little maltreated.

Tonino followed his advice and, pretexting work and social engagements, reduced the number of his visits. What a relief to be free of her importunity! Disquieted, Moira presented him with an amber cigar-holder. He protested, accepted it, but gave her no more of his company in return. A set of diamond studs produced no better effect. He talked vaguely and magniloquently about his career and the necessity for unremitting labour; that was his excuse for not coming more often to see her. It was on the tip of her tongue, one afternoon, to say that *she* would be his career, would give him anything he wanted, if only . . . But the memory of John's hateful words made her check herself. She was terrified lest he might make no difficulties about accepting her offer. "Stay with me this evening," she begged, throwing her arms round his neck. He suffered himself to be kissed.

"I wish I could stay," he said hypocritically. "But I have some important business this evening." The important business was playing billiards with Berto.

Moira looked at him for a moment in silence; then, dropping her hands from his shoulders, turned away. She had seen in his eyes a weariness that was almost a horror.

Summer drew on; but in Moira's soul there was no inward brightness to match the sunshine. She passed her days in a misery that was alternately restless and apathetic. Her nerves began once more to lead their own irresponsible life apart from hers. For no sufficient cause and against her will, she would find herself uncontrollably in a fury, or crying, or laughing. When Tonino came to see her, she was almost always, in spite of all her resolutions, bitterly angry or hysterically tearful. "But why do I behave like this?" she would ask herself despairingly. "Why do I say such things? I'm making him hate me." But the next time he came, she would act in precisely the same way. It was as though she were possessed by a devil. And it was not her mind only that was sick. When she ran too quickly upstairs, her heart seemed to stop beating for a moment and there was a whirling darkness before her eyes. She had an almost daily headache, lost appetite, could not digest what she ate. In her thin sallow face her eyes became enormous. Looking into the glass, she found herself hideous, old, repulsive. "No wonder he hates me," she thought, and she would brood, brood for hours over the idea that she had become physically disgusting to him, disgusting to look at, to touch, tainting the air with her breath. The idea became an obsession, indescribably painful and humiliating.

"*Questa donna!*" Tonino would complain with a sigh, when he came back from seeing her. Why didn't he leave her, then? Berto was all for strong measures. Tonino protested that he hadn't the courage; the poor woman would be too unhappy. But he also enjoyed a good dinner and going for drives in an expensive car and receiving sumptuous additions to his wardrobe. He contented himself with complaining and being a Christian martyr. One evening his old friend Carlo Menardi introduced him to his sister. After that he bore his martyrdom with even less patience than before. Luisa Menardi was only seventeen, fresh, healthy, provocatively pretty, with rolling black eyes that said all sorts of things and an impertinent tongue. Tonino's business appointments became more numerous than ever. Moira was left to brood in solitude on the dreadful theme of her own repulsiveness.

Then, quite suddenly, Tonino's manner towards her underwent another change. He became once more assiduously tender, thoughtful, affectionate. Instead of hardening himself with a shrug of indifference against her tears, instead of returning anger for hysterical anger, he was patient with her, was lovingly and cheerfully gentle. Gradually, by a kind of spiritual infection, she too became loving and gentle. Almost reluctantly—for the devil in her was the enemy of life and happiness—she came up again into the light.

"My dear son," Vasari senior had written in his eloquent and disquieting letter, "I am not one to complain feebly of Destiny; my whole life has been one long act of Faith and unshatterable Will. But there are blows under which even the strongest man must stagger—blows which . . ." The letter rumbled on for pages in the same style. The hard unpleasant fact that emerged from under the eloquence was that Tonino's father had been speculating on the Naples stock exchange, speculating unsuccessfully. On the first of the next month he would be required to pay out some fifty thousand francs more than he could lay his hands on. The Grand Hotel Ritz-Carlton was doomed; he might even have to sell the restaurant. Was there anything Tonino could do?

"Is it possible?" said Moira with a sigh of happiness. "It seems too good to be true." She leaned against him; Tonino kissed her eyes and spoke caressing words. There was no moon; the dark-blue sky was thicky constellated; and, like another starry universe gone deliriously mad, the fire-flies darted, alternately eclipsed and shining, among the olive trees. "Darling," he said aloud, and wondered if this would be a propitious moment to speak. "*Piccina mia.*" In the end he decided to postpone matters for another day or two. In another day or two, he calculated, she wouldn't be able to refuse him anything.

Tonino's calculations were correct. She let him have the money, not only without hesitation, but eagerly, joyfully. The reluctance was all on his side, in the receiving. He was almost in tears as he took the cheque, and the tears were tears of genuine emotion. "You're an angel," he said, and his voice trembled. "You've saved us all." Moira cried outright as she kissed him. How could John have said those things? She cried and was happy. A pair of silver-backed hair-brushes accompanied the cheque—just to show that the money had made no difference to their relationship. Tonino recognized the delicacy of her intention and was touched. "You're too good to me," he insisted, "too good." He felt rather ashamed.

"Let's go for a long drive to-morrow," she suggested.

Tonino had arranged to go with Luisa and her brother to Prato. But so strong was his emotion, that he was on the point of accepting Moira's invitation and sacrificing Luisa.

"All right," he began, and then suddenly thought better of it. After all, he could go out with Moira any day. It was seldom that he had a chance of jaunting with Luisa. He struck his forehead, he made a despairing face. "But what am I thinking of!" he cried. "To-morrow's the day we're expecting the manager of the hotel company from Milan."

"But must you be there to see him?"

"Alas!"

It was too sad. Just how sad Moira only fully realized the next day. She had never felt so lonely, never longed so ardently for his presence and affection. Unsatisfied, her longings were an unbearable restlessness. Hoping to escape from the loneliness and ennui with which she had filled the house, the garden, the landscape, she took out the car and drove away at random, not knowing whither. An hour later she found herself at Pistoia, and Pistoia was as hateful as every other place; she headed the car homewards. At Prato there was a fair. The road was crowded; the air was rich with a haze of dust and the noise of brazen music. In a field near the entrance to the town, the merry-go-rounds revolved with a glitter in the sunlight. A plunging horse held up the traffic. Moira stopped the car and looked about her at the crowd, at the swings, at the whirling roundabouts, looked with a cold hostility and distaste. Hateful! And suddenly there was Tonino sitting on a swan in the nearest merry-go-round, with a girl in pink muslin sitting in front of him between the white wings and the arching neck. Rising and falling as it went, the swan turned away out of sight. The music played on. *But poor poppa, poor poppa, he's got nothin' at all.* The swan reappeared. The girl in pink was looking back over her shoulder, smiling. She was very young, vulgarly pretty, shining and plumped with health. Tonino's lips moved; behind the wall of noise what was he saying? All that Moira knew was that the girl laughed; her laughter was like an explosion of sensual young life. Tonino raised his hand and took hold of her bare brown arm. Like an undulating planet, the swan once more wheeled away out of sight. Meanwhile, the plunging horse had been quieted, the traffic had begun to move forward. Behind her a horn hooted insistently. But Moira did not stir. Something in her soul desired that the agony should be repeated and prolonged. Hoot, hoot, hoot! She paid no attention. Rising and falling, the swan emerged once more from eclipse. This time Tonino saw her. Their eyes met; the laughter suddenly went out of his face. "*Porco madonna!*" shouted the infuriated motorist behind her, "can't you move on?" Moira threw the car into gear and shot forward along the dusty road.

The cheque was in the post; there was still time, Tonino reflected, to stop the payment of it.

"You're very silent," said Luisa teasingly, as they drove back towards Florence. Her brother was sitting in front, at the wheel; he had no eyes at the back of his head. But Tonino sat beside her like a dummy. "Why are you so silent?"

He looked at her, and his face was grave and stonily unresponsive to her bright and dimpling provocations. He sighed; then, making an effort, he smiled, rather wanly. Her hand was lying on her knee, palm upward, with a pathetic look of being unemployed. Dutifully doing what was expected of him, Tonino reached out and took it.

At half-past six he was leaning his borrowed motor-cycle against the wall of Moira's villa. Feeling like a man who is about to undergo a dangerous operation, he rang the bell.

Moira was lying on her bed, had lain there ever since she came in; she was still wearing her dust-coat, she had not even taken off her shoes. Affecting an easy cheerfulness, as though nothing unusual had happened, Tonino entered almost jauntily.

"Lying down?" he said in a tone of surprised solicitude. "You haven't got a headache, have you?" His words fell, trivial and ridiculous, into abysses of significant silence. With a sinking of the heart, he sat down on the edge of the bed, he laid a hand on her knee. Moira did not stir, but lay with averted face, remote and unmoving. "What is it, my darling?" He patted her soothingly. "You're not upset because I went to Prato, are you?" he went on, in the incredulous voice of a man who is certain of a negative answer to his question. Still she said nothing. This silence was almost worse than the outcry he had anticipated. Desperately, knowing it was no good, he went on to talk about his old friend, Carlo Menardi, who had come round in his car to call for him; and as the director of the hotel company had left immediately after lunch—most unexpectedly—and as he'd thought Moira was certain to be out, he had finally yielded and gone along with Carlo and his party. Of course, if he'd realized that Moira hadn't gone out, he'd have asked her to join them. For his own sake her company would have made all the difference.

His voice was sweet, ingratiating, apologetic. "A black-haired pimp from the slums of Naples." John's words reverberated in her memory. And so Tonino had never cared for her at all, only for her money. That other woman . . . She saw again that pink dress, lighter in tone than the sleek, sunburnt skin; Tonino's hand on the bare brown arm; that flash of eyes and laughing teeth. And meanwhile he was talking on and on, ingratiatingly; his very voice was a lie.

"Go away," she said at last, without looking at him.

"But, my darling . . ." Bending over her, he tried to kiss her averted cheek. She turned and, with all her might, struck him in the face.

"You little devil!" he cried, made furious by the pain of the blow. He pulled out his handkerchief and held it to his bleeding lip. "Very well, then." His voice trembled with anger. "If you want me to go, I'll go. With pleasure." He walked heavily away. The door slammed behind him.

But perhaps, thought Moira, as she listened to the sound of his footsteps receding on the stairs, perhaps it hadn't really been so bad as it looked; perhaps she had misjudged him. She sat up; on the yellow counterpane was a little circular red stain—a drop of his blood. And it was she who had struck him.

"Tonino! she called; but the house was silent. "Tonino!" Still calling, she hurried downstairs, through the hall, out on to the porch. She was just in time to see him riding off through the gate on his motor-cycle. He was steering with one hand; the other still pressed a handkerchief to his mouth.

"Tonino, Tonino!" But either he didn't, or else he wouldn't

hear her. The motor-cycle disappeared from view. And because he had gone, because he was angry, because of his bleeding lip, Moira was suddenly convinced that she had been accusing him falsely, that the wrong was all on her side. In a state of painful, uncontrollable agitation she ran to the garage. It was essential that she should catch him, speak to him, beg his pardon, implore him to come back. She started the car and drove out.

"One of these days," John had warned her, "you'll go over the edge of the bank, if you're not careful. It's a horrible turning."

Coming out of the garage door, she pulled the wheel hard over as usual. But too impatient to be with Tonino, she pressed the accelerator at the same time. John's prophecy was fulfilled. The car came too close to the edge of the bank; the dry earth crumbled and slid under its outer wheels. It tilted horribly, tottered for a long instant on the balancing point, and went over. But for the ilex tree, it would have gone crashing down the slope. As it was, the machine fell only a foot or so and came to rest, leaning drunkenly sideways with its flank against the bole of the tree. Shaken, but quite unhurt, Moira climbed over the edge of the car and dropped to the ground. "Assunta! Giovanni!" The maids, the gardener came running. When they saw what had happened, there was a small babel of exclamations, questions, comments.

"But can't you get it on to the drive again?" Moira insisted to the gardener; because it was necessary, absolutely necessary, that she should see Tonino at once.

Giovanni shook his head. It would take at least four men with levers and a pair of horses. . . .

"Telephone for a taxi, then," she ordered Assunta and hurried into the house. If she remained any longer with those chattering people, she'd begin to scream. Her nerves had come to separate life again; clenching her fists, she tried to fight them down.

Going up to her room, she sat down before the mirror and began, methodically and with deliberation (it was her will imposing itself on her nerves) to make up her face. She rubbed a little red on to her pale cheeks, painted her lips, dabbed on the powder. "I must look presentable," she thought, and put on her smartest hat. But would the taxi never come? She struggled with her impatience. "My purse," she said to herself. "I shall need some money for the cab." She was pleased with herself for being so full of foresight, so coolly practical in spite of her nerves. "Yes, of course; my purse."

But where was the purse? She remembered so clearly having thrown it on to the bed, when she came in from her drive. It was not there. She looked under the pillow, lifted the counterpane. Or perhaps it had fallen on the floor. She looked under the bed; the purse wasn't there. Was it possible that she hadn't put it on the bed at all? But it wasn't on her dressing-table, nor on the mantelpiece, nor on any of the shelves, nor in any of the drawers of her wardrobe. Where, where, where? And suddenly a terrible thought occurred to her. Tonino . . . Was it possible? The seconds passed. The possibility became a dreadful certainty. A thief as well as . . . John's words echoed in her head. "Black-haired pimp from the slums of Naples, black-haired pimp from the slums . . ." And a thief as well. The bag was made of gold chain-work; there were more than four thousand lire in it. A thief, a thief . . . She stood quite still, strained, rigid, her eyes staring. Then something broke, something seemed to collapse within her. She cried aloud as though under a sudden intolerable pain.

The sound of the shot brought them running upstairs. They found her lying face downwards across the bed, still faintly breathing. But she was dead before the doctor could come up from the town. On a bed standing, as hers stood, in an alcove, it was difficult to lay out the body. When they moved it out of its recess, there was the sound of a hard, rather metallic fall. Assunta bent down to see what had dropped.

"It's her purse," she said. "It must have got stuck between the bed and the wall."

The Claxtons

IN their little house on the common, how beautifully the Claxtons lived, how spiritually! Even the cat was a vegetarian—at any rate officially—even the cat. Which made little Sylvia's behaviour really quite inexcusable. For after all little Sylvia was human and six years old, whereas Pussy was only four and an animal. If Pussy could be content with greens and potatoes and milk and an occasional lump of nut butter, as a treat—Pussy, who had a tiger in her blood—surely Sylvia might be expected to refrain from surreptitious bacon-eating. Particularly in somebody else's house. What made the incident so specially painful to the Claxtons was that it had occurred under Judith's roof. It was the first time they had stayed with Judith since their marriage. Martha Claxton was rather afraid of her sister, afraid of her sharp tongue and her laughter and her scarifying irreverence. And on her own husband's account she was a little jealous of Judith's husband. Jack Bamborough's books were not only esteemed; they also brought in money. Whereas poor Herbert . . . "Herbert's art is too *inward*," his wife used to explain, "too spiritual for most people to understand." She resented Jack Bamborough's success; it was too complete. She wouldn't have minded so much if he had made pots of money in the teeth of critical contempt; or if the critics had approved and he had made nothing. But to earn praise *and* a thousand a year—that was too much. A man had no right to make the best of both worlds like that, when Herbert never sold anything and was utterly ignored. In spite of all which she had at last accepted Judith's often repeated invitation. After all, one ought to love one's sister and one's sister's husband. Also, all the chimneys in the house on the common needed sweeping, and the roof would have to be repaired where the rain was coming in. Judith's invitation arrived most conveniently. Martha accepted it. And then Sylvia went and did that really inexcusable thing. Coming down to breakfast before the others she stole a rasher from the dish of bacon with which her aunt and uncle unregenerately began the day. Her mother's arrival prevented her

from eating it on the spot; she had to hide it. Weeks later, when
Judith was looking for something in the inlaid Italian cabinet, a
little pool of dried grease in one of the drawers bore eloquent
witness to the crime. The day passed; but Sylvia found no opportunity to consummate the outrage she had begun. It was only in
the evening, while her little brother Paul was being given his bath,
that she was able to retrieve the now stiff and clammy-cold rasher.
With guilty speed she hurried upstairs with it and hid it under
her pillow. When the lights were turned out she ate it. In the
morning, the grease stains and a piece of gnawed rind betrayed
her. Judith went into fits of inextinguishable laughter.

"It's like the Garden of Eden," she gasped between the ex
plosions of her mirth. "The meat of the Pig of the Knowledge of
Good and Evil. But if you *will* surround bacon with categorical
imperatives and mystery, what can you expect, my dear Martha?"

Martha went on smiling her habitual smile of sweet forgiving
benevolence. But inside she felt extremely angry; the child had
made a fool of them all in front of Judith and Jack. She would
have liked to give her a good smacking. Instead of which—for one
must never be rough with a child, one must never let it see that
one is annoyed—she reasoned with Sylvia, she explained, she
appealed, more in sorrow than in anger, to her better feelings.

"Your daddy and I don't think it's right to make animals
suffer when we can eat vegetables which don't suffer anything."

"How do you know they don't?" asked Sylvia, shooting out
the question malignantly. Her face was ugly with sullen ill-temper.

"We don't think it right, darling," Mrs Claxton went on,
ignoring the interruption. "And I'm sure you wouldn't either,
if you realized. Think, my pet; to make that bacon, a poor little
pig had to be killed. To be *killed*, Sylvia. Think of that. A poor
innocent little pig that hadn't done anybody any harm."

"But I hate pigs," cried Sylvia. Her sullenness flared up into
sudden ferocity; her eyes, that had been fixed and glassy with a
dull resentment, darkly flashed. "I hate them, hate them, *hate*
them."

"Quite right," said Aunt Judith, who had come in most in-
opportunely in the middle of the lecture. "Quite right. Pigs *are*
disgusting. That's why people called them pigs."

Martha was glad to get back to the little house on the common
and their beautiful life, happy to escape from Judith's irreverent

laughter and the standing reproach of Jack's success. On the common she ruled, she was the mistress of the family destinies. To the friends who came to visit them there she was fond of saying, with that smile of hers, "I feel that, in our way and on a tiny scale, we've built Jerusalem in England's green and pleasant land."

It was Martha's great-grandfather who started the brewery business. Postgate's Entire was a houshold word in Cheshire and Derbyshire. Martha's share of the family fortune was about seven hundred a year. The Claxton's spirituality and disinterestedness were the flowers of an economic plant whose roots were bathed in beer. But for the thirst of British workmen, Herbert would have had to spend his time and energies profitably doing instead of beautifully being. Beer and the fact that he had married Martha permitted him to cultivate the arts and the religions, to distinguish himself in a gross world as an apostle of idealism.

"It's what's called the division of labour," Judith would laughingly say. "Other people drink. Martha and I think. Or at any rate we think we think."

Herbert was one of those men who are never without a knapsack on their backs. Even in Bond Street, on the rare occasions when he went to London, Herbert looked as though he were just about to ascend Mont Blanc. The rucksack is a badge of spirituality. For the modern high-thinking, pure-hearted Teuton or Anglo-Saxon the scandal of the rucksack is what the scandal of the cross was to the Franciscans. When Herbert passed, long-legged and knickerbockered, his fair beard like a windy explosion round his face, his rucksack overflowing with the leeks and cabbages required in such profusion to support a purely graminivorous family, the street-boys yelled, the flappers whooped with laughter. Herbert ignored them, or else smiled through his beard forgivingly and with a rather studied humorousness. We all have our little rucksack to bear. Herbert bore his not merely with resignation, but boldly, provocatively, flauntingly in the faces of men; and along with the rucksack the other symbols of difference, of separation from ordinary, gross humanity—the concealing beard, the knickerbockers, the Byronic shirt. He was proud of his difference.

"Oh, I know you think us ridiculous," he would say to his friends of the crass materialistic world, "I know you laugh at us for a set of cranks."

"But we don't, we don't," the friends would answer, politely lying.

"And yet, if it hadn't been for the cranks," Herbert pursued, "where would you be now, what would you be doing? You'd be beating children and torturing animals and hanging people for stealing a shilling, and doing all the other horrible things they did in the good old days."

He was proud, proud; he knew himself superior. So did Martha. In spite of her beautiful Christian smile, she too was certain of her superiority. That smile of hers—it was the hall-mark of her spirituality. A more benevolent version of Monna Lisa's smile, it kept her rather thin, bloodless lips almost chronically curved into a crescent of sweet and forgiving charitableness, it surcharged the natural sullenness of her face with a kind of irrelevant sweetness. It was the product of long years of wilful self-denial, of stubborn aspirations towards the highest, of conscious and determined love for humanity and her enemies. (And for Martha the terms were really identical; humanity, though she didn't of course admit it, *was* her enemy. She felt it hostile and *therefore* loved it, consciously and conscientiously; loved it because she really hated it.)

In the end habit had fixed the smile undetachably to her face. It remained there permanently shining, like the head-lamps of a motor-car inadvertently turned on and left to burn, unnecessarily, in the daylight. Even when she was put out or downright angry, even when she was stubbornly, mulishly fighting to have her own will, the smile persisted. Framed between its pre-Raphaelitic loops of mouse-coloured hair the heavy, sullen-featured, rather unwholesomely pallid face continued to shine incongruously with forgiving love for the whole of hateful, hostile humanity; only in the grey eyes was there any trace of the emotions which Martha so carefully repressed.

It was her great-grandfather and her grandfather who had made the money. Her father was already by birth and upbringing the landed gentleman. Brewing was only the dim but profitable background to more distinguished activities as a sportsman, an agriculturist, a breeder of horses and rhododendrons, a member of parliament and the best London clubs.

The fourth generation was obviously ripe for Art and Higher Thought. And duly, punctually, the adolescent Martha discovered William Morris and Mrs Besant, discovered Tolstoy and

Rodin and Folk Dancing and Lao-tzse. Stubbornly, with all the force of her heavy will, she addressed herself to the conquest of spirituality, to the siege and capture of the Highest. And no less punctually than her sister, the adolescent Judith discovered French literature and was lightly enthusiastic (for it was in her nature to be light and gay) about Manet and Daumier, even, in due course, about Matisse and Cézanne. In the long run brewing almost infallibly leads to impressionism or theosophy or communism. But there are other roads to the spiritual heights; it was by one of these other roads that Herbert had travelled. There were no brewers among Herbert's ancestors. He came from a lower, at any rate a poorer, stratum of society. His father kept a drapery shop at Nantwich. Mr Claxton was a thin, feeble man with a taste for argumentation and pickled onions. Indigestion had spoilt his temper and the chronic consciousness of inferiority had made him a revolutionary and a domestic bully. In the intervals of work he read the literature of socialism and unbelief and nagged at his wife, who took refuge in non-conformist piety. Herbert was a clever boy with a knack for passing examinations. He did well at school. They were very proud of him at home, for he was an only child:

"You mark my words," his father would say, prophetically glowing in that quarter of an hour of beatitude which intervened between the eating of his dinner and the beginning of his dyspepsia, "that boy'll do something remarkable."

A few minutes later, with the first rumblings and convulsions of indigestion, he would be shouting at him in fury, cuffing him, sending him out of the room.

Being no good at games Herbert revenged himself on his more athletic rivals by reading. Those afternoons in the public library instead of on the football field, or at home with one of his father's revolutionary volumes, were the beginning of his difference and superiority. It was, when Martha first knew him, a political difference, an anti-Christian superiority. Her superiority was mainly artistic and spiritual. Martha's was the stronger character; in a little while Herbert's interest in socialism was entirely secondary to his interest in art, his anti-clericalism was tinctured by Oriental religiosity. It was only to be expected.

What was not to be expected was that they should have married at all, that they should ever even have met. It is not easy for the children of land-owning brewers and shop-owning drapers to meet and marry.

Morris-dancing accomplished the miracle. They came together in a certain garden in the suburbs of Nantwich where Mr Winslow, the Extension Lecturer, presided over the rather solemn stampings and prancings of all that was earnestly best among the youth of eastern Cheshire. To that suburban garden Martha drove in from the country, Herbert cycled out from the High Street. They met; love did the rest.

Martha was at that time twenty-four and, in her heavy, pallid style, not unhandsome. Herbert was a year older, a tall, disproportionately narrow young man, with a face strong-featured and aquiline. yet singularly mild ("a sheep in eagle's clothing" was how Judith had once described him), and very fair hair. Beard at that time he had none. Economic necessity still prevented him from advertising the fact of his difference and superiority. In the auctioneer's office, where Herbert worked as a clerk, a beard would have been as utterly inadmissible as knickerbockers, an open shirt, and that outward and visible symbol of inward grace, the rucksack. For Herbert these things only became possible when marriage and Martha's seven hundred yearly pounds had lifted him clear of the ineluctable workings of economic law. In those Nantwich days the most he could permit himself was a red tie and some private opinions.

It was Martha who did most of the loving. Dumbly, with a passion that was almost grim in its stubborn intensity, she adored him—his frail body, his long-fingered, delicate hands, the aquiline face with its, for other eyes, rather spurious air of distinction and intelligence, all of him, all. "He has read William Morris and Tolstoy," she wrote in her diary, "he's one of the very few people I've met who feel *responsible* about things. Every one else is so terribly frivolous and self-centred and indifferent. Like Nero fiddling while Rome was burning. He isn't like that. He's conscious, he's aware, he accepts the burden. That's why I like him." That was why, at any rate, she thought she liked him. But her passion was really for the physical Herbert Claxton. Heavily, like a dark cloud charged with thunder, she hung over him with a kind of menace, ready to break out on him with the lightnings of passion and domineering will. Herbert was charged with some of the electricity of passion which he had called out of her. Because she loved, he loved her in return. His vanity, too, was flattered; it was only theoretically that he despised class-distinctions and wealth.

The land-owning brewers were horrified when they heard from Martha that she was proposing to marry the son of a shop-keeper. Their objections only intensified Martha's stubborn determination to have her own way. Even if she hadn't loved him, she would have married him on principle, just because his father *was* a draper and because all this class business was an irrelevant nonsense. Besides, Herbert had talents. What sort of talents it was rather hard to specify. But whatever the talents might be, they were being smothered in the auctioneer's office. Her seven hundred a year would give them scope. It was practically a duty to marry him.

"A man's a man for all that," she said to her father, quoting, in the hope of persuading him, from his favourite poet; she herself found Burns too gross and unspiritual.

"And a sheep's a sheep," retorted Mr Postgate, "and a wood-louse is a woodlouse—for all that and all that."

Martha flushed darkly and turned away without saying anything more. Three weeks later she and the almost passive Herbert were married.

Well, now Sylvia was six years old and a handful, and little Paul, who was whiny and had adenoids, was just on five, and Herbert, under his wife's influence, had discovered unexpectedly enough that his talents were really artistic and was by this time a painter with an established reputation for lifeless ineptitude. With every reaffirmation of his lack of success he flaunted more defiantly than ever the scandal of the rucksack, the scandals of the knicker-bockers and beard. Martha, meanwhile, talked about the inwardness of Herbert's art. They were able to persuade themselves that it was their superiority which prevented them from getting the recognition they deserved. Herbert's lack of success was even a proof (though not perhaps the most satisfactory kind of proof) of that superiority.

"But Herbert's time will come," Martha would affirm prophetically. "It's bound to come."

Meanwhile the little house on the Surrey common was overflowing with unsold pictures. Allegorical they were, painted very flatly in a style that was Early Indian tempered, wherever the Oriental originals ran too luxuriantly to breasts and wasp-waists and moonlike haunches, by the dreary respectability of Puvis de Chavannes.

"And let me beg you, Herbert"—those had been Judith's parting words of advice as they stood on the platform waiting for the train to take them back again to their house on the common— "let me implore you: try to be a little more *indecent* in your paintings. Not so shockingly pure. You don't know how happy you'd make me if you could really be obscene for once. Really obscene."

It was a comfort, thought Martha, to be getting away from that sort of thing. Judith was really too . . . Her lips smiled, her hand waved good-bye.

"Isn't it lovely to come back to our own dear little house!" she cried, as the station taxi drove them bumpily over the track that led across the common to the garden gate. "Isn't it lovely?"

"Lovely!" said Herbert, dutifully echoing her rather forced rapture.

"Lovely!" repeated little Paul, rather thickly through his adenoids. He was a sweet child, when he wasn't whining, and always did and said what was expected of him.

Through the window of the cab Sylvia looked critically at the long low house among the trees. "I think Aunt Judith's house is nicer," she concluded with decision.

Martha turned upon her the sweet illumination of her smile. "Aunt Judith's house is bigger," she said, "and much grander. But this is Home, my sweet. Our very own Home."

"All the same," persisted Sylvia, "I like Aunt Judith's house better."

Martha smiled at her forgivingly and shook her head. "You'll understand what I mean when you're older," she said. A strange child, she was thinking, a difficult child. Not like Paul, who was so easy. Too easy. Paul fell in with suggestions, did what he was told, took his colour from the spiritual environment. Not Sylvia. She had her own will. Paul was like his father. In the girl Martha saw something of her own stubbornness and passion and determination. If the will could be well directed . . . But the trouble was that it was so often hostile, resistant, contrary. Martha thought of that deplorable occasion, only a few months before, when Sylvia, in a fit of rage at not being allowed to do something she wanted to do, had spat in her father's face. Herbert and Martha had agreed that she ought to be punished. But how? Not smacked, of course;

smacking was out of the question. The important thing was to make the child realize the heinousness of what she had done. In the end they decided that the best thing would be for Herbert to talk to her very seriously (but very gently, of course), and then leave her to choose her own punishment. Let her conscience decide. It seemed an excellent idea.

"I want to tell you a story, Sylvia," said Herbert that evening, taking the child on to his knees. "About a little girl, who had a daddy who loved her so much, so much." Sylvia looked at him suspiciously, but said nothing. "And one day that little girl, who was sometimes rather a thoughtless little girl, though I don't believe she was really naughty, was doing something that it wasn't right or good for her to do. And her daddy told her not to. And what do you think that little girl did? She spat in her daddy's face. And her daddy was very very sad. Because what his little girl did was wrong, wasn't it?" Sylvia nodded a brief defiant assent. "And when one has done something wrong, one must be punished, mustn't one?" The child nodded again. Herbert was pleased; his words had had their effect; her conscience was being touched. Over the child's head he exchanged a glance with Martha. "If you had been that daddy," he went on, "and the little girl you loved so much had spat in your face, what would you have done, Sylvia?"

"Spat back," Sylvia answered fiercely and without hesitation.

At the recollection of the scene Martha sighed. Sylvia was difficult, Sylvia was decidedly a problem. The cab drew up at the gate; the Claxtons unpacked themselves and their luggage. Inadequately tipped, the driver made his usual scene. Bearing his rucksack, Herbert turned away with a dignified patience. He was used to this sort of thing; it was a chronic martyrdom. The unpleasant duty of paying was always his. Martha only provided the cash. With what extreme and yearly growing reluctance! He was always between the devil of the undertipped and the deep sea of Martha's avarice.

"Four miles' drive and a tuppenny tip!" shouted the cab-driver at Herbert's receding and rucksacked back.

Martha grudged him even the twopence. But convention demanded that something should be given. Conventions are stupid things; but even the Children of the Spirit must make some compromise with the World. In this case Martha was ready to compromise with the World to the extent of twopence. But no more. Herbert knew that she would have been very angry if he had given more. Not openly, of course; not explicitly. She never visibly lost her temper or her smile. But her forgiving disapproval would have weighed heavily on him for days. And for days she would have found excuses for economizing in order to make up for the wanton extravagance of a sixpenny instead of a twopenny tip. Her economies were mostly on the food, and their justification was always spiritual. Eating was gross; high living was incompatible with high thinking; it was dreadful to think of the poor going hungry while you yourself were living in luxurious gluttony. There would be a cutting down of butter and Brazil nuts, of the more palatable vegetables and the choicer fruits. Meals would come to consist more and more exclusively of porridge, potatoes, cabbages, bread. Only when the original extravagance had been made up several hundred times would Martha begin to relax her asceticism. Herbert never ventured to complain. After one of these bouts of plain living he would for a long time be very careful to avoid other extravagances, even when, as in this case, his economies brought him into painful and humiliating conflict with those on whom they were practised.

"Next time," the taxi-driver was shouting, "I'll charge extra for the whiskers."

Herbert passed over the threshold and closed the door behind him. Safe! He took off his rucksack and deposited it carefully on a chair. Gross, vulgar brute! But anyhow he had taken himself off with the twopence. Martha would have no cause to complain or cut down the supply of peas and beans. In a mild and spiritual way Herbert was very fond of his food. So was Martha—darkly and violently fond of it. That was why she had become a vegetarian, why her economies were always at the expense of the stomach—precisely because she liked food so much. She suffered when she deprived herself of some delicious morsel. But there was a sense in which she loved her suffering more than the morsel. Denying herself, she felt her whole being irradiated by a glow of power; suffering, she was strengthened, her will was wound up, her energy enhanced. The damned-up instincts rose and rose behind the wall of voluntary mortification, deep and heavy with potentialities of force. In the struggle between the instincts Martha's love of power was generally strong enough to overcome her greed; among the hierarchy of pleasures, the joy of exerting the personal conscious will was more intense than the joy of eating even Turkish Delight or strawberries and cream. Not always, however; for there were occasions when, overcome by a sudden irresistible desire, Martha would buy and, in a single day, secretly consume a whole pound of chocolate creams, throwing herself upon the sweets with the same heavy violence as had characterized her first passion for Herbert. With the passage of time and the waning, after the birth of her two children, of her physical passion for her husband, Martha's orgies among the chocolates became more frequent. It was as though her vital energies were being forced, by the closing of the sexual channel, to find explosive outlet in gluttony. After one of these orgies Martha always tended to become more than ordinarily strict in her ascetic spirituality.

Three weeks after the Claxtons' return to their little house on the common, the War broke out.

"It's changed most people," Judith remarked in the third year, "it's altered some out of all recognition. Not Herbert and Martha, though. It's just made them more so—more like themselves than they were before. Curious." She shook her head. "Very curious."

But it wasn't really curious at all; it was inevitable. The War could not help intensifying all that was characteristically Herbertian and Martha-ish in Herbert and Martha. It heightened their sense of remote superiority by separating them still further from the ordinary herd. For while ordinary people believed in the War, fought and worked to win, Herbert and Martha utterly disapproved and, on grounds that were partly Buddhistic, partly Socialist-International, partly Tolstoyan, refused to have anything to do with the accursed thing. In the midst of universal madness they almost alone were sane. And their superiority was proved and divinely hallowed by persecution. Unofficial disapproval was succeeded, after the passing of the Conscription Act, by official repression. Herbert pleaded a conscientious objection. He was sent to work on the land in Dorset, a martyr, a different and spiritually higher being. The act of a brutal War Office had definitely promoted him out of the ranks of common humanity. In this promotion Martha vicariously participated. But what most powerfully stimulated her spirituality was not

War-time persecution so much as War-time financial instability, War-time increase in prices. In the first weeks of confusion she had been panic-stricken; she imagined that all her money was lost, she saw herself with Herbert and the children, hungry and houseless, begging from door to door. She immediately dismissed her two servants, she reduced the family food supply to a prison ration. Time passed and her money came in very much as usual. But Martha was so much delighted with the economies she had made that she would not revert to the old mode of life.

"After all," she argued, "it's really not pleasant to have strangers in the house to serve you. And then, why should they serve us? They who are just as good as we are." It was a hypocritical tribute to Christian doctrine; they were really immeasurably inferior. "Just because we happen to be able to pay them—that's why they have to serve us. It's always made me feel uncomfortable and ashamed. Hasn't it you, Herbert?"

"Always," said Herbert, who always agreed with his wife.

"Besides," she went on, "I think one ought to do one's own work. One oughtn't to get out of touch with the humble small realities of life. I've felt really happier since I've been doing the housework, haven't you?"

Herbert nodded.

"And it's so good for the children. It teaches them humility and service. . . ."

Doing without servants saved a clear hundred and fifty a year. But the economies she made on food were soon counterbalanced by the results of scarcity and inflation. With every rise in prices Martha's enthusiasm for ascetic spirituality became more than ever fervid and profound. So too did her conviction that the children would be spoilt and turned into worldlings if she sent them to an expensive boarding-school. "Herbert and I believe very strongly in home education, don't we, Herbert?" And Herbert would agree that they believed in it very strongly indeed. Home education without a governess, insisted Martha. Why should one let one's children be influenced by strangers? Perhaps badly influenced. Anyhow, not influenced in exactly the way one would influence them oneself. People hired governesses because they dreaded the hard work of educating their children. And of course it *was* hard work—the harder, the higher your ideals. But wasn't it worth while making sacrifices for one's children? With the uplifting question, Martha's smile curved itself into a crescent of more than ordinary soulfulness. Of course it was worth it. The work was an incessant delight—wasn't it, Herbert? For what could be more delightful, more profoundly soul-satisfying than to help your own children to grow up beautifully, to guide them, to mould their characters into ideal forms, to lead their thoughts and desires into the noblest channels? Not by any system of compulsion, of course; children must never be compelled; the art of education was persuading children to mould themselves in the most ideal forms, was showing them how to be the makers of their own higher selves, was firing them with enthusiasm for what Martha felicitously described as "self-sculpture".

On Sylvia, her mother had to admit to herself, this art of education was hard to practise. Sylvia didn't want to sculpture herself, at any rate into the forms which Martha and Herbert found most beautiful. She was quite discouragingly without that sense of moral beauty on which the Claxtons relied as a means of education. It was ugly, they told her, to be rough, to disobey, to say rude things and tell lies. It was beautiful to be gentle and polite, obedient and truthful. "But I don't mind being ugly," Sylvia would retort. There was no possible answer except a spanking; and spanking was against the Claxtons' principles.

Aesthetic and intellectual beauty seemed to mean as little to Sylvia as moral beauty. What difficulties they had to make her take an interest in the piano! This was the more extraordinary, her mother considered, as Sylvia was obviously musical; when she was two and a half she had already been able to sing "Three Blind Mice" in tune. But she didn't want to learn her scales. Her mother talked to her about a wonderful little boy called Mozart. Sylvia hated Mozart. "No, no!" she would shout, whenever her mother mentioned the abhorred name. "I don't want to hear." And to make sure of not hearing, she would put her fingers in her ears. Nevertheless, by the time she was nine she could play "The Merry Peasant" from beginning to end without a mistake. Martha still had hopes of turning her into the musician of the family. Paul, meanwhile, was the future Giotto; it had been decided that he inherited his father's talents. He accepted his career as docilely as he had consented to learn his letters. Sylvia, on the other hand, simply refused to read.

"But think," said Martha ecstatically, "how *wonderful* it will be when you can open any book and read all the *beautiful* things people have written!" Her coaxing was ineffective.

"I like playing better," said Sylvia obstinately, with that expression of sullen bad temper which was threatening to become as chronic as her mother's smile. True to their principles, Herbert and Martha let her play; but it was a grief to them.

"You make your daddy and mummy so sad," they said, trying to appeal to her better feelings. "So sad. Won't you try to read to make your daddy and mummy happy?" The child confronted them with an expression of sullen, stubborn wretchedness, and shook her head. "Just to please us," they wheedled. "You make us *so* sad." Sylvia looked from one mournfully forgiving face to the other and burst into tears.

"Naughty," she sobbed incoherently. "Naughty. Go away." She hated them for being sad, for making her sad. "No, go away, go away," she screamed when they tried to comfort her. She cried inconsolably; but still she wouldn't read.

Paul, on the other hand, was beautifully teachable and plastic. Slowly (for, with his adenoids, he was not a very intelligent boy) but with all the docility that could be desired, he learned to read about the lass on the ass in the grass and other such matters. "Hear how beautifully Paul reads," Martha would say, in the hope of rousing Sylvia to emulation. But Sylvia would only make a contemptuous face and walk out of the room. In the end she taught herself to read secretly, in a couple of weeks. Her parents' pride in the achievement was tempered when they discovered her motives for making the extraordinary effort.

"But what is this dreadful little book?" asked Martha, holding up the copy of "Nick Carter and the Michigan Boulevard Murderers" which she had discovered carefully hidden under Sylvia's winter underclothing. On the cover was a picture of a man being thrown off the roof of a skyscraper by a gorilla.

The child snatched it from her. "It's a lovely book," she retorted, flushing darkly with an anger that was intensified by her sense of guilt.

"Darling," said Martha, beautifully smiling on the surface of her annoyance, "you mustn't snatch like that. Snatching's *ugly*." "Don't care." "Let me look at it, please." Martha held out her hand. She smiled, but her pale face was heavily determined, her eyes commanded.

Sylvia confronted her, stubbornly she shook her head. "No, I don't want you to."

"Please," begged her mother, more forgivingly and more commandingly than ever, "please". And in the end, with a sudden outburst of tearful rage, Sylvia handed over the book and ran off into the garden. "Sylvia, Sylvia!" her mother called. But the child would not come back. To have stood by while her mother violated the secrets of her private world would have been unbearable.

Owing to his adenoids Paul looked and almost was an imbecile. Without being a Christian Scientist, Martha disbelieved in doctors; more particularly she disliked surgeons, perhaps because they were so expensive. She left Paul's adenoids unextirpated; they grew and festered in his throat. From November to May he was never without a cold, a quinsy, an earache. The winter of 1921 was a particularly bad one for Paul. He began by getting influenza which turned into pneumonia, caught measles during his convalescence and developed at the New Year an infection of the middle ear which threatened to leave him permanently deaf. The doctor peremptorily advised an operation, treatment, a convalescence in Switzerland, at an altitude and in the sun. Martha hesitated to follow his advice. She had come to be so firmly convinced of her poverty that she did not see how she could possibly afford to do what the doctor ordered. In her perplexity she wrote to Judith. Two days later Judith arrived in person.

"But do you want to kill the boy?" she asked her sister fiercely. "Why didn't you get him out of this filthy dank hole weeks ago?"

In a few hours she had arranged everything. Herbert and Martha were to start at once with the boy. They were to travel direct to Lausanne by sleeper. "But surely a sleeper's hardly necessary," objected Martha. "You forget" (she beautifully smiled), "we're simple folk." "I only remember you've got a sick child with you," said Judith, and the sleeper was booked. At Lausanne he was to be operated on. (Expensive reply-paid telegram to the clinic; poor Martha suffered.) And when he was well enough he was to go to a sanatorium at Leysin. (Another telegram, for which Judith paid, however. Martha forgot to give the money back.) Martha and Herbert, meanwhile, were to find a good hotel, where Paul would join them as soon as his treatment was over. And they were to stay at least six months, and preferably a year. Sylvia, meanwhile, was to stay with her aunt in England; that would save Martha a lot of money. Judith would try to find a tenant for the house on the common.

"Talk of savages!" said Judith to her husband. "I've never seen such a little cannibal as Sylvia."

"It's what comes of having vegetarian parents, I suppose."

"Poor little creature!" Judith went on with an indignant pity. "There are times when I'd like to drown Martha, she's such a criminal fool. Bringing those children up without ever letting them go near another child of their own age! It's scandalous! And then talking to them about spirituality and Jesus and *ahimsa* and beauty and goodness knows what! And not wanting them to play stupid games, but be artistic! And always being sweet, even when she's furious! It's dreadful, really dreadful! And so silly. Can't she see that the best way of turning a child into a devil is to try to bring it up as an angel? Ah well . . ." She sighed and was silent, pensively; she herself had had no children and, if the doctors were right, never would have children.

The weeks passed and gradually the little savage was civilized. Her first lessons were lessons in the art of moderation. The food, which at the Bamboroughs' house was good and plentiful, was at the beginning a terrible temptation to a child accustomed to the austerities of the spiritual life.

"There'll be more to-morrow," Judith would say, when the child asked for yet another helping of pudding. "You're not a snake, you know; you can't store up to-day's overeating for next week's dinners. The only thing you can do with too much food is to be sick with it."

At first Sylvia would insist, would wheedle and whine for more. But luckily, as Judith remarked to her husband, luckily she had a delicate liver. Her aunt's prophecies were only too punctually realized. After three or four bilious attacks Sylvia learned to control her greed. Her next lesson was in obedience. The obedience she was accustomed to give her parents was slow and grudging. Herbert and Martha never, on principle, commanded, but only suggested. It was a system that had almost forced upon the child a habit of saying no, automatically, to whatever proposition was made to her. "No, no, no!" she regularly began, and then gradually suffered herself to be persuaded, reasoned, or moved by the expression of her parents' sadness into a belated and generally grudging acquiescence. Obeying at long last, she felt an obscure resentment against those who had not compelled her to obey at once. Like most children, she would have liked to be relieved compulsorily of responsibility for her own actions; she was angry with her father and mother for forcing her to expend so much will in resisting them, such a quantity of painful emotion in finally letting her will be overcome. It would have been so much simpler if they had insisted from the first, had compelled her to obey at once, and so spared her all her spiritual effort and pain. Darkly and bitterly did she resent the incessant appeal they made to her better feelings. It wasn't fair, it wasn't fair. They had no right to smile and forgive and make her feel a beast, to fill her with sadness by being sad themselves. She felt that they were somehow taking a cruel advantage of her. And perversely, just because she hated their being sad, she deliberately went out of her way to say and do the things that would most sorely distress them. One of her favourite tricks was to threaten to "go and walk across the plank over the sluice." Between the smooth pond and the shallow rippling of the stream, the gentle water became for a moment terrible. Pent in a narrow channel of oozy brickwork six feet of cataract tumbled with unceasing clamour into a black and heaving pool. It was a horrible place. How often her parents had begged her not to play near the sluice! Her threat would make them repeat their recommendations; they would implore her to be reasonable. "No, I won't be reasonable," Sylvia would shout and run off towards the sluice. If, in fact, she never ventured within five yards of the roaring gulf, that was because she was much more terrified for herself than her parents were for her. But she would go as near as she dared for the pleasure (the pleasure which she hated) of hearing her mother mournfully express her sadness at having a little girl so disobedient, so selfishly reckless of danger. She tried the same trick with her Aunt Judith. "I shall go into the woods by myself," she menaced one day, scowling. To her great surprise, instead of begging her to be reasonable and not to distress the grown-ups by disobediently running into danger, Judith only shrugged her shoulders. "Trot along, then, if you want to be a little fool," she said without looking up from her letter. Indignantly, Sylvia trotted; but she was frightened of being alone in the huge wood. Only pride kept her from returning at once. Damp, dirty, tear-stained, and scratched, she was brought back two hours later by a gamekeeper.

"What luck," said Judith to her husband, "what enormous luck that the little idiot should have gone and got herself lost."

The scheme of things was marshalled against the child's delinquency. But Judith did not rely exclusively on the scheme of things to enforce her code; she provided her own sanctions. Obedience had to be prompt, or else there were prompt reprisals. Once Sylvia succeeded in provoking her aunt to real anger. The scene made a profound impression on her. An hour later she crept diffidently and humbly to where her aunt was sitting. "I'm sorry, Aunt Judith," she said, "I'm sorry," and burst into tears. It was the first time she had ever spontaneously asked for forgiveness.

The lessons which profited Sylvia most were those which she learned from other children. After a certain number of rather unsuccessful and occasionally painful experiments she learned to play, to behave as an equal among equals. Hitherto she had lived almost exclusively as a chronological inferior among grown-ups, in a state of unceasing rebellion and guerilla warfare. Her life had been one long *risorgimento* against forgiving Austrians and all too gentle, beautifully smiling Bourbons. With the little Carters from down the road, the little Holmeses from over the way, she was now suddenly required to adapt herself to democracy and parliamentary government. There were difficulties at first; but when in the end the little bandit had acquired the arts of civility, she was unprecedentedly happy. The grown-ups exploited the childish sociability for their own educational ends. Judith got up amateur theatricals; there was a juvenile performance of the *Midsummer Night's Dream*. Mrs Holmes, who was musical, organized the children's enthusiasm for making a noise into part-singing. Mrs Carter taught them country dances. In a few months Sylvia had acquired all that passion for the higher life which her mother had been trying to cultivate for years, always in vain. She loved poetry, she loved music, she loved dancing—rather platonically, it was true; for Sylvia was one of those congenitally clumsy and aesthetically insensitive natures whose earnest passion for the arts is always destined to remain unconsummated. She loved ardently, but hopelessly; yet not unhappily, for she was not yet, perhaps, conscious of the hopelessness of her passion. She even loved the arithmetic and geography, the English history and French grammar, which Judith had arranged that she should imbibe, along with the little Carters, from the little Carters' formidable governess.

"Do you remember what she was like when she arrived?" said Judith one day to her husband.

He nodded, comparing in his mind the sullen little savage of nine months before with the gravely, earnestly radiant child who had just left the room.

"I feel like a lion-tamer," Judith went on with a little laugh that covered a great love and a great pride. "But what does one do, Jack, when the lion takes to High Anglicanism? Dolly Carter's being prepared for confirmation and Sylvia's caught the infection." Judith sighed. "I suppose she's already thinking we're both damned."

"She'd be damned herself, if she didn't," Jack answered philosophically. "Much more seriously damned, what's more, because she'd be damned in *this* world. It would be a terrible flaw in her character if she didn't believe in some sort of rigmarole at this age."

"But suppose," said Judith, "she were to go on believing in it?"

Martha, meanwhile, had not been liking Switzerland, perhaps because it suited her, physically, too well. There was something, she felt, rather indecent about enjoying such perfect health as she enjoyed at Leysin. It was difficult, when one was feeling so full of animal spirits, to think very solicitously about suffering humanity and God, about Buddha and the higher life, and what not. She resented the genial care-free selfishness of her own healthy body. Waking periodically to conscience-stricken realizations that she had been thinking of nothing for hours and even days together but the pleasure of sitting in the sun, of breathing the aromatic air beneath the pines, of walking in the high meadows picking flowers and looking at the view, she would launch a campaign of intensive spirituality; but after a little while the sun and the bright eager air were too much for her, and she would relapse once more into a shamefully irresponsible state of mere well-being.

"I shall be glad," she kept saying, "when Paul is quite well again and we can go back to England."

And Herbert would agree with her, partly on principle, because, being resigned to his economic and moral inferiority, he always agreed with her, and partly because he too, though unprecedentedly healthy, found Switzerland spiritually unsatisfying. In a country where everybody wore knickerbockers, an open shirt, and a rucksack there was no superiority, no distinction in being so attired. The scandal of the top-hat would have been the equivalent at Leysin of the scandal of the cross; he felt himself undistinguishedly orthodox.

Fifteen months after their departure the Claxtons were back again in the house on the common. Martha had a cold and a touch of lumbago; deprived of mountain exercise, Herbert was already succumbing to the attacks of his old enemy, chronic constipation. They overflowed with spirituality.

Sylvia also returned to the house on the common, and, for the first weeks, it was Aunt Judith here and Aunt Judith there, at Aunt Judith's we did this, Aunt Judith never made me do that. Beautifully smiling, but with unacknowledged resentment at her heart, "Dearest," Martha would say, "I'm not Aunt Judith." She really hated her sister for having succeeded where she herself had failed. "You've done wonders with Sylvia," she wrote to Judith, "and Herbert and I can never be sufficiently grateful." And she would say the same in conversation to friends. "We can never be grateful enough to her, can we, Herbert?" And Herbert would punctually agree that they could never be grateful enough. But the more grateful to her sister she dutifully and even supererogatively was, the more Martha hated her, the more she resented Judith's success and her influence over the child. True, the influence had been unequivocally good; but it was precisely because it had been so good that Martha resented it. It was unbearable to her that frivolous, unspiritual Judith should have been able to influence the child more happily than she had ever done. She had left Sylvia sullenly ill-mannered and disobedient, full of rebellious hatred for all the things which her parents admired; she returned to find her well behaved, obliging, passionately interested in music and poetry, earnestly preoccupied with the newly discovered problems of religion. It was unbearable. Patiently Martha set to work to undermine her sister's influence on the child. Judith's own work had made the task more easy for her. For thanks to Judith, Sylvia was now malleable. Contact with children of her own age had warmed and softened and sensitized her, had mitigated her savage egotism and opened her up towards external influences. The appeal to her better feelings could now be made with the certainty of evoking a positive, instead of a rebelliously negative, response. Martha made the appeal constantly and with skill. She harped (with a beautiful resignation, of course) on the family's poverty. If Aunt Judith did and permitted many things which were not done and permitted in the house on the common, that was because Aunt Judith was so much better off. She could afford many luxuries which the Claxtons had to do without. "Not that your father and I mind doing without," Martha insisted. "On the contrary. It's really rather a blessing not to be rich. You remember what Jesus said about rich people." Sylvia remembered and was thoughtful. Martha would develop her theme; being able to afford luxuries and actually indulging in them had a certain coarsening, de-spiritualizing effect. It was so easy to become worldly. The implication, of course, was that Aunt Judith and Uncle Jack had been tainted by worldliness. Poverty had happily preserved the Claxtons from the danger—poverty, and also, Martha insisted, their own meritorious wish. For of course they could have afforded to keep at least one servant, even in these difficult times; but they had preferred to do without, "because, you see, serving is better than being served." Jesus had said that the way of Mary was better than the way of Martha. "But I'm a Martha," said Martha Claxton, "who tries her best to be a Mary too. Martha *and* Mary —that's the best way of all. Practical service *and* contemplation. Your father isn't one of those artists who selfishly detach themselves from all contact with the humble facts of life. He is a creator, but he is not too proud to do the humblest service." Poor Herbert! he couldn't have refused to do the humblest service, if Martha had commanded. Some artists, Martha continued, only thought of immediate success, only worked with an eye to profits and applause. But Sylvia's father, on the contrary, was one who worked without thought of the public, only for the sake of creating truth and beauty.

On Sylvia's mind these and similar discourses, constantly repeated with variations and in every emotional key, had a profound effect. With all the earnestness of puberty she desired to be good and spiritual and disinterested, she longed to sacrifice herself, it hardly mattered to what so long as the cause was noble. Her mother had now provided her with the cause. She gave herself up to it with all the stubborn energy of her nature. How fiercely she practised her piano! With what determination she read through even the dreariest books! She kept a notebook in which she copied out the most inspiring passages of her daily reading; and another in which she recorded her good resolutions, and with them, in an agonized and chronically remorseful diary, her failures to abide by the resolutions, her lapses from grace. "Greed. Promised I'd eat only one greengage. Took four at lunch. None to-morrow. O.G.H.M.T.B.G."

"What does O.G.H.M.T.B.G. mean?" asked Paul maliciously one day.

Sylvia flushed darkly. "You've been reading my diary!" she said. "Oh, you beast, you little beast." And suddenly she threw herself on her brother like a fury. His nose was bleeding when he got away from her. "If you ever look at it again, I'll kill you." And standing there with her clenched teeth and quivering nostrils, her hair flying loose round her pale face, she looked as though she meant it. "I'll kill you," she repeated. Her rage was justified; O.G.H.M.T.B.G. meant "O God, help me to be good."

That evening she came to Paul and asked his pardon.

Aunt Judith and Uncle Jack had been in America for the best part of a year.

"Yes, go; go by all means," Martha had said when Judith's letter came, inviting Sylvia to spend a few days with them in London. "You mustn't miss such a chance of going to the opera and all those lovely concerts."

"But is it quite fair, mother?" said Sylvia hesitatingly. "I mean, I don't want to go and enjoy myself all alone. It seems somehow . . ."

"But you ought to go," Martha interrupted her. She felt so certain of Sylvia now that she had no fears of Judith. "For a musician like you it's a necessity to hear *Parsifal* and the *Magic*

Flute. I was meaning to take you myself next year; but now the opportunity has turned up this year, you must take it. Gratefully," she added, with a sweetening of her smile.

Sylvia went. *Parsifal* was like going to church, but much more so. Sylvia listened with a reverent excitement that was, however, interrupted from time to time by the consciousness, irrelevant, ignoble even, but oh, how painful! that her frock, her stockings, her shoes were dreadfully different from those worn by that young girl of her own age, whom she had noticed in the row behind as she came in. And the girl, it had seemed to her, had returned her gaze derisively. Round the Holy Grail there was an explosion of bells and harmonious roaring. She felt ashamed of herself for thinking of such unworthy things in the presence of the mystery. And when, in the entr'acte, Aunt Judith offered her an ice, she refused almost indignantly.

Aunt Judith was surprised. "But you used to love ices so much."

"But not now, Aunt Judith. Not now." An ice in church—what sacrilege! She tried to think about the Grail. A vision of green satin shoes and a lovely mauve artificial flower floated up before her inward eye.

Next day they went shopping. It was a bright cloudless morning of early summer. The windows of the drapers' shops in Oxford Street had blossomed with bright pale colours. The waxen dummies were all preparing to go to Ascot, to Henley, were already thinking of the Eton and Harrow match. The pavements were crowded; an immense blurred noise filled the air like a mist. The scarlet and golden buses looked regal and the sunlight glittered with a rich and oily radiance on the polished flanks of the passing limousines. A little procession of unemployed slouched past with a brass band at their head making joyful music, as though they were only too happy to be unemployed, as though it were a real pleasure to be hungry.

Sylvia had not been in London for nearly two years, and these crowds, this noise, this innumerable wealth of curious and lovely things in every shining window went to her head. She felt even more excited than she had felt at *Parsifal.*

For an hour they wandered through Selfridge's. "And now, Sylvia," said Aunt Judith, when at last she had ticked off every item on her long list, "now you can choose whichever of these frocks you like best." She waved her hand. A display of Summer Modes for Misses surrounded them on every side. Lilac and lavender, primrose and pink and green, blue and mauve, white, flowery, spotted—a sort of herbaceous border of young frocks. "Whichever you like," Aunt Judith repeated. "Or if you'd prefer a frock for the evening . . ."

Green satin shoes and a big mauve flower. The girl had looked derisively. It was unworthy, unworthy.

"No, really, Aunt Judith." She blushed, she stammered. "Really, I don't need a frock. Really." ..

"All the more reason for having it if you don't need it. Which one?"

"No, really. I don't, I can't . . ." And suddenly, to Aunt Judith's uncomprehending astonishment, she burst into tears.

The year was 1924. The house on the common basked in the soft late-April sunshine. Through the open windows of the drawing-room came the sound of Sylvia's practising. Stubbornly, with a kind of fixed determined fury, she was trying to master Chopin's Valse in D flat. Under her conscientious and insensitive fingers the lilt and languor of the dance rhythm was laboriously sentimental, like the rendering on the piano of a cornet solo outside a public house; and the quick flutter of semiquavers in the contrasting passages was a flutter, when Sylvia played, of mechanical butterflies, a beating of nickel-plated wings. Again and again she played, again and again. In the little copse on the other side of the stream at the bottom of the garden the birds went about their business undisturbed. On the trees the new small leaves were like the spirits of leaves, almost immaterial, but vivid like little flames at the tip of every twig. Herbert was sitting on a tree stump in the middle of the wood doing those yoga breathing exercises, accompanied by auto-suggestion, which he found so good for his constipation. Closing his right nostril with a long forefinger, he breathed in deeply through his left—in, in, deeply, while he counted four heart-beats. Then through sixteen beats he held his breath and between each beat he said to himself very quickly, "I'm not constipated, I'm not constipated." When he had made the affirmation sixteen times, he closed his left nostril and breathed out, while he counted eight, through his right. After which he began again. The left nostril was the more favoured; for it breathed in with the air a faint cool sweetness of primroses and leaves and damp earth. Near him, on a camp stool, Paul was making a drawing of an oak tree. Art at all costs; beautiful, uplifting, disinterested Art. Paul was bored. Rotten old tree—what was the point of drawing it? All round him the sharp green spikes of the wild hyacinths came thrusting out of the dark mould. One had pierced through a dead leaf and lifted it, transfixed, into the air. A few more days of sunshine and every spike would break out into a blue flower. Next time his mother sent him into Godalming on his bicycle, Paul was thinking, he'd see if he couldn't overcharge her two shillings on the shopping instead of one, as he had done last time. Then he'd be able to buy some chocolate as well as go to the cinema; and perhaps even some cigarettes, though that might be dangerous. . . .

"Well, Paul," said his father, who had taken a sufficient dose of his mystical equivalent of Cascara, "how are you getting on?" He got up from the tree stump and walked across the glade to where the boy was sitting. The passage of time had altered Herbert very little; his explosive beard was still as blond as it had always been, he was as thin as ever, his head showed no signs of going bald. Only his teeth had visibly aged; his smile was discoloured and broken.

"But he really ought to go to a dentist," Judith had insistently urged on her sister, the last time they met.

"He doesn't want to," Martha had replied. "He doesn't really believe in them." But perhaps her own reluctance to part with the necessary number of guineas had something to do with Herbert's lack of faith in dentists. "Besides," she went on, "Herbert hardly notices such merely material, physical things. He lives so much in the noumenal world that he's hardly aware of the phenomenal. Really not aware."

"Well, he jolly well ought to be aware," Judith answered, "that's all I can say." She was indignant.

"How are you getting on?" Herbert repeated, and laid his hand on the boy's shoulder.

"The bark's most horribly difficult to get right," Paul answered in a complainingly angry voice.

"That makes it all the more worth while to get right," said Herbert. "Patience and work—they're the only things. Do you

know how a great man once defined genius?" Paul knew very
well how a great man had once defined genius; but the definition
seemed to him so stupid and such a personal insult to himself,
that he did not answer, only grunted. His father bored him,
maddeningly. "Genius," Herbert went on, answering his own
question, "genius is an infinite capacity for taking pains." At that
moment Paul detested his father.

"One two-and three-and One-and two-and three-and . . ."
Under Sylvia's fingers the mechanical butterflies continued to
flap their metal wings. Her face was set, determined, angry;
Herbert's great man would have found genius in her. Behind her
stiff determined back her mother came and went with a feather
brush in her hand, dusting. Time had thickened and coarsened
her; she walked heavily. Her hair had begun to go grey. When
she had finished dusting, or rather when she was tired of it, she
sat down. Sylvia was laboriously cornet-soloing through the dance
rhythm. Martha closed her eyes. "Beautiful, beautiful!" she said,
and smiled her most beautiful smile. "You play it beautifully,
my darling." She was proud of her daughter. Not merely as a
musician; as a human being too. When she thought what trouble
she had had with Sylvia in the old days . . . "Beautifully." She rose
at last and went upstairs to her bedroom. Unlocking a cupboard,
she took out a box of candied fruits and ate several cherries, a
plum, and three apricots. Herbert had gone back to his studio
and his unfinished picture of "Europe and America at the feet of
Mother India." Paul pulled a catapult out of his pocket, fitted a
buckshot into the leather pouch and let fly at a nuthatch that was
running like a mouse up the oak tree on the other side of the
glade. "Hell!" he said as the bird flew away unharmed. But the
next shot was more fortunate. There was a spurt of flying feathers,
there were two or three little squeaks. Running up Paul found a
hen chaffinch lying in the grass. There was blood on the feathers.
Thrilling with a kind of disgusted excitement Paul picked up the
little body. How warm. It was the first time he had ever killed
anything. What a good shot! But there was nobody he could talk
to about it. Sylvia was no good: she was almost worse than
mother about some things. With a fallen branch he scratched a
hole and buried the little corpse, for fear somebody might find it
and wonder how it had been killed. They'd be furious if they
knew! He went into lunch feeling tremendously pleased with

himself. But his face fell as he looked round the table. "Only this beastly cold stuff?"

"Paul, Paul," said his father reproachfully.

"Where's mother?"

"She's not eating to-day," Herbert answered.

"All the same," Paul grumbled under his breath, "she really might have taken the trouble to make something hot for us."

Sylvia meanwhile sat without raising her eyes from her plate of potato salad, eating in silence.

Aldous Huxley was born in 1894, the third son of Leonard Huxley and grandson of T. H. Huxley. From a preparatory school (described in *Eyeless in Gaza*) he went on to Eton, which he left at seventeen owing to serious eye trouble which left him nearly blind. One eye recovered sufficiently for him to enter Oxford in 1913, but he had to abandon his hope of becoming a physician and was rejected for military service in 1914. In 1919 he married Maria Nys, a Belgian, and joined the *Athenaeum* magazine, writing biographical and architectural articles and reviews of fiction, drama, music, and art. Having already published three books of verse, he began with *Limbo* and *Crome Yellow* the series of stories and novels which combined dazzling intellectual dialogue and a surface cynicism with a ground of clear moral convictions, and exerted a strong emancipating influence. In the twenties Huxley lived mostly in Italy; in the thirties his home was near Toulon, France. To this period belonged *Brave New World*, a pessimistic futurist novel and his best known. In 1937 the state of his eyes led him to move to California, where he became convinced of the value of mystical experience, the theme of several of his later works. After the death of his first wife in 1955, Huxley married Laura Archera. Their home was destroyed by fire in 1961; little survived apart from the manuscript of *Island*, his last novel. Aldous Huxley died in November 1963.

ELEPHANT PAPERBACKS

Literature and Letters
Stephen Vincent Benét, *John Brown's Body*, EL10
Philip Callow, *Son and Lover: The Young D. H. Lawrence*, EL14
James Gould Cozzens, *Castaway*, EL6
James Gould Cozzens, *Men and Brethren*, EL3
Clarence Darrow, *Verdicts Out of Court*, EL2
Floyd Dell, *Intellectual Vagabondage*, EL13
Theodore Dreiser, *Best Short Stories*, EL1
Joseph Epstein, *Ambition*, EL7
André Gide, *Madeleine*, EL8
Irving Howe, *William Faulkner*, EL15
Aldous Huxley, *Collected Short Stories*, EL17
Sinclair Lewis, *Selected Short Stories*, EL9
William L. O'Neill, ed., *Echoes of Revolt: The Masses, 1911–1917*, EL5
Ramón J. Sender, *Seven Red Sundays*, EL11
Wilfrid Sheed, *Office Politics*, EL4
Tess Slesinger, *On Being Told That Her Second Husband Has Taken His First Lover, and Other Stories*, EL12
Thomas Wolfe, *The Hills Beyond*, EL16

ELEPHANT PAPERBACKS

Theatre and Drama
Robert Brustein, *The Theatre of Revolt*, EL407
Plays for Performance:
    Aristophanes, *Lysistrata*, EL405
    Anton Chekhov, *The Seagull*, EL407
    Georges Feydeau, *Paradise Hotel*, EL403
    Henrik Ibsen, *Ghosts*, EL401
    Henrik Ibsen, *When We Dead Awaken*, EL408
    Heinrich von Kleist, *The Prince of Homburg*, EL402
    Christopher Marlowe, *Doctor Faustus*, EL404
    August Strindberg, *The Father*, EL406